D0275239

Skinner's Drift

Skinner's Drift

LISA FUGARD

VIKING
an imprint of
PENGUIN BOOKS

VIKING

Published by the Penguin Group
Penguin Books Ltd, 80 Strand, London WC2R ORL, England
Penguin Group (USA) Inc., 375 Hudson Street, New York, New York 10014, USA
Penguin Group (Canada), 10 Alcorn Avenue, Toronto, Ontario, Canada M4V 3B2
(a division of Pearson Penguin Canada Inc.)
Penguin Ireland, 25 St Stephen's Green, Dublin 2, Ireland (a division of Penguin Books Ltd)
Penguin Group (Australia), 250 Camberwell Road,
Camberwell, Victoria 3124, Australia (a division of Pearson Australia Group Pty Ltd)
Penguin Books India Pvt Ltd, 11 Community Centre,
Panchsheel Park, New Delhi – 110 017, India
Penguin Group (NZ), cnr Airborne and Rosedale Roads, Albany,
Auckland 1310, New Zealand (a division of Pearson New Zealand Ltd)
Penguin Books (South Africa) (Pty) Ltd, 24 Sturdee Avenue,
Rosebank 2196, South Africa

Penguin Books Ltd, Registered Offices: 80 Strand, London WC2R ORL, England

www.penguin.com

First published 2005
1

Copyright © Lisa Fugard, 2005

The moral right of the author has been asserted

All rights reserved
Without limiting the rights under copyright
reserved above, no part of this publication may be
reproduced, stored in or introduced into a retrieval system,
or transmitted, in any form or by any means (electronic, mechanical,
photocopying, recording or otherwise), without the prior
written permission of both the copyright owner and
the above publisher of this book

Set in Monotype Dante 7/9 pt
Typeset by Palimpsest Book Production Limited, Polmont, Stirlingshire FK2 0NZ
Printed in Great Britain by Clays Ltd, St Ives plc

A CIP catalogue record for this book is available from the British Library

ISBN 0-670-91548-3

For Gavyn

I

September 1997

Eva pressed her forehead to the window and watched the ruffle of waves rimming the coastline recede from view as the plane nosed its way towards Johannesburg. The dirt roads were visible, clawed into a land pitted and scarred by drought. She knew the hell of driving them; how dusty and worn she'd feel after jolting along one, with nothing to look at for hour upon hour but rocks and thorn trees. Maybe, if she was lucky, a jackal, a snake. Africa lay stretched beneath her like the ravaged hide of some ancient beast, and something fierce shuddered inside her; a love that startled her and set off another round of tears, and she turned from the oval window and leaned back into her seat.

The girls sitting behind her were talking to each other. Sixteen hours into the flight and she still couldn't identify the language. Definitely not Xhosa, she hadn't heard any of the characteristic clicks, and not Sotho because she would surely have recognized the rhythms if not any of the words. At least they weren't singing.

It was September, the plane only half full. Unlike the other passengers who had shifted around after take-off to secure a bank of seats for themselves, the three girls had stayed together. They wore dark-blue pinafores and light-blue shirts. They looked too old to be schoolgirls, but then Eva thought of the overcrowded classrooms in the townships, where twenty-year-old pupils shared textbooks and wrote their matric exams sitting on cement floors.

They sang for the first time just before the dinner service

and their voices, full of sunshine and honey and dust, had disturbed in Eva some sodden longing for what used to be home. She wiped her eyes with a blue South African Airways blanket. She was crying for her father, because of her father. She shook her head in mild disgust at herself. Her mother was dead, worthy of her grief, and yet here she was weeping for that miserable ghost clinging to life in a hospital in Louis Trichardt.

She drank two small bottles of red wine with dinner and swallowed half a sleeping pill. She tucked the seat belts between her three seats and fashioned herself a bed, soft voices behind her murmuring something as she drifted off. In her sozzled state she imagined it to be a lullaby, the private twittering of doves in a thicket.

Now, with an hour left in what had seemed like a never-ending flight, Eva stared at the cratered red earth giving way to a smooth dun-coloured expanse mottled with dark green. Sand rivers, which flow for just a few weeks each year if the rains are decent, wound across the land like snail trails. Someone kneed her through the seat. The girls were giggling, piling on top of each other to look out of their small window and she impulsively leaned over her seat back, saying, 'Isn't it beautiful?'

They nodded, two of them immediately raising hands to demurely cover their mouths while the third, a young woman really, looked curiously at Eva. She wanted to ask them what they'd been doing in America. Were they members of a youth group or a choir? Had a church sponsored their trip? The forthright gaze of the young woman deterred her from asking as Eva realized that she, in turn, would be questioned. She already had her lines prepared: she would claim to be an American tourist. She would lie to the girls, as she had for most of her years in New York, changing her story each time; one moment she was an immigrant from New Zealand, another a student visiting from England.

She slid back into her seat, her exhilaration tempered with shame. It had been ten years since she'd left the country, and left her father standing in front of the Dutch Reformed Church in Alldays. Now, he was dying. Her aunt Johanna had telephoned her three nights ago and begged her to return.

The shadow of the plane slid across the turquoise pools of Johannesburg's northern suburbs, and buckled over ochre-coloured slag heaps piled beside exhausted gold mines. The wheels thudded on to the runway and the girls launched into 'Nkosi Sikelel'i Afrika'. Other passengers seated in her section joined in, the white South Africans humming because the Xhosa words of their new anthem still eluded them, the blacks giving full voice. A smiling American family seated in the bulkhead stood up to watch, the father filming it all with a video camera. They were going on safari; Eva had overheard them talking to the steward.

What did they think? That it was an African custom to launch into song whenever a plane touched down, a way of thanking the great spirit in the sky for bringing them safely back to earth? She looked out at the long, dry, once green grass and the exhausted blue of the mid-afternoon highveld sky. She doubted it would be an easy visit; hopefully it would be a short one.

Eva had left in 1987, a month after her mother's funeral. Lorraine had been cremated, which was an unusual occurrence in the Limpopo valley. Farmers and their wives and their dogs were buried, resting in the earth being reward enough for years of toil. Lorraine's final act of rebellion had been to deprive the community of the grim satisfaction of watching Martin shovel earth on to his wife's coffin. Instead, Eva and her father stood in the shade of the marula tree beside the church while the mourners nervously paid their respects. God forbid Martin should open his mouth and subject them to the jaw and tremble and buck of his stutter. They needn't have worried: Eva held the fort beautifully. She clasped their hands in hers. Some expressed condolences in English, others Afrikaans, and she addressed each person in their language of choice. Within an hour it was over, no one left, apart from two little African boys staring at them from beneath a thorn tree across the street, and the *dominee* approaching to talk about how God's hand is present in even the most hideous of accidents. Eva wanted to scream.

'I'm going to drive back to Jo'burg,' she said to her father without looking at him. She would not give him that, not even a glance at his hands to see if they were shaking, fingers of one hand worrying in the palm of the other.

She wept in the car. The goshawks perched on the telephone poles, the koppies rising out of the rock-strewn veld; the world that she loved seemed incapable of offering any solace, and Eva was grateful when darkness arrived and all she could see was the broken white line in the road, the signs announcing the kilometres to Johannesburg.

Weeks passed. Her uncle Hendrik, who worked as a stunt man in the South African film industry and had secured her a job as a production assistant on a soap opera, paid her a visit. She'd been fired; her hair was unwashed, her flat filthy. Alarmed he urged her to do something good for herself. Take a trip, he said, and he gave her enough money for a ticket overseas. Eva chose a night flight to Amsterdam. The lights of Soweto and Johannesburg were scattered beneath her like diamonds and rubies and tiger's-eyes when the plane took off. Darkness and stars for eight hours, then the impossible green and density of Europe, the sombre civilized ocean beneath them as they flew into Schipol airport. She checked into a hostel, crawling out once a day for an apple pancake and a beer, unable to contemplate a future. Then one morning, a week after her arrival, she realized one certainty: she would

4

not return home before his death. She went out and bought a train ticket to Spain.

He will want to be buried, Eva thought, as she waited with the other passengers in the line leading to passport control. And she knew where. The small cemetery outside Messina where the plastic flowers melted during the summer months. Damn him for dying. She handed over her South African passport and an African man with an explosive smile stamped it and said, 'Welcome home!'

With the end of apartheid, Jan Smuts International airport had become Johannesburg airport. The Witwatersrand, the area encompassing Johannesburg, Randfontein and a few other towns, and which was named after a cascade of white water that the early settlers had seen, was now part of Gauteng – Eva had no idea what Gauteng meant. The conservative Transvaal, province of stoic farmers, sofa-sized rugby players and insatiable hunters, had been divided into the Northern Province and Mpumalanga. A new country, and she sensed it the minute she passed through customs.

Gone were the young, nervy-eyed, white soldiers with their machine guns. Instead the terminal seemed overrun with black taxi drivers asking her if she needed a ride. No, no thank you, she said, her eyes sweeping across their faces. In the past she'd have handled them with a certain confidence, an ongoing rapid discernment – trust this one, have nothing to do with that character – her white skin at least giving her the illusion of security. Now, she felt uncertain of herself.

She stepped outside into the shock of the sunlight. Buses with spewing exhaust pipes and ads for Sun City painted on their sides trundling past, row upon row of cars in the vast parking lot – it would have been so cosmopolitan if it hadn't been for that light, wild and fierce, as if gleaned from the eyes of animals that kill. She took a minibus shuttle to the Holiday

Inn, listening to the earthy lilt of the driver's voice, the white family sitting opposite her with their flattened accents that turned each word into a roughly carved piece of wood.

After a plate of prawns peri-peri from room service and a long shower, Eva made her way to the bar. Two large fibre-glass tusks flanked the entrance; inside, a group of Indian busi-nessmen crowded the red Naugahyde banquets. She perched on a stool at the bar and ordered a glass of pinotage. In the mirror opposite her, she studied the reflections of the two blonde South African women seated to her right: long mani-cured nails, chunky gold jewellery and cell phones resting on the bar. She thanked God she had avoided that fate and glanced at her own reflection. She'd worn lip gloss and it hadn't helped, her mouth appeared to be more downturned than usual, her eyes vacant. She was twenty-eight years old, but with her short haircut – it had been so chic in New York – and the emotional tumult of returning etched across her face, she looked odd, like a middle-aged teenager. She reached quickly for her glass of wine.

The blondes departed and Eva ordered another glass from the bartender who wore a Nehru jacket cut from Kente cloth.

'An American who knows that pinotage is South Africa's finest wine.' He set the glass in front of her. 'So, what part of the States are you from?'

'I live in New York.'

'Ah, the Big Apple.'

She laughed. He made it sound like a piece of fruit. The bartender wrinkled his brow as if he didn't understand her amusement and, emboldened by the velvety pinotage, she said, 'Yup. *Maar ek's gebore in Humansdorp en het op 'n plaas –'* The words tumbling out of her mouth like clods of earth flus-tered her. She hadn't spoken Afrikaans out loud in ten years, and she knocked her wine glass over.

'No problem.' He wiped the bar clean. 'Welcome home, Mrs – or could it be Miss?'

'Miss, Eva –' Her eyes fluttered away from his in embarrassment. She must have sounded like a holdover from the old South Africa; Miss Eva was the way the Africans who worked on Skinner's Drift had addressed her. 'I mean, it's just plain Eva.'

'Welcome home, not so plain Eva.'

Again she avoided his eyes. Surely he wasn't flirting with her. 'Van Rensburg,' she added.

'Oh, that's a nice *boere* surname.' He refilled her glass and slid it towards her. 'A few years ago I would have been scared of someone with a name like that.'

'Cheers!' She raised the glass to her lips, unsure of how she should respond.

A smile curled ever so slowly across his face until his cheekbones jutted out like rock ledges.

'Eva, is everything A-okay?' He leaned towards her, close enough for her to read the name tag pinned to his jacket.

'Great, Rapulana.'

'No, no, you make it sound too American. Listen. Rah –' his mouth opened wide as a lion's. 'Puu –' his lips pursed as if he were kissing her. 'Lana!' He swallowed and sighed.

Eva turned scarlet. She ran her fingers nervously up the stem of her wine glass. And abruptly stopped, realizing that the gesture might seem provocative. 'Rapulana –' God, even saying his name felt like a sexual act. 'Thank you. You've – well, you've given me quite a welcome!'

She finished her wine, reached for her bag and scooted off the bar stool.

'Eva. Wait!'

'Yes?'

'I like you, Eva, but . . . you need to pay your bill.'

'Oh, my God, I'm so sorry!'

She fumbled with her wallet and pulled out a one hundred rand note. When he walked to the register at the other end of the bar she fled, leaving him a generous tip.

Back in her room she was pacing. Would she have been so flustered if a black American had come on to her? Of course not. It was being back in the country where, just a decade ago, a black man would never have flirted with her that had shaken her confidence. She opened the blinds and stared at three planes parked on a distant runway. Swissair with its comforting red cross, and two others, which were obviously from an African country, cheetahs in full stride painted on the fuselage below a row of tiny windows. She had a Visa card, escape was still a possibility. But it wouldn't be once she called Johanna. Her stomach turned over.

The cheetah planes glided towards the terminal. Gambia, Guinea Bissau, the names of African countries came to mind, countries that Eva could not place on a map. She looked at her watch – it was nine thirty – and picked up the phone. God knows what Johanna thought of her, wicked Eva abandoning her father when he needed her so. She dialled the number.

'Hello, Johanna.'

'*Skattebol?*'

'It's me.'

'You've come home. *Liewe Here* –' Johanna sobbed.

'Yes, I'm in Johannesburg.'

Johanna blew her nose and wheezed. 'Eva?'

'Yes, I'm here.' A deep sucking sound followed and Eva knew her aunt had reached for her inhaler.

'But you are sounding like an American,' Johanna said, and then, as if it were quite possible that an American was playing a horrible trick on her, she demanded, 'Eva? Are you sure that's you?'

Eva grinned. She piled two pillows together and lay on the bed, relaxing into the asthmatic gullibility of her aunt.

'Johanna, I swear, it's me.'

They chatted about the flight. Johanna wanting to know about the food on board and whether the plane had managed to fly the whole way without stopping for petrol.

'Yes, we didn't run out of fuel. So, how is he doing?'

Another trumpeting nose blow. 'Oh, *skat*, I think he had another stroke while he was incinerated in the hospital –'

'Incarcerated, but that's not –'

'What's that, Eva?'

'Nothing . . . never mind. Go on.'

'Well, it's terrible. He doesn't recognize anyone. He just lies there and cries.'

Eva's smile faded. The thought of her father in tears rankled her and she sat up and told her aunt she'd be in Louis Trichardt late the following afternoon. Johanna gave her a brief lecture on how she must not give any blacks a lift. 'Even to the old women who carry all their belongings in a bundle on their heads. A person just can't tell these days.'

She hung up the phone, the image of her weeping father still vexing her, and switched on the TV in time to watch the news. Fist-clenching black workers picketing the Pepsi bottling plant, a white game warden detailing the efforts to track a rogue lion that had killed several head of cattle belonging to a tribe contesting the borders of the Kruger National Park. And the Truth and Reconciliation Commission had wrapped up its hearings in Pietermaritzburg with testimony from a distraught African woman who spoke of gathering pieces of her husband after police firebombed their house. In two weeks the commission would reconvene in the Northern Province.

She switched to MNET, the twenty-four-hour movie channel, and swallowed the other half of her sleeping pill. Her thoughts drifted uneasily to Stefan.

She'd been tempted to call him from JFK to tell him she was flying to South Africa. A need for earnest decent Stefan to say, 'That's great, Eva. You're going home.' But she still felt ashamed of the way she'd behaved with him.

She'd met him in the winter of 1992 on the set of a TV commercial where she was working as a gofer. De Klerk had released Mandela from Pollsmoor prison and to say you were a South African was to be an ambassador of hope. No longer a pariah, you were now a desired guest at parties where you were supposed to speak eloquently about the struggle, you were supposed to tear up and talk about the walk from the darkness into the light. But Eva didn't reveal her nationality to Stefan right away. She mumbled her usual nonsense about New Zealand, and then had to field several questions concerning fjords and sheep.

They began seeing each other, Stefan patiently pursuing, Eva feeling squirrelly about it all. He worked as a part-time set painter and photographed New York with a pinhole camera. He also took photographs of Eva. The transformation of her face into an eerie poltergeist-like blur appealed to her, and soon she had over a dozen of them taped to her refrigerator.

'I should have one for my passport photo,' she joked one August afternoon after they'd idly been discussing travelling somewhere together. They'd just made love and she stood naked in front of the refrigerator, trying to prise a tray of ice cubes from the depths of her ice-blocked freezer.

'So let's see your passport,' Stefan replied.

She turned, the cool air a blessing on her back, and studied him. He hadn't put his glasses on so she knew he couldn't see her. He was unassuming and so terribly gentle and polite, like Neels, and she was tired of lying and feeling so lonely. Abandoning her quest for ice, she dug her passport out of a drawer, handing it to him with his glass of cool water from the tap.

'South Africa? But you come from New Zealand.'

'I lied.'

'Why? Eva, my God, I read about it in the papers . . . your country is astonishing!'

She was stunned – sensitive Stefan had tears in his eyes. The tears she was supposed to have. She pulled on her panties. 'You don't know what it was like in the late eighties. When I first arrived in the city a Jamaican threw me out of his cab after I told him I was a South African.'

Stefan patted the bed. 'But you don't have to lie about it any more.'

Reluctantly, she sat beside him.

'Tell me something, Eva van Rensburg. Anything.'

It was the hour when sunlight graced her studio apartment. Sparrows were hopping through the ginkgo tree outside her window and her neighbour had the baseball game on his TV.

'I grew up on a farm,' she said.

Within the week, Stefan had bought a copy of *Cry, the Beloved Country* that he carried in his backpack. Alarmed by his growing passion for all things South African, Eva told him that she was not interested in politics, or discussing her childhood. But often, after making love, she'd stare out of her window at the yellowing leaves of the ginkgo tree, the sleet, and tell him about life on Skinner's Drift. The day she was riding her horse and came across a huge knot of python uncoiling in the morning sun, the Limpopo running muddy and strong after summer storms.

It was Stefan who told Eva that expatriate South Africans, even those holding foreign passports, 'Even kiwis like you,' could go to the UN and vote in the country's first democratic election. He urged her to go and she did. And she lied, telling him how wonderful it was to cast her vote when in truth she'd felt too ashamed, too filthy to join the line and she'd fled to a bar and ended up in a stranger's bed. Soon after that, in a wash of self-loathing, Eva broke up with him.

A year later they were seeing each other again and South Africa had set up the Truth and Reconciliation Commission. Stefan followed it avidly in the papers, reading about Vlakplaas, the farm outside Johannesburg where hit squads were trained, where *die manne*, members of the Security Police, could relax, have a drinking session, a *braaivleis*. He was on fire with the country's suffering and the more he talked about justice and healing and compassion, the more alienated Eva felt.

'What do you think?' he asked her one evening as she poured a jar of pasta sauce into a pot. 'Do you think people like Dirk Coetzee should get amnesty?'

Eva shrugged and began chopping black olives for the sauce.

Stefan paced the length of her apartment. 'He tortured people. You know, they did that on Vlakplaas. And yet' – he stopped, ran his hands through his sandy-coloured hair – 'I find this so remarkable. I think that South Africa could forgive him. The heart of your country –'

'Please, can we have one night when we don't have to talk about all of this. I told you, I'm just not interested in politics so why you keep on –'

He looked at her in confusion. 'I don't get it. How can you know about all of this and not care?' His voice began to tremble. 'They burned a body on that farm, Eva. They sat around and drank beers and watched –'

'Don't you dare cry!' Eva flung the chopping board to the floor. 'Don't you dare snivel in my apartment over my country, my history, my life!' She was on the verge of tears but when she spoke again her voice was calculating. 'You're so in love with that fucking country. Well, guess what? I'm not. I'm never going back. And you want to know something else? I lied to you. I didn't even care enough to vote.'

Stefan took off his glasses and rubbed them on his turtle-neck.

They ate their pasta in silence. If he'd been a dog his ears would have folded back in appeasement. In bed that night, the fingertips tracing the length of her spine told her that he still cared about her, despite her outburst. It didn't matter, she could not forgive herself, and when she didn't roll over and move into his arms he stopped and left her alone. A few days later she once again ended the relationship.

Thanks to the sleeping pill, Eva slept until ten. She devoured a plate of fresh pawpaw then took the shuttle bus back to the airport where she rented a car for the five-hour drive to Louis Trichardt.

She headed north on the N1. Beyond the outlying suburbs of Pretoria flat-topped thorn trees dotted the veld on either side of the road. Donkeys grazed near clusters of shacks built out of rusted car doors, sheets of corrugated iron, sacking, and anything else their broken inhabitants could find. Occasionally she passed a farmhouse surrounded by a tall security fence. A dry thirsty light washed over everything.

She knew the road well. There stood the one-pump petrol station, now abandoned, that her father had patronized. The owner had been a lean, thin-lipped Afrikaner who sat in a deck chair, cold Castle in one hand, pack of Lucky's in the other, and watched his black employee pump the petrol. There the bend in the road where her father once ran over a rinkhals, reversed over it to make sure it was dead, and then, despite Lorraine's protestations, invited Eva to look at the long grey-brown snake, its tail still violently whipping about.

Two hours into the drive she passed Boshoff's Nursery where her mother had bought her rose bushes. Eva braked sharply. She made a U-turn and pulled into the gravel drive-way and scanned the aisles. There were no roses in bloom. A

table with Eva and murmur, 'Are you sure you wouldn't like to try the tongue, Evie?' Unable to contain her laughter any longer Eva would flee the table for the toilet where she would try to compose herself. On her return, she'd find her mother, eyes rolling like an excitable horse, pestering Johanna, waving her serviette at her sister-in-law and demanding that she speak more slowly so she could understand her Afrikaans. It was only during the car ride back to the farm that Eva resumed the vigil she kept over her father's moods, anxiously watching the set of his jaw while her mother dissected the hours they'd spent at Voortrekker Suites, ready to change the subject if she sensed that her mother was going too far.

'*Skattebol*, another slice of pie?' Johanna asked.

Eva started. 'No, I'm fine right now.'

'A little more sherry?'

'Sure.'

In the unflattering light of the dining alcove her aunt's face looked wrung out and deeply lined. She'd never married and Eva had a vision of a teenage Johanna, stocky legged and frowning, in a school playground, one arm wrapped tight around her stuttering little brother, a fist raised at his tormentors.

Eva relented, after all the fritters were delicious. '*Tannie, die pampoen is baie lekker.*'

Johanna's lips quivered, she removed the hanky that she kept tucked between her breasts and dabbed her eyes and thanked God that her niece was home. She prayed for Martin's recovery and stared at the ceiling as if to check that her words had taken flight.

Eva promptly drained her sherry glass.

Johanna did the same, eyes flitting to the ceiling once more as she cried, 'And please forgive me for not making him leave the farm!'

'I'm sure you did everything you could,' Eva soothed.

'No, I went to the farm a few weeks ago. I hadn't seen him

in months and I cooked him a tongue, three chickens and a *melktert*. Like an expedition, I'm telling you. All that dust and that twisting road down through the koppies. It was terrible! I got there in the middle of the day and found him sleeping on the sofa with all the curtains closed. I made us some tea and when he stepped outside I saw that he hadn't shaved in days and – forgive me for saying this,' Johanna clutched Eva's hand, 'he smelled, bad, like he wasn't washing himself. I wanted to cry when I looked at his feet, all swollen and red.'

Through a thickening fog of Old Brown Sherry and jet lag, Eva stared at the veins on her aunt's hand, winding like rivers on a map, dividing into tributaries. She knew she should have some sort of emotional response, her aunt was telling sad stories about her father's decline – when Johanna had called her in New York and said, 'he's dying', her heart had almost stopped – but all Eva felt was immense fatigue, her head about to fall into the plate that held the last pumpkin fritter. She blinked at it, too good to waste. She picked it up and tried to concentrate on Johanna's words.

'I should have made him come home with me. But by the end of the visit he'd cheered up. You know why? That bloody dog stole the tongue. Ach, I was angry. But my *boetie* was laughing and if that's what it took I would serve tongue to that animal once a week. I thought he was going to be all right. Two weeks later I got a call from the hospital.'

Johanna tilted the sherry bottle, less than an inch left. Eva declined and Johanna finished it.

'He gave me something to give to you. I was in the car and he came out of the house with a box and said, "When my time comes, give these to Eva." I told him to stop talking such rubbish, but he insisted.'

Eva struggled to keep her eyes open. 'He gave you something?' she mumbled.

'Those diaries, the ones your mother kept. I put them in

your room. *Kind? Is jy wakker?* Come, come, you must go to bed.' Johanna ushered Eva down the hallway to the spare room. She peeled back the sheets on a sturdy single bed with a dark wooden headboard. Eva kicked off her shoes and pulled off her jeans and flopped on to the bed.

'Do you want your pyjamas?' Johanna asked when she returned with Eva's suitcase.

'Don't own any,' she murmured.

'Brush your –'

Eva shook her head.

Johanna stood beside the bed, chuckling. 'Look at you! Miss America with no pyjamas in my spare bed. Sleep well, *skattie*.'

At three in the morning Eva's eyes snapped open. She fumbled for the switch on the bedside light, uncertain of where she was. Two paintings hung on the wall opposite her, one of pale-skinned women with pastel headscarves sitting in the shade of an oasis. In the other, haggard men with white beards were leading a string of camels down a sand dune. Ah, yes, Johanna's house. She remembered her aunt talking about the diaries and wriggled out of the tightly tucked in blankets to search for them. In the corner of the room she spied a thick crocheted blanket folded on top of a cardboard box marked CASTLE LAGER. She tossed the blanket on to the bed, lifted the flaps and saw the familiar pebbly grain on the black leather covers of her mother's diaries. A small envelope rested on top of them. She withdrew a sheet of paper and recognized the spidery child-like handwriting.

For Eva. From your father.

Goose bumps rippled across her forearms. She'd had no contact with him for a decade; because of his stutter Martin had never befriended words, spoken or written, and it was through letters from Hendrik and Johanna, letters she reluctantly opened, that Eva learned about her father's decline.

She read the two short sentences again, then closed her eyes as she guessed at what remained unwritten.

Angrily, she crumpled the sheet of paper and tossed it to one side. She knelt beside the box and carefully removed the diaries, arranging them on the floor in three rows in chronological order. The first was a composition book, the kind Eva had used at school, and on the cover Lorraine had written 1974. The last diary – she noted this with a twist in her stomach – was for 1984.

She scooted a few feet away from them as if to get an overview. They're nothing more than daily entries about life on the farm, she told herself. Still, the notion of what her mother might have discovered unsettled her.

Eva stood up abruptly and moved back to the bed. She would not read them. There was no need to. She knew all there was to know about the farm. And her father knew, and why the hell had he asked Johanna to pass these on? She didn't have one jot of sympathy for the ruin of a man that her aunt had described, almost destitute in his own house.

Yet, when she was a child she'd always been curious about those diaries, wondering how her mother saw her and her father and their life on the farm. A quick look, that's all she'd need now. She scooped up the composition book and turned to the first entry of 1974.

3 FEBRUARY
We have a home! Not a farm that we are managing but our very own. Skinner's Drift! It is roughly three thousand hectare with the most extraordinary red sandstone rock formations marking the eastern border. The interior is harsh with a few baobabs and lots of stunted mopane trees, but we are living close to the Limpopo in a rundown double-storey farmhouse with a red-tile

roof and iron grille work on the windows. We walked the river this afternoon. It's dry but that happens for a few months each year. And the floodplain is rich and perfect for crops. Martin carried Eva on his shoulders and I've never seen him so happy. Eva kept asking questions and insisted on answering them herself. Later we found a puffadder coiled behind the toilet. Martin shot it and in the process cracked the cistern. So much to do and I should go to sleep, but I'm so excited! As I write this, Eva is sleeping on a camp bed in our room and Tosha is at my feet, wondering what to make of the sound of a hyena calling. As am I!!!

Eva could see the river winding through the trees beyond the farmhouse like a deserted highway. The sand was the colour of milk and honey in the lazy light of late afternoon, the silence broken by the mewling cries of the grey louries.

4 FEBRUARY

A day of unpacking and trying to understand this house, this new life. The world here is so different from the Eastern Cape. No ocean, no smell of the sea, instead we smell potatoes! There's a plant that grows on the banks of the river and it smells exactly like chopped raw potatoes. Dolf Claasen our neighbour visited today with tales of leopards and elephants. The era of big game roaming in this area is coming to an end, but there is still plenty of wildlife on the Botswana side of the Limpopo. It's just dawning on me what it means to be living on the border. Right now I could take my cup of tea, walk across the dry riverbed (nervously, because Dolf has spooked me with his elephant stories) and be in another country. And I love the fact that I am finally living in a double-storey house. Call me hoity toity if you like but we're coming up in the world. No more one-bedroom farm managers' homes for us, buckets in the kitchen to catch the leaks and an outside toilet. Eva will have her own room and we'll have an office downstairs. In a few days I'm driving into Louis Trichardt and Johanna will show me the shops.

6 FEBRUARY

An African man showed up at the door this morning, hat in hand, saying that he would work hard, asking us to please give him a chance. His name is Ezekiel and he worked for the previous owners and my sense is that he's a good, trustworthy man. Martin has him tearing down old chicken coops, clearing away a lot of rusted junk. He lives in a shack near the river. I gave him a few slices of bread for lunch and asked him if he wasn't scared when the elephants come through. He laughed and said that when he hears them he lies very still on his bed.

Eva closed the composition book and placed it back on the floor. She wrapped her arms around herself, trying to tear away from the image of Ezekiel standing at the kitchen door, crumpling his hat in his hands, hoping the baas will give him a job and he won't have to move on. It would have been better if he had. She hadn't seen him since the day her mother was killed. She'd left, travelled far away from Skinner's Drift, and he'd continued to work for Martin.

Her chest felt tight, the room airless and she opened the window and slipped her hand through the burglar bars. She rubbed her fingers together as if feeling the texture of the night. The Soutpansberg were two, maybe three miles away. It was still wild country, and her thoughts skittered around the leopard that would be prowling the ravines at this hour, the anxious baboons huddling together on rock ledges. No jackals though. *Phukubje*, that was the Sotho word for jackal, Ezekiel had told her. They mated for life and they preferred flatter, more open terrain.

2

September 1997

Louis Trichardt's hospital, a modest avocado-green brick building, sat on the foothills of the mountains, a twenty minute walk uphill from Johanna's house. Eva was out of breath by the time she pushed open the front door and inquired where she could find Dr de Vet, the physician monitoring her father's condition.

A woman at the front desk told her to take a seat and an intercom crackled to life. '*De Vet? De Vet? Daar's imand vir jou in die wagkamer.*'

The windows were wide open, the smell of disinfectant slight. The standards of medical care in South Africa were slipping, but if she had to choose between an antiseptic American hospital and this one where a bird could fly in, where a gecko was clinging to the wall just above the sagging sofa – well, she'd want to die here. She browsed through the classified ads in an old copy of *Farmer's Weekly*. Across the country people were selling muscovy ducklings, Rhodesian ridgeback puppies, breeding crocodiles, bees, ostriches and imported capuchin monkeys.

'Miss van Rensburg?'

The voice startled her 'Yes!' She leapt up, the magazine slipping to the floor.

Doctor de Vet bent down to pick it up, then shook her hand and introduced himself.

An ancient-looking stethoscope with a cracked rubber casing hung around his neck and in a rough Afrikaans accent he talked to Eva about her father's debilitated liver and alcohol cardial myopathy. 'It creates a flabbiness of the heart. The South African disease, I call it. Too much drinking in this country.' A series of small strokes had left Martin partially paralysed on the right side of his body. Some recovery was expected, but for the moment he did not recognize any of his visitors.

'Visitors?' The use of the plural surprised Eva. In one of his letters Hendrik had mentioned that her father was leading an increasingly isolated life, cut off from the community.

'Your aunt, of course.' Eva sensed an edge to his voice and she imagined he'd found Johanna rather taxing. 'There's a Mrs Louw who comes to see him. And an old black man recently visited. Your aunt was upset by that, wanting to know who he was, why we let him in. Can't stop him, I told her. I think he must have been one of the workers on the farm. So, visit your father and we will talk again tomorrow morning.'

'Can I ask you something? It sounds crude, I know. But – well, what I'm hearing is that my father is *not* on his deathbed.'

'I will be blunt with you. No. Not yet. We will release him, but it will be just a matter of time before he comes back to us.'

'O-kay.'

'Your aunt told me you have a farm.'

Eva nodded.

'He cannot go back there. He needs care. I've discussed some of this with your aunt and she seems to want to take him into her home. I notice you have an American accent.'

'Yes, I live there now.'

De Vet smiled. 'Americans are inching their way towards immortality. Do you know their life expectancy exceeds ours? We're talking whites, of course.' He extended his hand. 'Your father is in Ward D.'

The names posted on the wall told Eva that Martin occupied

bed number three. She entered quietly to find five wandering-eyed old men and a buxom black woman: an orderly she assumed. One bed was empty. She stopped at the foot of bed number two where a rotund sweating man feebly tossed his head from side to side. The woman tended to her father in the adjacent bed, and Eva heard huffing and puffing and the snap of sheets being changed.

'Your nightmare, hey, Mr van Rensburg, to have me looking after you? You know what my revenge is for all you old white farmers? To do such a good job that I bring you back to health. Maybe I get some *muti* from the *sangoma* and mix it into your jelly and custard and make you younger. Mmm hmm, start a conspiracy, all across the country, turn all the dying old *boere* into young men!' She walloped Martin's pillow several times. 'So you have many, many years to experience the joy and freedom of our new South Africa!'

Eva burst out laughing. The woman spun around, generous hips jiggling, and clapped a hand over her mouth.

'Oh, it's all right,' Eva reassured her. 'Make them all as young as you like!'

The woman relaxed. 'Mr Snyman is your father?'

Eva looked once more at the head tossing man, his false teeth grinning in a glass of pink liquid on the table beside him. She wondered what his story was. 'No,' she finally replied, and she motioned to her father's bed.

'Ah, Mr van Rensburg's daughter. Come, come!'

She approached the foot of Martin's bed and glanced at the woman's name tag. She wasn't an orderly, she was a nurse. Her name was Fortune Ramothiba and with a deft movement she pulled a green curtain around the bed leaving Eva alone with her father.

He had become an old man in the years that she'd been gone and she immediately felt guilty for leaving. But the idea of staying with him in that farmhouse set her heart kicking.

She would have died if she'd done that. Martin had once been a boyishly handsome man with intense blue eyes, the lines on his high forehead giving him a slight quizzical expression; now his cheeks were sunken and salted with stubble, and one of the strokes had smeared the left corner of his mouth into a grimace. His pyjama top was unbuttoned, revealing a slack freckled chest and his underarm hair. When she was a little girl, Eva had thought the tips of two lion's tails were peeking out from his armpits.

His rheumy blue eyes wandered across the room and she began to sweat, a tentative smile appearing on her face, even as she feared the moment when he locked eyes with her and dragged her into the strange mad ocean in which he was floating.

'. . . Dad . . .' The word cracked in her throat.

Martin's eyes swept across her face with no hint of recognition.

She moved to his side. 'Dad?' she whispered in an agitated voice. Again they drifted past her, vacant, flat as buttons. She could have been a stranger.

It wasn't relief that Eva felt, but a growing sense of outrage.

She stomped down the hill, past maids hanging washing and dogs that didn't bother to bark at a white person. Johanna was waiting at her garden gate, hanky in one hand, her eyes wide and questioning.

'He's fine,' Eva snapped.

The eyes grew even wider. 'He spoke to you?'

'No. But he's going to make it. I spoke to de Vet.' She snorted, relishing the irony of the name, and headed inside, Johanna on her heels asking, 'Is he still crying, suffering so?'

Eva sat heavily on one of the *riempie* benches. 'Those aren't tears. De Vet said they are of no emotional significance whatsoever.' She'd fudged the truth, just a fraction, de Vet had said he doubted the tears were an emotional response. 'His eyes are leaking because the stroke must have affected part of his auto – auto something nervous system.'

'Liars. All doctors are liars!' Johanna shoved the hanky between her breasts and set them shivering like two baked custards. 'Your pa has a lot to cry about, to lose a wife in such an awful way.' She reached out a plump, veiny hand and squeezed Eva's forearm. '*Skattebol*, he knows you've come back.'

Eva looked despairingly around the room. The prospect of afternoons spent reminiscing with Johanna alarmed her, and knowing that the sun blazed outside made the gloomy lounge, with its sacrificial springbuck and dour wooden furniture that conjured up images of women in *kappies* and men with beards down to their navels, even more oppressive.

'I have a craving for samosas,' she suddenly said to her aunt. 'Does the Greek on the corner of Main Street still sell them?'

He did. Eva immediately drove into town and bought three deliciously greasy, curried potato and onion samosas for lunch. She sat in her car and ate them, munching on the crispy corners first, the way she used to as a teenager. Then she drove past a few of Louis Trichardt's hotels – a dull group except for the Misty Mountain on the outskirts of town. She followed the driveway lined with pine trees to the reception building where several monkeys had ganged up on a ginger cat that stood, fangs bared, in a bed of geraniums. A stout middle-aged man wearing a safari suit and a paisley print waist-coat, and carrying a beaky looking chihuahua under his arm, watched the skirmish from the doorway. Eva was won over, the rates were reasonable, and she made a reservation for the following night.

On her return to Voortrekker Suites she announced her plans. Johanna looked grim.

'This is so emotional for both of us and I think we could use the space. I promise I'll stop by for tea every day,' Eva reassured.

After much frowning Johanna finally said she respected a young woman's needs. 'And I must make that spare room nice for your pa.'

The chihuahua was asleep on the guest register when Eva checked in the following afternoon. Jock Ferreira, the manager of the Misty Mountain, was sporting another flamboyant waistcoat, and he asked the dog to move, both in English and Afrikaans, before lifting it up so that Eva could sign the book. Standing on the other side of the counter she could have sworn that Jock's eyebrows were lightly pencilled in. He was den mother of a sort to the hotel's predominantly male clientele – the jovial businessmen from Zimbabwe who wore wide colourful ties and carried battered leather briefcases; the mournful Afrikaner salesmen who favoured khaki; and the four helicopter pilots who appeared as Jock handed Eva her key and announced they were staying six months while they completed a geological survey of the Venda and Louis Trichardt area.

Eva drove to the upper terrace and parked in front of her room. De Vet's confidence that her father was going to pull through had made things clear to her, a few more days of being the dutiful daughter and she would return to New York. She took a phone card from her wallet and dialled her number to check her answering machine.

Uh, hi, Eva. It's, uh, Nathan, uh, Nathan Borowitz. You, uh, gave me your number a few nights ago in, uh, Rudy's. Remember? Anyway I'll, uh, try you again.

Ms van Rensburg, this is Gloria at Dr Abramsky's office. Your last cleaning was a year and a half ago. Please call 369-5050 for an appointment.

Hi, it's, uh, Nath—

Eva deleted the message and ran her tongue across her teeth. Rudy's was the neighbourhood bar on her corner, the haunt of the 'help, I've got to slog through yet another day' crowd.

She switched on the lamp next to her bed, with its startling cover of charging elephants, and unpacked her belongings, stacking the diaries on the chest of drawers. Night had fallen, plonked down on her – none of that graceful, slow slanting light that settles on the brownstones in New York. In Africa night pours out of a bucket in the sky. She felt glum. Hesperian Depression, she decided. It affected baboons, the onset of night and the possibility of an attack by a leopard making them keen and clutch each other. In an attempt to cheer herself up, she dressed for dinner. Lip gloss and mascara, suede boots with a narrow two-inch heel and a clingy blouse.

Elderly black waiters wearing red fezzes and white tennis shoes slowly criss-crossed the dining room, bearing trays laden with grey roast beef and lumpy mashed potatoes. The Zimbabwean businessmen sat together and laughed and shook their forks at each other. The white salesmen, seated here and there at tables for one, looking like tufts of dry grass in their safari suits, kept glancing at her. After dinner Eva joined the helicopter pilots in the bar where the liquor bottles stood on a shelf book ended by two mounted warthog heads.

They were dreadful chauvinists which annoyed her, then amused her. Three rum and Cokes later, she had abandoned all attempts to join their conversation and sat sprawled in her chair, the dopey smile on her face saying: Heavens, no, I'm not as clever as you, I know nothing about the genetic bottle-neck in the cheetah population and I'm totally ignorant when it comes to South African politics and America's affairs for that matter.

When Greg, the blond pilot who had initially feigned mild

disinterest in her, offered to walk her to her room, Eva almost replied, good, I want to sleep with you.

They went to his room instead where his puppy, a female boerbul with boxing glove-sized paws, snoozed in a pile of his dirty laundry. He was strong, different from the men she'd known in New York. His arms were ropey and there were smells on his body that reminded her of the bush. They made love quickly.

Afterwards, he drifted off to sleep and she lay beside him in the dark, eyes open, watching the headlights from the few lorries climbing up the mountain sweep across the ceiling. She wondered if she'd been foolish. She felt vulnerable, making love to him had made her touch the earth somehow – night folding around her, her breath dissipating in the cool air of the Soutpansberg, and a familiar longing pressing against her heart like tiny thumbs. She rolled away from him, remembering her first time, on the banks of the Limpopo; Neels pleading with her and then spreading his camouflage shirt on the sand, later, sitting at dinner and thinking *I'm a woman now*, slicing the meat on her plate, drinking a glass of Coke, and tumbling into fantasies of escape and a life away from Skinner's Drift.

The puppy ambled over and licked Eva's hand. She heaved it on to the bed next to Greg and quietly got dressed and left his room.

She met the monkeys the following morning when she drew her curtains and startled three of them in the midst of a flea-nipping session on the hibiscus hedge outside her window. One of them hissed at her, revealing tiny fangs in a seashell pink mouth. Eva slowly dropped to her knees so her head was level with the windowsill. She stared at the animal and it stared back through piercing black eyes that, for a few moments, made Eva and her struggles seem utterly unimportant. When the animal sauntered off, she did exactly what the sign in her room cautioned against: removed the coffee supplies from the jar on the dresser, scattered packets of sugar on the tray, and opened the door. She went to the bathroom, left that door slightly ajar, lowered the lid of the toilet and sat down and waited. Within ten minutes, monkeys with cremora beards were eating the sugar, performing a benediction with their wrinkled black palms as they romped across her unmade bed.

Ensconced in the Misty Mountain, Eva quickly settled into a routine. She resumed her reading of the diaries and woke each morning by nine, made a cup of coffee, placed sugar on the windowsill for the monkeys, and climbed back into bed. Day after day her childhood spooled out in her memory. Sightings of aardvarks and aardwolves; the purchase of irascible Shylock, Eva's first pony; the excitement of the early harvests; a flask of afternoon tea beside the Limpopo and a swim when the river was flowing swiftly and crocodiles weren't a threat. Eva hadn't wanted to know how sweet the early years on Skinner's Drift had been, and to have them documented so left her feeling tender.

When Eva reached the diary for 1981, the pace of her reading slowed. She'd gone to boarding school and, apart from the African workers, Martin and Lorraine were alone on the farm. No longer her mother and her father, they'd become husband and wife and Eva felt uncomfortable, as though she were prying. Lorraine never wrote about her marriage, but in the descriptions of still days when not even the breeze from the river visited the garden, the noting of the pitiful rainfall, and the occasional entry about attacks against farmers in other parts of the country and her concern for their safety, Eva sensed her mother's isolation, her father's growing obsession with defending his land. She used to feel it when she came home for the school holidays, the air in the house tinged with disillusionment.

Around noon, she drove into town for her lunch of three samosas, a neon-green cream soda, and one of the sweets from her childhood – chocolate Flakes, tooth-rotting Beehives, marshmallow mice with liquorice tails.

By two o'clock she was in Ward D, struggling to reconcile all that she'd encountered in the diaries with this moment, sitting beside the husk of her father.

After an hour of silence at his bedside, she headed for Johanna's house and a cup of tea and slice of whatever calorie-laden treat her aunt had baked. She dodged all discussion of future plans and weepy reminiscences about the past by encouraging her aunt's penchant for gossip. Did Eva know that after the election, Patience, the maid who used to work for Mrs Meiring up the street, had camped on the lawn with her babies, had washed the dirty nappies in the fishpond, and insisted that Mandela told her that she could have Mrs Meiring's house? And what did Eva think about the queen keeping her dead corgis, preserved for ever by the royal taxidermist, in a velvet-lined room in the back of Buckingham Palace? When their laughter grew too loud, after all Martin was *suffering so*, just up the hill, Eva placated Johanna by slipping into a few sentences of Afrikaans.

By dusk she was back at the hotel, soaking in the bath. She joined Greg and the other pilots for dinner, then drinks at the bar from which she and Greg excused themselves after about an hour, and made their way to his room. Later, when he was snoring, she slipped away. She took the cement walk that zig-zagged up the slope; past rooms where the Zimbabweans were laughing in front of their TV sets; past the Afrikaner sales-man, each night there was a different one standing in the park-ing lot, smoking a cigarette and looking at the stars. He always greeted her, this lonesome Afrikaner, the glimmer of hope for a quickie in his eyes, or so she thought, if not that then surely a few minutes commiseration about how South Africa

31

was going to the dogs. Good evening, Eva always said in a voice laced with America and she quickened her pace.

Back in her room, she would curl up on her bed and stare at the diaries on the dressing table. The pile of those she'd read was growing taller and taller and she admonished herself: You know how this is going to end, stop reading them.

In the eight days that Eva had been visiting her father, a courtship had sprung up in the trees outside the window beside Martin's bed. *Whoop* sang the first barbet, *dudu* answered the second, but their conversation was so swift that to the untrained ear they sounded like one bird. *Whoop-dudu whoop-dudu* they sang, coaxing Eva to return to the bush.

She craned her neck, trying to catch a glimpse of them, then gave up and once again studied her father. There was a definite touch of pinkness to his cheeks. His breathing seemed deeper and easier.

The sweating man in bed number two had been discharged the previous day and a Mr Grobbelaar, still lucid enough to blanch at the sight of the indomitable African nurse approaching him with a thermometer, had taken his place.

'Sissie . . . I'm fine . . .' he whined to Fortune, using the term of familiarity with which whites addressed their maids on the days they wanted to cosy up to them.

'That's right, *Meneer* Grobbelaar. And this is Sun City and just down the hall are the gambling tables. Was it last week that you hit the jackpot, Eva?'

Eva smiled. Her relationship with the nurse pleased her. It felt clean, the first time she'd ever had such an uncomplicated interplay with a black person, and she wondered if other whites secretly wore their 'easy friendships' as badges of pride, evidence that the transition into their new country had been a smooth one.

'One hundred and two.' Fortune shook her head and slipped

the thermometer into her pocket. 'I tell you what, *Meneer* Grobbelaar, stay for just a few days. And then you can go back to the farm. Ja, what's the name of your farm?'

'Jakalsfontein,' Grobbelaar groaned.

'Jackal Springs . . . very nice . . .' She winked at Eva and made a notation on his chart.

'Fortune?' Eva asked. 'Do you also have an African name?'

'Mmm, Mahlatse. You know what it means?' She hung the chart on the railing at the end of bed number two and moved on.

'No.'

'Guess.'

'She who will turn the old white *boere* into strapping young men?'

Mahlatse chuckled. 'It means fortune. I will have good fortune. I will know the fortunes of others!'

'Mahlatse,' Eva repeated. 'And do you know people's fortunes?'

'Ha! If I did, do you think I would have married Clever Boy? Do you think I would have paid the most *un*skilled builder in all of Vivo to fix the roof on my mother's house? Ai, too much fun with you in the ward, Eva.'

Eva glanced again at her father. Another fifteen minutes and she'd head to Johanna's for tea. She angled her chair so she also had a view out the window and listened to the nurse as she continued on her rounds.

'Mr Jakobs, you are not looking so well. We must pray for you. Mr van Rensburg, when are you going to say hello to your daughter?'

Whoop-dudu whoop-dudu sang the barbets. One settled on a low branch in front of the window, bobbing up and down as it called, and Eva could clearly see its bright-red face and breast, its stubby black beak.

Then Mahlatse began to sing.

Bird song and the nurse's mellow voice licked through the ward and a wave of bittersweet homesickness engulfed Eva. Yes, she was in South Africa, but she longed to go all the way home, back to those golden late afternoons when she'd ride her horse down a path on Skinner's Drift and feel utterly embraced by birds and sunshine and the distant sound of African music on a radio in one of the kraals.

'Oh, don't stop,' she said as Mahlatse's voice dropped to a hum. The barbet flitted away and Eva turned to the nurse. 'What were you . . .' Her words evaporated. Her father was watching her, his blue eyes questioning. She flushed with indignation, feeling as though he'd spied on her.

'Somebody knows you,' Mahlatse said from the foot of his bed.

Martin glanced at the nurse and then returned his watery gaze to his daughter. 'Eva?' he asked weakly.

'Hello, Dad.' Her voice felt small and tight. 'I flew in from New York. I've come to see you.'

Seconds passed and his eyes fluttered shut. She placed a hand on her chest, her heart threatening to thump free.

'He's happy to see you,' Mahlatse crooned.

'No-no –' Eva shook her head, grabbed her bag and hurried out of the ward.

She yelped in the car as she sped down the hill, past Johanna's house and back to the hotel. She still loved him. Nothing would ever be as intoxicating as those moments she had had with him as a child, sitting beside him in the bakkie when they drove the dirt roads on Skinner's Drift at night, seeing an animal and whispering *jackal . . . honey badger . . . rooikat . . .*

Things started to go wrong when she returned from her first term at boarding school. The smell of the river in the air, small birds with turquoise breasts dust-bathing beneath one of the rose bushes – Eva was thirteen, encountering home after eight weeks of French lessons and thrilling afternoons in the hall listening to the older girls debating, sparring with ideas and dazzling sentences. And there was her father approaching her across the verandah, wanting to ask her something. For the first time she was horrified by his stutter. The donkey-like sounds that he made, the tendons in his neck stretched tight like sinews. Shame clouded his eyes and she immediately knew that he'd sensed her disgust. She blinked back her tears and vowed to keep on deciphering the rhythms of his breath, the barely noticeable jerking movements of his left hand that told her what he was thinking and feeling. He was her father and she would do anything for him.

Eva pulled into the parking place at the hotel. Monkeys scampered along the roof as she opened the door to her room. She stared at the dresser and the diary for 1984 which she had yet to read. She'd gone mad that year. Just thinking about it set something shameful burrowing into her gut. How she wanted to drown it with a few drinks, masturbate it away, crawl into someone's arms. Too late for that. She picked up the diary and read the first entry, weighing every word.

1 JANUARY 1984

New Year's Day. And I'm trying to be hopeful. It's unthinkable that yet another year of drought awaits us, of course the rains will come. But then, I imagine that if I look at the first entry in last year's diary I will see myself trying to conjure up the same optimism. The borehole keeps pumping up water. On a still day, when I'm sitting in the kitchen, I can hear the motor kick in. It used to be a sound that Martin loved, our water, sloshing into the holding tank. Now I see him tense up when he hears it. It makes no sense for water to be coming out of the ground when it's not falling from the sky, he said.

3

8 JANUARY 1984
It's awful, but the drought has a language all of its own. At the civil defence meeting today Rolene told us that Detlef, who is quite proficient in tracking, can see the hunger and the desperation in the game on their farm. Elephants are digging up and down the Limpopo searching for water and around these holes he's finding impala tracks with drag marks. A sign that the animals are extremely stressed and will soon die. And during the spring rut (what spring? to write the word is a travesty) they lost several males. After expending what little energy they had left defending their herds, they were unable to mate, unable to even stand and search for grazing and they died of exhaustion.

Martin was flung out of sleep, a buffalo of a memory bearing down on him, making him gasp, adrenalin shooting into his heart, his gut in spasms. *Jesus fucking Christ!* He looked wildly around the dimly lit bedroom. The extravagant spiralling horns of the kudu mounted on the opposite wall, Lorraine's white nightgown draped over a chair, the drone of the floor polisher, brought him back to his surroundings.

Watching the two flies that had settled in the tangle of sheets between his legs, he reached across the night table, eased a lace doily off the glass of milk that he had placed there and brought the glass to his lips, sending the milk to work, waiting for it to neutralize the drinks from the night before. When he'd drained it, he carefully placed the glass back on the table, not startling the flies. Pain carved at his forehead and he lay still beneath the sheets. He was in danger

– somewhere in his thoughts lay the memory of what he had done in the darkness of the previous night's hunt.

He marshalled his attention around the day's work. Irrigate the fields of young tomatoes. Repair the fence on the southern boundary. Make sure Jannie has taken care of the oil leak in the delivery truck. And then there was a three o'clock meeting at the bank in Messina with Fanie Booysen, when a little matter concerning monthly payments would be discussed.

Martin listened, the floor polisher was suddenly silent. Seconds passed. He heard the gate to the front garden click shut. The maid was going home for breakfast, but instead of leaving through the gate near the carport, as she was supposed to, she had walked through the rose garden. He raised his left hand – only a slight tremor – and brought it down swiftly on the fly closest to him. The other one scattered and he untangled himself from the sheets and glanced at the clock. Eight in the morning already.

Martin had slept three hours later than usual. Still, he dressed slowly, staring out of the bedroom window which offered the best view of his land. The double-storey house, unusual for the Limpopo valley with its squat hunkered down farmhouses, sat on the edge of a gentle rise. Beyond the garden of roses and fruit trees and fragrant vines, all kept well watered despite the drought, the land dipped until it reached the border fence. When Martin bought Skinner's Drift, this fence consisted of only three strands of barbed wire erected for quarantine purposes to keep out stray cattle from Botswana. But a few years ago, with concerns about terrorist incursions mounting – a cache of weapons and food was found on De Hoop, several prime Afrikaner oxen on Nie Te Ver were blown to bits when the boy herding them down a dirt track near the river came across a land mine – the SADF had fortified most of the border and erected two parallel fences well over fifteen feet tall with curls of razored wire in between. The fences were a few hundred feet shy of the actual border which lay in the middle of the Limpopo. Tall locked gates built into the fence every few kilometres allowed farmers access to the river.

There had been a summer of torrential rain when the Limpopo breached its banks and spilled across the floodplain, and Martin had stood at this window and seen blue fracturing the sunlight between the ancient trees. Now there was nothing but dry earth and way off in the distance between the nyala trees and the sycamore figs, a glint of sand, searing white, the bones of his river. The Limpopo hadn't flowed in two years.

Most mornings at this hour Lorraine would be tending to her roses, but the garden below him was deserted except for a pair of crimson-breasted shrikes fossicking amongst the fallen leaves beneath the fig trees. He remembered that it was Wednesday and she must be at her civil defence meeting. And Eva? He rushed the thought through his head. Never in the house. Never slept late. Probably out riding.

Ignoring the suggestion of breakfast waiting for him downstairs in the dining room – boxes of cereal, bread, a jar of Lorraine's green fig jam – he lingered in the doorway. He'd been in here the night before, he remembered. He and Eva standing in a messy kitchen, Lorraine's teacup beside the sink. Lorraine had been upstairs, asleep as was always the case with her when they returned from a night drive. She hadn't wanted them to go hunting. There was enough meat in the freezer, they could make do, she'd said. She'd glared at him when he slid his keys across the table to Eva, his signal for her to get his rifle from the cabinet in their office. He knew Lorraine disapproved of the way he hunted at night, catching antelope in the headlights, but it wasn't sport, just food for god's sake. Sometimes he wondered if his wife had any understanding of the demands of running a farm.

Martin stared at the clean dishes stacked on the draining

board beside the sink. He couldn't remember what Eva had done when they returned from the night's hunting, probably made herself a plate of leftovers. The next thing he did remember was sitting in the darkened lounge. He had his brandy glass in his hand and he was listening to the soft tread of her footsteps as she moved around upstairs.

He checked the lounge, now filled with sunlight. No brandy bottle or glass next to his chair. The maid must have already cleaned the room. He moved to the bar, gulped a shot of brandy straight from the bottle, shuddered from the bite of it, gulped another and then returned to the kitchen where he opened the back door and stepped into the garden.

The heat of the day felt smothering, thick-furred, as if he were crawling underneath the belly of a monstrous animal squatting over the house. Beyond the chain-link fence that surrounded the garden, Ezekiel and Wellington lay sprawled on the ground in the shade of a bougainvillea, blue overalls tied off at their waists. Martin moved closer. Two magenta blossoms had fallen on to Wellington's dark chest. On his side of the fence, Martin saw his dogs motionless on the lawn: Tosha with her legs splayed, Leeutjie the young ridgeback on his back, rose pink tongue hanging out of his mouth.

Panic scuttled through him as he wondered what else he had done with his gun the night before. He stumbled back towards the house and tripped over a dog's bowl and dropped his keys. Leeutjie sprang up, saw Martin and then flung himself against the fence in a flurry of barking. Ezekiel and Wellington scrambled to their feet and Martin hurled his voice at them with relief. 'Sleeping! You l-l-lazy buggers!'

He opened the gate and grabbed Leeutjie by his collar so the young dog could not escape while Tosha, his almost blind, brindled bull terrier, bumped her way through.

'Morning, baas!' Ezekiel lifted Tosha into the flatbed of the bakkie, then climbed in.

Wellington vaulted in easily after him and grinned as Martin approached. *'Pha'la! Pha'la!'* he chanted, drumming the side.

Martin paused before opening the door. That's right, he'd forgotten about it – he *had* shot an impala. And there was the garden hose. It had been dragged over to the carport so Wellington or Ezekiel could rinse the blood out of the flatbed.

'You see it?' he asked Wellington.

'No, baas. Miss Eva told me.'

The mention of her name set his stomach churning and he wondered just where his daughter might be. He opened the bakkie's door. Something didn't feel right. He shifted his weight, patted his shirt pocket. Cigarettes? Yes. He reached behind him with his left hand. Rifle? No. He always went out with a rifle, but this morning he had forgotten it. He walked swiftly back into the house and went to his office where he unlocked the gun case and reached for the closest one. Then he went out to check his cool room and saw an impala ram, with a long clean slit running the length of its belly, stretched out on the steel table. He had no recollection of eviscerating it, couldn't even remember carrying it from the bakkie to the cool room. The animal was painfully thin, barely worth butchering. He walked back into the house and took another swig from the brandy bottle before driving the short distance to the pump station.

The rains of 1981 and 1982 had been scant, last year's even more pitiful, and since then Martin had not trusted his water in the hands of Ezekiel and Wellington. He did it all himself, flicking the switches at the pump house, adjusting the movement of the centre pivot irrigation system that spun skeins of water over his three immense circular fields. After several stammered lectures about how precious the water was and the hell they would have to be pay if they wasted a drop – *make sure I never find a leak, anywhere!* – an uneasy ritual had developed amongst the three men.

'D-do you know what that is?' Martin would ask as he covetously watched the rows of tomatoes and potatoes glistening beneath the spray of Limpopo valley water.

'*Ja*, baas,' Wellington would respond.

'Is that w-water, W-w-wellington.'

'No, baas.'

'Are you sure? It looks like water to me, Wellington?'

Martin always found it easy to say Wellington the second time around, he remembered the shape of the word, could catch it in his mouth and present it intact to the world. And Wellington, looking relieved when his name slid out the second time, would grin at Ezekiel.

'Hell, d-d-don't be so stupid.' No need to risk Wellington's name for a third time. 'If it's not water then why don't you tell me and old Ezekiel what it is.'

'Gold and diamonds, baas!' Wellington would sing with a slappy soft-shoe shuffle. 'Gold and diamonds!'

That's right, Martin would think, on the Reef they have their gold, just down the road De Beers has its diamonds, and here I have my water.

There was no ritual this morning. Martin entered the small building that housed the pumping equipment, flicked the switches and listened anxiously to the roar of the water surging into his holding tanks. He then drove half an hour to the southern boundary of the farm where he dropped Ezekiel and Wellington, telling them to spend the day checking the fences.

He returned to his fields alone and parked in the shade of a large nyala tree. Stay! he told Tosha. The heat was merciless, already into the nineties, and he walked the line between the scorched earth and the verdant irrigated rows of young tomatoes. Within five minutes he reached the far curve where he found several trampled plants. He noticed a small footprint and scuffed it with his shoe. He found another and another, then they vanished as if whoever had made them had suddenly taken flight. He stared at the stocky mopane bushes and the knobthorn tree beyond the nearby dam, trying to orientate himself.

They had been driving east along the river road when they came across the small herd of impala. Martin switched off the engine and Eva handed him his rifle. He was still smarting from Lorraine's disapproval and he whispered to his daughter, 'No. You do it, my girl.' He waited, watching her hands briefly touch the gun and then curl back into fists. She refused. Since she had started at boarding school he'd been coaxing her to take her first animal and she always said, next time, I promise. Now, she shook her head adamantly and said that she didn't want to. He was stunned, and hurt. He reached across the passenger seat and pulled his old silver hip flask out of the glove compartment. A silent bitter toast to his wife. *So you finally claimed our daughter.* He drained the flask and Eva sat silent beside him, arms folded, rifle resting on her lap. The impala that had been blinded by the headlights suddenly broke away, startled by a jackal that trotted into view. Martin pulled the pistol that he kept tucked in the waistband of his trousers and fired several shots at the jackal. Predators were the only creatures thriving on his drought-stricken farm and he hated them.

He started the engine and they looped into the interior. Amidst the eerie-looking termite mounds and the squat mopane bushes he spotted that starving ram. He shot it and made Eva help him place it in the flatbed.

They were heading home, driving slowly along the road that led past the empty dam and on to the fields, a stagnant silence in the bakkie, when he saw it running through the far reach of his headlights. He slammed on his brakes. The early moon had not set and he saw it even when it darted out of the light and he pulled out his pistol and fired at it. 'Dad! No!' Eva cried out. He pushed her to the floor of the bakkie and told her to stay down. He switched off the engine and walked along the edge of the field, the shadow of that gunshot still flying through him, gathering up all the other sounds of the night, the piercing whistle of a pearl-spotted owl, the crisp leg brushing and wing rubbing of numerous beetles and moths, until all that remained was the scuff of his shoes on the ground. By the time he found it he was beyond caring.

He was standing in front of it when he heard the gasping, and he fired again. But that ugly gasping sound continued and he was furious, was on the verge of firing for a third time when he realized the sound came from behind him. He turned to find his daughter's terrified eyes, terrified and terrifying, as if they'd become unmoored, were floating towards him.

He couldn't hold her gaze and quickly swung his head away, only to be blinded by the bakkie's headlights. He felt off balance and flailed at the air, teetering on his heels, the ground seeming to shift under his feet. The gasping stopped and he knew Eva had moved away. She hadn't brushed past him, but he felt something flowing from himself. A part of him was leaving. It was her. He lifted his head to the stars, a cool light that bathed his burning eyes. Just for a moment he thought he heard rain, the unmistakable fat sounds of the first heavy drops hitting the ground. A laugh spiralled inside him and then vanished. *If this is what I needed to do to bring rain I would have shot one a long time ago.* It wasn't rain. He looked down to see Eva scratching at the ground, throwing sand and dry leaves on to the small body. He yanked her to her feet and slapped her across the face. Eyes now eerily calm stared back at him as he reached for her cold hand and led her firmly to the bakkie. In the headlights, driving home, they picked out another jackal. He let it be, the keen pointed face looking at him as he drove by.

★

It took Martin half an hour to find the grave. He guessed Eva had used a branch to brush the ground, covering her tracks and those of the night before, but as he roamed the bushveld between the fields and the empty dam he found footprints. She was cunning and clever but it was always in the service of something soft. That was her problem, he thought, no matter how cunning and clever she was her emotions could get the better of her, and emotions led to mistakes.

He looked for drag marks, for freshly turned soil. Ants finally pointed him in the direction of the grave. Hours earlier she'd dislodged a nest on the side of a small donga and the ants were still streaming in all directions. Martin stared at them and listened for the sound of movement.

Was she still here? Hiding? Watching him?

No, not Eva, she couldn't sit still that long.

He climbed down into the shallow ravine where the earth was softer, easier to dig. He broke off a branch from a nearby bush, squatted next to an area that seemed uniformly smooth and probed the ground. The stick slid right in. He pulled it out and stood up, quickly wrapping his indignation around his violently leaping heart.

Mine! This is my land!

He calmed himself. Years of hunting had taught him never to panic in the bush. He stood absolutely still and listened. There was nothing to fear. No one was out there. He was safe.

He remembered the way, the night before, he had started the engine, turned the steering wheel, headlights illuminating the edge of the tomato fields, then the dirt road. He had felt it in his body, a visceral relief, a knowing of the way night worked, darkness descending on the tangle of mopane scrub where he and Eva had just stood, a tide of blackness obliterating everything that had happened there.

He froze. Someone *was* approaching, leaves and twigs

crunching under foot. He ducked until he heard a familiar panting and Tosha's battle-scarred muzzle came into view. Her devotion to him, and the relief that it was just her, brought him to the verge of tears. The dog was almost blind and yet she had jumped out of the bakkie to search for him.

'Tosha!' he whispered and he helped her as she scrambled down the side of the donga. She paid little attention to him and sniffed the ground ravenously. She lifted her head, swinging it this way and that, then, nose down, she began to dig.

No! He lunged for her collar. She pulled away, her thick neck tensing. Martin sank to his knees and yanked harder. He punched her in the haunches, but she was a bull terrier and a punch felt like a pat. She licked his face, tail beating against his thigh.

With one arm wrapped tight around his dog, he took off his belt and looped it through her collar. Past the dried-up dam he led her and on to the bakkie where he opened his door and pushed her over to the passenger seat. His shirt was soaked with sweat and the dog panted heavily so he started the engine and flipped the air conditioning switch to high. Soon Tosha settled her head on his lap and he stroked her muzzle. She was twelve, getting on for a farm dog. When the cataracts developed Martin worried that he would have to put her out of her misery, but with her sense of smell she still managed to get around.

According to Jannie, the one person Martin tentatively considered to be a friend, the only way to understand a dog's sense of smell was to think of colours. The young white man, sixteen years his junior, worked for Martin during harvest time, driving the delivery truck to the produce market in Johannesburg. But his real passion was the bush. He'd become a skilled taxidermist and had mounted the animals on display at Skinner's Drift. 'All the time, you and me are walking through smells so thick they're like clouds of colours,' he told

He pulled his four-year-old daughter close and stammered out a story about a wonderful world of lakes and rivers just below the hard-baked earth. Eva listened, wide-eyed. When he was finished she darted around, stamping the ground. Is it here? Is it here? Cocking her head like a bat-eared fox, listening for the sound of water.

Fourie had died ten years ago. The new diviner working the farms used a magnetometer, but even with that machine he couldn't address Martin's concerns about the water table. How much do I have? How much longer can I drink from the Limpopo? Skinner's Drift was heading towards foreclosure, there wasn't one cent to spend on drilling a new bore hole, and they were approaching the third year of the drought. For the past nine months not one drop of rain had fallen. Martin had weathered other droughts, but even with the ones in the past there had been a sprinkle, a little shower. Not enough to break a drought, but enough for a man to keep faith.

The previous night's drinking bout had left him with a terrible thirst and he drove back towards the farmhouse. Amidst the dusty bushes and dying trees it shimmered into being, white and startling, surrounded by trees and a velvet square of lawn.

He balked at going any closer and parked at the side of the road. This time he helped the dog out of the car and she nosed behind as he followed the footpath to the stables. He squatted next to the outside tap, switched it on and drank from his cupped hands. Then he stuck his head under the flow of water and drenched his face.

'Ezekiel?' a listless voice called.

Christ! It was his daughter!

He bolted into the thick bush opposite the tap and crouched out of sight. Eva walked out of the gloom of the stables and into the sunlight.

'Tosh? What are you doing here?'

She patted the dog and Tosha snorted with delight. Then Eva noticed the tap still running. With a flick of her wrist she silenced it.

A prickling spread across the back of Martin's neck as Eva stood absolutely still, eyes scanning the bush. The moment was eerily familiar; an animal registering his presence, an instant of recognition, his reward for hours of patient stalking, before he lifted his gun. A split second communion before he pulled the trigger, hoping his bullet would fly faster than the adrenalin about to surge through the animal, toughening the meat.

From his hiding place Martin could almost feel the tension rippling into his daughter's muscles. Her heart would be pumping wildly. His hands trembled and he wanted to call her name. He had the shape of it in his mouth, but could not get air to it. He wanted to hold her. He wanted to hit her. He felt the weight of his rifle, hanging off his shoulder as he crouched in the bush. The expression on her face crumpled into one of confusion and sorrow and he couldn't bear to look at her and he lowered his eyes and heard her say in a bold but broken voice, 'I'm going now. But, Tosha, you stay!'

He raised his head several minutes later and saw his nearly blind dog staring at him. And in the way that dogs often do, she sensed his eyes upon him and hung her mouth open and smiled.

In the bakkie Tosha once again rested the familiar weight of her head on his lap as he rattled along the dirt road that eventually joined up with the tar road to Messina. He would miss that weight when she finally went. God, he so hoped he wouldn't have to do it. Marshall their old Alsatian had died in his sleep, but he'd had to shoot Blitz, the young border collie. He'd found him on the front lawn barely breathing, his head grotesquely swollen, two puncture marks in the white splash across his muzzle. A Saturday afternoon and a two hour drive to the nearest vet who might not even be there. He knew Blitz could not survive the venom and so he'd shot him. Afterwards Lorraine hovered around as he dug the hole right in the middle of the lawn, asking why it was in the middle of the lawn and shouldn't they plant a tree next to Blitz's grave. No! he shouted. He refused to tell why, refused to talk about his oupa's farm where the old man had planted Persian lilacs above the graves of his farm dogs. Dogs bitten by snakes and kicked by horses, dogs dead from tick fever or found stinking and maggot-infested in snares. On warm spring nights he often reached for his seven-year-old grandson's hand, saying, 'Come, my dogs are flowering.' Stoically Martin would walk beside his oupa, the fallen flowers moist under his bare feet, waiting for the rotting head of a dog to fall from the trees. The scent of lilacs still left him nauseated.

When Martin reached the tar road he increased his speed. Every dam he passed had dried up, the surrounding bush a wasteland. The sky ahead was pale blue, a memory of blue, as if something with sharp teeth had reached up and sucked the blue right out of it.

And yet, according to Fourie, there was this hidden landscape of water. There had to be. He had just passed the turnoff for the diamond mine where De Beers used hundreds of thousands of gallons of water a day. There were restrictions in Messina, no one had watered their lawns for two years but they still had baths, drank from the tap, flushed toilets.

Eva's stories flashed to mind. As a little girl she had elaborated on his stuttered tale of underground rivers and lakes. *If we slide down this aardvark burrow, if we crawl through the hole in the trunk of that tree maybe we can get there.*

He reached the outskirts of Messina and passed the cemetery with its graves, well ordered in the scorched earth. Why not do the same for a dog, he thought, give it a decent burial? When Tosha's time came he would do just that.

And kaffirs? And terrorists? The questions barked out at him.

He pounded the steering wheel. God, he was furious with Eva! He had half a mind to go dig it up. No, ask Ezekiel and Wellington to dig it up, that would put everyone right on the farm, guaranteed things would run smoothly then.

The bakkie hit a bump and jolted, the shocks momentarily bottoming out. He was no longer on the tar road, but rather two rutted tracks scored into the veld by donkey carts. He had turned on to it instinctively, the bone-jarring indirect route to Katinka's house.

Hers was a name that would trip up any stutterer, darting around the tongue like a swift. Before Martin began visiting the tall, young, dark-haired widow he had never dared say it; when he saw her in town or at a church function, her name soared high above him. Now, into the seventh month of their affair, he still never called her by her name. But often, while rattling along this donkey cart track, he would lure it into his mouth where it sang *Katinka-Katinka-Katinka*.

Today her name fell out of his mouth. Katinka. The sound of a stone breaking a window.

She lived at the end of a tar road that jutted into the veld, a new development on the outskirts of town. Martin shifted into neutral and stared at her small brick house.

One of the last things that Katinka's husband Dirk had done before he was killed was replace the scorched lawn with white gravel. He'd decorated it with a large heron that some African on the side of a road somewhere had fashioned out of wire, and two knee-high Dutch windmills that were now turning slowly in the hot breeze. A few pink impala lilies bloomed in a heart-shaped bed in one corner, and a sturdy drought-resistant pepper tree cast a lacy shadow on the gravel.

Martin had visited Katinka just three days ago. It was

foolhardy to be seen here too often and a bitter smile jagged across his face.

Me, with a need to talk? There is nothing more pathetic.

But it was true, the words were right there and when she opened her front door, after obviously catching sight of him, there in his bakkie on the edge of the veld, he felt them snarled up in his throat.

. . . Ihavedonesomethingterrible . . . andmydaughtershe . . .

He parked in the shade of a large baobab, rolled down both windows for Tosha and crossed the road. The garden gate squeaked as he opened it. Dirk hadn't oiled it and Martin had got used to it, had stopped thinking every time he opened the gate that he should fix it. He could tell Katinka was pleased to see him, but also a little unsure. Without the ritual of handing over the Tupperware container they didn't quite know how to proceed.

'Did your dog drive you here?' she asked.

Martin glanced over his shoulder. Tosha had shifted to his seat behind the steering wheel.

Katinka laughed. She never made jokes like this. He wondered if she was nervous, maybe she'd read something on his face. He felt awkward and regretted the decision, though he couldn't recall making it, to see her. Then she smiled her lovely sad wet smile and he followed her down the hall, past two china ballet slippers hanging on the wall, past the photo of Dirk in his uniform.

Dirk was the Limpopo valley's dead hero; a recce missing in Angola for a year before the military claimed to have found his remains. There had been a funeral with a sealed coffin that had everybody wondering. The SADF never revealed the full details about Special Services and their missions. Afterwards the town adopted Katinka, the Limpopo valley's war widow. In another part of the country this might not have happened, but here, close to the border, close to the edge of their world, they needed her. Pies, casseroles, jars of jam, rusks, were dropped off at her house. A few days after the funeral Martin had stopped by, on Lorraine's insistence, with a large Tupperware container filled with cuts of impala and a bag of kudu biltong. Katinka received them graciously. Martin tried to speak, but his genuine concern was butchered by his tongue.

'You don't have to,' she said. 'I'm so tired of listening to it. They don't make any difference, all the words that people say.'

It was that simple, he was taken off the hook. A sudden feeling of spaciousness, as if the sky were inside him. She opened the refrigerator and they smiled at each other; there was no place for the meat. Cool air touched skin. Katinka gestured with a tilt of her head at the bottles of Castle tucked in amongst the foil-covered dishes and other Tupperware containers. Martin nodded. The refrigerator sucked shut. The beers hissed open. They both kissed the cold glass rims and drank. Another sip. Then she put her bottle down and slowly walked towards him. In the bedroom, afterwards, he again tried to speak. She shushed him, leaning in to kiss him, nip his throat. Later that night Katinka threw the meat over the back wall. She'd lost her taste for it. Each week he brought another offering. The shivering glistening liver carved out of a kudu he'd just shot, velvet steaks from an eland. They made love and in the evening she tossed the meat out. Genets, civets and stray dogs from the nearby African location foraged behind her house.

Katinka was barefoot, dressed in a filmy yellow cotton dress, her long black hair swinging loose. She gave Martin a beer, then switched on the kitchen tap to pour herself a glass of water. He stammered out some nonsense about how-how-how he just hap-hap to be d-driving – all the while watching her flutter her hand under the running water. Such a careless gesture in the middle of the drought. It filled him with anxiety to think of the water travelling through the mains under Messina's streets, down her particular road, under Dirk's white gravel, into the warm pipes that ran through her house to be scattered like diamonds across her sink.

He shook his head. 'N-no, no –'

'What?' she asked, filling her glass, 'what?'

Their awkward restless words hung in the air and Martin saw her blushing. He would never be able to say what he needed to, and to suddenly leave would embarrass both of them. He moved to the sink and put his lips on hers. With his tongue, with his teeth, he wanted her to know. The words would never crystallize in his mouth, but maybe there was a way she could reach in and take them out of him, like sucking venom from a snake bite. Maybe with her body next to his she could draw it from him. Women were mysterious like that. Life was mysterious. There was water one hundred feet below the ground and not a drop had fallen from the sky for almost a year. And so Martin led her to the bedroom.

A month into his affair with Katinka, he had realized that what he truly craved was the little stretch of time after they had made love, the few minutes while she dressed – she always left the bed first – made a sandwich, fetched another beer. He would lie in her bed, all the curtains drawn except for a small high rectangular window that framed the tip of a koppie, resting in a brief moment of peace, as if their love-making were a passageway to a secret room where he could visit the fineness of himself, a golden place where he found all his hopes and dreams intact. Later, while driving back to the farm, his guilt would rage. He found a way to somehow leave his relationship with her at the gate and vowed never to think about it on his land. Brandy also helped, gulped down as if to wash dirt out of a wound.

Katinka had switched the air conditioner off when they entered the bedroom. Now, he lay with a thin film of sweat on his body, feeling the blades of the ceiling fan above him carving away the cold, feeling the return of the familiar weight of heat. Long strands of her black hair slid across his chest as she sat up. He grabbed her hand. He didn't want to be left alone in the space of the moments afterwards, he was scared of what he would find. He kissed her again and summoned up a whispered sentence. 'It's too hot outside for the dog.'

'Martin?' She placed his name delicately in the air.

He put a finger to his lips, taking them back into silence. He left the bed and went to the bathroom where he splashed lukewarm water from the cold tap on his face. Dirk's razor rested on a shelf above the bath. The brass handle was tarnished, the razor too sturdy to have been used by a woman. Besides the photo in the hallway it was the only trace of Dirk in the house. His clothes had all been given to a local church. Out of respect the minister sent the items over the Soutpansberg to Louis Trichardt so Katinka wouldn't see a garden boy in one of Dirk's shirts. As he always did, Martin picked up the razor, feeling the weight of it as he measured himself against Dirk the recce with his face blackened for camouflage. Martin knew he could never have been a recce. Not with his stutter. But what did people think? That it was a condition that affected his nerves, his tracking skills, his reflexes, his ability to take immediate action in the face of a threat? Bullshit! He was fighting his own war, defending his land, defending his family. In a war nothing is as it seems. In Angola SWAPO walks around in shoes that leave lion tracks on the ground. Today's child could be tomorrow's terrorist.

He wished he could find a pencil and just write Katinka a note. Instead he returned to the bedroom to tell her he had to go. This time it was she who held the silence, bidding him not to speak as she kissed him goodbye.

He took another beer from her refrigerator and stepped outside. At the gate he paused. He'd never brought his dog to Katinka's house and there she was, torpedo-shaped head resting out the bakkie's window. He opened the squeaking gate and Tosha's ears pricked up; he hadn't even called her name, but she knew it was him. He stood in the middle of the road, beer in hand, watching her pick up a new smell. The scent of his love-making with Katinka like a bruise on his body, an aura of mulberry and dirty yellow.

The windmills creaked behind him and he turned and walked back inside. Katinka had tied her hair into a pony tail as long as the horns of a sable antelope. With her eyes she questioned his return and he motioned towards the bathroom.

He switched on the tap. Water bubbled up from far below, a lost babbling language from the country beneath the one he was living in. He dropped his pants and as best he could he washed himself.

Martin forced himself onwards into his day, chore after chore. Each time he parked in the shade and each time he returned with smells for his dog. The pungent aftershave of Fanie Booysen who would decide whether to extend Martin's credit one more time. The chemical seep from the bottles of pills that would stabilize blood pressure, give a frightened wife a good night's sleep. And each time he watched the dog lift her head and take them in – these small gusts of truth from his life – lips which looked like they'd been snipped with pinking shears crinkling into a smile. A tail slapping against the warm vinyl of the bakkie's seat.

Finally he pulled in front of the Limpopo River Lodge opposite the railway station. The bar was dark and womb-like, the bottles waiting patiently against the wall, Rolf the bartender reaching for the Fish Eagle as he sat down. No words, just a nod to say, hit me again, when he'd downed the first.

Someone sat beside him, the scrape of the stool on the floor as they made themselves comfortable. He recognized the thickly freckled sunburnt forearms on the bar.

'I saw you parked outside. Just a beer, Rolfie. Truck's ready. You want me to drive next week?'

Martin nodded.

Jannie took a long swig of his beer and pressed his palms, damp from the bottle, to his forehead. 'Claasen got a cheetah. Cornered it against a fence on his farm and rammed it with his bakkie. And now he wants me to mount it. He carries it into my place, wrapped in a bloody blanket. Like a woman in his arms, for Christ's sake. It breaks my heart. Next time I'm going to say no, I'll only work on something that you shoot like a man.'

Rolf approached with the bottle and Martin placed a hand over his glass. The tremor was still there.

'You okay?' Jannie asked.

Rolf poured himself a glass. 'Let me tell you something, if it doesn't rain soon we will all go mad, every single one of us.'

'We must go to the rain queen, make an offering.'

'I heard she's three hundred pounds and likes boys with red hair.'

Jannie tapped his empty beer bottle. 'You joke, Rolfie, but I think she's the *moerin* with us and that's why it won't rain.'

Rolf shrugged and slid another beer towards Jannie.

Martin eased off the stool. He laid a ten rand note on the bar and waited for his change.

'You okay?' Jannie asked again.

'*J-ja*. I-I I'll see –'

'At the farm tomorrow. I'll be there at eleven.'

The world was split open when Martin drove home. The hour of the day when the heat lifts and the bush begins to breathe easy. Once he reached the farm he followed a barely used dirt road that led towards the red sandstone cliffs. When the road ended he parked and continued on foot. There was not a cloud in the sky and the light from the setting sun washed the earth, leaving everything golden. He heard the dog scrabbling across the rocky ground. The huffing of her breath. Some of the rocks were quite large and he turned and watched her stumble into them. In terrain like this she could easily break a leg and yet she lurched on, determined to find him. When she finally reached him she touched his leg with her nose, before settling down a few feet away, blind head looking out over the dry Limpopo below. He wished he could pluck out her eyes and hold them in his hands like marbles. Rub them together, make thunder, bring rain. Instead, he nudged the safety off his rifle and shot her.

4

10 JANUARY 1984

There's been no sign of Tosha for a week and I fear the worse. Maybe she was bitten by a snake or caught in a snare, nothing dies peacefully in this part of the world. Martin is terribly upset, she was his favourite and this morning he spoke to Ezekiel and told him to not spend any more time looking for her as other chores are piling up. I suppose he's right. But I miss her and Leeutjie seems to as well. Am I being too sentimental for a farmer's wife? Tonight I don't care. And so life goes on. I'm thinking about taking Eva into LT tomorrow for a shopping trip to buy her some new clothes. She'll be in standard eight this year and suddenly she's fashion conscious. Fancy Parkmeade is getting to her. And I like it! One of these days we will go to Rosebank and visit those shops. In the meantime Truworths and Foschini will be plundered.

Lefu lay on his lumpy coir mattress, awake, he'd slept for half an hour and in forty-five minutes he had to return to the fields. One of his dogs whined and he heard voices outside, his grandson talking to someone. He shut his eyes again, the interior of the old stables where he lived with his daughter and his grandson was cool and dark, while outside the cicadas thrummed.

Someone sniffed, someone said, 'Grandfather?'

Lefu pretended he was asleep.

Someone said it again and he grunted and opened his eyes to see the silhouette of nine-year-old Mpho in the darkened doorway.

'Naledi wants you,' the boy said. 'She's outside.'

Lefu pulled on his blue overalls, stepped into his shoes that were held together with small twists of wire and walked outside to find Eva astride her horse Casper in the scattered shade of the old leadwood tree.

Eva was the only white child that Lefu had so honoured with a Sotho name, Naledi being his word for star. And fifty years ago Lefu's grandmother had given five-year-old Lefu a white-world name, one that would not baffle his future employers.

'Ezekiel,' Eva said, 'I want you to dig a hole for me. I will give you one rand.'

Lefu nodded. He would do anything for his Naledi, he would especially dig a hole for one extra rand. He approached Casper and the grey horse snuffled its mottled pink lips into Lefu's outstretched palms.

Eva yanked the reins, jerking Casper to attention. 'Let's go now.'

Lefu noticed her bloodshot eyes. She is still crying for old Tosha, he thought, and he slapped Casper on the rump and followed Eva back to the new stables where he collected a spade. On reaching the dirt road that led to the farmhouse and the cultivated lands, Eva swivelled around in her saddle to face him.

'My father mustn't see us,' she said quietly. 'We have to go the long way.'

She crossed the road and followed a path winding through the thorn thicket that lay beyond the rear garden of the big house. A water pump coughed to life and a flock of guinea fowl scurried deeper into the bush.

In the garden Lorraine called, 'Grace! Grace!' using the white-world name that Lefu had given his daughter. And there was Nkele's lilting response, 'Yes, ma-dam!'

Casper broke into a lazy trot and Lefu jogged behind. There was much to complain about on Skinner's Drift – the lack of electricity in the old stables, the too long work day and now his Naledi was upset – but the play of voices and machines and creatures on the farm filled Lefu with a plunging sense of belonging. The farm cradled his life, his years being trod into the land between the sometimes flowing Limpopo, the fierce sandstone cliffs and the ancient baobab tree three miles south of the river that marked the southern boundary.

Eventually they rejoined the dirt road where Eva skirted the last field of tomatoes and rode into the open veld on the far side of the dried-up dam. She dismounted, looked around as if to make sure no one had followed them and tied Casper to a tree. She stamped on the ground. 'Dig here.'

'How big must the hole be?' Lefu asked.

Again she glanced around, then pointed to a small cluster of mopane bushes. Even before he saw the animal Lefu heard the buzzing of the iridescent green flies congregating on its body.

'Naledi, this is a jackal.'

Her request that he dig a hole for the animal struck him as odd. Jackal were considered vermin and farmers often shot them. He thought that perhaps she had mistaken it for one of the farm workers' dogs and because they had not found Tosha's body she wanted to bury this animal.

'Do you know my word for a jackal? *Phukubje.*'

'I know what animal it is.'

He waited for her to repeat the Sotho word. If she stumbled over it he would gently correct her, but she didn't respond. Lefu began to dig, puffs of dust rising into the air each time the spade struck the ground. When he paused he saw that Eva had dragged the jackal closer. He'd never known her to be so quiet, usually she was always chatting about boarding school or the horses. Believing her silence to be impatience with the length of time it was taking him to dig the grave, he said, 'The earth is very hard because of the drought. I must make a deep hole otherwise another animal will dig it up.'

A gust of wind swirled the dust and Lefu registered the faint rotting smell of the jackal; there was still a peculiar sweetness about it and he knew the animal had only been dead a few hours.

'I don't want anything to dig it up,' Eva said.

Lefu nodded. 'Then we will put rocks on the grave.'

When the hole was ready Eva pushed the jackal to the edge and tipped it into the earth. Lefu noticed the lower half of the animal's body had been ripped apart by gunfire; someone had used a great many bullets just to kill a jackal.

'Thank you.' Eva placed a one rand coin in the palm of his hand. She looked at him briefly, a sad and almost mistrustful expression on her face, and then without so much as a good-bye she mounted Casper.

He watched her trot into the bush. She was fifteen years old, almost a young lady, and as his palm closed around the one rand coin he remembered a day many years ago when a five-year-old Eva asked him to dig a hole so she could bury her budgie that had been killed in its cage by a hawk. He'd willingly done so and when he was finished she pressed ten cents into his hand. The gesture tore at his heart, all the shame and waste and stupidity of his country was instantly laid bare. He wanted to tell this little girl with the hair so blonde it was almost white that he didn't want her ten cents, but he sensed that her desire to give it to him came from some place good. It was all she could do and so he accepted it. Over the years as their friendship grew Eva had continued to give him money; for creating a small pool next to the dam in which she kept her tadpoles; for building jumps in the horses' camp; for braiding Casper's mane and oiling his hooves to a gleaming ebony when she rode him in the Boere Dag horse show in Messina. And now, for burying a jackal.

Still puzzling over her request, he returned to the last row of tomato plants and kicked soil over the congealed blood. He found a rock and placed it on the grave. Remembering her insistence that her father not see them, he retraced his footsteps and took the long way back to the stables.

Lefu hid the one rand coin in the tack room – for some reason he did not want to bring it home. But that did not mean he would not spend it and, early that evening, as he carried a bucket of water to the small clearing in which he cultivated his mealies, he considered the various items he could purchase with that coin. One loaf of bread or a can of sweet condensed milk? Maybe he would treat himself to six cigarettes from Mr Retief who sold them loose at his shop in Messina.

He carefully gave each of his stunted mealie plants a splash from the bucket. It was barely enough to keep them alive, but if he let them drink deeply they would grow tall and green and the rustle of their leaves would tell Martin that Lefu was stealing precious water that needed to be saved for the crops in the fields.

Suddenly, the sound of the sky being rent just inches above his head made him drop the bucket. Several times a month Cheetah 100s from the air force base at Louis Trichardt tore through the sky above the border farms. Even though Lefu had heard the sound for years, the manner in which the jets seemed to creep up and then pounce always startled him. As fast as the terrible roar arrived it vanished.

'Fighter jet! Fighter jet!' Mpho yelled.

He streaked up the footpath with outstretched arms and swerved in and out of the rows of struggling mealie plants. He pretended to shoot his grandfather and Lefu flailed his arms and staggered backwards, smiling, because he knew just what he was going to buy with that one rand coin.

*

The following day Lefu sat in the back of the bakkie as Lorraine made the hour and a half drive into Messina for her weekly shopping trip. He loaded the sacks of horse pellets and dog food and when she entered the supermarket he hurried to the café on Main Street. In the corner of the window, propped against a pyramid of dusty cans of Lucky Star Pilchards in Chilli Tomato Sauce, was a black and white photo comic. *The Adventures of Buck de Vaal*. The cover photograph showed a white man with a thick neck and a crew cut, dressed in camouflage, standing in front of an aeroplane. A fighter jet.

Lefu entered the shop and waited patiently. Mr Retief, a jowly Afrikaner, helped the white customer who came in after Lefu and then turned to Lefu who solemnly placed his one rand coin on the wooden counter. 'For the book with the pictures.'

'Can you read, Oupa?' Retief demanded.

'It's for my grandson.'

The shopkeeper plodded to his window display. '*True Romance*? No, that's not good for boys. *Tarzan*?'

'No, baas, the one with the fighter jet.'

'Ah, *Buck de Vaal*.' Retief lumbered back with the comic and tossed it on the counter. 'Keeping the Russians out of our skies. Okay, Oupa, he's yours.'

Lorraine returned to Skinner's Drift in the late afternoon with Lefu sitting on the sacks of feed, amidst shopping bags and boxes loaded with bottles of wine and beer and brandy. All his life he had travelled in the flatbeds of farmers' bakkies, facing the rear, watching trees and hills and farmhouses grow smaller and smaller. This way of seeing the world often made Lefu melancholy, he felt as though he was always leaving, always seeing where he'd just been. But that day, with the comic book for Mpho hidden in his overalls and the vapour trail of a Cheetah 100 dissolving in the sky, it seemed a truly splendid way to see the world.

Back at the old stables, Mpho yipped with joy when his grandfather handed him the comic.

'This is not fun. This is reading lessons!' Lefu teased. 'You must read one page a day.'

With his mother sitting on one side and Lefu on the other, the young boy wiped the rickety kitchen table clean, laid *The Adventures of Buck de Vaal* in front of him, and carefully turned to page one.

In the first photograph Buck de Vaal stood in front of a bathroom mirror, pinning medals on to his jacket, while a woman in a lacy nightgown stood beside him.

I can't tell you – anything – about my – mis? Mpho read slowly.

'Mish . . . mish . . .' Nkele encouraged him to find the word.

Mission!

Lefu listened with pride as his daughter and his grandson worked together. His schooling had come to an end when he was eight years old and he could barely read or write.

Top . . . secret! Mpho hooted.

Buck de Vaal kissed the woman.

Nkele chuckled.

I love you.

End of page one.

'Grandfather, I must see him fly,' Mpho pleaded.

Lefu relented. 'You get two pages tonight. But only tonight.' He folded the comic book so Mpho could see the second page, but not the third.

There, in the photograph at the bottom of the page, stood Mr de Vaal stroking the fuselage of his plane.

'Fighter jet!' Mpho crooned, stretching the words out.

Word about the wonderful stories being told in the old stables spread quickly amongst the African children on Skinner's Drift and the next evening Thapelo's twin daughters knocked on the door and politely asked if they could please join Mpho for the reading of the comic. For three nights, Lefu and a growing crowd of children followed the adventures of Buck de Vaal as he filled his plane with petrol, and flew high above South Africa. Misfortune awaited him. On page five he crashed in South West Africa. To the children's relief he was not harmed. He wiped the dust off his jacket and patted his pockets.

My gun? Mpho read solemnly. *My two-way radio?*

He crawled up a sand dune, the jet exploded and visitors showed up.

Terrorists!

Three African men armed with machine guns stood on the crest of the dune.

'AK 47s!' said Mpho.

Lefu, who had been drinking a mug of black tea that could never be sweet enough, snapped to attention. 'What did you say?'

'AK 47s,' recited the twin sisters, nodding their tightly braided heads in unison.

'And how do you know about this?'

'Everyone knows those guns, Grandfather,' Mpho answered.

'Enough!' Lefu whisked the comic book off the table. 'It's bedtime. For all of you!'

When the rising moon set the nightjars trilling at one in the morning, he was still awake berating himself for being so foolish as to buy the comic for Mpho. He knew how it would end, who would be killed and who would be saved, and the ease with which the words AK 47 had fallen from the mouths of the children, tumbled out soft as the patter of rain, distressed him.

He slept fitfully until the hour before dawn when Lady's sharp bark woke him. He sat up in his narrow bed and listened. Someone was softly calling his name. He left the bed, lifted the sacking stretched across the small window and saw Lucky and Lady wagging their tails in the middle of the tamped down dirt clearing in front of the old stables. Again he heard his name. He pulled on a pair of old trousers and a shirt, stepped into his shoes, and quietly opened the door. The moonlit shadow of the old leadwood tree spilled towards him. Beneath the tree stood a ghostly horse with someone astride it.

'Ezekiel,' a small voice whispered, 'I want you to come riding with me.'

It sounded like Eva. But she was asleep in the farmhouse, and even if she weren't she would not be near the old stables at this hour, and she would certainly never ask him to ride. Her father forbade it. Martin van Rensburg did not want a black man sitting on any of his horses.

A snuffling sound rippled into the night and the horse tossed his head in greeting. It *was* Eva and Casper. She beckoned him and he moved through the night air until he reached the warm breath of the horse. She was riding bareback and what she said astonished him. 'I will give you money if you will ride into the bush with me and do me a favour.'

'Miss Eva . . . I cannot,' Lefu whispered. 'You know I am not allowed to ride. And soon, very soon, I must feed the horses, clean the stables. The baas will be very angry if I am late.'

'I have cleaned the stables and my father will not know. He is drunk. I will give you ten rand.'

As if she were certain that this amount had settled it and Lefu would follow her, Eva tugged on the halter and urged the horse back towards the stables.

Lefu did. He found himself walking up the familiar footpath that each morning led his family back into the lives of the van Rensburgs, his feet knowing just when to step over the knotted roots of the strangler fig, his hand reaching out to brush the leaves of his dying mealies. Eva had lit a lamp at the stables and in the centre of the concrete floor he saw the wheelbarrow filled with soiled wood shavings. She slid off Casper, hurried into the tack room, and returned with a saddle and bridle that she handed to Lefu, saying, 'Ride Donder.'

Bewildered, he stood there not moving.

'Hurry!' Eva urged and she opened the stable door and motioned for him to enter.

Donder butted his head against Lefu's chest and he slipped the bit into the horse's soft mouth, eased the saddle on to his back and tightened the girth.

'Let's go,' Eva said and she nudged Casper up the footpath.

So many times Lefu had led the large dark-brown horse outside for Martin to ride, now, as if in a dream, he put his foot in the stirrup and hiked himself up.

Donder shuddered into a generous trot and Lefu jostled in the saddle and gripped the horse's mane in terror. Perhaps Martin was not so drunk that he couldn't drive across the farm to search for his wayward daughter; if he saw a black man riding his horse at five in the morning he would shoot him. No questions asked. Half a mile down the dirt road Eva veered on to a footpath snaking through the bush and Lefu, still gripping Donder's mane, followed right behind her. He felt powerless to turn back, to even voice his fears, he was at Eva's mercy and he was disoriented: the paths that he knew so well on foot looked different from astride a horse. He bounced in the saddle, briefly touching the rhythm, touching it again, until suddenly he had slipped into it, a surging river of horse, and it felt familiar, easy, the way it had been when he was a youngster pinching rides on the donkeys around the kraals, on sad sway-backed horses that he pushed into ragged trots. The massive border fence loomed ahead. Eva urged Casper into a canter and turned on to the dirt track running parallel to the river. Lefu pressed his fists into Donder's neck, feeling the animal's warmth and sweat, its muscular legs eating up the earth. Faster and faster they rode until there was no separation between Lefu and Donder and the acres of land called Skinner's Drift. Somewhere far behind he slipped free of his tired aching body and the sadnesses his heart had accumulated.

'Naledi!' he gasped when she finally reined in. He looked at her in a way that he would never look at her again; there was no past between them, no hint of their future, just a black man and a white girl who had shared an exhilarating ride together.

For the briefest moment Eva was radiant. 'You ride well!' Then her eyes flickered away from his. Lefu followed her gaze. In the long grass, beneath the blackened branches of a tree that had been struck by lightning two years ago, lay a tawny-coloured caracal, a cat a little larger than a jackal, with tufts of long black hair on the tips of its ears. Dark clots of blood on its flank marked where several bullets had entered its body.

Eva dismounted and squatted next to the animal, her hands hovering over it. 'We need to take it back to the dam.'

She opened the leather saddle bags slung in front of Casper's saddle, retrieved a rope and a large piece of sacking and handed them to Lefu. He was baffled as to why she wanted the animal's body, but having been taught never to question a white person he didn't ask her and he wrapped the caracal in the sacking. Eva stood a few feet away, watching him, the expression on her face one of sorrowful uncertainty. Lefu tried to lay the animal across Donder's back but the horse snorted and shied away.

'It's the blood. He does not like the smell, Naledi.'

'He must do it!'

Lefu tried again and with some coaxing he managed to tie the bundle behind the saddle. No sooner was he astride Donder, than Eva said, 'There are more.' She trotted along the rutted track in the direction of the sandstone cliffs until she reached a cluster of fragrant water acacias. Beneath them Lefu saw two jackals, and like the one he had buried several days ago, these animals had been shot numerous times. Eva took two more sacks out of her saddle bags and he bundled the jackals into them, tying one on to Donder and the other on to Casper who was quieter and didn't flinch.

In the dawn light they cantered for most of their return, a circuitous route that took them far away from the kraals of the other workers. They reined in when they reached the clearing alongside the empty dam where just a few days ago Eva had asked him to bury the first jackal.

'I hid a spade near the last row of tomato plants. Bury them.'

Lefu dismounted and quickly untied the three bundles.

'Hurry!' Eva urged and she trotted back to the stable leading Donder by the reins.

It was almost six o'clock and already the sun felt too hot. Beyond the tomato fields Lefu saw the dust and the thirst of the land. He sank to his knees, horrified by what he had just done. A hyena standing on its hind legs, walking into the big house and pouring itself a drink was no more of an aberration than Lefu galloping across Martin van Rensburg's farm on Martin van Rensburg's horse. With the drumbeat of hooves still reverberating in his body he pressed his forehead to the earth and begged God's forgiveness.

Flies were already gathering on the three sacks and he found the spade, walked ten paces from where he had buried the first jackal and began to dig. Two feet deep and the earth was bone dry. The movement quieted his heart. Just dig, just work, he kept telling himself.

Eva reappeared on Casper as he was shovelling earth on the caracal. In a business-like fashion she gave him the ten rand note. 'You know my father is shooting these animals,' she said before she rode away.

Martin van Rensburg unsettled Lefu more than any other white farmer that he had worked for. He wasn't the cruellest, they all had their moments of heartlessness, rather it was his manner of speech, the way words snagged on his tongue like thorns, that disturbed Lefu. Makakaretsa, the children on the farm called him, the man who cannot catch his words. It seemed to Lefu that within Martin there was another man and the two of them were always arguing over what to say.

Several hours after riding Donder, Lefu spotted Martin walking briskly towards the stables with Leeutjie at his heels.

'Get out!' he hissed at Mpho who had been spinning across the concrete floor singing, *My gun! My two-way radi-oh!-oh!-oh!* Mpho scampered off and Lefu resumed sweeping the tack room.

Martin entered and glanced around. He'd recently taken to carrying a semi-automatic instead of a rifle and the stocky gun gleamed darkly in the sunlight.

'Afternoon, baas,' Lefu said.

Martin did not respond. He took a fistful of pellets and walked to the camp where the horses spent their days clustered amongst a stand of trees.

The broom felt unwieldy in Lefu's hands, but he kept sweeping. After burying the jackals and the caracal, he had cleaned Donder's saddle twice and hosed the horses to wash away any smears of blood. Still he was petrified. Maybe Martin could read the minds of his horses. Perhaps the young dog would smell the dead animals.

'Ezekiel!' Martin bellowed.

Lefu hurried out of the tack room, broom in hand, and Leeutjie immediately latched on to the bristles and tried to tug it away.

'D-d-d-did you clean the stables?'

'Yes, baas!'

'Well, they looked filthy! I wouldn't even l-l-let a kaffir sleep in them.'

'Yes, baas. I will do them again.'

Martin strode away. Leeutjie released his hold on the broom and dashed after his master and Lefu, who was now drenched in sweat, leaned against the wall and thanked God for being so merciful as to keep him safe. At least for now.

His body, however, would not let him forget his stolen hours on horseback and muscles he hadn't used in decades began to ache. By day's end he was hobbling and he told Nkele he had slipped and hurt his leg.

After the family ate their simple supper, Mpho marched outside to invite the other children to join him for the evening's entertainment. Lefu opened the comic book to page six and stared at the adventure awaiting them – two Africans were marching de Vaal across the ridge of a sand dune, one of them holding an AK 47 to the white man's head. He eased himself off his chair, walked stiffly to the stable door and announced, 'No comic tonight.'

Mpho stamped his foot. 'But you said –'

'Ai, I said nothing,' Lefu snapped.

'One page a day is what you said,' Nkele corrected from the horse stall that now served as a small bedroom for her and Mpho.

'It's too much,' Lefu tried to explain to the children.

'Too much what?' His daughter joined him at the stable door.

'Too much –' As he struggled for words he turned from Nkele's frown, her folded arms, to the disconsolate faces of the children. 'It's too much reading! Too many stories!'

De Vaal sinking a knife into the chest of one of the African men; de Vaal eating a snake; three white men holding parachutes and machine guns; de Vaal and the men stepping over the bodies of the dead Africans – Lefu flipped through the pages in disgust. He'd taken *The Adventures of Buck de Vaal* when he knew Nkele or Mpho would not be around and now he held a match to the comic. His relief at seeing the bad luck pages catch fire – if he hadn't bought that comic then he would have been sleeping so soundly, he would never have heard Eva whisper his name and he would never have been so mad as to mount Martin's horse – soon gave way to guilt as he realized how devastated Mpho would be. Too bad, Lefu thought, as the comic book fell apart in ashy pieces. I don't want him reading about AK 47s. But when he considered having the conversation with Mpho – *Little one, even though this country, your life, will sometimes break your heart, sometimes make you very, very angry, picking up a gun is not the answer* – something inside him balked. Perhaps he could say the dogs tore the comic to pieces? No, Lucky and Lady knew not to enter the old stables. Someone stole it? Then Mpho would accuse the other children.

'I was boiling a kettle on the fire,' he told the boy, 'and looking at the pictures and one of the dogs jumped against me and the book fell into the fire.'

A stunned Mpho stomped outside, kicked each of the dogs in the ribs and burst into tears.

'It's not their fault!' Lefu cried and he hobbled outside to console his grandson. 'I will buy you another one. This Friday when the madam goes into town I will buy you two!'

'You opening your own comic shop?' Retief grumbled as Lefu handed over the ten rand note that Eva had given him.

The old man gathered a selection from the window, where a second pyramid of rusty rimmed cans of All Gold Mutton Curry had been created, and spread them in front of Lefu. *True Romance, Tarzan, Nurses on Holiday*, another *Buck de Vaal*. The array was confusing.

After five minutes Retief lost his patience. 'Oupa! This is not a lending library. You must hurry up and choose.'

'Pieter, please tell me you have glacé cherries!'

Lefu froze. That was Lorraine's voice. Retief moistened his lips, reached under the counter, and with a wheezy flourish produced a murky looking jar of cherries.

Lorraine clapped her hands. 'I knew you'd have them!' She placed her handbag on the counter and dug for her purse. 'Oh, it's you, Ezekiel. What's this?' She noticed the open comic books in front of him and smiled and frowned in her particular way. 'I didn't know you read comics.'

'So this is your boy,' Retief said, 'I told him this is not a library.'

'The books are for Mpho, madam. He's a good reader.'

'Really? That's wonderful! Well, he definitely needs something better than these.'

She stacked the comic books in a neat pile and handed them to Retief who reluctantly returned the incriminating ten rand note. Lefu slipped it into his pocket and kept his eyes on the old-fashioned scale on the counter, the pile of dubious oval-shaped weights beside it, and waited for Lorraine to ask, How come you suddenly have ten rand to waste on comics?

'Meet me at the bakkie in a few minutes,' Lorraine said. 'I'm going to CNA to buy Mpho a book.'

On their return to the farm she handed Lefu a brand-new hardcover book. Again the wobbly table with its crust of sky-blue linoleum was wiped clean, the book lovingly opened. Instead of photographs the family gazed at colourful drawings of a baby, darker than any white child Lefu had ever seen but not as dark as an African, resting between the paws of what looked like a huge grey jackal.

It was seven o'clock of a very warm . . . eve-evening . . . Mpho grinned at his mother. *When Father Wolf . . .*

*

74

Days passed, temperatures soared well above one hundred degrees – too hot to go riding – and Eva stayed away from the stables. At night Lefu sipped his black tea – three teaspoons of sugar and still it didn't taste sweet enough – and listened to Mpho reading from his hardcover book. Whenever thoughts of riding Donder entered his mind he forced himself to concentrate on the story. The baby was now a young boy and had befriended a black leopard. *And once upon a time there was an African man who went riding at night with a white girl.* The young boy was in danger, a terrible snake, larger than any python that Mpho had seen, wanted to kill him. *The man rode a horse that was brown like him and strong.*

On the last afternoon of the summer holiday, ten days after he had ridden with Eva, Lefu sensed someone watching him as he fed the horses. He spun around and there she stood, tall and thin and unsmiling, looking like the ghost he thought he had seen astride Casper.

'Why do you give me such a fright?' he cried.

'I'm going back to boarding school,' she said without looking at him. She reached into a plastic bag and pulled out a slab of peanut brittle that she broke in pieces and fed to the horses. First Zambezi, then Donder, Casper and old Shylock.

'Work hard at school, Miss Eva,' Lefu said and he disappeared into the tack room. He thumped a hand to his chest to try to calm his rapidly beating heart. He'd never been frightened of Eva before. Other children, yes. As a young man white children had unnerved him more than the adults. It was their eyes, the way they flickered with life, they were curious and eager, they brought friendship that in seconds could transform into something treacherous.

When he left the tack room and entered Zambezi's stall, she was still there, picking burrs out of old Shylock's mane. 'How do you say caracal in Sotho?' she asked.

Lefu pretended he had not heard her and he scolded the

nervy black horse who would not offer his hoof to be cleaned. Eva leaned over the stable door. 'Ezekiel, please tell me the Sotho word for caracal.'

'*Lengau*,' he mumbled.

'*Lengau* . . . *Phukubje* . . .' She recited the names with care. 'Well, I'll see you in a few months.'

Out of the corner of his eye he saw her hands gripping the edge of the stable door. Then they were gone. He remembered the torn bodies of the jackals and the caracal and the way he'd cleaned the blood from his hands with sand. He knew the shuddering power of Donder's stride and the hardness of the earth underfoot after riding. He had buried four wild animals behind the tomato fields for his Naledi and yet, as she walked out of the stables, he could not find the words to ask: Why do you want to bury these animals? And why am I helping you do it?

With Eva back at school Lefu threw himself into his chores, polishing the tack and touching up the walls of the stables with a bucket of whitewash. He groomed the horses and couldn't help but pay extra attention to Donder. When the horse shook his head the muscles rippling along his strong neck filled Lefu with hope. Yes, he felt it in his heart. Hope!

Ai! What is it that you are hoping for old man? Life here is hard and van Rensburg is an angry man, but you have a job and every evening there is just enough food on the table for your family.

Perhaps it was the sight of his horses with their manes and tails combed, their flanks gleaming, that prompted Martin, who'd ridden less and less since Eva started boarding school, to walk over to the stables late one afternoon to tell Lefu to saddle Donder.

Martin mounted his horse, flicked his sjambok and Donder extended into a brisk walk. Within seconds they were out of sight and Lefu set about breaking apart a bale of luccrne.

While slipping the saddle on curious-eyed Donder, he'd felt enraged at Martin for having such fine horses, for not allowing him to ride, now Lefu mocked this fury, still hobbling around like some club-footed cripple. He thanked God that Martin had shown up to remind him of the parameters of his world. Donder belonged to the baas. When the young gelding arrived on Skinner's Drift his name was Hunter and Martin changed it to Donder, the Afrikaans word for thunder.

Martin returned after half an hour, dismounted, and handed the reins to Lefu. 'It's hell out th-there. Everything is d-dying.'

Lefu led Donder to the water trough where the horse drank deeply. Martin stood in the shade, watching him.

'Y-you're a Christian,' he said.

'Yes, baas.'

'Pray for rain. May-maybe he will l-l-listen to you.'

That night Lefu brooded through supper. Afterwards he lectured his family about the virtues of hard work. He droned on and on while Mpho stared glumly at the chest of drawers where he kept his hardcover book and Nkele studied her fingernails. The speech was for his own benefit. There was the Lefu who spoke the words and then there was another Lefu, a man whose face did not betray the sense of injustice that he held in his heart, a man who grew impatient with tired old Lefu saying something about working even harder, '. . . because one day our Naledi will be living in the big house. With a good husband, a kind man. And Makakaretsa will be so old there will be nothing to fear. We work hard now to secure our reward in the future . . .'

The words guttered out. The smell of their paraffin lamp was making him nauseous and the room felt unbearably small. 'We need more water,' Lefu mumbled and he grabbed the bucket and strode outside.

In the night air he breathed more easily. He walked up the path, turned the stable tap on, and listened to the horses stamp their feet. He carried the water to his mealies. Since riding with Eva he had neglected them. It was too late, standing there in the warm dark night he knew the plants were dead.

April drew near, temperatures dropped into the low eighties and summer's haze and the constant cymbal-like sound of insects died down. Starving impala stripped acres of every leaf and twig. Trees released their souls and the land quietly closed her eyes. Only Martin's tomato plants, voluptuous with reddening fruit, flourished under the seemingly endless supply of water sucked from beneath the dry Limpopo.

But right before harvest time a strange blight affected the crop; overnight the fruit blistered on the vine and the plants had to be destroyed. The fields were ploughed and Martin took a chance. He planted one sector with fast-growing lettuces and two with potatoes that would be ready for harvest in July as long as there was no frost in June.

At the end of a long day of tucking seed potatoes into the loamy field furthest from the big house, Lefu walked into the veld behind the dry dam. It was the first time he had been there since Eva had asked him to bury the animals. He feared each grave would be clearly visible, but time and dust were obliterating his secret and the only person who knew about it was still at boarding school.

'When is Easter?' he asked Nkele later that evening, knowing that Eva's autumn holiday always coincided with Easter.

Nkele checked the calendar with the elephant illustration. Lorraine received one every year from the chemist in Messina and sent it to the old stables. 'Next week,' Nkele answered.

The following morning Lefu found a young jackal floating in the water trough at the far end of the horses' camp. Later in the day Martin told him to investigate the rotting smell coming from the water tank that collected water from the roof of the carport. He prised the lid off the tank, shone a flashlight on the remaining few inches of water and saw five rats in various stages of decomposition, a sixth swimming in slow circles.

One by one he fished them out, crushing the lone survivor with his spade. He heard a small cry and turned to see Lorraine, arms folded tight across her chest, watching him from the kitchen steps.

'Can you do something to keep them out?' she asked, a wince of distress on her face.

Lefu told her he would put wire mesh over the gutter that fed the tank. He felt uncomfortable about killing the rat in front of her and anxious about Eva's impending return, and the question somehow tumbled out. 'When is Miss Eva coming home? I want to wash her horse,' he added quickly.

'She didn't want to come home. I don't know why. I said to her father that we shouldn't –' Lorraine caught herself, she pursed her lips and tucked her hair behind her ears. 'Make sure nothing can get down that gutter.'

Lefu nodded.

'She's gone with a school friend's family to Jeffrey's Bay.' Lorraine offered him the small smile that meant she was sorry for being abrupt with him. 'Do you know where that is?'

'No, madam.'

'Very far away, Ezekiel. By the ocean. The sea.'

He spent the rest of the afternoon cleaning and resealing the tank. When he was done he fed the horses, and then groomed Donder until his haunches gleamed like the stinkwood table in the van Rensburgs' dining room. There was something else mixed in with his relief at knowing that Eva would not be spending her holiday on the farm – a trace of disappointment.

In mid June a surprise dusting of frost two days in a row silvered the thorn trees and sugared the parched earth. The leaves of the potato plants crinkled black and all the workers and their children were sent into the fields to dig for whatever potatoes they could find. In the open-sided packing shed a grim-faced Martin counted twenty-eight boxes filled with tiny potatoes.

'Chuck them,' he stuttered.

'No,' protested Jannie who'd accompanied him. 'I'll drive them in. It's better than nothing.'

'Forget it,' Martin whispered. 'It won't even pay the petrol.'

'Not true. We sell them for fifteen rand each –' He lifted his eyes to the ceiling where the swallows made their nests and struggled with the arithmetic. By the time he'd figured it out, Martin had stalked away.

Undeterred, Jannie clapped his hands. 'Ezekiel! Wellington! Load the boxes! People in Jo'burg like their potatoes small. Ja, they call them new potatoes.'

'New potatoes?' Lefu asked as he swung the boxes into the truck. He liked Jannie, he was an easy-going white man, and bantering with him – respectfully done, always with Jannie in the lead – was one of the nuggets of sweet life to be found on Skinner's Drift.

'I'm telling you, there are people in the big city who won't buy a potato bigger than a quelea's egg!'

Within the hour Jannie was on the road.

The following morning Lorraine and Martin left the farm before dawn in the old blue diesel Mercedes, the car used for long drives and trips to church, and Lefu knew that Eva must be returning for her winter holidays. He spent the day painting creosote on the fence posts. In the late afternoon he noticed a trail of dust billowing above the plateau. He determined to pay the car no attention, but as it passed by his head jerked up and he saw Eva staring at him from the back seat.

She did not visit the stables that afternoon, nor the following day.

Two nights after her return, while filling the bucket at the stable tap, Lefu saw the headlights of the bakkie wavering along the dirt road that dead-ended at the southern boundary. There was nothing out there except aardvarks digging up termite mounds and roving jackals, perhaps a few dying impala. Lefu suspected that Martin had gone hunting.

He woke at five the next morning, his grey blanket pulled up to his chin, and lay there and worried. What if Eva called him again? This time she might wake the whole family. He didn't want any trouble and he dressed swiftly, putting on two shirts and an old jacket, a hand-out from a Mr Viljoen who he had worked for many years ago. Soon enough he heard the horses snorting their hellos to someone who must have entered the new stables and he walked up the footpath and stepped into a tangle of bush to watch.

Eva led a saddled Casper outside. She was bundled up in a dark-brown anorak, a wool scarf and leather gloves. She appeared to be riding alone, but then she looped Casper's reins around a post next to the water trough, walked back into the stables and returned with Donder. The horse looked magnificent – Makapelo, the storm the Limpopo valley was waiting for – smoke pouring from his nostrils as he tossed his head and snorted at the approaching dawn.

Lefu whistled low and Eva spun around.

'Naledi,' he whispered and he stepped out of the bushes.

She didn't smile as he'd expected, but nodded curtly. He felt mortified, he'd acted presumptuously, forgotten his place, and he was on the verge of apologizing when she gestured towards Donder. Lefu pressed his palms against the horse's muzzle and mounted the dark shadow. A touch of the reins and he gathered up all that was shivering and restless beneath him.

'Haria!' he whispered and Donder leapt forward.

Lefu didn't give further thought to Eva's cool demeanour.

Once again he was flying across the foreign land that was Skinner's Drift experienced from the back of a horse. They cantered along the dirt track that led to the rarely visited interior, dawn revealing acre upon acre of stunted mopane bushes wearing their copper-coloured autumn leaves like rags. Here and there a conical termite mound reared out of the earth and tilted slightly to the south.

Eva reined in near the old baobab tree on the southern boundary and Lefu cupped his numbed hands and breathed on them. He heard a match striking and the smell of cigarette smoke wafted in his direction.

'You better not tell my parents that I'm smoking.'

He nudged Donder around and Eva blew a severe stream of smoke into the air.

'Promise me.'

'I promise I will not tell.'

She eyed him a few seconds longer as if to gauge his trustworthiness. 'I never knew smokes would taste so good. The first was lousy, I almost puked. It was in the blue gum trees behind the swimming pool. I suffered through that first one.'

Lefu listened politely. Eva had changed. She seemed unhappy with a touch of something mean-spirited about her, something that reminded him of her father. He missed the young girl who would spend afternoons sitting on a bale of lucerne reading aloud from a book about a horse named Black Beauty. Sometimes she would stop and half smile at him and his heart would hurt, but nicely so, because of the tender way in which she seemed to know him.

Eva finished her cigarette and tossed the butt on the ground. 'It's somewhere between here and that tree.'

She looped away to the right and after making sure the stompie was not going to start a fire, Lefu headed to the left. He zig-zagged his way towards the baobab, until the ever reliable green flies alerted him to death's presence. He dismounted, pushed aside the branches of a small mopane and saw a young, thick-jawed hyena lying in a pool of dark blood. He recoiled, he hated hyenas. Eva was some distance away and he considered moving on, pretending he hadn't found the animal. He couldn't. She trusts me, he thought, I must call her. He whistled and Eva trotted over and dismounted.

She reached into the bush, grabbed the rear paws of the hyena and tried to tug it into the open. Although small of stature the animal was heavy.

'Ezekiel, help me.'

'I can't.'

'What do you mean you can't?'

'*Fetse* . . . the animal, it is dirty –'

'Don't be stupid.' She let go of the dusty black-padded paws and stood facing him, hands indignant on her hips. 'Just help me, for god's sake!'

Lefu shook his head. Eva reached into the pocket of her anorak and pulled out her cigarettes.

'You want them?'

He lowered his eyes and she flung the box at him, cigarettes spilling to the ground.

'They're yours. *And* I'm going to pay you. Ten rand. Is that enough? Now, help me!'

'Miss Eva – I am sorry. I will dig the hole for you, but I do not want to touch that animal.'

'Shit! Ezekiel, do it!'

She sliced the bush with her riding crop and Casper flinched and tossed his head and backed away. 'Stupid!' she yelled at her horse, bringing the crop down on his neck. He shied. She hit him again and he reared up, hooves dangerously close to her face.

'Naledi!'

Donder rolled his eyes and snorted and backed away. Lefu

knew that if he didn't intervene Eva might get kicked, the horses would gallop away and he'd be left with nothing but trouble. 'Stop it!' he shouted, and with one hand on Donder's reins he dodged the flailing hooves and grabbed Casper's reins from her. Eva held the crop, trembling, in mid air, then dropped it and stumbled away in tears.

The horses were nickering in panic, jostling each other, and Lefu crooned at them, finally coaxing them to walk in a wide circle. He needed to calm them, he also needed to still his anger. He knew who Eva had really wanted to hit. And she had spoken so harshly to him. No worse than her father, he told himself, not as bad as some of the other white children you have known.

After several minutes he approached a disconsolate Eva. 'Here is your horse, Miss Eva.'

She had gathered up the cigarettes and she offered the box to him. 'Some of them are broken. I'm sorry.'

He shook his head.

'Please,' she begged, and to appease her he tucked the box into his jacket pocket. 'You think I'm horrid. I know you do. But I hate it here so much, I hate my parents, I hate having to . . .' She looked at him for several seconds, her grey eyes searching before she lowered them, saying, 'I'm sorry, Ezekiel.'

'It's okay, Miss Eva.'

She prodded the hyena with her foot. 'Casper won't like that ugly thing tied on his back, will he?'

'I don't think so.'

'Then we'll leave this one.'

They mounted in silence and trotted west along the fence, stopping for a bloodied bat-eared fox and a sleek genet, small animals that slipped easily into the sacks. They cantered back through the acres of mopane scrub until they sighted the circular fields in the distance and they slowed to a walk.

'We still have time.' Eva dug into her jeans pocket for a disposable cigarette lighter that she handed to Lefu. 'Why don't you smoke one of your cigarettes. And give me one.' She cocked her head and smiled at him. 'Please.' They lit up and she said, 'Just like cowboys. Have you ever seen cowboy films?'

'No. But I see pictures of them in the advertisements for the cigarettes.'

'You mean Texans? They're my favourite brand. Watch!' She blew several smoke rings. 'So, Ezekiel, what are you going to do when I ask you to help me with an elephant?'

An elephant?

Eva spluttered with laughter and Lefu relaxed and savoured the cigarette. What a relief it was to joke with her.

'Then, Naledi, we are in big trouble!'

'Or a hippo! No chance of that. No *kuba* until the river comes back.'

She *did* remember some of the Sotho words he'd taught her.

'*Thutlwa*,' he said slowly. 'Imagine the hole I would have to dig for *thutlwa*, a big long ditch for the –'

'I know, I know. Don't tell me. Giraffe!'

Her giddy laughter subsided and she looked around. 'Ssh, we must remember to be quiet.'

Winter stillness swooped back down around them and Lefu shivered. He could well imagine that Martin and every other farmer had heard them. They were putting down their cups of coffee, they were listening the way they listen for the full-chested moan of a lion, the sawing cough of a leopard, they were reaching for their guns.

At the dry dam he dismounted, untied the two hessian sacks and handed Donder's reins to Eva. He collected the spade, then stood for a few moments beside the thorn tree, testing his fear. His heart beat fast and his mouth was dry, but there was also the winter sun warming his face. The sturdy handle of the spade felt good, dependable in the palm of his hand. He picked up the first animal and scanned the veld beyond the dam. In digging the graves he did not want to unearth the animals he had already buried.

The weight of death – cold stiff bodies bundled in sacking – had become familiar to Lefu and when someone handed him a baby, the squirming power in the plump little legs shocked him.

'You look like you're holding a snake!' a voice cried from across the crowded room. A tiny hand swatted at Lefu's face and he awkwardly passed the baby to Nkele.

Eva had left for boarding school two weeks ago, and he and Nkele and Mpho were visiting one of the men who worked on Claasen's farm. The man lived with his wife and her sister, the mother of the baby, in quarters more cramped than the old stables. But, wonder of wonders, they had electricity and where there is electricity there is television. Rugby matches, game shows, American soap operas, nature programmes – crowds of people showed up after Sunday church services to watch the TV. After an hour or so, those in the room would reluctantly give up their place for someone who was waiting outside. A grumbling democracy at work.

Nkele rocked the infant and looked at her father with concern. 'Are you all right?'

'Too much . . . Too many people! And it's hot in here!' He elbowed his way out of the noisy room.

Mosanku, a friend of his, sat on a tree stump some distance away from the dwelling place and he gestured for Lefu to join him. He offered Lefu the cigarette he had just rolled and opened his bag of Drum to fashion another. He was a tall thin man with a narrow face and the white people knew him by the name of Gabriel. He worked as a skinner for Jannie who, though he still drove Martin's truck, had recently opened a small taxidermy business in Alldays. Mosanku knew many of the Limpopo valley farmers' secrets: who crossed into Botswana to poach eland; who baited and shot nine hyenas in the dry river bed.

He wasn't much of a talker and to sit in the sun with him, smoke a cigarette, and look at the spill of land beyond the workers' quarters, pleased Lefu. Winter had subdued the birds and the silent song of the earth and rock swept his mind of all thoughts, until Mosanku asked, 'How are things on your farm?'

Lefu shrugged, feigning an attitude of indifference. A question from Mosanku was a dangerous thing; he never asked questions unless he knew the answers. Lefu wondered if something in his manner hinted at the exhilaration he felt when he was astride Donder, perhaps it was the way he spoke, or rather didn't speak of the drought – when he flew through the bush on the back of the dark-brown horse the dying trees meant nothing to him.

'No problems on Skinner's Drift,' he finally responded.

Mosanku inhaled deeply and savoured the fruity taste of Drum tobacco. 'I was with Jannie when he visited your farm a few weeks ago. He and van Rensburg sat down for business and I was told to skin the impala in the cold room. And he's the only farmer who also wants me to cut up the meat. All the others do it themselves – they think I will steal from them – but van Rensburg says to me, 'G-g-gabriel, I know every ounce of meat that is on these animals. The second I saw-saw them in the bush I could tell. So if you take any I will know and I will come wh-wh-wh-wh-wh-wh-whip you!' Mosanku flashed his teeth in a smile. 'I make jokes now, but I was frightened when I saw what was in that cold room. Van Rensburg is usually a careful man, those eyes know just where to shoot. A bullet in the neck, one that breaks the spine, or in the heart. But these impala had been shot many times. The skins were torn and the meat was full of pieces of metal. Your van Rensburg is not hunting with a rifle any more, he is using a machine gun.' Mosanku sucked again on his cigarette until the embers reached his calloused fingertips. 'I'm telling you this because – ai, you know what I am going to say.'

Lefu nodded, hoping to silence his friend. Mosanku said it anyway.

'We do not live separate from these white people. There is Mosanku and then there is Jannie. Mosanku is smoking a cigarette with his friend Lefu and Jannie is there' – he pointed to the distant cluster of shade trees surrounding Claasen's house – 'drinking whiskey with Claasen and talking about the leopard Claasen baited last night. I say to myself that I do what I want with my life, but I am here because Baas Jannie is here. I am like this with Jannie Louw,' he said, and he entwined his arms. 'And you, my friend? You are like this with a crazy one.'

With the sun low in the sky, Lefu and his family said their goodbyes and trudged along the footpath traversing the plateau and Claasen's land. Even if they hurried they would still arrive home in the dark.

'You look tired, Father.' Nkele touched Lefu's shoulder.

'Too much –' Lefu turned away from his daughter's fretful face. The words tumbled constantly from his lips, *too much, too much*, when maybe what he wanted to say was, *not enough*.

How far the walk from Claasen's seemed. If he was on horseback he could be home in under an hour. The shock of footsteps on unyielding earth lingered for days after he rode. His legs felt tired, his heart exhausted from the weight of his secret.

A man who is married and cheats on his wife at least shares

his deception in the warm arms of the other woman. If he was a thief he might find another, in a shebeen perhaps, who had committed similar acts. But he could tell no one of his blood carried forth on the powerful legs of a horse, his heart soaring, and then hours later the impatience he felt when the smoke from the paraffin lamp stung his eyes and he watched his shadow crashing into his grandson's on the grimy walls of the old stables.

Too much. Not enough.

Mpho marched ahead and he heard the boy singing softly. *My gun! My two-way radi-oh-oh-oh!* The ghost of Buck de Vaal was still with them and Lefu didn't have the energy to banish him.

Halfway down the winding road to the farm, Martin drove up behind them and braked to give his workers a ride. They scrambled into the back of the bakkie and Lefu noted the machine gun resting on the seat beside Martin. He took his familiar position, his back pressed against the rear window. For years he'd prided himself on the way he conducted his life, not gossiping about his employers, determined to hold on to the thing that Mosanku said did not exist, his 'separateness'. 'Who invited them?' he'd ask his daughter when she brought home stories about the goings on in the big house. But in riding with Eva he had trespassed into Martin's life, and what he'd found scared him. Mosanku was right. Martin wasn't hunting any more – in the past he would have asked Jannie to mount that golden caracal – he was killing. And Naledi seemed intent on burying every predator that her father shot.

Terrorists, snarled the white farmers. The word was made of barbed wire and it tore their mouths open. Several months later on a hot November night, Mike and Tinus Laubscher, a father and son who farmed alone, were hacked to death with machetes on their farm near the Kruger National Park, their two female sheepdogs shot in the head.

The border fortification was not sufficient protection, and along with his fellow farmers, Martin replaced the simple fence that had enclosed his house and garden with a twelve-foot-high security fence. Lefu and Thapelo worked for a week, digging holes, hammering poles into the ground, stretching the wire taut until the house was surrounded. A white man from Pietersburg, a professional when it came to the business of security, added the finishing touch and topped the fence with loops of glinting razored barbed wire.

Two weeks later Eva returned for her long summer holiday. With her hair cut short as a boy's she was barely recognizable. Lefu planned to tell her that he couldn't ride with her any more – farmers carried guns at all times now and white people, who knew you, wouldn't stop to give you a lift when they passed you on the road. What he and Eva were doing was madness. But the indifferent manner in which Eva said hello to him and walked around the stables patting the horses unnerved him. They had never once talked about what they had done together and a ridiculous fear surfaced; he would speak of stolen hours on the back of a horse and she would laugh and say, what are you talking about? Or perhaps she would threaten him: You've been riding? Wait till I tell my dad.

The day after Eva's return, Nkele told him that Martin wanted to see him at the stables during his lunch hour. Lefu could not eat the bread and jam his daughter hastily set in front of him. He headed up the footpath and waited in the cool of the tack room. Soon Leeutjie trotted in and whined.

'Ezekiel!' Martin bellowed.

A bank of cloud had marshalled at the southern rim of the sky and the air felt scorching. Martin was leaning against the fence of the horses' camp and he beckoned Lefu to join him.

'If you could ride any of my horses w-which-which one would it be?'

Lefu stared dully at the horses flicking their tails in the shade. Van Rensburg knows and he is playing with me, he thought. He willed himself not to care, to mentally leave in anticipation of the beating. Thin heart, thin spirit.

'I'm w-waiting for an answer.'

His tongue felt fat and useless in his mouth. He had to say something, even if they were the words that took him to the prison in Pretoria where he would be hanged.

'All of them.'

For a second Martin looked stunned, then he laughed, 'Hell, y-you're a g-greedy bugger!'

'Baas, it is because I have looked after them and I know they are the best horses.'

'Ja, you're clever, Ezekiel. But you also know your place, hey? Well, you get to ride one of them. From now on I want you to g-go with M-m-miss Eva.'

Lefu did his best not to look surprised, then he thought that maybe he should look surprised, then he wasn't sure if he had even heard Martin correctly.

'Yes, baas,' he answered.

'Don't say yes like a monkey until you understand what it is I'm saying. You think the d-d-drought has made the baas mad. No. I'm thinking very clearly. I *don't* trust you. You hear me? I don't trust any of your kind.' Martin's voice dropped to a whisper, his sentences slipping out as easily as a snake gliding through a thorn bush. 'So why will I let you ride with my daughter?'

'I don't know, baas.'

'I think you know what is going on in the bush. And you know me, Ezekiel, and what I will do if anything happens to my daughter. So, when she wants to ride you go with her and you look after her. You hear me?'

'Yes, baas.'

'He needs a horse that can keep up with me. Let him ride Donder.'

Lefu slowly raised his head to see a sullen-looking Eva leaning against the tack room door, twitching her riding crop.

'You have a p-p-problem, my girl, with the way I'm d-d-doing this?'

She shook her head.

Martin's words crawled out jagged. 'You c-can ride, can't you, Ezekiel? Hell, th-that would be a bloody j-joke. All this time you've been working with the horses and you can't ride.' Without waiting for an answer he walked off with Leeutjie at his heels.

Eva opened the gate to the camp and whistled for the horses. She clipped ropes to each of their halters.

'Saddle them,' she instructed Lefu.

'Naledi, it is very hot.'

'You heard what my dad said. I want to ride now.'

She tossed the rope across Casper's neck, pulled herself on to his back and cantered away. Lefu had no choice but to ride bareback. Branches whipped across his chest as he chased after her. They broke into a clearing and he urged the horse forward until he rode alongside Casper. Eva looked stricken, as if she were galloping away from something terrible.

'Naledi!' He grabbed Casper's halter and slowed the horse down. 'It's foolish to ride like this in such hot weather!'

'I'm sorry,' she gasped. Her T-shirt clung to her back and her face was flushed. The horses jostled down to a walk and Lefu circled around to head back to the stables.

'Ezekiel, I don't want to go home yet.'

'I must be working in the fields.'

'Please. Just for a few minutes longer. He said you could ride with me.'

Once again Lefu followed Eva, this time to a pair of small

shepherd's trees just beyond the far end of the horses' camp. They dismounted and tied the horses to the gnarled trunk of one of the trees. Eva sat cross-legged in the small pool of shade beneath the other, Lefu squatted a few feet away from her.

She reached into the waistband of her shorts and removed a small .22 calibre pistol. 'Look what my dad wants me to carry.' She placed it on the ground between them, in a manner that made Lefu uncomfortable as though she were challenging him with it. 'Did you know Mike and Tinus?' she asked in a hesitant voice.

'Everyone knows everybody,' he replied.

Mike and Tinus. Two more white men. What made them stand out was that they worked their land with a minimum of workers. They worked like workers.

'Who do you think did it?' she asked, so softly, and Lefu reeled from what remained unspoken: Would you do something like that?

'I don't know, Miss Eva.'

If he could have spoken honestly he would have said, Why do you ask me that? Do you not trust me? If he trusted her he would have said, You see where I live, Naledi. No electricity, no running water. You see that soon Mpho will have no school to go to. You hear the way your father talks to me. If I thought a stranger was hiding in the bush, someone that would help my people, and I chose to look the other way you could not blame me. But Lefu had no words, just his hands always working, and a heart that did not always know how to hold Eva van Rensburg.

The heat of the day shimmered and rolled towards them, lapping at their shade.

'We must think about cool things,' Eva said after a long silence. 'Like swimming. You remember swimming in the Limpopo?'

'I haven't swum in the river.'

She looked astonished. 'Never?'

'Never.'

'Then when did you last go swimming?'

Lefu shrugged.

'You must have swum sometime. When you were a boy?'

'Maybe.'

It was too hot to fashion the memory into words and he closed his eyes. As a boy he and his friends had swum naked in the Nyls river. He remembered the leap into the muddy water, the shade under the bridge, the songs they sang as they walked home feeling so cool and free, and the smell of fried fish. Not once, since coming to the Limpopo valley, had he eaten fried fish.

He woke sometime later and saw several dusty blue birds perched on the twisted branches above him, their beaks open like dogs. Eva untangled the horses' reins from the other tree and he rose to his feet to help her. Thunderheads reared in the sky above them and the sun was soon blotted out. It had happened before; too dangerous to hope for rain.

They mounted and made their way back to the stables in full view; anyone could see the white girl and the African man riding together. When they passed Thapelo's daughters and the twin sisters gaped at such a wondrous sight – old Lefu riding Makakaretsa's finest horse – he felt oddly ashamed. He wanted to say to those little girls: You should have seen me when I was flying on this horse. Instead he spoke in Sotho so Eva would not understand. 'You think I don't have enough work? Now he makes me ride his horse.'

They passed the big house and an anxious voice called, 'Eva!'

Eva nudged Casper in the direction of the gate in the security fence and Lefu followed.

'Did you have a good ride?' Lorraine asked, slipping off the short leather gloves she wore while pruning her roses.

'It was okay,' Eva mumbled.

'Look at you, Ezekiel. On that horse!' She smiled at Lefu, then noticed the absence of saddles and bridles and scolded Eva. 'Don't make him ride bareback. She must at least make you comfortable, Ezekiel.'

'Yes, madam.' He found it hard to look at Lorraine from astride Donder. Her voice sounded so bright and friendly, but her smile was different, slippery, as if she couldn't hold on to it.

Eva clicked her tongue and her horse walked briskly to the stables.

'Don't forget to water the roses tomorrow,' Lorraine said, a familiar frown on her face once more as she waggled her pruning shears at Lefu.

'Yes, madam.'

She put her gloves back on and nodded vigorously, he could go now.

As Donder followed Casper, Lefu realized it was fear that he'd seen on Lorraine's face. Eva was also fearful. Beneath her anger, the gallop through the bush, the flaunting of her gun, she was a frightened girl. And just below his fear, a membrane that enveloped all of his encounters with white people – his respectful, Yes madam! the quick jump into the bakkie when a lift was offered, his hand out for the ten rand note after he buried Eva's animals – lay his anger.

He slipped off the horse's back and filled the water buckets and Eva broke open a bale of lucerne and carried armfuls into each stall. She waited for him to lock the tack room, then said good night, and mentioned something about riding the following day. Lefu didn't know if he would be burying what her father had shot or riding alongside her, at her father's command, making sure she came to no harm.

Birds skimmed above his head and into the bush to roost as he made his way down the footpath. Lucky and Lady sat still as statues on either side of the doorway to the old stables, and Mpho perched on the bottom half of the door, swinging his feet. He called out to his grandfather, 'Maybe tonight–'

'Ah! Don't say it!' Nkele shouted from inside and Mpho pulled a face at Lefu. 'If you say it you might chase it away,' she explained, and she scooted her son off the door.

In the hours before the downpour a deep silence tumbled from the clouds above the Limpopo valley. Only Lefu seemed oblivious to the impending storm. The day's events, the year's events, had left him exhausted. He was a tired old man wanting nothing more than a piece of fried fish.

It rained on and off for a week. Streams leapt down the ravines of the Soutpansberg, the Blaauberg and the Waterberg; they spilled into the Sand river, the Crocodile and the Mogalakwena, which in turn breathed life into the wide sandy Limpopo. It rained so hard that Nkele relented and let Lucky and Lady sleep in the old stables.

On Sunday people who hadn't attended services in years were spotted in the pews of the Nederlandse Reformeerde Kerk in Alldays. On the benches in Claasen's packing shed, which served as a church for many of the farm workers, Mosanku, who rarely attended, sat straight-backed and solemn. It had rained. Thank God. But so much? Prayers for those whose homes had been flooded were offered up.

For the walk back to Skinner's Drift, Nkele carried her good shoes in a plastic bag and serenaded her father and her son with hymns and pop songs. Mpho gripped his grandfather's hand then released it, only to reach for it moments later. And each time the path crested a rise Lefu saw puddles of water glinting in the sunlight.

'Look, Frisco in the dam!' Nkele cried as the path led them past the coffee-coloured water.

Lefu noticed a pile of debris blocking the mouth of the small donga that fed the dam and he told his daughter to continue on without him as he was going to unblock it.

'But it's Sunday. You don't have to work,' she protested.

'Freeing the water is not work. And neither is planting mealies, and that is what I will do later on this afternoon.'

Plant them now and in three months Nkele would steam them over the fire and he could sink his teeth into the sweetness of earth and rain and sunshine.

'Mealies!' Mpho yelped.

'Yes! And you and your friends will swim in the dam.'

'But Makakaretsa will catch –'

'I will stand guard for you,' Lefu promised.

He waited until Nkele and Mpho were out of sight before he turned his gaze to the expanse of land beyond the dam where he and Eva had buried the animals. He couldn't pinpoint a single grave. Wind, sun and now rain had all subtly changed the features of the land and Lefu felt his heart had been rinsed clean.

He crouched at the end of the donga, heaved a tangle of branches and several plastic bags from the mouth of the small stream, and watched the water surge into the dam, foam scudding across the surface. He ran his hand lightly above the earth, searching for the fuzz of new growth. A few more days, he told himself, and he stood up and followed the watercourse, intent on removing all the debris.

While lifting an old tyre out of the water, twenty feet away from the dam, he noticed bones jutting out of the bottom of the donga. An animal of some kind, one that must have died of natural causes because he certainly would not have buried it there. He turned his attention back to the tyre; the tread was worn but it would make a nice swing for the children. And then, because he couldn't shake the memory of bundling bloody bodies into sacks, he once again peered into the water.

The silt was settling and Lefu saw the small skull and the delicate curve of ribs. He drew back, fearful. It can't be, he thought, then he once again knelt down and stared into the donga. A scrap of blue cloth, caught on a piece of bone, swayed gently in the water.

His first impulse was to pretend he had not seen it; he was walking away, shrugging off notions of how it might have got there, when it occurred to him that someone else might find it and who knows what would happen. They might start digging, they might uncover all the animals he had buried and his transgressions with Eva would come to light.

He hurried to the stables where he took off the jacket of the old suit he wore for church and hung it from a nail in the tack room. When he gripped the worn smooth wooden handle of the spade he knew he had to see Eva. He walked up the road to the big house, spade in hand, and stood helplessly in the shade of the nyala tree opposite the gate in the security fence. Martin hated seeing his workers around the house on Sunday and he was hesitant to call her name.

Through the fence he saw Lorraine and Eva standing on the front lawn and the blur of Leeutjie's body as the dog tore through the puddles, chasing the tennis ball that Eva was throwing for him. After some time he heard the ball *thunk* against the fence and seconds later Eva pressed her smiling face to the diamond mesh. 'Ezekiel!' She opened the gate and stood there barefoot, still wearing the smart yellow dress she'd put on for church.

'Do you want to ride? I was thinking about it, but it's Sunday and I'm not supposed to ask you to work.' She noticed the spade in his hand. 'Is something wrong?'

'I found something, Miss Eva.'

'What do you mean?'

'You must please come and look.'

Her eyes swam away from his. 'Where?' she asked.

A terrible thought flew into Lefu's mind. Nonsense, he told himself, but he suddenly felt wary about talking to Eva.

'Nothing, Miss Eva. It's Sunday . . . don't worry . . .' he said and he walked away.

'Ezekiel, wait!'

He walked faster, berating himself for being so foolish as to think he could confide in her. And there she was, right behind him, breathing fast, pleading with him to tell her what was going on. He wanted to turn on her, to shake the spade at her and shout *Bona!*, the way one does when a stray mongrel follows you home.

He left the road, skirted the field and made his way to the donga, a mad hope leaping into his heart. *I didn't see what I thought I did.* But, no, there was the small skeleton. He heard Eva breathing heavily. She stood some ten feet away. She was barefoot and frightened and Lefu saw the five-year-old girl who had sought him out to bury her dead bird.

'Come look, Miss Eva.'

She did not move. 'It's just a jackal. I remember. I buried it. One of the first my dad shot and because it was close to the house I did it myself.'

'No, Miss Eva, look at this. It is not a jackal.'

'I told you. My father shot the jackal and I came back and buried it.'

'Naledi . . . this is not right. Maybe we must go to the police.'

'Ezekiel!' Eva pounded her hands at her sides. 'I've told you what happened. You go to the police and there will be trouble. Big trouble!'

Lefu was stunned by the threat.

'You think they'll believe you? Especially when I tell them how you went riding when you weren't supposed to! Don't you dare say anything. Don't you dare!' she cried and she ran off in tears.

The earth was still heavy with rain and it took Lefu close to an hour to dig the grave. Eva watched from some distance away, her yellow dress standing out against the green of the fields. He clambered into the water and removed the bones – the skull, the thigh bones, the ribcage with its longing for breath. He tried to lay the bones in some kind of order as if he were reconfiguring the small body. Then he shovelled the earth back into itself and stamped on the grave.

He did not know how to return to his family; there was a story on his face that he did not want Nkele and Mpho to read. At dusk, frogs long buried in the earth splashed into the dam. The moon rose and he heard the hum of the bakkie's engine and soon spotted headlights crawling down the dirt track that led to the interior of the farm.

He rose to his feet, and as he slowly walked home Lefu had his vision. As if he were an eagle in the sky, he saw Skinner's Drift, the neighbours' farms and the land in Botswana all spread out beneath him. The Limpopo was sand, but it shone the way it did when it was flowing and a full moon floated high in the sky. Men with guns were crossing the river, they carried AK 47s and they streamed over from Botswana and the foxes and the jackals and the hyenas and the lions let them be. Lefu saw the black hell of the hyena's thick mouth and the moonlight shivering on the silvery hairs on the back of the jackal. He saw the small veins in the ears of the bat-eared fox, hundreds of them, like the footpaths lacing Skinner's Drift, the footpaths that he and his family and families before them made as they walked the land, the map the white people didn't know about, the one his brothers with their AK 47s were following. The bat-eared fox stood silently in the bush and heard the grass sighing under the feet of Lefu's brothers. The jackal lifted its head and smelled their sweat. Then Lefu saw Martin's headlights, now shining this way, now that. The animals leapt into the air, they offered their throats and their skulls and Martin's gun blazed. Lefu knew then that they were offering their lives so his brothers could slip by in the darkness. He saw them dancing, machine-gun fire spinning them into the air.

5

We are at that in-between place, when it seems as if all that rain was in vain. Our world still looks the same: desolate, parched and it's brutally hot. But when I went for a walk I could sense the explosion of green that will happen in the next weeks. And the air is humid. I feel like I'm living in the tropics and yet when I step outside the garden it looks godforsaken, a strange and unsettling combination. I took the soldiers a tin of rusks earlier today, and tomorrow I'll bake them some more treats. They seem to be settling in. Their names are Mark, Wynand and Neels and they have dreadful ostrich-egg haircuts. Every once in a while a jeep trundles along the road. And yesterday I saw the soldiers patrolling the border fence. I know that is supposed to comfort me, instead it made me terribly nervous.

When Martin whispered he never stuttered and though he never whispered endearments the ease with which the words flowed from his mouth always made Lorraine shiver with the intensity of her love for him, even as she listened to the most dire news. *Dam's flooding! There's a spitting cobra in the kitchen. Lorraine, I'm putting a security fence around the house.*

During the rains he'd rolled over to her side of the bed and whispered, 'The army is going to post soldiers on the farm. They'll be here next week.' She nestled her head against his chest and the sound of his heartbeat reminded her of a windmill turning steadily in a strong wind. On and on he whispered about patrols and curfews and commando units, moist warm murmurings that tickled the top of her head. They made love for the first time in months and the inner voice that had been nudging her, scaring her, a voice that said, I don't want to live on Skinner's Drift any more, was momentarily quieted.

Three days after the rains ended, Lorraine stood on the patio once again surveying the world that Martin had created when he fenced their home. He'd included the entire front garden with her extravagant rose beds. He'd also been generous in the back of the house, enclosing at least fifteen feet of lawn beyond the washing line.

Smells unleashed by the rain prowled this new world, over-powering the scent of her roses. The musky miasma of several pawpaws rotting beneath the trees, the growl of moisture-laden earth, the cloying sweetness of the mandevillia vine dripping on to her as she crossed the verandah with a tin of rusks tucked under one arm. Muscling its way through all of these odours was the alien metallic smell of the fence that gave her a dull headache just above the eyes.

At the gate she traced the diamond pattern of the wire. She flicked out her tongue and lightly touched her finger. The fence left a strange taste in her mouth. Less than two hundred feet in front of her stood the brown mushroom of the soldiers' tent. The first thing to sprout since the rains.

They'd arrived on Skinner's Drift the day before in two army jeeps that didn't kick up any dust because the dirt road was still soaked. While a technician installed a radio system in their hallway, the family and Jannie, who'd just made a run to Johannesburg, sat in the lounge and chatted with the local kommandant.

'Just a precaution,' the kommandant said, referring to the military presence on the farm. He sipped tea from a china tea cup decorated with four tiny blue maidens dancing beneath a tree. 'Go about your business as usual.'

Lorraine asked him if it was still safe for Eva to ride. 'She's always out on her horse.'

The kommandant paused and Eva shot in, saying that she wasn't interested in riding any more.

'She r-rides with one of our boys,' Martin said.

'Is he a good kaffir?' the kommandant asked and he reached for another scone.

'As good as any kaffir can be,' Martin stammered.

At that point Eva politely left the room, but Lorraine knew from the set of her mouth that it was a nasty politeness. She glanced at Jannie. His hair stuck up in tufts as if he hadn't combed it and his socks were mismatched, the one a darker shade of khaki than the other. He stared at the hartebeest head on the far wall. He was being respectful, pretending that he had no inkling of the tensions corded through her family.

'And night driving?' Lorraine asked the kommandant. 'Sometimes Martin and my daughter go out looking for game in the evening.'

'Just for the time being, I'd advise you not –' The kommandant's last words were drowned out by the radio that spluttered to life, connecting the farmhouse to the soldiers' post, neighbouring farms and the military base in Messina.

Before the kommandant left he had the three soldiers introduce themselves. By dinner their names had escaped Lorraine.

The soldiers hadn't seen Lorraine approaching. She cleared her throat and the soldier closest to her spun around, a look of panic on his face. The other fellow burst out laughing and teased his mate, then, as if suddenly remembering army protocol, they both stood upright and at attention.

She laughed nervously and held out the tin. 'I brought you some rusks. You can have extras, can't you?'

To her relief they reintroduced themselves. Mark, the freckled fellow cleaning the gun, was a Krugersdorp boy. The gangly, dark-haired nervous one hailed from Port Elizabeth and his name was Neels. She took in their pimples, their soft eyes, the way Neels, who clutched the tin of rusks, chewed on his lower lip. The army had sent children to protect her.

'And there's Wynand.' Mark pointed across the low scrubby bush. 'He's also from Krugersdorp.'

Lorraine shaded her eyes. Wynand was there and then he wasn't, now dappled in the shade, now lost in the long dry grass, slipping in and out of the landscape until he stood in front of her, sweat beading on his forehead. She put a hand out to steady herself on one of the guide ropes of their tent. The taste of the fence was making her feel nauseated.

'Are you all right, Mrs van Rensburg?' Mark asked.

'I'm fine. But you boys must be careful. You don't know how hot it can get here.'

'Do you want to sit down?' He pulled a wooden crate closer.

'I'm fine. Don't fuss,' she scolded. 'I need to go home now, but if you boys need anything you must please ask.'

'I'll walk with you.' Wynand hugged his rifle close to his body and escorted her back to the farmhouse.

'Thank you!' she called after she shut the gate. She squinted, trying to see through the diamond mesh, but it had a way of dancing in front of her eyes, making it hard to focus on the land beyond.

Lorraine ate two squares of the Cadbury's Fruit and Nut she kept in the refrigerator and took a furtive sip of Martin's brandy, straight from the bottle. The casual cleaning of the rifle, a gun that was not going to be used for game hunting; the ease with which Wynand, dressed in camouflage shirt and pants had walked in and out of the mouth of the earth; the taste of the fence – she had only just comprehended the seriousness of the situation.

Wing beats of panic replaced the relief she'd been feeling

daughter into the house. She was too thin, dark pockets under her eyes told Lorraine she wasn't sleeping and she feared the months away from the farm were proving too much for her. She tried to reach out to Eva, to console Martin on the rare occasion that he expressed his concern over water levels, but as time passed and the tension in the house grew unbearable Lorraine gave up, abandoning even the writing of invoices, her share of the office work. She visited Dr Krieger. He wrote her a prescription for tranquillizers and implied she wasn't the first wife in the area to request them.

Reassuring herself that those grim days were over, Lorraine flipped forward to 12 December and picked up her pen. She would be a good wife and a good mother, she would continue to keep the record.

> We are at that inbetween place, when it seems as if all that rain was in vain. Our world still looks the same: desolate, parched . . .

She paused, that's what she found so unsettling. Once she saw signs of life, grass, water in the river, she was certain she'd feel better.

Lorraine's afternoon nap was long and deep, a well of sleep out of which she crawled an hour and a half later with much effort. The bedroom felt chilly and she switched off the fan and opened the window. Fists of warm air nudged past her as she gazed down on her rose beds. Apricot Dawn and Barnard's Beauty were in bloom. Her sylphs, she called them. Each time she and Martin dropped Eva at boarding school she returned with a rose bush or two. And they had sustained her in unexpected ways.

During the drought she had often stood at this window at night, half hidden behind the lacy curtain, stealing tenderness from Martin, watching him stroll around the garden, pre-occupied until he found himself caught in the perfume of her roses. He'd stop, tilt his head back, close his eyes, and the sweep of his neck, so boyish and vulnerable, would fill her with longing and she'd take deep breaths, imagining she was breathing with him as he drew in her sweet air.

Lorraine decided to dress for dinner. She chose a simple pale-green sun dress, clipped on a pair of rose quartz earrings, a birthday present from Eva, brushed her blonde hair, and daubed on her coral lipstick. She was about to dip a tissue into a jar of cold cream – it looked so silly out here in the bush – when the scratchy song of the butcher bird drew her back to the window.

The fiscal shrike was a new resident in the garden, arriving just days after the fence was erected. She'd named him Cromwell and was keeping a tally of the prey he impaled on the barbed wire. Four moths, one locust, a frog and two small lizards. Tonight he sang the death song for a strand of spaghetti pilfered from the leftovers she'd put in the dogs' bowls.

When she glanced back down at the garden she saw her daughter standing amidst the roses.

'Eva? We're going to have a braai tonight.'

Eva didn't respond.

'Wait! I'll be right down.'

Lorraine hurried downstairs. These days Eva was in the habit of disappearing, sometimes even in the middle of a conversation she'd be out the door. She'd change the subject, come up with an excuse, words couldn't hold her. The sheep-skin rug on the polished wooden floor in the corridor skidded under foot and Lorraine slowed down, preparing herself for disappointment as she went into the dining room and through the French doors that led to the verandah.

Eva was still there, barefoot, dressed in frayed shorts and a tank top. Her brutally short haircut made her appear younger than fifteen. She looked exhausted, the radiant rain-soaked girl who loved the smell of wet horses had vanished. And so quickly. On Sunday, the day after the rains ended Lorraine had joked with Eva as she threw a tennis ball for Leeutjie into the huge puddles on their front lawn. Six hours later she sat at the dinner table, her eyes red and swollen from a crying episode, she barely ate and said nothing except, I'm going with you, when Martin picked up his gun for yet another evening of hunting.

Lorraine wanted to take her daughter in her arms, she wanted to implore Eva to trust her enough to tell her what was making her so unhappy. She also knew that such a response would surely make Eva recoil. 'Too much rain. I know it sounds silly, but I think it rained for a day too long.'

Eva didn't even bother to look at her.

'Then the soldiers. Too many of them. And I didn't like that kommandant. Did you? What was his name? Wessels?' Damn, now she was close to tears, Eva could be so dismissive at times. 'Eva – if there's ever anything you need to talk about –'

Eva glanced up, a flicker of something moving across her face. Simultaneously Lorraine heard the groan of the gate in the security fence swinging open. Martin was home. She was certain that Eva stiffened slightly at the approach of her father.

'B-bats –' Martin stammered as he walked the stone path between the rose beds. 'Bats c-c-come out at n-n-night and so does my daughter?'

'What on earth are you talking about?' Lorraine snapped.

Martin looked hurt and she flushed. She had been cruel, any impatience she felt with regards to his stutter was always followed by remorse. But dammit, Eva had been so close to talking to her.

He gestured into the washed grey sky where a bat flitted above them and Lorraine recognized it as his way of reaching out. She looked from her daughter to her husband – he looking at the bats, she refusing to acknowledge them – and a fero-cious prayer rose up inside her. *Keep us safe.*

Just then two soldiers skirted the garden as they patrolled the border fence that loomed just one hundred feet beyond the fence surrounding the house.

'*Hoe-hoe gaan dit, korporale?*' Martin stammered, and he walked to the edge of his fence to greet them.

'Mark, Wynand and Neels,' Lorraine whispered to Eva. 'I finally managed to match their names to their faces this after-noon.'

She wanted Martin to have a moment alone with the young men, sensing that their presence invigorated him, but Eva had tossed off her words and went to join her father. Lorraine followed.

'*Gooie naand,*' said the freckled soldier from Krugersdorp.

Mark or Wynand? Now, Lorraine couldn't remember. He smiled at her and added a greeting in English for her benefit.

Martin chuckled. '*Ja, ja, ons is tweetalig op hierdie plaas. Engelse vrou.* Daughter goes to English boarding school to keep *engelse vrou* happy. N-n-not yet sure if d-daughter is English or *regte Afrikaner.*'

The corporals laughed awkwardly.

'English,' said Eva.

The boys' smiles faded. Lorraine watched them as they glanced at each other, searching for the best way to negotiate this terrain where father and daughter sparred.

'*Maar sy-sy verstaan – ons –*' Martin bowed his head, his speech slowing as he gathered his words, '*baie goed.*'

Eva folded her arms. 'So, we used to watch elephants walk-ing along the banks of the river. Now it's soldiers.'

'Elephants?' asked the tall soldier.

Poor boy, he looked so anxious. He was the one from Port Elizabeth, Lorraine remembered, nervous Neels, and the other fellow was Mark.

'Plenty of elephants! And once in a while a lion.' Eva arched her eyebrows dramatically. 'Have you heard the hyenas yet? I hope the army gives you good strong tents. Keep them zipped at night. A hyena can chew a man's face off. Then there's the terrs, but of course that's why you're here, in case they come after us.' She turned to her mother. 'What else, Ma?'

'Oh, I–I . . . I don't –' Lorraine found herself stuttering as she stared in amazement at the new creature in front of her. A flirtatious daughter.

Eva smiled again at the soldiers. 'So, are you scared?'

'*No!*' the young men bellowed and snapped to attention.

'And do you like our cage?' She gripped the wire and shook it, sending a twanging vibration into the air. 'Do you think we need it?'

'Evie, leave them alone.' Lorraine put a hand on her daughter's shoulder, but she shrugged her off.

'You m-m-must – must –' Martin breathed heavily.

Lorraine lowered her eyes and tried to concentrate on the quavering call of a nightjar, the first of the evening. Listening to her husband search for words, no, he didn't search for words he dug them out of himself, was sometimes more than she could bear. She imagined the soldiers felt nothing but pity for him and she wanted to tell them that he was the bravest man she knew, that his effort made her love him even more.

'– must excuse us,' Martin laboured on, 'these – these are hard –'

'What my dad is trying to say is that these are hard times for us,' Eva interrupted. 'We're confused. Yes, we are. Because what exactly does a terrorist look like? Do we have to worry about the people working on our farm?' Her voice trembled slightly, the tone suddenly not so self-assured. 'Do they wear uniforms like you? Or do they just look like the Africans that visit our workers? Must we now remember the face of every kaffir that works on our neighbours' farms?'

Hearing the word 'kaffir' come out of her beautiful daughter's mouth made Lorraine wince. Most farmers used the derogatory term freely, as did their wives and their children. Lorraine refused to and had corrected Eva when she was a little girl parroting what she'd picked up from her school mates.

'We're here to protect you,' one of the soldiers said gallantly.

Lorraine could barely see his face, in the minutes that she had stood at the fence with her daughter and her husband, night had fallen. She ran her tongue over her teeth. She could still taste the fence, a puddle of metal waiting to spill down her throat.

Martin nodded and the soldiers slipped into the darkness.

In the kitchen Lorraine poured herself a glass of white wine, and stacked plates, knives and forks, the sosaties, boerewors and salad on to a tray that she carried outside. She set the patio table for dinner, then sat in her wicker chair and sipped her wine. She noticed the lipstick smudge on her glass, wiped her mouth with a paper napkin and leaned back, waiting for the knot in her neck to loosen.

The rains had birthed insects, clouds of tiny silvery fluttering things that swarmed above the lawn and larger moths that blundered into the patio lights. The tattered flight of another bat caught her eye and she called, 'Martin, Evie, look! Is it a fruit bat?'

Martin ignored her and placed the sosaties on the grill and Eva rough-housed with Leeutjie.

Martin had been Eva's playmate when she was little. A chameleon, a huge moth – on certain nights the littlest thing could set them off, both of them excitedly calling for Lorraine to look at it. As much as she'd delighted in the two pairs of glistening eyes focused on her, she had a suspicion that it was not her that they were talking to, rather they were reaching to each other through her, sniffing and touching like wild dogs, calling in an intricate ritual dance. Inevitably Martin would jiggle the keys and he and Eva would leave for a night drive.

Lorraine had been envious of their bond, but to see it now so strained pained her. God, she wanted to understand her daughter. As if sensing her mother's hunger, Eva shoved Leeutjie away and ranged into the garden. She never developed a dark tan like Martin, and Lorraine watched her long pale legs dipping in and out of the pools of darkness.

'Keep away from the fence!' As soon as the words tumbled out her mouth Lorraine regretted them.

'We have a fence, Ma, so we *can* walk around our garden. This is the whole point of this f –' Eva scowled, *fucking* still held in her mouth.

'I'm sorry. But, Evie, it's just that it's dark and –'

'But what?' Eva challenged. 'Let me guess. You think the terrs are just waiting for us to get close to the fence so they can grab us. Don't you realize that if someone wanted to they could shoot through this.' She laughed cruelly. 'I don't believe it? You think Dad built a magic fence, a bullet proof –'

'*Eva!*' Martin bellowed.

She had been rude and deserved a reprimand, but the swiftness with which Martin strode toward his daughter alarmed Lorraine. She leapt to her feet. 'Martin, no! Both of you! Stop it!'

Martin flung the long steel braai fork across the lawn and strode back to the coals. Eva walked even deeper into the garden.

'Please!' Lorraine pleaded. 'Please, let's just start again and have a nice evening together.'

She sat down in the wicker love seat and picked up her glass with shaky hands. Wine slopped into her lap as the bloody spectres of the murdered farmers, Mike and Tinus Laubscher, visited her yet again. The brutality of the killings had stunned Lorraine, but unlike her neighbours who wanted to stay, to assert their god-given right to farm the fertile land of the Limpopo's floodplain, she wanted to leave.

Again she went through the details wondering if it could happen to her family. The border fence along that stretch of the river was not as elaborate as on Skinner's Drift and of course Mike and Tinus had not fenced their house. She doubted they even had a garden; Mrs Laubscher was long dead. Perhaps long grass whispered where there should have been a neatly clipped lawn. It would be very easy for killers to crawl through that grass. But why didn't the dogs bark? Because the men were lonely. Yes, they let their dogs inside for company. Lorraine could see it now – Mike and Tinus sitting at their dining table, knives scraping on plates as they cut into their chops, the dogs underneath the table, panting, waiting for the bones. And – She restrained herself, there was no need to imagine the attack. Just the facts. They had been macheted to death and Tinus's arm had been hacked off. No one shot them. So Lorraine *was* safe behind Martin's fence. Then she remembered the dogs, two female sheepdogs, both shot in the head.

Lorraine drank too much during dinner. Hating and then loving and then hating again her unknowable husband, the rude blonde girl who was her daughter, unrecognizable with that ugly short haircut. Could someone please tell her why a beautiful girl would butcher her hair like that?

Wine always made her thirsty and she left the table to get a glass of water from the kitchen. On her return she stopped at the door. Something was moving just beyond the fence? Yes, it had seen her. It was trying to stay very still so she would think it had disappeared.

The water glass slipped out of her hand. Eva and Martin spun around. She tilted her head slightly and motioned with wide eyes toward the fence. Martin stood up casually. He touched Eva on the forearm and whispered to her to clear the table. Once he passed the large plate-glass window in the lounge, he ran to the office and returned with his semi-automatic. He motioned for Eva and Lorraine to lie down on the floor. As he flicked on the outside floodlights and stepped outside, Eva crept towards the window. Lorraine grabbed her ankle, but Eva kicked free and rose on to her elbows and peered out.

'Dad!' She scrambled to her feet and dashed outside. 'Dad! It's just Ezekiel's dogs. I saw them! All they did was smell our food!'

Lorraine dashed after her. Eva tried to pull the gun away from Martin, the barrel of the semi-automatic swinging wildly as he held fast.

'Please, Mom! Stop him!' she begged.

'You little idiot!' Lorraine slapped her daughter across the face. 'I don't even think you realize what is going on here? Do you? So caught up in your own selfishness!'

Her hand flew up again and Eva's eyes flashed furious. Then the tears came.

Lorraine clapped her hands over her mouth. 'Evie?' she whimpered. She reached with trembling fingertips to touch her daughter's cheek. Eva flinched. 'Oh God, Eva, I'm sorry. Forgive me, please! I got frightened and –'

'You don't know enough to be frightened,' Eva spat, and she ran inside.

'Eva?' It was useless. She faced Martin, stabbing the air with a finger. 'Don't! Don't even try to say anything!'

He patrolled the perimeter of the garden and she poured another glass of wine. When he was done he returned to the patio, drained his brandy glass, hurled it over the top of the fence and stalked inside. Lorraine remained outside for a few more seconds, long enough to see Ezekiel's dogs – a grey pair that were whippet-thin like all African dogs – trot through a splash of light.

Before going to bed Lorraine tapped on Eva's door. She turned the handle to find the door was locked. In a halting voice she spoke her apologies. She listened. The silence behind the door was so dense, so complete, she wondered if she even had a daughter any more.

She felt appalled by her rage, and the look on Eva's face changing from disbelief to deep hurt. Lorraine knew that pain well. Her own father's hands cuffing her across the top of her head. A leg kicking out at her when he was frustrated. Always the left one, the metal brace that he wore as a result of his childhood polio hidden beneath his trousers. The sudden clatter of metal – a horse jiggling its bit against its teeth, the sound of a rifle being reloaded – still made her start.

And so she took another of the pills that Dr Krieger had prescribed for her.

She woke the next morning to find Eva and Martin already out of the house. Unable to sit alone with her remorse, she ate her breakfast in the kitchen while Grace washed the dinner dishes.

'Have you seen Eva? Do you know where she is?' Lorraine asked.

'Wellington saw her with the bees, madam.'

The two hives sat at the far end of the horses' camp. Eva had a way with bees and after one sweltering summer she'd abandoned the protective clothing Lorraine insisted she wear.

'She must be cleaning the hives. The drought killed all the bees. We'll have to get Eva some more.'

Grace shuddered and let out a small cry.

The arrival of the bees, well documented in Lorraine's diaries, had astonished the Africans. The queen and hundreds of workers came in the post, in a brown box labelled 'DANGER'.

'They can send anything in the post these days, Grace, snakes even.'

'I just want letters, madam.'

As Lorraine watched her maid dip her slender arms into the soapy water, she recalled the dirty blue envelope – addressed to Grece Ramothiba, C/O Rinsbreg, Box 21, Masina – that she'd found in the postbox several years ago. The uncertain misspelled words looked like tiny boats adrift at sea and the envelope had come unglued. When Lorraine peeped inside, she saw one page of lined paper torn from an exercise book. It was the only letter that Grace had received.

'Think of it. If we get the bees then we get the honey.' She took her half-eaten slice of toast and tossed it into Leeutjie's bowl on the other side of the kitchen door. 'And, Grace, make us a chicken curry tonight. It's Eva's favourite.'

On the first Wednesday of every month farmers' wives in the Limpopo area met for tea and target practice, gossip and home-baked jam squares. Lorraine considered skipping the meeting, but at 11.30 that morning Rolene telephoned.

'For the morale of the community, Lorraine, it's vital that you attend,' she barked.

Lorraine doodled on the pad beside the phone, deeply gouged curls resembling the barbed wire on top of the fence. She wondered if Rolene had sensed her doubts the last time they saw each other, dressed in black, handkerchiefs in hand, at the funeral for Mike and Tinus. Were the women of the Limpopo valley sniffing out her growing desire to leave?

'Certainly, Rolene, I'll see you at two.'

She hung up the phone. Martin was standing in the hall-way, watching her.

'Oh, you startled me! That was the Field Marshal, reminding me about target practice.'

He nodded his approval.

She made him an early lunch of two cold sosaties and a few slices of brown bread. She put the kettle on for tea and set a beer on the table for him, all the while feeling out what lay between them.

Regret for the ugliness of the previous night?

Was he feeling tender inside the way she was?

He had something to say, she could almost see it like a cloud forming just above his head. She swirled the tea bag in her cup and raised an eyebrow. *Come on, Martin. Speak.*

'R-r-river's back.'

Lorraine broke into a smile. He had come back for lunch just to tell her that their river was flowing once again and in that instant it seemed that their fortune would be determined by the erratic life of the Limpopo. She moved to the kitchen door, hoping to feel the touch of the cool breeze that sometimes danced off its waters.

Martin placed a hand on the small of her back which meant, don't move, I'll be right back. A minute later he returned with her pistol. He placed it on the counter, stroked her hair and left the house. At the gate he crouched to talk to Leeutjie. Another time he seldom stuttered, when speaking to a dog.

She set off in the bakkie at one in the afternoon, the hottest time to be driving, with Ezekiel sitting in the back. The sandstone cliffs that she called the Gods were to her left, ox-red and unforgiving, and as she negotiated the switchbacks she saw the river, churning and coffee-coloured. Within a few weeks it would settle down, transform into the wide blue Limpopo that she so loved.

Just before reaching the tar road, she stopped for a gate. Ezekiel climbed down and opened it and she was struck by how sombre he looked. He'd always had an air of private dignity about him, but these days he seemed even more withholding. Once through she waited for him to climb back in, instead he squatted on the ground next to her window and ran his hands over the earth.

'What is it?'

'New grass, madam.'

She stepped out of the bakkie, walked a few feet away from him, and bent down and saw hundreds of stubby green shoots pushing out of the earth.

The road to Rolene's led her past the stone pillars and wrought-iron archway that marked the entrance to Ons Hoop, the Kingwells' old farm. Marjorie Kingwell hadn't made it. It wasn't soldiers and guns and fear of terrorists that broke her, just the challenge of daily life in the Limpopo valley. Lorraine recalled how bright and eager Marjorie had been at the welcoming tea the farmers' wives held for her. 'I give her four years,' Rolene said when Marjorie left the room. Within three and a half Ons Hoop was up for sale. Kate Venter with her newborn was another deserter.

Cars lined the length of Rolene's driveway and Lorraine parked opposite the recently built concrete pen in which Rolene and her husband Detlef bred crocodiles. According to the sign on the wall – *Krokodille! Stilte asseblief!* – crocodiles liked the quiet life.

For several minutes she sat in the bakkie, girding herself for what was to come. She still felt like an outsider, an English-speaking oddity amidst the sturdy Afrikaner women with their capable hands and sinewy hearts. In hindsight she knew the others had made bets on her at her welcoming tea. Too refined. Too English. I give her one year.

That was nine years ago.

Ezekiel's gravelly cough brought her back to the present. He'd climbed out of the bakkie and stood a few feet away from the crocodile pen, attempting to peer over the wall.

'I'll be about an hour and a half, Ezekiel.' She shut the door of the bakkie and asked him to please not go too far, she didn't want to waste time looking for him when it was time to leave.

Rolene greeted her at the edge of her patio and Lorraine apologized for not having time to bake anything. She took a seat and Rolene welcomed Sergeant Lourens from the Pontdrif police station. Everyone knew him, everyone had a worker who at some time or another had been carted off for pass book infractions, stabbings, drunken incidents.

'Thank you, thank you, ladies!' Lourens stood in front of the bar with its crudely carved scene of voluptuous bare-breasted figures holding pineapples. He had a touch of the showman about him and he bowed as the gathering of eighteen women applauded. 'Most of you now have a group of soldiers living on your farms. I've spoken to Kommandant Wessels of the Far North and he has told me that in the next several weeks graders will be coming to improve the roads along the border fence.'

Lorraine remembered him, the tea-sipping kommandant.

'He sends you his best.' Lourens fished a piece of paper out of his pocket and read, 'The ladies are every bit as important as the men in our first line of defence. Please give them my respects. I'm counting on them.' Lourens paused as Rolene's maid brought the tea tray. Rolene poured, Lourens added sugar, took a sip, and when the maid was out of earshot he resumed, in a lowered voice. 'Don't be fooled by your garden boy or the girl who works in your kitchen. Most of you do have good trustworthy workers, but you must still keep your eyes open. The enemy will often make contact with the local people and intimidate them. We're counting on you to be sensitive to any changes in the behaviour of your staff. Any suspicions and you report to me or the military personnel. Ladies, you are of prime importance, as important as your husbands, as important as the boys now posted on your farms, as important as the local commando units. One more thing, and I'm embarrassed to say this because I know I'm talking to a platoon of Annie Oakleys. You must be proficient with your small firearms. When Rolene informed me of today's target practice, I offered to give some tips. You should have seen the look she gave me. But, jokes aside, ladies, I'm here to watch and if I have any suggestions, please don't take offence. Just think of what a mess I'd make if I tried to bake a *melktert!*'

The women laughed and reached into their handbags for their Glocks and Lugers and Colts. Two at a time they tore into the black silhouettes hanging between the palm trees at the bottom of the garden.

Rolene and Charmaine.

Anna and Elsabiet.

Sondra and Katinka – tall, widowed Katinka Theron with her swaying, gleaming waist-length hair and long legs. The women of the farming community had befriended her, adopted her. She was their mascot. Reason to fight, to stay, to become an expert with a Webley, a Smith and Wesson.

The length of Katinka's hair irritated Lorraine. Why, for god's sake, was she wearing it loose? At Dirk's funeral, close to two years ago, Katinka's hair had fallen just below her shoulder blades. Lorraine had seen her a handful of times since then, but her hair had always been tucked up. Why didn't she cut it? Lourens moved in to adjust Katinka's stance, and she draped her black hair over one shoulder.

Like an animal's pelt, thought Lorraine. It was her turn now and she stepped forward, narrowed her eyes and emptied the clip.

'Not bad for an English woman.' Lourens eyed the partially shredded target. 'Martin know you're this good?'

'I hope so,' Lorraine said curtly, and she walked to the bar and reloaded.

Rolene's young children dashed across the lawn to hang fresh targets. Each woman emptied another clip and Lourens announced that Fidel Castro and the Russians and 'anyone else who wants to monkey with us' better watch out. 'Don't forget to reload!' he reminded the women as the gathering dispersed.

Lorraine said her goodbyes and headed for the bakkie. While glancing around to locate Ezekiel, she watched Katinka open the door of her small maroon-coloured car. She imagined the walk, though she'd never been to Katinka's house, down the hallway so empty and quiet and lonely without her husband. 'Katinka!' she called out, feeling guilty for judging her so. 'Are you safe at your house? Make sure you have someone secure it for you.'

Katinka started, a look of alarm on her face that quickly melted into a generous smile. 'Thanks, I'm fine. By the way I heard your entire garden is fenced.'

'It's as good as a fence can be. From certain places you can't even see it.'

Katinka was about to step into her car when Rolene approached them. 'Haven't you seen Katinka's wall?' She joined Lorraine at the bakkie. 'It's very impressive. Hundreds of broken beer bottles lining the top. Did you do that yourself, Katinka?'

Katinka shook her head, no, she didn't, and the sunlight skittered through her hair.

'*Ja,* that's a big job. I thought you must have had help.'

'Lourens came by one afternoon.' She drummed her fingers on the roof of her car. 'It was very sweet. Martin also helped me.'

Rolene turned to Lorraine with wide, unblinking eyes. 'I tell you, Lorraine, your husband could protect all of us. I got the creeps just looking at her wall. If anyone tried to climb over it they'd cut themselves to ribbons. Katinka!' Again Rolene stopped her from driving away. 'Did you drink all that beer and break the bottles yourself?'

Lorraine didn't register the response, she was still taking in what she'd just heard. Martin secured Katinka's house? Why didn't he tell her?

'You should have. It's fun!' Rolene put a firm hand on Lorraine's forearm, bringing her back into the conversation. 'I did that with my mom's place outside Kimberley. She lives close to the township. You take a towel, wrap it around an empty beer bottle, and then –' She mimed cracking a bottle against the side of Lorraine's bakkie. 'Just so, at an angle, so you get a nice jagged cut.'

Katinka's car rumbled to life.

'Call me if you need anything!' Rolene shouted. She squeezed Lorraine's shoulder. 'Shame, we must all look after her. You have time to look at my crocs?'

Lorraine dutifully followed Rolene. A dozen motionless crocodiles lay scattered around a murky pool. 'That sign you put up – asking for quiet – doesn't the shooting upset them?' she asked politely.

Rolene laughed. 'No, gunfire makes their eggs nice and strong. Makes them wonder when we're going to toss another kaffir over the wall.'

It was late afternoon and Lorraine drove fast. She told herself that it made absolute sense that Martin had secured Katinka's house. Everyone else helped her, why shouldn't he? After Dirk died they'd given her cuts of meat, Lorraine had even baked rusks for her. But she couldn't shake free of the encounter she'd just had; Rolene grinning like one of her crocodiles, her capable hand gripping Lorraine's forearm, Katinka awash in her long black hair. Her stomach caved in as images of Martin kissing the young woman, fondling her breasts, played out in front of her. The thought that finally consoled her also cut her with shame: *Why would anyone want to have an affair with Martin?*

She had just left the tar road near Pontdrif when she saw several figures standing in the middle of the road some distance away. She slammed on her brakes. The week before, in Ellisraas, a farmer on a dirt road had been shot and left for dead, his bakkie stolen. She reached into her handbag and grabbed her pistol. Ezekiel, who was sitting in the flatbed, tapped on the glass and she shrieked. He mouthed something and violently shook his head. She turned back to the figures in the distance, they waved their arms in the air and came running towards her. She fumbled with the safety and the gun, slippery with her sweat, fell to the floor. Ezekiel pounded on the glass with both fists. 'Baas Claasen's men! Moving cattle, madam! Look!'

Of course, she saw them clearly. The men were waving their herding sticks and there were the cows in the veld on the side of the road. She bowed her head over the steering wheel and wept.

She tried to calm down during dinner, telling herself that any woman would feel as if her life were unravelling if she'd endured a three-year drought, had soldiers camped outside her door, and a teenage daughter whose expression could, within the space of a minute, change from utter vulnerability to stony disdain. It didn't help. When she raised her head and looked at her family she felt as though she were drowning. They were sitting at the stinkwood table as they had hundreds of evenings before, eating Grace's impala stew, but there was nothing for Lorraine to hold on to, her life was unrecognizable.

She waited until Eva was in her room before she joined Martin in the lounge where he sat nursing a brandy.

'Martin, I want to talk to you,' she blurted.

The request immediately struck her as ludicrous.

Lorraine had met Martin during her last year at UCT. A rainy winter's day in the Cape and she'd reluctantly gone to an intervarsity rugby match. Fifteen minutes into the game and the players were covered with mud and the spectators berserk with the decades long rivalry. *Vrystaat!* bellowed the Maties, while the UCT students screamed in vain for their Ikeys to clobber the Stellenbosch team. Lorraine was pressed up against a man with light blue eyes. He kept looking at her, an amused expression on his face as if he was aware of her boredom, her feeble attempts to join in. God, she hated team sports. It was only at half-time that she heard his stutter. Her friends snickered and, acutely embarrassed by their insensitivity, Lorraine made it a point to talk to him in her simple Afrikaans. It took a while for him to respond – he managed a citrus farm in the Eastern Cape and was visiting his stepbrother who was a student at Stellenbosch – and she did not look away, but kept her eyes on him. She wanted this man to know that she could be a place of refuge, that she did not think less of him. Perhaps it was the ferociousness of her desire that made her friends shut up, that made Hendrik ask her if she would meet them for drinks. When he walked into the ladies' bar later that night, Lorraine, who was taking a class in Greek and Roman mythology for her bachelor's degree, had already made up a myth about Martin van Rensburg. Every word in the world had been poured into him, but he had fallen out of favour with the Gods and they had stopped up his throat with rocks. She was the one who could free him.

Lorraine's discovery of how words failed her was more recent. They slipped out of her mouth like sand through an hourglass, they never held what she truly meant and formed lies and half-truths that she recalled days later.

'Martin.' She said his name again as if that one truth could lead her further. She wished she could abandon all words, speak with her hands, with her eyes, the way they used to, but she felt so far away from her husband. Guns and patrols and security fences had infused him with a new vitality. He wasn't frightened like she was. He was thriving.

She sat on the sofa opposite him and spoke about her concerns, as best she could. This was a dangerous time, she didn't feel comfortable with Eva roaming the farm.

'It's not that dangerous,' he stuttered, 'and besides there are soldiers on the farm. You must stop worrying.'

'But it will be dangerous, Martin!' Her voice rose in pitch like the silvery whine of a jackal. She still hadn't said what she meant.

He joined her on the sofa and clasped her hands in his. She kept silent. After a few moments he released her and she gathered up her courage and said the words a farmer's wife is never supposed to utter.

'I want to leave.'

He stood up as if he hadn't heard her, and walked to the liquor cabinet.

'I want to leave Skinner's Drift. This part of the world doesn't want us any more. Drought and now this danger –'

'We c-can't.'

Which she'd expected. A fight, an argument. 'Martin, there's life beyond this farm. We'll go elsewhere. See if we can manage another farm in the Eastern Cape. We'll sell Skinner's Drift, get what we can for it –'

'We c-c-can't,' he repeated, and he opened a new bottle of Fish Eagle.

The details came slowly, mulish words kicking out of his mouth and she loathed them. There had been problems with the farm during the drought, bore holes running low, the loss of the tomato crop, the frost in the winter. They were sinking deeper and deeper into debt. And, yes, there was a point when he thought they might have to leave, but then he learned that the SADF would give him a loan, a big loan if they stayed on, if they managed the farm according to Defence Department guidelines. He'd applied for the loan and it had come through the previous month, just in time for them to fence the house. As he paced the lounge and travelled deep into his story, Martin appeared transformed, taller, his face fashioned out of burnished wood, his eyes bright as stars. I love this country, he stammered, and now they want me, they want *us*, we are their first line of defence.

Lorraine stood in the upstairs bedroom, rolling a sleeping pill in the palm of her hand. No, she decided, not two nights in a row. She slipped it back into the bottle and changed into her nightgown. Out the window she saw Leeutjie, full of young dog bravado, sitting on the lawn, sniffing the night. The moonlight illuminated her roses, sculpting the blooms in creamy marble. The fence gleamed and in the distance the gods rose up grey and solemn, surveying their world.

The nightjars sang. In her battered copy of *Roberts' Birds of Southern Africa* the rhythm of the bird's call was evoked by the phrase 'Good Lord deliver us', but after ten years of living on Skinner's Drift Lorraine still couldn't hear that prayer in the bird's wavering call. Who had come up with that phrase anyway? Some missionary travelling north on the old trade routes that wound through the Soutpansberg, across the mopane fly-infested scrub and into Matabeleland? A sweaty Scottish missionary listening to the rumble of drums, waiting for Shaka or Dingaan or Sheteswayo to attack. Both he and the bird imploring, Good Lord deliver us.

She thought about Martin's eagerness to be part of the first line of defence and her fear rose liquid, a snake curling up her spine, flaring its burning hood in her skull. Perhaps without her knowing, while she'd been standing at the window her eyes had skimmed a scraggle of bush where blacks with AK 47s huddled.

She tugged the curtains shut, and opened the diary to distract herself. She still had to write the day's entry.

13 DECEMBER
We had a braai last night, the first since Eva –

She savaged the page, gouging out the sentence she had just written. She wouldn't do it, write about the farm when it wasn't even theirs any more. How dare he take the loan from the defence force without discussing it with her. If an African showed up with a gun she would hand over everything they owned. She would run screaming. Not for a second would she fight. She flung the diary across the room, anger bucking through her body scattering her fear.

With the moon almost full, the nightjars would not be silenced. *Jag weg die wewenaar.* That was the Afrikaans phrase that mimicked the bird's call: Chase away the widower! Of course the Afrikaner would come up with something cruel like that. It probably originated during the Great Trek, some poor bastard losing his wife to who knows what – yellow fever, black water sickness, green fever, fever from living in the godforsaken bush. Some poor chap alone with his dim-witted oxen, hardly Great Trek material which was all about the family. She still remembered the frightening illustrations in her junior school history book, the women and children huddling in the protective circle of ox wagons, the bearded Voortrekker men shooting at wide-eyed black men who wielded assegais and wore strips of leopard skin on their arms and legs.

Chase away the widower! How typical. While the English trembled and prayed for mercy, the Afrikaner banished anyone who needed mercy.

An English-speaking woman and an Afrikaner. Maybe it would finally come down to that with her and Martin. Her parents had warned her and yet she'd felt confident that they would survive. They were both outcasts. He with his stutter, an obvious affliction. With her it was something else, mood swings that frightened her mother and later on the men she met at university. But not Martin, his steadiness had calmed her in their first years of marriage.

When her anger finally exhausted itself, Lorraine curled up on her bed with an aching familiar loneliness, a cold-vaulted emptiness inside her that only Martin could fill.

A moth thumping against the window pane.

A hyena whooping at half past two and the slicing whistle of a pearl-spotted owl.

A footstep?

The low rumble of an African voice?

With her daughter sleeping down the hall and her husband on the sofa downstairs, Lorraine rode out the night, buoyed on a sea of sound until the first bird called. The rectangle of sky in the small side window had just begun to lighten, an almost imperceptible shift in the night sky, a relaxing, and then she heard it, just a twitter, a flutter of sound that didn't have the fear of the nightjar about it but rather a curiosity, a testing of the waning night. Within an hour the bush would be summer-raucous with shrieks and trills. She drifted off when the sky was grey blue.

In the days leading up to Christmas, Lorraine became a nocturnal creature. She flushed her sleeping pills down the toilet, convinced that if she hadn't taken them night after night during the drought she would have prevented Martin from signing the loan from the Defence Department. She fell asleep at dawn, and woke close to midday. While her neighbours, the women with the capable hands, made lunch for their men and their uncomplicated children, she ate bowls of cornflakes with cold, cold milk. Except for one trip into Messina for groceries and a check of their postbox, she stayed in the confines of the fenced-in house, spending her afternoons in the garden. She didn't lack for company.

The soldiers always stopped in mid patrol to say hello and she asked the boys for the addresses of their mothers so she could write and reassure them that all was well with their sons.

Ezekiel entered the garden each day at half past three and worked for an hour before feeding the horses. Lorraine noted the particular way he had of carrying a spade on his shoulders as if it weighed nothing and yet at exactly the same moment was the weight of the world. Once, she saw him momentarily seduced by the perfume of her roses. Old Ezekiel with the cough that made her think of TB arched his wrinkled neck and breathed deep and for an instant Lorraine found herself breathing with him.

Jannie visited one day, sweaty and dishevelled, after making the ten-hour round trip drive to the produce markets in Johannesburg. As usual he had stopped at a bakery that she liked on the outskirts of Pretoria and bought her two croissants, and as usual he stumbled over the French word and blushed and finally said, 'I got you your crescents.' She told him he'd brought civilization to the Limpopo valley and greedily bit into one and he laughed and blushed even deeper and said he had to get back to work.

'No, no. Sit with me for a bit. Tell me about the rest of the world.'

Jannie straddled one of the wicker chairs. 'When I was leaving Pretoria I saw a man in a sports car with a dog with long blonde hair sitting in the passenger seat, just like his wife.'

'Maybe an Afghan hound.'

'I swear it looked like a woman from the back.'

'Something else!' She knew he found her a bit dramatic and she played it up whenever they were alone.

'Okay.' He thought for a moment. 'There's an Italian hunter at Shangri-La. They say he's a prince –'

'Probably a count. I've read that Italy is full of them.'

'Kobus took him to Zim and now he's got seven zebras. Nice ones.'

'Rugs for his girlfriends?'

Jannie laughed. 'Seven girlfriends? I don't know. He's an ugly bugger.'

Lorraine sipped her tea. 'I'm curious about something. You went to school with Dirk Theron, didn't you?'

'*Ja*. We also did basics together.'

'His wife was at the civil-defence meeting the other day. Katinka. I imagine you've stayed in touch with her.'

Jannie nodded.

'She looked lonely. Is she doing okay?'

'As far as I know.' He rocked back on the chair and stood up.

'Well, I think people judge her harshly, because of the dancing, all that business in Jo'burg –'

'Maybe. I don't know. Listen, I got to go. Seven zebras are waiting for me.' He lingered at the table for a second, then he said, 'I'm driving next week and they have these little cakes with strawberries –'

Lorraine's heart dived into the pit of her stomach. It was true and he knew and he felt sorry for her. 'No, no, I can bake little cakes. But you have to be French to make these.'

'I don't know, Lorraine. The *ou* who runs the bakery is a *regte Afrikaner*.'

'Go – go –' She waved her saucer at him. After he'd left the garden she pushed the second croissant to the edge of the table. The pied starlings who had been eyeing her tea – they were such bold birds – hopped up and tore it apart.

The only thing that brought a smile to Lorraine's face was her daughter. She seemed less surly. Dare she say it, almost happy? Lorraine suspected she had a crush on one of the soldiers. When she asked Eva as much, Eva feigned sticking her finger down her throat. '*Sies*, Mom! A soldier? They have no hair!'

There was a rhythm to her afternoons in the garden and it lulled her for a few hours until dusk when the cattle egrets flew overhead and Martin came home. Her anger roused itself then. He hadn't looked so alive in years, his eyes a burning blue. He was of his land, as vigorous and robust as the trees and vines and grasses that were drinking deeply in the Limpopo's floodplain.

She'd been married to Martin for eighteen years. In the hours after midnight she browsed through her diaries alone in their bedroom, retracing her journey, attempting to understand how she had arrived at a time in her life when she was living in a cage with a husband whom she suspected of having an affair, no, she was certain of it, and who spent nights sleeping downstairs on the sofa. What she found was her absence, at least in words. She'd barely written about herself, often it seemed as though just Martin and Eva lived on Skinner's Drift. And yet the truth of her life was there, shadowed beneath the entries, unwritten, unknowable to any other's eyes but her own.

The entry from March of 1981 read:

Confucius is missing. He hasn't shown up for days. Eva is back from boarding school and is spending hours on her horse looking for him. The staff are also on the lookout. Of course, I suspect the worst. I don't think it was a snare, they're set at the height for bushbuck. Probably a snake which is too dreadful to dwell on. Sometimes I think we shouldn't have pets.

What she hadn't written about was her belief that the disappearance of the Siamese was fitting punishment for the kisses that came with the cat. The man who had advertised the pedigreed animals in the *Farmer's Weekly* lived in Tzaneen, a five-hour drive away. He was listening to classical music when she arrived, Chopin, his hands were soft and there wasn't a speck of dirt under his fingernails. She'd stumbled upon the life she should have been living. They talked for over an hour and she learned he was recently divorced. As planned, she stayed overnight in a hotel. He took her out to dinner where they toasted her new kitten with a bottle of wine. Afterwards, in the parking lot, she kissed him, his mouth so gentle and generous and warm. It went no further. The next day she drove back guilty and in love with her little blue-eyed devil. She named him Confucius. The staff called him Confusing. He lasted eight months.

A few years earlier she had written an entry about the elephant hunt that took place on the farm.

Martin finally got the elephant. Eva and I came back from Cape Town to hear the news. Hopefully this will put an end to the crop damage. The staff couldn't stop talking about it and so to fully record life on Skinner's Drift I am documenting their comments.

Evelina – That elephant was so angry. It screamed and then I heard the gun. Like thunder. The baas told us he was going to kill the elephant that day so we all stayed at home.

Wellington – It looked like a mountain in the field. Suddenly there was an elephant mountain.

Ezekiel – Thank you for the meat, madam.

(He wouldn't say anything about the elephant. He claimed he slept through the whole episode.)

The truth was Martin had left the large gate in the border fence open, encouraging the elephant to amble through night after night and feast on the tomato plants, until he had sufficient evidence of crop damage. The permit to shoot the animal was pushed through in three days because Mr Grobbelaar was a friend. She'd fabricated an urgent trip to Cape Town – her father was sick with nothing more than a mild touch of the flu – so she and Eva wouldn't have to be on the farm when he shot it. She recalled how, on her return, she'd sensed the absence of the animal, the land unusually still and sorrowful. And her puzzlement when she asked Martin if he was going to mount the head and he looked shocked and told her elephants were too special to have mounted in the house.

An entry from October 1975, their second year on the farm, was particuarly painful to revisit.

What lives in our garden? I will make a list. Crimson-backed shrikes, a mole snake, the visiting monkeys, several –

Rarely did she abandon an entry but on that morning, nine years ago, a slight cramping in her stomach and a moist feeling between her thighs made her slip her fingers into her panties. Her heart sank when she saw the rust-coloured discharge and she telephoned the doctor. Nothing could be done. That night she miscarried. She'd been hoping for a boy – a son who would have been all hers, the way Eva was Martin's.

After these late-night excursions into the past, Lorraine opened the pages of 1984, her current diary. Since discovering that Martin had taken the Defense Department loan there was nothing left to write. Or was there? The blank pages were white and pure, they smelled clean. Any life could be recorded on them. Her life. She started on 17 December, the appearance of the words so startling, like small friends on the page. *I barely know myself.*

Two days before Christmas Martin entered their bedroom at six in the morning with a cup of tea. He stammered his concern; she should leave the house, he didn't want her to be so frightened, and with the rains the bush had come to life in the most glorious way. He'd arranged for one of the soldiers to accompany her on a walk. He almost begged her to go.

Lorraine got dressed and headed downstairs to the lounge. She collected her field guides and carried them into the kitchen where Eva was making toast.

'You're up early,' Eva said. She was wearing her shorty pyjamas.

'Your dad –'

'I know. He told me you're going on a *jol* with one of the soldiers.' She buttered her toast and Lorraine placed the books on the kitchen table.

Reptiles, Birds, Trees, Butterflies, Wild Flowers, Mammals, Amphibians. Lorraine couldn't decide which guides to take, couldn't even figure out which area of the farm she wanted to visit. 'I'm not going,' she said abruptly. 'This is ridiculous.'

'So you'll stay in the cage?'

Lorraine was silent for a moment, then she turned to her daughter. 'Help me choose.'

Eva closed her eyes and shifted the books around. 'Abracadabra.' She handed *Wildflowers* and *Butterflies* to her mother.

Lorraine took it as a sign. There was only one place to visit with these two guides, the small natural amphitheatre hidden at the base of the sandstone cliffs. Martin rarely went there, it didn't offer much in the way of hunting, and for Eva, who went everywhere on horseback, the extremely rocky terrain made it inaccessible.

She placed the field guides in a rucksack along with her binoculars, a tube of sun block, two canteens of water, a plastic bag filled with shaved biltong, another with cheese and tomato sandwiches.

'Eva!' She scolded her daughter who perched on the counter, dipping her finger into a jar of peanut butter. Leeutjie barked furiously and through the kitchen window Lorraine saw an army jeep pull up next to the fence.

'He's here,' Eva said, and she slid off the counter and walked to the door.

'Not in your pyjamas!'

Too late. Eva swung open the top half of the kitchen door. Well, at least the soldier couldn't see her legs.

'My mom will be right there!' She turned to Lorraine. 'It's the weird one from Port Elizabeth.'

'They do have names and his is Neels. Oh God, do you think I'll be safe with him? He doesn't even look like he knows what to do with his gun.'

Eva grinned. 'None of them do. Calm down, Mom. You'll be fine.'

Lorraine grabbed her rucksack and hurried outside and through the gate. 'Well, I gather you're to take me anywhere I want,' she said as she settled herself on the front seat beside Neels.

'Yes, Mrs van Rensburg!'

'Firenze, then!'

'Mrs van Rensburg?'

'Please, call me, Lorraine,' she said rapidly, covering up her embarrassment at having her little joke fail.

'Have fun!' Eva shouted. The kitchen door swung wide and there she stood, all legs as she waved goodbye.

Neels blushed violently. He put the jeep in gear and it lurched forward, pitching Lorraine towards the dashboard.

A few honey-scented water acacias were still in bloom, but she barely noticed their fragrance. Neels seemed petrified of her and it was making her nervous. She glanced at him. Big hands, broad shoulders, large dark eyes which briefly met hers, then fled. He hunched over the wheel. Everything about him was just a touch too big for someone trying so hard to disappear.

After three kilometres the road climbed a small rise and ended abruptly. They had reached the north-west corner of the farm and the sandstone cliffs rose up in front of them. To her left Lorraine saw the river running brown in the shade.

'Now we walk!' she said brightly.

While Neels awkwardly slung his rifle over his shoulder and clipped two canteens of water to his belt, she scanned the river with her binoculars. 'I thought so, the crocodiles are coming back. There's a huge one on that sandbank.'

'I know him. We often see him when we patrol this area. We have a name for him.'

'And what is it?' she asked, delighted that he seemed to be loosening up. If he would just relax then she could relax.

'Korporaal Krokodil. He probably does a better job patrolling the border than we do. Not that we're doing a bad job!' he added, a mortified look on his face.

'I'm sure you're doing fine.' Lorraine patted his arm and he flinched. Oh God, she wondered, does he think I'm too forward? 'Perhaps we should turn back? I'm sure you have other more important things to do.'

'No. I must take you wherever you want to go. Mr van Rensburg told me to.'

Lorraine registered the edge to his voice. She most often noted the fear that her husband could induce in people in the farm workers, and to see it in this young man made her sad.

He offered to carry her rucksack and they set off, Lorraine leading the way for a few moments, before he coughed and awkwardly stepped in front of her. 'Excuse me . . . Mrs van Rensburg, I must be in front.'

They walked through the boulder-strewn bush to the foot of a small koppie, adjacent to the towering rock formation, and climbed to a ledge jutting out of the flank of the hill. Lorraine drank thirstily, and rested for a few minutes, before they made their way up and over the koppie to reach a small gully not visible from the ground. Their descent was eased by several natural steps of red rock and they rounded a large boulder to stand at the edge of a small clearing.

Baboons sounded an alarm call and a troop scattered up the cliff opposite them. A nyala tree with a magnificent sweep dominated the clearing. Sprawling ilala palms grew next to the tumble of rock blocking the view of the river while off in another corner stood a cluster of the trees Lorraine loved most, fever trees with their yellowish-green trunks.

The expression on Neels's face told her that he appreciated the natural beauty of the place. 'Elephant can't get in here,' she explained proudly as if she herself had landscaped it, 'so that acacia has been able to mature for hundreds of years. Look behind you!'

A rock fig had taken hold thirty feet up a rock face. Whitish roots snaked into crevices, while one, thick as a man's thigh, plunged straight into the earth. There were secrets here. A bushman painting of a thin leaping antelope on the underside of a rock overhang. A ledge where she'd spotted a nesting crowned eagle.

They strolled into the middle of the clearing and she handed him the sandwiches. 'I'm going to look around,' she said, and she left him sitting on a rock, rifle laying across his knees, mouth stuffed with a cheese and tomato sandwich.

A veil of privacy dropped over Lorraine as she made her

way to the small pool at the base of the cliffs and she found herself longing for Martin. He should have been the one to bring her here; when they entered the clearing she would have seen the delight on his face instead of that of the young soldier, and she would have once again embraced Skinner's Drift, given her heart to the farm, knowing that it was the only way that her husband could ever feel her love.

The sunny yellow skimmers flitting at the water's edge were easy to identify. When she saw a pale-blue butterfly a little larger than a postage stamp resting on a rock beside the pool, her excitement peaked. 'Neels! Quick! Come here!'

He dashed to join her, gun in hand, a panicked expression on his face.

'Oh, God, I didn't mean to alarm you. I'm so sorry. But see that little blue butterfly? I think it's a Sand River Blue. This is only the second time I've seen one. They're very rare. They usually feed on carrion. Ah, dammit, there it goes!'

'Carrion?' Neels asked.

'Dead animals.'

'Butterflies do that?'

She laughed at his surprise. 'Odd for such a pretty little thing, but it's true. That butterfly is endemic to our farm and a few others, this narrow band of land running up to the Sand River. I always thought the farm should have been named Sand River Blue.'

Lorraine's face grew warm. She decided to tell him the story that Fourie the old water diviner had told her years ago when she ran into him in Messina.

'Around the turn of the century a hunting party travelling north out of the Soutpansberg set up camp on the banks of the Limpopo, near an area shallow enough for them to cross. A French naturalist named Le Mesurier accompanied the hunters and kept a record of their journey, including this incident. One of the hunters spotted a large crocodile basking on a sand bank – just like your Koporaal Krokodil – and naturally shot it. The African skinners travelling with the men worked quickly and chucked the carcass back in the river, which of course attracted more crocodiles which the men promptly shot. Le Mesurier wrote that by mid afternoon they had killed over a dozen crocodiles and their African skinners were working like fiends. Needless to say the men had a few shots of brandy to congratulate themselves.' Lorraine paused. 'Do you hunt?'

Neels shook his head.

'You've never shot an animal?'

'No.'

'Do you want to? No, never mind, you don't have to answer. That night the men lit a fire to protect themselves and the donkeys they were using as pack animals. They continued to drink and fired at the jackals and hyenas drawn by the smell of death. A lion arrived in the hour before dawn and they immediately shot it, but when they examined it in the morning light they found it to be old and mangy and didn't bother skinning it.

'By now the animals they'd slaughtered began to reek. You would think the hunters would have moved on, but no, a kind of madness overcame them. They kept on drinking and taking pot shots at every scavenger drawn to the pile of rotting flesh. Le Mesurier wrote in his diary that by dawn of the third day the heap of carcasses was eerily quiet. That rarely happens in the bush – there's always something sniffing around death. He went back to sleep. When he woke an hour later he saw a blue cloud rippling above the carcasses. The smell almost made him throw up, but he moved closer and saw hundreds of Sand River Blues feeding on the carrion.'

'This happened on your farm?' Neels asked.

'About a mile along the river road. A museum in Cape Town has Le Mesurier's watercolours, including several of the sandstone cliffs on our farm.'

Wonder played across the young man's face; he believed her. And Lorraine lingered a while with the image of the blue butterflies, slivers of sky fallen to earth, before saying, 'Le Mesurier only saw a few butterflies. Not a cloud. I made that up. Otherwise it's too ugly.'

She turned her head so he wouldn't notice the tears that suddenly came to her eyes. 'That's why the farm is named Skinner's Drift. All the skinning that happened at that ford.'

'But still,' Neels said after an awkward silence, 'if the butterflies are that rare then that man Le –'

'Le Mesurier.'

'He was lucky to see them. Right?'

He was being kind. He must have sensed her distress and her heart reached out to him, even as she kept her head turned. 'Yes, you are right. He was very lucky.'

Lorraine wiped her eyes. She felt exhausted. She'd barely had two hours' sleep the night before, and she set the field guides on a rock in case Neels wanted to use them and settled down in the shade of the nyala tree for a nap.

When she woke an hour later Neels had vanished. He must have gone exploring, she thought, and she stood up and looked around for him.

'Mrs van Rensburg!' a voice shouted. 'Up here!' He'd scaled the steepest rock face and squatted on a ledge several feet above the rock fig. He waved something in his hand. 'Look out,' he called, and tossed it.

A strip of leather thudded at her feet. She bent down and picked up a dog's collar. Visible on the rusty name tag was the dog's name: TOSHA.

Lorraine frowned. Martin had told her the dog had been sniffing around the packing shed while he worked on the truck's oil leak. When it was time for him to leave there had been no sign of Tosha, and assuming that she'd wandered home he drove into Messina for his appointment at the bank.

The packing shed was more than two kilometres away from the cliffs.

She was still fingering the collar when Neels scrambled down and joined her.

'Mrs van Rensburg, please – I know I wandered off, but I had my eye on you all the time.'

'This is a collar from one of our dogs. She was almost blind. One day she vanished. She must have fallen –' She stopped, the scene too horrible to contemplate.

Neels held a fragment of a bleached skull in his hand. 'The whole skeleton is up there. I also found this.' He fished a stubby piece of metal from his pocket.

'That's a bullet.'

He nodded. 'Mrs van Rensburg – I'm sorry – but it looks like someone shot your dog.'

Lorraine shook her head at the bullet as if declining his offering. 'But why?'

'Maybe she found someone hiding in the bush.'

'But she was blind. She could never get into this clearing.'

'She wasn't in the clearing she was up there and –'

'Stop! I can't do this!'

Lorraine looked around at the lush trees, the warm silent rock. She was far from home and what could he really do to protect her? What if there were two, or more? She dropped to her knees, nauseated from fear, and shoved the dog's collar into her rucksack. 'I want to go back. It's getting late.'

'I'm sorry, I shouldn't have told you.'

'I don't care. I just want to leave.'

She piled in the field guides and the sunblock. 'Let's go!' she said, a touch of hysteria spilling into her voice.

He gathered his canteens and with the butt of his rifle he quickly gouged a hole in the ground.

'What are you doing?'

'She was your dog.'

He slipped the bone fragment into the hole and covered it up.

They walked back swiftly and in silence. When the familiar images of Mike and Tinus's hacked bodies receded, Lorraine was left with a fury that hummed through her entire body. Martin had sentenced her to life on Skinner's Drift and she tramped her hatred into his land.

On reaching the jeep she saw how dejected Neels looked. 'Don't feel bad. It's not your fault. But do me a favour. If you speak to my daughter don't say anything about the dog. It will just upset her.'

'Cross my heart.' And he did with solemn swipes. 'I'm going to find out who did it.'

'You don't have to.'

'I will. Wynand's father is a policeman and he's been telling us stories about murders that his dad solved. All you need is the bullet.'

He dropped her back at the farmhouse and she thanked him for the 'almost lovely' day. 'One more favour. Don't mention anything to Mr van Rensburg either. Tosha was his dog.'

Once inside the house, Lorraine went upstairs and placed the collar in a shoe box in the back of the built-in cupboard. She remembered sitting in the garden and hearing Eva's desperate voice as she called for the dog. She remembered asking Ezekiel to please check his snares. 'No snares, madam. I don't do that,' he'd said. She'd lost her temper. 'Don't you lie to me! I know you boys set snares all over the farm. Just check them!'

Night after night the ghastly scenarios had played through her mind: Tosha bitten by a snake or choking to death, Tosha poisoned by an African with a grudge. Never once did she think the dog had been shot. She made up her mind to wait until after Eva had gone back to boarding school before telling

Martin. Besides it was two days to Christmas and she hadn't even begun to bake. She would start with the mince pies tonight.

Christmas was a muted affair, a far cry from the festive years of the past when the mounted animals wore paper hats and Eva hung angels from the horns of the buffalo. Lorraine invited the soldiers for dinner; they couldn't all leave their post at the same time so they came over in relays, each one wolfing down a plate of roast beef and Yorkshire pudding and pulling Christmas crackers with her and Eva. When Neels arrived she avoided making eye contact with him, even though he was the one who brought their gifts; three cubes of bath salts for her and three for Eva, obviously a set that the soldiers had divided in two, and a cheap bottle of brandy for Martin. Each soldier left the house with a rum-soaked cake and a leaden Christmas pudding. 'If they had a cannon, they could fire your puddings into Botswana,' Eva joked.

She knew the hour of their afternoon patrol and in the days after Christmas she retreated to her bedroom at that time, hoping to avoid an encounter with Neels. She did not want to hear any more about Tosha's death.

Wynand broke the news. She had returned from a shopping trip when he approached the bakkie and told her that from the bullet and Neels's description of the skeleton he suspected the dog had been shot with a machine gun. 'My pa would know for sure. But I'm pretty certain –'

'*Hoe g-g-gaan dit koporaal?*' Martin appeared in the door of his workroom that stood adjacent to the carport, beer in hand.

'*Baie goed, Meneer.*' Wynand shook hands eagerly with Martin.

'P-pretty cer-certain about what?' questioned Martin.

'I'll tell you later,' Lorraine murmured. 'Thank you, Wynand.'

'Good afternoon, Mrs van Rensburg. And, *Meneer*, I'm sorry about your dog.'

Martin stared at Lorraine, the question still in his eyes and she waited until Wynand was out of sight.

'I was going to tell you after we took Eva back to school. You remember that day I went walking with Neels? He found Tosha's skeleton. Someone shot her.'

He drained his beer, then bent down to check the tyres on the bakkie.

'Martin? Did you hear me? Someone shot your dog!'

'I know what you're thinking,' he stuttered, 'and it's crap. It was probably a jackal skull and the soldiers shouldn't be wasting their time with such rubbish.'

'But he found her –'

Martin slammed a fist against one of the tyres. 'L-listen to-to me! T-t-terrorists did not shoot the b-bloody dog!' He stood up and strode off, returning seconds later to place a hand on each of her shoulders. He whispered, 'She died of thirst. Or got caught in a snare. The skeleton that the boy found was not Tosha's. Okay?'

'Okay,' she whispered back.

She felt the lingering damp heat of his breath on her cheek, an eddy of dread rippling through her as he walked away, machine gun swaying from his shoulder.

The most awful gun shot Lorraine ever heard was the one that killed Blitz. A blistering summer day and humid, the dog grotesque, his head swollen from the snake bite, and Martin striding into the house, returning moments later with a rifle. He seemed not to notice her and would have shot the dog in her presence. She begged him to please take Blitz to the vet. He would not. It happened right before her eyes, his grief hardening into something touched by cruelty. She ran into the house and lay face down on their bed, a pillow pressed over her head. Still, she heard the gun shot. And such a silence afterwards, broken finally by the sound of Martin digging a grave for his dog.

He mercifully put Blitz out of his suffering, she reminded herself whenever it came to mind. If he shot Tosha – and please God, surely he didn't – she would never be able to say the same. Her husband could not be so cruel as to let his daughter call and call for the dog when all the while he knew what had happened to it.

In her bedroom that night Lorraine kept her eye on the clock, the hands coming together at midnight. It was 1985. The worst year of her life had ended. She opened the previous year's diary and looked at the last few entries. They were not for Eva, they had no place in a diary chronicling their days on Skinner's Drift. She tore out the six offending pages and reread them, thinking that after doing so she would destroy them. She couldn't. They were something to hold on to and so she hid them, taping them to the underside of one of her drawers in the chest opposite the bed.

In the days leading up to the start of Eva's new year at Parkmeade Lorraine baked treats for her daughter to smuggle into her dorm. She made sure that Grace had sewn name tags into Eva's new school shirts. The prospect of two months without her daughter scared her – not that Eva had been much company, she'd taken to roaming the farm on an old bicycle – but she brought vitality and purpose into the house.

The morning they were to drive to the boarding school, just outside Johannesburg, the family woke before dawn. Martin wanted to leave promptly at five, but their daughter had slipped away.

'Eva!' Lorraine called. 'Eva!'

The remembered echo of her daughter calling *Tosha!* . . . *Tosha!* . . . had all reason flying out of her head, and she rechecked the car at least five times to make sure all of Eva's belongings were there. Eva finally showed up forty-five minutes later wearing a pair of sunglasses that she kept on for the entire journey.

The atmosphere in the car was tomb-like. Utter silence for three hours until out of desperation she asked Martin to stop at Boshoff's nursery – usually they did it on their drive back. She stepped out of the car and into the fragrant promising dawn, the aisles crammed with plants, and all the hope and comfort that her roses had given her withered into bitterness as she recalled those evenings when watching her husband walk amidst their perfume was the extent of the tenderness between them. She couldn't bear to search for a new cultivar and she headed back to the car where Eva stood, unsmiling, her folded arms on the roof. Lorraine bit her lip hard to stop the tears that threatened to pour down her cheeks. She'd wanted to wrench all love for her husband out of her heart, and, appalled that her daughter must have seen such vicious-ness swirling across her face, she forced a smile and said, 'Evie, why don't you choose one?' Still hidden behind her sunglasses, Eva glumly reached for the closest rose bush and carried it to the register where Lorraine paid for it.

Three hours later they parked at the bottom of the jacaranda tree-lined avenue that led to Parkmeade School for Girls. Amidst a crowd of parents lugging suitcases and hockey sticks and garrulous teenagers, Lorraine carried Eva's duffel bag weighted down with her contraband – four date loaves wrapped in tin foil and a Tupperware container of crunchies – to the dormitory. She hugged her daughter goodbye and ran her hands through Eva's short hair as if by doing so she could restore it to its former length.

'Grow it, please,' she murmured as she removed Eva's sunglasses. Her downcast eyes were puffy. 'What is it? Oh, Evie, please tell me what is wrong.'

Eva shook her head and dived into her mother's arms. Life

is a catastrophe, a disaster, a fucking mess, thought Lorraine. Tears filled her eyes and this time she couldn't stop them. 'Don't worry, I'm fine,' she said between sobs.

Eva gently extricated herself from her mother's embrace. 'You can use my sunglasses if you like.'

They both smiled. One more hug and Lorraine said, 'It was a hard summer, but we'll be all right.'

'Hard year,' said Eva.

Lorraine looked at her daughter's grey eyes, her slightly mournful down-turned mouth. There was a touch of weariness about Eva, a smudge of experience that added depth to her face. She was growing up and she was honest, more honest than her mother. 'You're right. Hard year. I'll see you in March,' Lorraine said, and she tore herself away.

She walked back down the avenue, past the hockey fields and the swimming pool. She imagined not returning to the farm, disappearing into Johannesburg, finding a job, perhaps telephoning the man who had sold her the Siamese cat. She drew closer to the blue diesel Mercedes where Martin was napping, head leaned back against the headrest. She watched him for a moment, before opening her door, the rise and fall of his chest, the sweep of his neck which had always reminded her of how vulnerable her husband really was.

Again they drove in silence, through Pretoria, past Boshoff's and into Pietersburg where he finally spoke, asking if she was hungry. She shook her head. They continued north. At Louis Trichardt there was always a choice – take the road that skirted the Soutpansberg, the route he preferred, or take the winding road through the mountains, her favourite. He chose the mountains. The gentleness of the vegetation, the surprise of mist, hurt her eyes. She refused to roll down her window to feel the coolness and moisture of the air.

They wound out of the Soutpansberg and he turned on to a small dirt road, not the most direct route to Skinner's Drift.

She guessed that he, too, wanted to delay their arrival on the farm, maybe he sensed that from the moment they pulled into the carport, no, before that, from the moment they descended the dirt road and saw the lights that Grace had switched on in anticipation of their arrival, their life together would be over. Even though she wasn't going to leave.

Within an hour they would be home. Lorraine closed her eyes. The rose bush Eva had chosen for her had several fading blooms and she smelled a hint of their perfume. Perhaps – yes, it could be, perhaps she had got it all wrong. She willed herself to speak calmly. And she did, no trace of a tremble in her voice.

'I have terrible thoughts in my head and I want you to tell me they're not true. One of them is about you . . . and Tosha . . .'

She stared at his tanned hands, the white nubs of his knuckles as he gripped the steering wheel, and the swell of his silence lifted her, carried her farther and farther away. She doubted she could be so graceful when it came to asking about the other things on her mind and so she kept quiet. Skinner's Drift lay sprawled in the valley below and she let the beauty of the farm at dusk break her heart.

6

January 1985

Nkele slung the carpet over a sturdy branch of one of the fig trees and beat it with Eva's old hockey stick. She thumped and walloped it until clouds of dust and dog-hair filled the air and her arms ached, then she heaved it off the branch and stood for a moment, hands on hips, catching her breath. Murdering a carpet was a deeply satisfying chore. She kicked the carpet into a bundle and was dragging it back to the verandah. She had just reached the corner of the house when she saw Lorraine standing alongside Lefu who was digging wide and deep around one of the rose bushes.

Was it her father's hesitancy, the way he dug and then stopped and turned around to look at Lorraine, that peaked Nkele's curiosity, made her drop the carpet to observe them? Perhaps it was the manner in which Lorraine almost placed her hand on Lefu's shoulder as if to reassure him. Once the rose bush was unearthed Lefu rolled it on to a piece of sacking and hoisted the bundle into the wheelbarrow.

Over the course of the summer the wheelbarrow had developed an awful squeak. Lefu had oiled the wheel but now it suddenly gave voice, a fleeting sound, like hundreds of mice being tortured, that made Nkele's teeth and ears ache. It was immediately followed by the deep shuddering groan of the gate in the fence as Lefu pushed it open. Even inanimate objects on Skinner's Drift were apt to complain.

Nkele was still grinding the wheelbarrow sound out of her teeth when she saw Lorraine glaring at her. She reached for the carpet, Lorraine had caught her loafing, then realized that Lorraine wasn't staring quite at her. Martin stood a few feet away, a glass of what looked like brandy in his hand. His eyes stuttered away from his wife's face and came to rest on Nkele's. For a moment she held his gaze, and what she saw shocked her; Martin van Rensburg, one of the most unpredictable, broody farmers in the Limpopo valley, was nervous. Her eyes darted back to Lorraine. The fluttery woman, who always seemed slightly agitated in her husband's presence, looked livid. It was as if each one's spirit had swooped into the other one's body.

Nkele seized the carpet and dragged it, lumping and bumping behind her, into the house. Through the window she could see that neither Martin nor Lorraine had moved.

Trouble was brewing. The van Rensburgs, unlike some of the white people she had worked for in the past, were private and usually kept their arguments and squabbles out of sight of the servants, if not out of earshot. Nkele trotted upstairs, gathered a pile of Lorraine's laundry and checked Eva's room. The girl had gone back to boarding school the previous day, leaving a mess in her wake. Nkele had already cleaned up, but when she got down on her hands and knees and looked under the bed she spotted two T-shirts and a bra. She added them to the pile, then sat on Eva's bed for a moment, her eyes scanning the shell necklaces and copper bangles scattered across the dressing table.

A few days ago Nkele had come across Eva and Neels kissing on the shady riverbank and she'd positioned herself behind a nearby tree to watch. Little Eva with one of the soldiers! It was better than television the way the couple slowly toppled to the ground and writhed in the sand. Neels rose to his knees and tore off his olive-green T-shirt. Eva scrambled a few feet away, pulled her shirt over her head and tossed it into the air. The garment snagged on a branch and while Eva frowned at it, perhaps puzzling how she would retrieve it, Neels crept behind her and cupped her small breasts. Eva's head lolled back on to Neels's shoulder, and the delight in Nkele's heart twisted into envy. She had last seen Mpho's father eight years ago. She'd lain in Bonisile's gentle arms while he urged her to come with him to Johannesburg where he would get a job in the mines and she would find work as a maid. When you are busy in the house, he'd said, you will know that I am deep in the earth beneath you.

Nkele stared at the large curved seed pod on Eva's dressing table. It came from an ana tree, the kind of tree beneath which Eva and Neels had lain. She squeezed the bundle of laundry in her arms; she could smell Lorraine's deodorant, Martin's sweat. Her heart felt shrivelled. Bitterness had laced her envy; resting in the arms of the man you love was yet another white world luxury.

The steady tolling of a spade slicing into earth drew her attention. She padded back to the master bedroom where the window overlooked the garden and saw her father unearthing another rose bush. After swaddling the root ball in damp sacking he went to work on a third. Some of the roses must be sick, Nkele decided, and he was probably going to burn them.

An hour later, whilst oiling the banister, she heard it again, the sound of a spade slicing methodically, if a touch wearily, into earth. She walked quietly downstairs to the lounge and saw her father disappearing with his wheelbarrow, violet and yellow roses stabbing above his head. Lorraine was still standing in the fierce summer sun, motionless as a heron next to the gouged out rose beds, but Martin had taken a seat on the patio.

Definitely trouble. Martin never stayed around the house on a weekday morning. Was she supposed to set the table for lunch? No, she thought, those two will not be sitting together.

At noon she left for lunch and met her father on the footpath with the empty wheelbarrow.

'Why is she throwing her roses away?' Nkele asked.

He trudged by without uttering a word. Typical of him, she thought. In the past year her father had turned into an irritable man, prone to snapping, lecturing and fits of silence. She continued down the footpath and saw Thapelo, an oil-stained rag in hand, sparkplugs on the ground in front of him, sitting on the small rise that overlooked the old stables. And there was Sankwela, a brush and a can of turpentine beside him. Both men were transfixed by Lefu's mealie field. And as Nkele made her way down the footpath she saw that a row of her father's young mealies had been chopped down and replaced with five rose bushes.

'The madam doesn't want them any more,' Sankwela offered.

'What do you mean, she doesn't want them any more?'

Sitting in his pool of shade Sankwela the sage had nothing further to say.

Nkele left the path, giving the roses a wide berth and picked her way down to the old stables where she made a sandwich. Roses in the mealie field? It could not be. They were Lorraine's treasures – Lefu had told his daughter as much when she came to work on Skinner's Drift – they were named after prime ministers and towns and Afrikaner pop singers.

She finished her lunch, scooped a mug of water out of the kitchen bucket, carried it outside to the shade of the lead-wood tree, and stared at the dollops of colour amidst the verdant green of the remaining young mealies. The leadwood tree sighed. Nkele licked the sweat from the corner of her mouth. Surely she was caught in a hallucination brought on by the waves of heat washing across the Limpopo valley. The tree sighed again. Gently easing away from the trunk, she peered into the branches and saw Mpho and several of his friends roosting in the crown. Her son's bright eyes skimmed over her face, then he stretched out on a branch and resumed his observation of the mealie field.

Lefu appeared with two more rose bushes. Nkele listened to her father's laboured breathing, the *thwack* of the panga, the soft forgiving sound the mealies made as they dropped to the ground, his grunts as he dug into the soil. Seven rose bushes in the field now, and a ghastly thought occurred to her.

All nineteen of those rose bushes are going to end up in our mealie field!

Alternately numb with disbelief and fearful, Nkele returned to the house where she ensconced herself in the small pantry next to the kitchen and scrubbed every shelf, wiped every can. The gate in the security fence groaned all afternoon, the spade sounded like a death knell. She didn't dare enter the lounge for fear of seeing either one of the van Rensburgs.

There were no instructions as to what she should prepare for dinner and she went home at dusk to find the field almost completely taken over by roses and a rose promenade leading to the old stables. Lefu was asleep on his bed. 'Father?' she asked desperately. He did not stir and she covered him with a blanket. She lit the fire and prepared samp and beans. She and Mpho did not eat outside as they often did on a warm summer evening, rather she marched her son inside and shut the door. Breathing was dangerous, an act of theft. She knew the fragrance of those roses, but she had smelled them in the confines of the garden surrounding the big house. It was a white world smell. Mpho sat quiet as a tortoise and she stared fiercely at him. *If I catch you dreaming about roses!*

That night, in the bed she shared with her son, Nkele dreamed about Bonisile. He was larger than a giant and she roamed his body. It was hard to get a grip with her feet as she wandered over his firm muscles, other places where his flesh was soft and pliable were easier. He was so vast and she searched for his eyes and his mouth. Warmth lifted off his skin and his smell was strong. There are places here where a woman can sleep, she thought, and she began to walk in a small slow circle, the way her father's dogs did when they made beds for themselves in the grass.

Nkele was always the last to leave the old stables in the morning. Lefu fed the horses by six at the latest. Mpho left at half past six for his hour long walk to Mrs Zietsman's farm school where a cup of milk and a slice of bread were served to each child at half past seven. Nkele usually woke with them, but when she opened her eyes the clock said ten to seven and she scrambled out of bed and into her maid's uniform, a powder-blue house coat. No coffee this morning. Still thick with sleep she stumbled out the door and flinched. Roses everywhere.

The madam doesn't want them any more, Sankwela had said, but Nkele didn't believe that for a second. Up the path she hurried, her stomach fluttering as she recalled her father pushing wheelbarrow load after wheelbarrow load of beautiful roses down the dirt road, a slow motion crime, the longest burglary in the world. She wondered if Martin and Lorraine were still staring at each other across the garden? Anything was possible and one thing certain: if the world down at the old stables had changed with the arrival of the roses, then so had the world up at the big house and she was about to find out how.

She approached the farmhouse where Leeutjie threw himself against the fence, barking. She crooned to the dog in Afrikaans, '*Luister, Leeutjie, ek is jou vriend.*' Keep them on your side, her father had instructed her, don't be scared to pat them, if you hate them then they will hate you back. And yet she couldn't help herself. *You ugly, ugly boere dog. So ugly only a boer could own you. If I was a leopard I would rip your head off!*

She was certain that in the seconds before Leeutjie's snarl softened into a slobbering smile he was looking at her and thinking violent dog thoughts.

With the dog pacified, Nkele opened the gate and began to sing, a habit she'd picked up when, at sixteen years of age and sporting the name Grace, so easy for the white people to remember, she began working for Mrs de Bruin, a timid widow who lived in Pietersburg.

Every morning Nkele had entered through the kitchen door, promptly at eight as instructed by the widow, and every morning she had startled her. In the kitchen, the hallway, the bathroom, Mrs de Bruin gasped and dropped spectacles, false teeth and cartons of milk. She pricked her finger with a sewing needle and scalded her lap with upended cups of tea. 'You're so quiet,' she'd exclaim. 'You scared me!' What am I supposed to do, Nkele wondered, knock on the door and wait for her to let me in, even though the door has been unlocked in anticipation of my arrival? She did just that. Mrs de Bruin hurried to the kitchen door, aghast. 'Oh! It's you, Grace! I couldn't imagine who it was!' Nkele felt frantic. *If I don't stop scaring this woman she will have a heart attack.* And so she sang. From the moment she left her tiny maid's room, just fifteen paces from the kitchen door, she sang a hymn or snatches from a pop song. On opening the door she'd drop down to a hum, just a few bars and then silence. Plenty of warning that Grace had arrived in the house. She carried the habit from job to job, a ritual summoning of Grace the quiet maid who was prompt, obedient and well mannered; Grace the cleaning presence, who was almost a non-presence, so much so that the white people would sometimes forget she was even there.

With Leeutjie trotting after her and the Lord's Prayer in Sotho quivering in her throat, she climbed the three steps and opened the kitchen door. It wasn't Lorraine who waited for her, but Martin.

'G-g-g . . . G-g-grace.' Her name struggling free of his mouth sounded like the bakkie's engine cranking to life on a cold morning.

Nkele curved inwardly in supplication, remembering the previous day's encounter. She had witnessed something she shouldn't have and now, listening to the horse-like snorts he made when words eluded him, she knew what it was. He didn't want those roses moved, he didn't want stoop-shouldered Lefu carting away all that sweet-smelling beauty. Nkele had been privy to a white man's humiliation at the hands of his wife. If a sjambok had come down on her back she would not have been surprised.

Please, baas, please! I have no eyes!

Martin's breathing quieted down. She registered a new sound, something insistent, something scratching. A rat in one of the kitchen drawers? She stared at the beginning-to-crack lino on the kitchen table and Martin slid something into her field of vision. He had written a note in large block letters.

THE MADAM IS SICK. DO YOUR WORK.

Out the kitchen door he strode, leaving Nkele with the still-ness and the smells and the already breathed feeling of the air inside the house.

Lefu never approved of the titbits of gossip that Nkele brought home, but she couldn't help it. Cleaning and cooking every single day was mind-numbing but, if a person threw in a bit of snooping, a touch of speculation, why then, the activities were transformed.

Even before the rattle of the bakkie's engine faded, Nkele scanned the kitchen and noted the sink bereft of dirty plates. The van Rensburgs had not made dinner last night. Perhaps Lorraine had been as exhausted as Lefu after the exodus of roses and had fallen into bed, and – Nkele padded into the lounge – Martin had resorted to his liquid diet. One empty beer bottle and a drained dry bottle of Fish Eagle had rolled underneath his leather chair. The pillow on the sofa told her he'd slept downstairs. This wasn't too surprising, but – and here she congratulated herself on being so astute – the pillow did not have a pillow slip which meant he'd taken it from Eva's room where Nkele had stripped the bedding the previous day. Was Martin still so nervous of his wife that he'd been afraid to enter their bedroom? Or had Lorraine realized what she had done and, suddenly terrified of her husband, locked the door?

Nkele's eyes flitted around the lounge until they came to rest on the large window and the absence of roses. The dug-up flower beds looked like two huge lumpy graves, the surrounding garden desolate. She stared and stared until that ominous green silence engulfed the lounge. She wanted to plug in the floor polisher and fill the house with noise, but Lorraine was sick. It was a day for silent chores.

She fetched the long-handled feather duster from the broom closet and went to work on the spiders on the ceiling. She was supposed to dislodge them and kill them but, terrified that they would drop on to her head, she had long ago settled for rearranging them. A few tickles with the feather duster and she rushed to the entrance of the lounge and watched a new constellation of dark stars forming on the van Rensburgs' ceiling.

That job done (she waited at least five minutes to make sure the spiders were securely attached to their new positions) she launched into the most ludicrous of chores, dusting the leopard behind the sofa, the antelope sticking their heads out of the walls and the big buffalo that leered at her from the top of the stairs.

At noon Nkele tapped on the bedroom door and asked Lorraine if she should bring her tea and marmite toast, standard fare for sick white women. There was no answer. She tried the handle, it wasn't locked. She opened it a crack, just to make sure Lorraine was all right and saw her sprawled on the bed, nightgown hiked above her knees, her skin a pulsing scarlet.

'Oh, madam!'

Nkele had never seen such a ferocious sunburn and she winced and tiptoed to the edge of the bed. Blisters studded Lorraine's face. Her eyes rolled white and listless.

'Grace . . .' she moaned through swollen lips, 'I suppose . . . it's punishment . . .' Her face cracked into the beginnings of a smile.

'Oh, madam, what can I bring you?'

Lorraine didn't answer. Smiling seemed to be painful and tears trickled down her temples. Nkele recalled Lorraine swabbing Eva with a particular lotion when she had a bad sunburn, and she searched through both bathrooms until she found the bottle with the crusted cap. She soaked a wad of cotton wool with the calamine lotion and daubed Lorraine's face. She methodically covered her arms with wide chalky stripes and then her calves. She didn't have enough for her feet which were laced with pale bands of skin, the pattern from her sandals.

Downstairs in the kitchen she squeezed the loaves of bread in the bread box. Nkele would have cut four fat slices from the freshest one; good girl Grace cut two slices from the stalest loaf. She ate in the garden, leaning against one of the pawpaw trees. Leeutjie trotted over, demanding his crust, and Wynand passed by on foot patrol. He stopped at the fence and peered into the garden and Nkele sat utterly still, hoping to blend into the tree. Apparently it worked, he didn't notice her.

After lunch she ironed the remainder of Eva's laundry and baked a shepherd's pie. Eventually someone in the house would eat. At half past four she climbed the stairs, stacked the T-shirts and shorts in Eva's cupboard, and walked down the hall to check on Lorraine. She was sleeping, the blue sheets tossed aside and smeared with chalky stains. One side of her face screamed scarlet where the lotion had rubbed off.

Whatever you have done, madam, Nkele thought, it was not worth it. We never wanted those roses and now look how ill you are with the sunburn.

It was close to sunset, her freedom hour. She was almost out the kitchen door when, acting on impulse, she wrote Martin a note. She placed it next to his but her fine cursive script made his look child-like so she tore it up and wrote another in crude lettering.

THE MADAM IS STILL SICK.

The soft slam of the kitchen door and she stepped outside, a groan from the gate and she was almost free. One obstacle remained. The roses. She walked down the dirt road and turned on to the footpath where she noticed, with grim satisfaction, the droop of their leaves, the smudge of lilac and yellow petals on the ground.

Yes, my friends, life here at the old stables is hard. You will not make it.

She heard her radio singing weakly and the chickens making their fat secret sounds as they dug deep into the bushes for the night. Mpho fanned the flames of the evening's cooking fire and the smell of wood smoke was sweeter than that of any rose.

The following morning Dr Krieger drove up to the farmhouse in his battered green station wagon. After examining Lorraine he spoke in hushed tones to Martin, and then summoned Nkele who just happened to be scrubbing the downstairs toilet with an ear cocked for snippets of their conversation.

'Mrs van Rensburg has got a terrible sunburn. I have never seen anything like it. It's almost a second degree burn. She needs cold compresses, pills for the pain, the blisters must be allowed to run.' He held up a hand. 'Martin, I'm telling you, it's the English blood.' He would resume talking to Nkele in a moment, right now he needed to expound on his theory concerning the geographic distribution of those of English descent. They were not meant to live north of the Orange river, whereas the Afrikaner could travel deep into the continent. The Great Trek was proof enough. Why, he was generous when he gave the English the Orange River. Hadn't they petered out at Grahamstown in 1820? His speech slowed down and he resumed talking to Nkele. 'Mrs van Rensburg – is badly sunburnt – and you – will look after her. The baas tells me – you're a good girl. Your name is – Grace?'

She nodded.

He repeated his instructions. Cold compresses, Bayer aspirin, let the blisters run. He sighed heavily. 'You'll never remember this. Can you read?'

'Yes, baas Krieger.'

He plucked a note pad from his pocket and set it on the side table. Big carefully drawn block letters, again! She watched them labouring across the paper like slow deliberate elephants.

When he was done Krieger mopped the sweat from his brow with a handkerchief and rolled his head as if to ease the tension in his shoulders. Mid roll he straightened it with a jerk. 'Good God!' He lumbered to the window and left a nose impression on the glass. 'What happened to the roses?'

The night before Nkele had wanted to ask Lefu that very question, but her father had that look on his face that said, *Bona!* don't talk to me, and after a few mouthfuls of food he had gone to bed. She stared at the wooden floor she would probably still be polishing when she was a hundred and two, and wondered how Martin would respond.

'The roses?' Krieger prompted.

Nkele didn't even hear an intake of breath to indicate that, if they waited long enough, Martin would say something. Instead he left the room, just like that, and disappeared into the downstairs toilet.

Krieger turned to Nkele. She shrugged and the toilet flushed.

'Look after her,' Krieger muttered, and he plodded out of the house.

Nkele wished she could do the same.

That evening, she found Lefu on his hands and knees next to one of the rose bushes, Mpho squatting at his side. Lefu drove a long steel pipe into the ground, removed it, and Mpho tossed something into the hole and tamped the soil with his small hands

'What are you doing?' Nkele demanded.

'Feeding the roses,' Mpho said. 'With chicken bones!'

'Why?'

Lefu looked up at her as if she had asked the silliest question in the world. He spoke in a tone that was faintly reminiscent of Dr Krieger's. 'Because – if we don't look after them – they will die.' With that, he and Mpho moved on to the next bush.

Nkele stomped down the path and slapped together their supper. Her father and her son gobbled their food and, to her dismay, returned to the roses.

'What now?' she yelled from the door.

'They need water,' came Mpho's plaintive voice.

She marched up the path and tapped him on the shoulder. 'Go practise your reading.' He scampered away and in a measured tone she addressed her father who was fingering the wilting leaves on one of the plants. 'Can you please tell me what is going on?'

'She doesn't want them any more.'

'And we don't want them either! They are nothing but trouble –'

'They are my reward.'

'Reward?' she spluttered.

'Yes. Reward. Men who work in a factory get a watch. I work for baas van Rensburg and I get roses.' He laughed weakly and Nkele thought that maybe her father was as mad as Lorraine.

'And now we have less mealies,' she grumbled.

'I will plant more.' He moved stiffly to the next rose bush, his hands hovering over it as if it were a small child. 'They do not know it is my reward. But it is. Such beautiful flowers, but they cannot have beauty at the big house.'

In the fading light he looked old. A slight rounding of his shoulders, the generous sprinkle of white hairs on his head. When had this happened? His voice had grown even deeper and sounded as though it issued from the earth beneath his feet. 'And you, Dikiledi?' Still bent over the rose he called her by her full name. 'What is making you so unhappy. It cannot be a few thirsty rose bushes.'

Lefu rarely call Nkele by her full name, and she felt as if she were suddenly adrift in an ocean of tears, her birthright. Dikiledi means 'one who weeps'; she had been named for the sorrow her father felt after her mother died when she was just a baby.

Night folded around them and Lefu murmured as if he understood her.

Long after her father and her beautiful son were asleep, Nkele remained at the small table in their makeshift kitchen. She was exhausted, yet didn't feel like sharing a bed with Mpho. She stood up and as she turned in a small circle, wondering whether she could fashion a bed with the three creaking wooden chairs, the tired pat of her feet evoked her dream. The slow circle into sleep on Bonisile's warm body. She weighed the dream against the words in the smudged blue envelope she had received five years ago. He had written that he missed her and his son and that he had finally got the much prized job in the mines. He would send money

164

soon. Was it a mining accident? Or a smart, sly woman from the city? Perhaps just a careless postman. She never heard from him again.

Lorraine healed slowly. The blisters on her arms and face wept clear fluid; crusty scabs formed, and when the scabs fell off the skin underneath looked pink and new. The newness soon faded except for two faint ovals on her cheeks.

And the roses did not die. How could they with so much attention lavished on them? The generous watering, the piles of mulch nestled around each plant, the prayers and mutterings and ministrations of Lefu and his troop of gardeners-in-training, Mpho and Thapelo's twin daughters. Nkele had declared a truce with the roses. Without their flowers, they looked innocuous, a few more green thorny residents of the African bush. And Nkele knew, she just *knew*, they would never bloom again.

Besides she had more pressing concerns. After five years of snooping through the van Rensburgs' lives, Nkele, to her discomfort, found herself under scrutiny. Lorraine was lonely and with Eva back at school and no roses to fuss over she focused her attention on Nkele. In the past the two women had talked, which meant Lorraine talked and Nkele listened. Lorraine still nattered away, but occasionally her words would cease, a lull in the wind for a few seconds, sometimes even minutes, and then out would pop a question, the kind of question that no employer had ever asked Nkele, because no employer had ever been interested in her.

Do you have brothers and sisters?

How far did you go with your schooling?

To which Nkele mumbled the briefest of answers.

No brothers or sisters, madam.

Standard six, madam.

Nkele had questions of her own, but of course she would

never dare ask them. Why did you give my father the roses? Did you know about your husband and the woman with the long dark hair?

Lorraine grew increasingly curious. She traipsed after Nkele while she dusted, she sat at the kitchen table while Nkele washed the dishes, even the smell of oven cleaner couldn't shoo her away. And no matter how hard she tried to convince herself that Lorraine's interest in her was genuine, that there was no catch, she felt on guard whenever she entered the house.

One afternoon, while cleaning the refrigerator, Lorraine asked a question of such a personal nature that Nkele decided she hadn't heard it. She narrowed her eyes and stared at a jar of mustard lost at the back of the top shelf. Every white person's refrigerator had one of these jars, a teaspoon of something in the bottom that they never finished. She fished the mustard out and plonked it on the table next to the mayonnaise and chutney and the last remaining jar of green fig jam. She moved to the sink and dampened a cloth. *What was your mother like?* No, Lorraine would never ask such a question. She wiped the tops of the jars, including the lost mustard. Would Lorraine notice it and say throw it out, she wondered, or would she and Martin eat that last teaspoon?

Lorraine persisted with her question. 'Ezekiel told me that she died several years ago.'

'When I was a baby, madam. I never knew her.' Nkele crouched in front of the refrigerator and wiped the trays for the eggs.

'That's terrible. Not to have known her.'

Nkele shut the door firmly. If she had the nerve she would have scowled at Lorraine.

'Oh, I'm sorry, Grace,' Lorraine said softly. 'I didn't mean to pry.'

Soon after that encounter the women found a topic that

pleased both of them. Mpho. Nkele felt fat with pride when Lorraine asked questions about him. He loves going to school, madam. He is still reading the book you gave him last year. Lorraine seemed delighted and during her next trip to Messina she bought him a zippered pouch to hold his pencils and two white school shirts. She told Nkele that Mrs Zietsman considered Mpho to be her star pupil and that of all the children in her farm school he stood a chance. She gave him another brand-new hardcover book. 'Keep him reading!' she exhorted Nkele.

Three months after being transplanted Star of the Reef flowered. Nkele was stunned. A day later a shy pink beauty nodded coyly in front of the tall green mealies. Two mauve roses with an intoxicating fragrance unfurled at the bottom of the footpath, not fifteen feet away from the old stables, and Ge Korsten – a bush named after an Afrikaner pop singer – erupted with blood-red blossoms with just a hint of, was it chocolate? in their perfume.

Lefu dropped several choice remarks about the roses after the Sunday church service, and by mid afternoon every worker on Skinner's Drift and a few from neighbouring farms 'just happened to be passing by'. An old petrol drum, a few logs, and chairs from the old stable were arranged in a semicircle opposite the transformed mealie field. Choice viewing seats for everyone, except Nkele who chose not to join the lively gathering and remained inside. When Thapelo's sister, who was visiting from Seshego, came in search of matches for her cigarette Nkele asked her to please explain the fuss and bother. Had these people never seen a rose before? The woman laughed and said, yes, but Lefu's roses were so beautiful and – this slick township mama turned all girlish and giggly – they made her feel so romantic.

From the door Nkele watched her father bobbing up every

few minutes to hurry over to a rose as if he were introducing it. She even heard people applauding. Mpho ran in and asked for the chair she was sitting on, the crowd was growing larger. She tried to seduce her son into joining her boycott by waving his new hardcover book at him, but he looked at her as if she were crazy. She retreated to the bed and flipped through the pages; there was the leopard without his spots, there the crocodile pulling the nub of the baby elephant's trunk. How astonished she and Mpho had been when they realized that the story took place on the banks of their river. After reading it they had walked to the border fence and stared at the river. 'The great grey-green greasy Limpopo?' he asked. 'Not today,' Nkele replied with a grin, for the blue sky was reflected in the lazy water.

Reading those words again infuriated her. Who was this Mr Kipling? Writing stories as silly as roses. Here she was trapped in the old stables while outside the fools admired the flowers. She thumped the book on the bed, slunk out the door and on to a footpath that veered past the outhouse with its resident flies. Now if those idiots really wanted a smell, she thought, this is where they should be sitting.

She walked with no particular destination in mind. By the time she reached the overgrown track that led to the abandoned dipping pen, her anger had evaporated and she was filled with sorrow. She couldn't bear living with roses. Their perfume drifted into the old stables at night, washed over her heart and made it beat out he is gone! gone! Bonisile is gone! gone! There was a warmth she had felt on winter nights in her small maid's room in Pietersburg, Bonisile's arm around her and Mpho sleeping at her breast, that all the sunny days on Skinner's Drift would never equal.

And it was no use thinking about it, she scolded herself, she had to go home, even if it meant smelling those roses. She took a step and stumbled to the ground. She tried to right herself but her ankle had caught on something and in seconds she tumbled through the bush and into a deep donga running parallel to the track. She shrieked and a rough palm clapped over her mouth.

'Bona!' a man's voice hissed. He pinned her to the ground with his body and shoved the barrel of a gun into her cheek. 'Anyone with you?'

Her head trembled, No! No! Sweat slopped from his face on to hers and she beseeched with her eyes, begging him not to hurt her. He grimaced and lifted himself up on one elbow, his hand dragging across her mouth. She felt the gun easing away from her face. His fierce eyes softened and fluttered shut and he slumped on top of her, head on her forearm as if she were cradling him, his legs and hips still pinning her down.

The man didn't stir. Nkele wrenched herself out from beneath the dead weight of his legs and took him in with one glance: an African in a blood-stained camouflage shirt and brown trousers, a large knife in a sheath at his waist, a worn leather boot on one foot, the other one bare with a terribly swollen ankle. Somehow he had slipped through the border fence and avoided the soldiers.

His eyes flickered open and she crouched rigid. He seized his gun, trained it on her and scrambled to his feet, but the moment he put weight on the swollen ankle his face contorted with pain and he buckled to the ground.

'Sister, please!' he whispered, searching her face. 'I do not want to hurt you . . . or anyone on this farm . . . I just need water, some food.'

Despite his words, visions of Martin and Lorraine being killed played across Nkele's mind. She wanted to run back to the big house, tell Martin and the soldiers, and have him removed. She didn't care. He shouldn't be here. She had a child to think about and she didn't want trouble on the farm.

'Please . . . help me . . .'

'Yes,' she nodded vigorously. 'I will come back tomorrow.'
She took a small step backwards, eyes fixed on the gun.

'I promise I will not hurt you,' he said.

She watched him lay the gun on the sand, watched him
slowly move his hands away from it and place them in the air
as if she were a policeman. She did not look at his face, no
point in knowing anything else about the man she was going
to turn in. She backed her way along the donga until it veered
to the left. He was out of view and she clawed her way through
a tangle of bush and on to the sunny track.

On the way home huge gulping sobs overtook Nkele and
she squatted on the ground and buried her head in her arms
until they passed. Lefu and Mpho were talking to the last of
the rose admirers and she slipped into the old stables. She
burned their supper, ate two mouthfuls of it and excused
herself. She threw up behind the outside toilet and decided
that she would tell Martin and the soldiers the next morning.

Terrorist. The word pulsed white hot in her mind as she
spent a sleepless night in the bed she shared with Mpho. But
there was also *Freedom Fighter* and *Comrade.* Why did she have
to find him? What if he killed the van Rensburgs? What if
Mpho came across him. She could barely restrain herself from
seizing her son and imploring him not to wander through the
bush.

Mpho was two years old in 1976, the year of the Soweto
uprisings. In the township outside Pietersburg Nkele had
rocked him in her arms and listened to the radio announcer's
voice break as he spoke of schoolchildren gunned down in
the streets of Soweto. During the months that followed she
heard about the speeches delivered at the funerals where boys
and girls became heroes, young lions, and she thought not
my boy, *never* my boy. When she was growing up the hope
of her Future had been a handsome man with a good job
who would put food on the table for their children. Now there

was a generation for whom Future meant only one thing. Freedom. She didn't want Mpho throwing stones, dodging armoured cars, vomiting in clouds of tear gas or running through a hail of bullets that the newspapers said were rubber but everyone knew otherwise. When Lefu sent word that the van Rensburgs needed a maid she had whisked Mpho off to Skinner's Drift, a farm in the middle of nowhere where there was no Future and no time to think of Freedom because there was too much work. Until now.

She stared at the curve of her son's small brow, his quiet mouth. She'd lost two babies before Mpho. His name meant 'gift' and she lavished him with imaginary kisses. He was extraordinary, even the white people could see it. Hadn't Mrs Zietsman who ran the farm school said that he stood a chance? A chance to be more than a stone-throwing comrade. Mrs Zietsman's words had delighted Nkele, and later, in her quiet reflective moments, roused her anger. The farm school only went up to Standard Five, in two years Mpho's education would come to an end. A decade ago she could have sent him to relatives in the townships where the schools were marginally better, at least they went up to matric, but since the early eighties a school boycott had been in effect, and now Mpho's chance was to be a stable boy or a grocery boy, a delivery boy, a road worker if he was truly fortunate.

Nkele buried her head into her old pillow that leaked feathers. She wanted to talk herself out of it, but she kept thinking about helping the man hiding in the donga. She groaned softly and bit the cotton cover stained by a cup of tea that Lorraine had spilled years ago and then passed on. No, it was madness. Every day the soldiers were out patrolling. What if he stayed there for days on end? She might get careless, slip up and somehow the soldiers would catch her with him.

Let him crawl away. Forget about him.

And if they catch him and torture him?

If they hang him in Pretoria?

Rather risk one life than two. Forget about him.

She abandoned him, then rescued him a hundred times that night.

At noon the following day Nkele wrapped her lunch bread in newspaper and tucked it in the pocket of her apron where it seemed to bulge in a most conspicuous manner. Earlier she had found a half full can of flat coke in the lounge, a leftover from Martin's liquid dinner – rum and coke main course, brandy for dessert. She took a sip, letting the warm sweetness give her courage.

With a heartbeat that could surely be heard from the Botswana side of the Limpopo, she embarked on her mission. A hundred feet down the dirt road she stopped and in an elaborate pantomime patted her pocket as if she'd lost a key, a letter. More likely her mind. She retraced a few steps and casually lifted her head, fully expecting to see Wynand, gun trained on her, as he followed her to the comrade in the donga.

During a run-in with him before Christmas, Wynand had cupped her chin, forcing her to look into his narrow eyes. 'Be careful, *Sissie,* walking in the bush. You don't want one of your freedom fighters to rape you. That's what they do pretty *sissie,* and then *bevokked* and *lus* they stumble into one of us and –' He made a gesture of slitting his throat and, with a squeeze of her breasts, he strolled off.

Nkele turned in a slow circle, in either direction the road stretched midday silent and deserted. Lefu was working all day at the far end of the farm and Mpho was in school. She continued on to the stables where she gulped her last shot of flat Coke and refilled the can with water. With a few swift steps she veered into the bush. Each crackling twig and crunching dry leaf bellowed *Kaffir aiding and abetting a terrorist!* Clumps of distant mopane looked suspiciously like well-camouflaged farmers rehearsing their commando manoeuvres.

When she reached the dirt track, she squirmed through a bush with too many thorns and stumbled into the donga. The branches hung low and she set off at a crawl. She heard the quick pant of his breath before she found him huddled in the sand.

'I brought you water,' she whispered, and she knelt in front of him.

He jerked his head up, hand fumbling for his gun.

'It's me!' For a moment he did not seem to recognize her. 'I promise I am alone.' She offered the coke can in an outstretched hand.

His ankle looked even more swollen and he seemed disoriented. Water dribbled down his chin as he drank.

'Slowly, you are wasting it. I will bring more . . .' She stopped, she had unwittingly told him she was willing to return. She offered him the bread, but he shook his head and drew his knees to his chest and shivered.

'I'm cold, little sister.'

Nkele frowned, the day was warm. She untied her blue apron patterned with white daisies and draped it over his shoulders.

'So cold!' he moaned.

'Ssh! you must talk soft. There are soldiers on this farm. They patrol the bush.'

His eyes flashed wide. 'That frightened white boy? *Homola!*'

'Yes,' she urged. '*Homola*, you must be quiet.'

He nodded guiltily. 'It is Umkhonte we Sizwe that has men in it. Men like Comrade Lucky Vula!' He shivered violently and before she knew what was happening he had burrowed into her lap. 'Cold! Cold!' His voice grew louder and, terrified that someone would hear him, Nkele embraced him. She hugged him tight, wrapped her arms around muscles and heart and blood and breathed deep the smell of his sweat.

His teeth chattered, he gripped her thighs. Suddenly he shook free of her and looked around fearfully. 'Where are we?' he asked in a hoarse voice.

'Skinner's Drift. Please!' she implored. 'You must be quiet!'

'Botswana?'

'No, South Africa.'

'South Africa?'

'Yes, yes, South Africa.'

The words seemed to lull him and she repeated them until he took them and held them gentle in his mouth. 'South . . . Africa . . .' He put his arms around her waist and crawled closer, nestling his head back into her lap as if it were the most natural thing to do.

His disorientation led Nkele to believe that he had a touch of malaria. She hoped the fever had broken, but after several minutes his brow furrowed and he began muttering. She considered clapping a hand over his mouth the way he had silenced her the previous day. Instead she rocked her upper body and stroked his cheek and discovered that when she leaned close to him he lowered his voice. Whisperings about ANC training camps and Russian comrades and a woman named Zindi tickled her ear.

It was half an hour before he calmed down and the easy pull and release of his breath told her that he had fallen asleep. Her back ached. She straightened up, stretched as best she could without disturbing him, and took a long hard look at the man in her arms. His face was broad, his mouth generous. He looked to be a few years older than she was, in his early thirties. A thin scar curled below his left cheekbone. She'd known a few Luckys in the township – careless, seductive young men who broke hearts – and each one sported a scar.

Nkele tried to move her legs, but they had fallen asleep. If she heard the soldiers coming she doubted she would be able to crawl away and yet she felt curiously calm, an almost visceral sensation, her blood thickening, moving with slow determined force.

When the weight of him changed and she sensed him waking up she grew terrified. His shoulders tensed and he moved stiffly from her lap, hand patting across the sand, reaching for his gun.

She scrambled to one side. 'You were cold. I was keeping you warm,' she said in her defence, not sure what he was going to do.

The thin scar now lent him an air of menace. He blew the sand off his weapon, then unwrapped the food she had brought him. 'I will need more.'

'Yes, I will come back tomorrow.'

'Whatever I said –'

'I have already forgotten.'

He nodded, dismissing her. She wanted to leave, but her apron was still draped across his back, strings dangling over his shoulder

'What is it?' he asked brusquely. He followed her gaze and tugged at one of the apron strings, spilling the daisy strewn cloth on to the sand between them. The beginning of a smile broke across his face and she grabbed her apron and crawled away.

Wild imaginings plagued Nkele as she prepared the evening meal. With his knife and his gun the man in the donga walked to Pretoria, slaughtering anyone who stood in his way. She and her family moved into the farmhouse and ate dozens of lamp chops each night for dinner. Martin worked in the fields and was so hungry he threw his sjambok in a pot to make soup. Lorraine worked as Nkele's maid – no, she lived by herself in a small house in Alldays and became Nkele's friend.

Nkele moved closer to the fire, there was a slight chill in the air. And she was being greedy. Just a small change would do. A little more money, a smile from Makakaretsa. A car. Too much. New bicycles for all three of them. A flushing toilet? Yes, that was it. An addition to the old stables with a flushing toilet . . . and a shower.

The fire hissed.

'Ai, what's happening to our supper?'

Nkele fanned her hands to clear the smoke and saw the pot boiling over, her father standing opposite her.

'Sorry, sorry,' she mumbled.

They ate in silence, too hungry to talk until their plates were almost empty. Then Lefu said, 'Your Miss Eva is not going to be happy.'

'*My* Miss Eva?' Nkele put her fork down. 'Why do you give her to me? I do not want her. She is your Naledi.'

Lefu ignored her comments. 'Her boyfriend, the soldier, he is missing.'

'Since when?'

'Miss Eva is going to be *very* happy!' Mpho said, and he speared the last potato on his plate. When he had their attention, he continued. 'He's gone to see her, that's what Dipatso told me.'

'Who is Dipatso?' Lefu asked.

'The soldier with the red hair. He's making me a gun for my birthday.'

'What?' Nkele and Lefu demanded at the same time.

'Out of *wood.*' Mpho's eyes flared as if he couldn't believe his mother and his grandfather were so stupid. 'He's almost finished.'

'Listen to me –' Nkele knelt in front of her son and squeezed his knees. 'I don't want you visiting the soldiers, I don't want you wandering through the bush. Do you understand?' She stood up and pulled her chair close to his. 'Now, tell me what you know about the missing boy.'

'Dipatso and the other one both say he was always scared . . . and in love!'

'Yes . . . and? . . .'

'He told them he was going to walk near the river and that was the last they saw of him. They say he's AWOL,' he said proudly, 'and he's gone to see Miss Eva at her school.'

Nkele turned and saw Lefu looking at her with a question on his face. 'What? You think I shouldn't worry about that white boy?'

'All I know is that he's missing,' he said, and with a nod of his head he told her that supper was over.

Nkele cleared the table with a feeling of dread in her belly. She could see it. The two men stumbling across each other, the struggle, the white boy shot dead, the black man limping into the donga to hide. No, no, best to believe what the soldiers said, best to imagine Neels and Eva kissing, rolling around in the bushes behind the hockey field where Eva scored the goals. Her father was sipping his evening mug of tea. She longed to tell him about the man in the donga, but she was uncertain as to how he would respond. Would he sit quietly at the table with her when Mpho was in bed and come up with a plan to help him? Would he be proud of the way she brought him food today? Or would he walk up to the big house in the dark and bang on the kitchen door to rouse Martin and his gun, calling, 'Baas! Baas, we have found somebody!' She thought about evenings when they listened to the news on her transistor radio, and along with her father she tsk, tsked and shook her head and frowned at the reports of riots and strikes and arrests of ANC members. Such terrible goings on. But were they really? She'd always avoided catching his eye for fear that he would see her thinking that maybe it was all there was left to do, for fear that she would see that he did not hold the same desire in his heart.

'Still ran dingo . . . yell . . . yellow dog dingo . . .' Mpho pressed his lips in concentration and stared at his hardcover book.

'. . . *Always . . . hungry, grin . . . grinning like . . . a rat trap!*'
Triumphant at catching a sentence, he swung his feet wildly
and glanced at Lefu.

Nkele noted the shadow of disappointment on her son's
face when he saw that his grandfather had dozed off, then,
undeterred, he dived back into the words.

'*Yellow dog dingo!*'

She imagined her son as old as Lefu, stunted from years of
saying *yes, baas!*, his head bobbing in obeisance, and she saw
herself ancient and withered, useless and toothless, living in
a hut somewhere, nothing but a burden with barely enough
to eat. It could happen, it was almost guaranteed to happen.
Her only hope was the man in the donga.

Nkele took the ivory bracelet with the gold clasp from the
top of the chest of drawers and placed it on Lorraine and
Martin's bed. Next she reached for a small enamel box shaped
like an egg in which sat three pairs of studded earrings. She
would have carried the bracelet and the box at the same time,
but her hands felt leaden and she did not trust them. Lorraine
had wandered in when Nkele was making the bed and now
she stood near the window, quietly watching. Nkele felt as
though she were dismantling Lorraine's life. And hadn't it
already begun? The roses now lived at the old stables. *Dumelang
baratiwa baka*, Lefu had called to them early that morning as
he walked up the path to feed the horses. Hello, my darlings.
When she left half an hour after him Nkele saw that two more
bushes were in bloom.

She reached for the framed wedding photograph, Lorraine's
long blonde hair and white dress billowing, Martin looking as
young as Neels. She glanced at Lorraine. She looked anxious.
A white person was missing and all the other white people in
the Limpopo valley feared the worst, feared that they would
be next.

Last she picked up the leather-bound diary for 1985. She was carrying it to the bed when Lorraine put her hand out for it.

'Have you heard about Neels?'

'Yes, madam.' Nkele daubed a cloth with furniture polish, and wiped the deeply grained surface of the chest of drawers.

'Wynand and Mark said he often talked about going AWOL to see Eva. Did you know that he was her boyfriend?'

'No, madam.'

'Neither did I.' Lorraine sat on the bed and picked up her wedding photograph. 'I called Eva at boarding school early this morning . . . I had to . . .' Her voice trailed off.

Nkele approached the bed. She took the bracelet and the box and placed them back on the dresser. Lorraine handed her the photograph and as she positioned it, delicately, with precision, a surgeon putting Lorraine's heart back together, Nkele felt a surge of love for this white woman with her moods and her jumpy enthusiasm. She did not want her to come to any harm. Nkele then moved back to the bed where Lorraine was holding the diary.

'Do you want it?' she asked.

'Want what, madam?'

'The diary. I'm not using it.' She fanned the pages. 'Look. They're blank. I haven't touched it.' She set the diary down and opened it to 3 April. 'Start with today. Write whatever you like.'

Two hours later Nkele crawled beneath the overhanging branches in the donga towards the barrel of a gun. He knew it was her, he'd motioned for her to approach and yet he pointed the gun as if he were about to shoot her. Her hands were shaking when she set the bread and the Coke can on the ground in front of him. He barely acknowledged her and kept staring in the direction from which she'd come. She could feel him listening. 'I promise I am alone,' she said, offended that he would think that she would turn him in.

He laid the gun across his knees and reached for the water. 'But someone might have followed you.'

Now, she listened intently and registered the subtle sounds splintering the silence. A beetle sliding down the side of the donga, spilling grains of sand on to the leaf litter. The strain and friction of muscle and feather as a bird flew out of the branches above them. The newspaper rustled and she heard him bite into the bread. She had smeared margarine and jam on the slices and he ate ravenously.

'You didn't tell anyone . . . your husband, your children, about the man you found in the bush?'

'How do you know I have a child?' she asked, suddenly suspicious.

'Because,' he spoke in an apricot jam-smoothed voice, 'someone pretty like you is definitely married. And if you were my wife I would give you lots of children.'

Her face grew warm. When she dared look at him again she saw that he was smiling, the scar on his cheek curling into a second smile. She murmured, 'My name is –'

He shook his head. 'No. Perhaps something happens. It is better if I do not know your name and you do not know who I am.'

'Of course.'

Nkele wanted to ask him if it was attainable, this Freedom. She wanted to tell him that she would never, ever, give up her son. She didn't care how much Freedom his life would bring. And she'd been thinking about the particular way he had said the words, South Africa. When she thought about the country – Cape Town, Durban, the Drakensberg mountains, the oceans that she had never seen – her head began to spin. It was too vast for her. Skinner's Drift, Messina, and maybe

Pietersburg and Seshego, that was her world. But he had said the words as if he owned South Africa, as if it were a beloved possession, a lover, as if in a few strides he could walk across the country.

'What is going to happen?' was all she could ask.

'It is already happening,' he answered.

When she returned to the old stables late that afternoon, after preparing dinner for Lorraine and Martin, Nkele handed Mpho the diary. He flipped through the pages, a puzzled look on his face. 'The book is empty?'

'Yes, and when you have something to say you can write in it.' She took it from him and placed it on the chest of drawers between the *Jungle Book* and the *Just So Stories*.

After supper she carried a chair outside and sat in front of the old stables while Lefu and Mpho walked amongst the roses. Another cool night. He would sleep lightly, as she had the few times she'd slept outside, evenings when she couldn't get a lift all the way home and the safest thing to do was to crawl into a storm drain on the side of the road, hold Mpho close and doze, waking to hear the rumble of the odd car passing by late at night. She clicked her tongue at Lefu's dogs stretched out on the sun-baked earth. They flicked their ears and rolled their eyes in her direction. 'Come,' she said quietly. They were not used to invitations from Nkele. She was the one who chased them out of the old stables, who shook the broom at them. She persisted and Lady roused herself and ambled over. Nkele scratched her ears. 'Lucky,' she coaxed. He ignored her and so, giving Lady one more scratch, she left her seat and squatted next to the rangy grey dog. 'Lucky . . . Lucky Vula,' she whispered and smoothed a hand across the dog's white-flecked muzzle.

*

The following day was chicken carcass day. Every Saturday Nkele roasted two large chickens. Lorraine and Martin carved them for Saturday dinner and Sunday lunch, ate chicken sandwiches on Monday and Tuesday. Come Wednesday the brown, drying bones were set on the table for Nkele to scavenge.

She picked them clean, ate one sliver of chicken, and laid the rest between two thick slices of bread. As she had the previous times, she moved with prickling nonchalance, feigning a casual lunchtime stroll.

'What day is it?' Lucky Vula asked as he opened the newspaper-wrapped package of food.

She smiled as she watched him bite into the sandwich. 'Today is Wednesday.'

He moaned. 'You've brought me a feast!' He licked each of his fingers when he was finished. 'I need something. A stick. To help me walk.'

'I will bring it tomorrow.'

'See if you can find it now.'

He was leaving. Six days ago she wished she'd never stumbled into him, now she wanted to keep him in the bush for a few more days. She would bring him chicken and flat Coke and when the fever returned she would hold him and let him breath his strange murmurings into her ear.

'Now.' He spoke like a soldier giving a command. 'And quiet – be quiet.'

She crept twenty feet down the donga, eased back on to the dirt track and walked casually to the old dipping pen. Within minutes she found a stout stick and something even better, an old metal fence post. Carrying both of them, she retraced her steps.

She squatted next to him and watched him break off a short length of the stick.

'You are going,' she said.

He took off his T-shirt and tore it into strips, one of which he used to bind a length of stick to the fence post.

'When are you going?' she persisted.

He placed his hand gently over her mouth, bidding her to keep quiet. She kissed his palm. Her eyes winced shut with embarrassment; what was she thinking? He stared at his hand for a moment, as if looking for the imprint of her lips, then returned to the business of fashioning his crutch and wound the remaining strips of material around the wood to pad it.

She throbbed with the need for him to know her. And yet she recalled his warning. No names. She could not tell him about anything that mattered to her. And so, with downcast eyes she spoke about the roses and told him how they had been thrown out of the garden surrounding the big house and now lived in the mealie field. She spoke of how ridiculous it was to have nineteen rose bushes – nineteen! – in such close proximity to the old stables.

'Why?' he asked.

She raised her head and saw the puzzlement on his face. 'Because . . . because they are so beautiful!' Warmth flooded the corners of her eyes and she shook her head as if trying to chase away her tears. 'If I could I would burn them,' she said vehemently. 'Please tell your comrades that . . . when it happens . . . we never asked for those roses, we never wanted to have more than anyone else.'

She looked at her wrist watch. It was time to return to the big house. She dusted the sand from her lap and got to her knees. He was leaving and she had a dinner to cook, life had muscled its way between them.

'You must do one more thing for me.'

She waited.

'You must bring me a rose.'

She laughed. Surely he was teasing her.

'Yes,' he insisted.

'But I cannot. They are not mine.'

'This is your first lesson, little sister. You must learn how to take.'

'But . . . but . . . I cannot walk through the bush holding a rose.'

'You will find a way,' he said firmly.

'And if I don't?'

'If you *do* I will tell my comrades that the little sister who lives next to the Limpopo river is also a comrade, a very special one. And if you are lucky she will give you a rose.'

The soldiers found Neels's body in the fork of a tree on the banks of the Limpopo. Wynand stood on the kitchen steps and delivered the news. 'Like some leopard, some bloody kaffir leopard had climbed up there and cut his throat. They're fucking animals.'

Lorraine shrieked. 'Oh God! When did you find him?'

'This morning, Mrs van Rensburg.'

'Oh God . . . no . . .' she sobbed.

Nkele and Wynand looked at each other. Soldier or maid, who would comfort Lorraine? Perhaps Wynand thought, you're a woman, it's your job. Only for the briefest of moments did Nkele think, you're white, it must be you. 'Madam,' she soothed, and she led Lorraine back to the table and sat her down.

'Oh, Grace, he was so sweet. And frightened . . . I knew it the first time I saw him.'

'I know, madam. He was a good boy.'

Wynand lingered at the door. 'He died for his country, Mrs van Rensburg.' He offered Nkele a shrug of his shoulders and slipped away.

Nkele switched on the electric kettle. With trembling hands she took Lorraine's special teacup from the cupboard and placed a tea bag in it. She remembered Eva leaning her head against Neels's shoulder. She hadn't been close enough to see the expression on his face but now she held it in her mind, just as if she'd been standing right in front of him, the white boy's eyes closing as he touched Eva's small breasts, his mouth drifting open in a smile.

The following day Lorraine left for Eva's boarding school. It was three days before the start of her Easter holiday, but Lorraine did not bring her daughter home. A soldier named Garth was posted to the farm. Nkele felt too frightened and also too angry, too sad, to return to the donga. Surely Lucky Vula had moved on. She stopped scolding Mpho for his friendship with Mark, Dipatso as he called him, the one with the freckles. She let him keep the clumsily carved wooden gun and each evening she asked him to tell her what the soldiers had to say about the search for Neels's killer. They were looking for tracks along the border fence, they put up roadblocks near Alldays. One day a helicopter flew low over Skinner's Drift.

Weeks passed and there was no talk of any insurgents being captured in the Messina or Alldays area. The nights grew colder and the rose bushes dropped their flowers, first Ge Korsten, then Free State Dawn and Cape Beauty. Nkele had to admit that she would miss them, so bright and cheery, like silly women watching her go to work each morning. Petals littered the footpath, until all that remained were three peach roses, spilling open in surrender.

One morning after Lefu and Mpho had left, Nkele took a knife to the last of the flowering bushes. A sawing back and forth – there were no sharp knives in her home – and she had a rose in her hand. She held it between thumb and forefinger, avoiding the thorns, and set off along the footpath. Halfway to the dipping pen she lost her nerve. How could she explain herself if she encountered one of the soldiers? She pulled the petals loose and nestled them in her bra.

In the donga she found the faint tracing of a large daisy drawn on a patch of smoothed sand. She squatted next to it and closed her eyes. She heard a leaf fall to the ground and the thin whistle of a nearby bird. She recalled his scar curling into a smile and the way he held South Africa so gentle in his mouth. She dug a small hole, took the rose petals from her breast and buried them, then ruffled her hands in the sand and erased the daisy.

Out of the donga she climbed. A stamp of a foot, a testing of the ground, a look around to make sure no one was watching, and she tried it out as she walked slowly down the path. South, said her left foot, Africa, said the right one. When she reached the dirt road, she paused. There was the farmhouse, a glimpse of the green fields, the soldiers' ugly brown tent. It would take some practice, but she would grow accustomed to it. Walking across South Africa.

7

Eva lay on the bed in her room at the Misty Mountain, the last of Lorraine's diaries resting face down beside her. She'd read halfway through it. Initially she feared coming across an entry suggesting that her mother knew about the madness of their night drives, but as she travelled through February and March, on into May and June, she grew increasingly despondent. How could her mother not have suspected that something was terribly wrong on Skinner's Drift?

Green for grazers, red for predators her father had taught her. There were exceptions but for the most part it was true. The eyes of the impala glowed green when the antelope were caught in the bakkie's headlights, the jackals and the small cats red. With the silencer muffling his gun, the shots sounded like popcorn popping. They stopped for the impala and she helped haul them into the back of the bakkie. She tried to remember where the others had fallen, a prayer, and a promise to return and bury them. The nightjars were the worst of all. It sickened her the way he saw the birds trapped in the headlights and just drove right over them. That made her want to scream and she never found them the next day, carried off and eaten she imagined.

And of course my mother knew nothing about it, Eva reminded herself. I never told her. She was at the farmhouse, drinking her tea out of the cup with the ivy curling up the handle, she was scratching her cheek with the nub of her pen, searching for another way to describe the beauty of yet another blue sky.

On their return the door to her parents' bedroom was always closed. Eva would stare at it, longing for her mother to appear, face creased with sleep, and ask her, Evie, what's wrong? I can tell something has happened. But even now as she rolled on to her side, knees pressed to her chest and revisited that moment, Eva couldn't free her words. She would always lie to protect her father.

Headlights swept across the wall opposite her and someone pulled into the parking lot close to her room. A door slammed. 'Make sure you have the cables and mics,' a woman called out. Tiny feet pattered across the roof, the swish of a branch as one of the monkeys leapt into a tree. Eva switched on the bedside light and continued to read, searching for a phrase, an image, anything to use as a balm.

There was nothing. Lorraine's last diary was a fugue on the drought – the grass on the side of the road turning from blonde to death grey, emboldened monkeys lapping water out of the dog's bowl. By July, her mother was skipping days. September and October and November were blank. Eva fanned the pages, their white silence mocking her. In December it finally rained, unleashing a torrent of words from Lorraine. A few pages later there was mention that Neels and the other soldiers had arrived on the farm. Eva touched his name. It looked so small on the page, as if he were already lost, doomed the minute he entered their lives. And that was the last entry. Several pages after that had been torn out. Eva ran her thumb across the jagged stubs. Was this where her mother had begun to write, *I've just found out that Martin and Eva . . .* and then, so appalled by what was appearing on the pages, she'd ripped them out?

No, her mother didn't tear them out. He did. She was certain of it, she could see it. The drunk old man Johanna had described, haggard, unshaven, sitting in the shuttered house with the dog beside him, glancing through the diaries as he placed them in the box for his daughter, then coming across the the incriminating words.

Stop it, she whispered. It was useless trying to delve into her father's mind. For Christ's sake, she said to herself, get on with your life.

It was just after seven, dinner was underway, but Eva couldn't face sitting with Greg and his friends. The Misty Mountain didn't offer room service and she hoped to slip into the lobby, avoid the pilots and cajole Jock into giving her something to take back to her room.

A few steps into the lobby and she registered the change of music. Instead of tired old Vivaldi and his Four Seasons – winter's agitated cello with your shepherd's pie; buoyant spring for your apple crumble and custard – Jock was playing disco music. Two of the maids who cleaned the rooms were peering into the dining room, while behind the reception desk Jock paced back and forth, phone cord dragging behind him.

'No rooms! Full up!' He listened for a moment. 'No, I can't help you. No, there's nowhere to stay in town.' He hung up, a harried look on his face as Eva approached. 'You staying in your room?'

'I'm *paying* for my room.'

'*Ja*, sorry, sorry. I've got reporters phoning, asking me if I have any rooms.'

'Why?'

'You don't know? The TRC is in town.' He lowered his voice. 'I've got some SATV people staying here. *And* three of the commissioners.'

'Why are they staying here?'

Jock dusted his thumbs across the lapels of his brown silk waistcoat. 'Because this is a *fine* establishment.'

'You're right. I'm sorry. But the music?'

'When they walked in all of my white guests looked guilty. I had to lighten the mood. It's the Bee Gees.'

Eva fidgeted at the desk as an image of Stefan came to mind. He was smiling at this twist of fate, Eva van Rensburg who doesn't give a damn about her country in the same town as the Truth and Reconciliation Commission. 'So where do they have the hearings?'

'The show grounds. Ouma's prize-winning *konfyt* one week, the truth' – Jock raised his hands and gestured quotation marks – 'the next.'

'I can see you're not a fan.'

'Listen, all of us have done bad things. Doreen!' The slip of a girl who cleaned Eva's room and who was standing snug against the dining-room door spun around. 'I'm sorry for throwing the mop at you the other day. You forgive me?'

Doreen giggled while the other matronly woman muttered rapid fire in Sotho, before scolding, 'Master Jock!'

'What's the matter, Mama? Doreen and I are reconciling.' He rested a hand on the chihuahua, sitting as usual on the sign-in book, and once again spoke to Eva. 'Jokes aside. I try to be decent and so do most of us. I pay a good wage, in line with what everyone else gets. And old Samuel and the other boys get to take leftovers back to their families. That's right, half the bloody township is eating roast beef and English trifle. Now, here's what I want to know. Are the blacks going to come forward? My cousin lives on a farm near Zeerust and his neighbour's sister and her two children were killed when they drove over a land mine. Bits and pieces of them found hanging in a tree. Is the bastard who planted that land mine ever going to show his face? It wasn't just us, Miss van Rensburg.'

Jock slipped a palm under the somnolent chihuahua's head, raising it up. 'Today one of my Zim boys, a regular I might add, asked me if this was a dog. What the hell did he think? I keep an overweight *nag aapie* as a pet?'

'Fool. Anyone can tell it's a pedigreed animal.' Eva gave him her sweetest smile. 'I'm not in the mood for a bar scene tonight. Any chance of a snack to take back to my room? And something to drink – a few drinks, in fact – maybe a bottle of –'

'You and the pilot have a fight?'

'No-o.'

Jock twiddled his fat signet ring. 'No need to blush, my dear. This place is a hotbed of romance.'

He headed for the bar and Eva stepped a few feet away from the desk until she had a clear view of the dining room. Seated at a table in the centre were a black man wearing small spectacles and an Indian man and woman. Pilots, salesmen, jolly Zimbabweans, all demographics of the Misty Mountain were staring at them. The waiters had gathered at the entrance to the kitchen, red fezzes bobbing, while the two cooks peered through the glass windows in the swinging doors. They had to be the commissioners. Ordinary looking people, holding the country's heart in their hands.

'Miss van Rensburg.' Jock handed her a bottle, a shot glass and two bags of Simba chips.

'Southern Comfort?'

'I thought you being an American –'

'I told you – I grew up here. Why won't you believe me?' After years of dodging her heritage it had become terribly important to Eva that Jock acknowledge this fact.

'Ja. But you left.'

The bluntness of his statement silenced her. She was searching for something to say in her defence when the pilots, still dressed in their jumpsuits, filed out of the dining room. A few steps into the lobby and they visibly relaxed.

'Nice music!' Greg called out. 'Howzit, Eva. Not in the mood for rice and fish?'

'It was a *kedgeree*,' Jock muttered.

Greg registered the bottle in Eva's hand and grinned at the carpet like a schoolboy anticipating a wild romp. 'Nooit!' he suddenly cried, a look of dismay on his face. 'Did something happen to your aunt?'

'My aunt?'

'Ja, the one who's in the hospital.'

Eva kept quiet while her lie trotted towards her, she barely recognized its markings. 'Oh, she's pulling through. She'll be fine. But I received troubling news from New York and –'

'S'okay.' Within seconds Greg's countenance changed from embarrassment as he sensed the brush off to one of supreme indifference.

Eva immediately felt guilty. 'Tomorrow night?' she offered.

Before he could respond, one of the other pilots who had witnessed their exchange, pulled him away.

Eva stalked back to her room where she put the chips to one side. Pickled onion flavour? Maybe the monkeys would like them. She poured a glass of Southern Comfort and imagined what she would have said to Greg if she'd been honest. *I lied to you because I'm terrified. It's my father who's in hospital and the fucker is going to make it.* The ease with which he said her name as if he'd been carrying it on his breath still had her feeling agitated.

He would soon be discharged. All she had to do was make sure he was comfortable at Johanna's and that her aunt understood which medication he had to take and when. It was foolish to hope for a . . . She frowned, she wasn't even sure what she wanted from him. A heartfelt conversation leading into an apology? A confession. Reconciliation?

She remembered Stefan talking about *ubuntu*. I know what it is, she'd lied. He'd been quite thrilled with his new African word and she let him talk for a few minutes about humanism, about forgiveness before shutting him up. In hindsight there was something creepy about his interest in South Africa, bleeding his heart with other people's pain. He actually used to touch his chest, pet it.

Eva drained her glass and poured another. She prowled the room, checked the return date on her plane ticket. She was leaving in eight days. She'd fly back to fall in New York, the best season. Buy a few new pieces of clothing, pull out her black hat with the shearling trim. It had taken her a few years to understand this business of layering one's clothing. But she knew it now, she'd be ready for frigid December and January and February and, if it was a rough year, March. Really, it wouldn't be so bad, warm drinks, a man – oh, who the hell was she kidding? Winter almost did her in every year.

She glared at the stack of diaries on the dressing table. Then, just for the hell of it, she opened one at random.

26 MARCH 1977

A quiet, uneventful day on Skinner's Drift. Eva is working on a school project about chameleons. She has one in a box and needed to put it on some gaily coloured fabric to watch it change colour. What a dreary lot we are. Everything Martin wears is khaki-coloured and even my clothing looked a bit 'bush'. We finally found some wrapping paper from last Christmas. The poor creature is now paralysed with indecision. Should it remain on Father Christmas's sleigh or move across the deep blue sky to the pine tree?

Her mother had written ten years of entries like that, nattering away about nothing like one of those European starlings that – thank you, Cecil John Rhodes – infested the country. She reached for the Southern Comfort and took a swig straight from the bottle. Oranges and bourbon, who would have thought to mix them together? Another swirly, sloshy mouthful and she toasted her mother. You left me nothing, she fumed. And then there was her father with what, maybe one word left inside of him? *Help*. No, she knew what it was. *Me*.

A third of the bottle gone and Eva heard something rooting beneath the hibiscus hedge. She pushed the window and almost fell into the bushes. She hauled herself back in and rested her chin on the windowsill, her nostrils flaring as she breathed in the night, a magnificent unpredictable black African night where creatures were hissing and pissing and hunting and mating. A night that she simply had to explore.

Bottle in hand she left her room and weaved across the parking lot. 'Shit! . . . Shit! . . .' The gravel hurt her bare feet. She staggered to the end of the lawn, a vertiginous experience with the town's lights spilled below, her father snug in one of them. *Voowu-hoo*. Eva recognized the call, opening like a blossom in the night. A spotted eagle owl proclaiming its territory. And that annoying pinging sound, the aural equivalent of Chinese water torture was a fruit bat. She took another swig from the bottle. One summer a fruit bat visited the garden at Skinner's Drift, and after two nights her mother had taken to scanning the trees with a flashlight, determined to find the bat so Martin could shoot it.

Something croaked and she knew it wasn't a frog but a . . . a . . . Well, it was something else. She made it halfway up the stone steps leading to a terrace dominated by a massive mahogany tree, before her head started to spin and she plopped down. Just for a little rest.

Half the bottle gone and Eva squinted, something tall and scrawny and moving with a steady gait was making its way across the lawn. An Afrikaner salesman, khaki socks standing at attention around his wiry calves, face wrecked by too much sunshine, the inevitable drink in his hand that would end up killing him. Ggrugh! Ghorggh! He spat it out a few feet away from her.

Watch . . . it . . . arsehole . . . String the words together and she'd put him in his place, but she couldn't corral them. The salesman sighed, looked up at the sky and turned in a slow circle as if he wanted to take in every star. She too looked up and saw Scorpio with his fiery heart, the southern cross, the milky way streaming over the dark mountain. She began to cry. How awful could her father be when she'd seen him dazzled by the stars above the farm, awed by a kudu leaping through the bush, chin raised high so its spiral horns rested flush against its neck? Eva snivelled and the salesman stiffened.

'*Wie's daar?*' he demanded.

She gripped the stone steps, she felt dizzy from moving her head too fast. 'Me,' she finally answered.

He stared into the darkness until he found her. 'Good evening. I didn't see you sitting there.' He bowed slightly and asked if he could join her. Eva nodded slowly and he sat two steps below her.

'A drink?' She waggled the bottle.

When he registered that it was Southern Comfort he seemed to look at her with great sympathy. 'Just a little *dop*.'

His name was Piet Malherbe. For thirty years he'd been selling a small spring that kept windmills pumping, he'd never been married, and he claimed there wasn't a dirt road in the country that he hadn't driven across. His favourite trips were to the eastern Transvaal – Piet had no patience with its new name, Mpumalanga – because there he could dip into the Kruger National Park. The best day of his life? He drove through Kruger and saw three lionesses bring down a buffalo; six hours later he received a five thousand rand order from a farmer's cooperative in Nelspruit. South Africa was the best country in the world. Could still be. 'I'm trying to be optimistic,' he said. 'I really am, but these are trying times.'

Eva prepared herself for the come on, but he insisted that she return to her room and get some sleep. He helped her down the stairs and she left the bottle with him. At the edge of the parking lot she stopped. *Ping! Ping! Ping!* 'Hear that?' she called out to him.

'Egyptian fruit bat,' Piet Malherbe answered.

The sun seemed impossibly bright, even with her sunglasses on, and Eva petered out halfway up the hill to the hospital and parked in the shade of the trees opposite Johanna's house. She rested her head on the steering wheel. What was she going to say to her father? All the rehearsals, the how dare yous – the moment had arrived and there was nothing, a lake in her throat where her accusations used to be. She rolled her head to one side. Across the street her aunt stood in the garden, hanging a bird feeder in a leafless jacaranda tree about to bloom. Eva felt pouty and orphaned, in need of sympathy.

'I drank too much,' she grumbled to a surprised Johanna, as she pushed open the gate.

'Hair of the cat?' Johanna nudged the feeder and set it swinging.

'What cat?'

'The one that scratched you. My girl, I've had a few too many in my day and I'm telling you, the best remedy is the hair of the cat –'

'No, it's a dog. Ah!' Eva pressed her thumbs to her temples, she'd spoken too emphatically. 'It's a dog,' she whispered, 'hair of the dog that bit you.'

'Whose dog? Eva, why are you whispering?'

'Tea,' Eva moaned. 'Please, a cup of tea and aspirins. *Asseblief.*'

She walked gingerly into the lounge and lay down on the stumpy legged sofa. Through the ricocheting ache in her head she heard her aunt clattering about the kitchen and a strange slow swishing sound. A deep voice said, *'Tannie, ek moet nog 'n blikkie verf koop.'*

She slitted her eyes open to see a young man in khaki shorts with thighs thick as tree trunks attempting to tiptoe past the lounge. 'Verskoon my . . . excuse me,' he said to Eva who grunted in reply.

The front door closed and Johanna bustled in. Today's apron was bordered with tiny Zulu shields and assegais. 'Hansie's going to buy some more paint for your father's room. But tell me, skat, when did you ever think you'd see a white man painting a wall?' The kettle whistled. 'The blacks have taken all the jobs,' Johanna said with a conspiratorial whisper, before returning to the kitchen.

Minutes later she placed a tray with two mugs of tea, a plate of rusks and a bottle of aspirin on the coffee table. She sat opposite Eva. 'I just spoke to de Vet –'

'That name,' Eva grumbled.

'What about it?' Johanna stopped in mid reach for a rusk.

'You don't think it's – Never mind, go on.'

'De Vet said your pa is going to be released any day now. That's why I've got to make chop chop with that room.'

Eva sat up and swallowed three aspirin.

'That's too many, Eva, you'll get a hole in your stomach.' Johanna dunked the rusk in her tea and sucked the soggy end.

Eva sank back on to the sofa. She never dunked rusks, the final sips of your cup of tea all soupy with crumbs. The notion of it was going to make her throw up.

'So listen, skat, I'm going to hang some landscapes in that room. You saw the bird feeder. What do you think?' Johanna didn't wait for her reply. 'What's left of his heart is going to break, but he can't stay at Skinner's Drift any more. Do you want it?'

'His heart?'

'Don't be funny. The farm.'

'What?' Eva spluttered.

'It's a big decision. But it must either be sold or you must take over and start farming. And turn a fast profit. Plant crops,

worry about water levels. Marry a good man to help you.'
She nodded in the direction of the room where Tree Trunk
had been working.

'Johanna!'

'Eva! This is your family. Your father. I cannot make these
decisions. What are your plans?'

'Meaning?'

'How long are you staying? Are you ever going to visit the
farm?'

Johanna dunked the remainder of her rusk and Eva averted
her eyes.

'That's right. Every time I bring up these questions you
avoid me.'

'I'm booked to leave in eight days,' Eva mumbled. 'But I
can lengthen my stay. Or shorten it!'

'My girl, you have things to think about.'

Eva nursed her cup of tea and stared at the painting of the
ancient men and the camels stacked in the hallway. Her father's
wispy hair was almost that long.

'I will look after him,' Johanna suddenly declared. 'I love
him!' Her voice quavered and she shot Eva a wild look. 'But
you must take responsibility for your family's affairs. You
disappeared. For ten years. I know there's been tragedy in
your life, but disappearing doesn't do anybody any good.'

Eva swallowed another aspirin when Johanna wasn't looking and slunk out of the house.

'Remember *skat, boer can altyd 'n plan maak!*' Johanna called
from the gate as Eva opened her car door. A farmer can always
come up with a plan.

She waved goodbye, thinking about her favourite proverb
– a monkey crapped in the rice pot. In Afrikaans it had such
a satisfying collision of consonants at the end: *Aapie het in die
ryspot gekak.* A visit to the hospital hunkered in the shadow
of the Soutpansberg was still out of the question. Instead, for

the first time since she'd been back, Eva drove into the mountains.

It felt good to be looking at wild things; the secret kloofs, tangled with dense vegetation, where leopard surely prowled; the tree ferns growing on the banks of the stream that raced alongside the winding road. Several miles into the range Eva parked and tramped into the bush to pee. Neon green grasshoppers exploded out of the long grass and on to her jeans and she brushed them off. Johanna's question nagged. Did she want the farm? What a ridiculous idea.

She drove on through the tunnel that led to the leeward side of the range where the rainfall diminished, the mountains yawning open, showing their dry brown throats. Sky and rock and stunted thorn trees, a vista of the land galloping away in the distant haze. She recalled the words her father had stammered one afternoon as they returned from Johanna's house, stuffed with lamb and tongue and tipsy tart: Africa – and he'd said it with the hunger and passion that only Afrikaners and Africans have for the land – *Afrika* begins on the northern flanks of the Soutpansberg. He was right. Even the sky seemed fiercer. On the lower slopes Eva saw her first baobab tree, crazy branches scribbling secrets in the air. She couldn't help but yip with delight.

At the bottom of the mountain pass where the women from Venda sat by the side of the road selling fruit and wooden giraffes and salad bowls, she turned left on to a dirt road that traced the northern length of the range. A glance now and then in the rear-view mirror to relish the cloud of dust kicked up by her car.

An hour after leaving Johanna's, Eva passed Shangri-La. The hunting lodge was still in business, the huge elephant trunks made out of bronze and set in concrete at the head of the dirt driveway had recently been buffed. A few miles on and she drove into Alldays. She was thirsty and she stopped in front of Oasis General Store where several barefoot black children were idly dragging sticks through the dust. Jannie had purchased the shop after he'd closed his taxidermy business and according to Johanna he'd even stopped working for Shangri-La. The most shocking haunch of gossip, however, that she and Johanna had gnawed on during one of their tea-time visits was that Jannie had married 'that Jezebel with the evil black hair, the one who used to dance for men in Johannesburg'.

'Katinka? Oh god, no!' Eva had shrieked. Jannie was such a sweet man, she'd even forgiven him for being a taxidermist. And Katinka – well, she couldn't put her finger on it but there was something about her that Eva didn't like.

'Yes!' Johanna said, a look of wicked pleasure on her face. 'It gets worse. Their child –'

'What about their child?'

'*Skattebol*, you think people in New York get up to no good. Let me tell you, in South Africa there are those amongst us who also wander into the devil's playground.'

'Tell me!'

'I can't spread rumours,' she protested. 'Let's just say if it *is* his child then I need to be inspected. And so does he!'

Eva hesitated before stepping out of her car. Jannie was family, in a way that Johanna wasn't. An unassuming presence in their life for so many years. The last time she'd seen him was at her mother's funeral and she still remembered his eyes; gentle and brown, brimming with sorrow and also pity and dismay as if he knew the intimate details of their ruin, the failures of her and her father.

A dull bell clunked when she entered the shop which, like all general stores in small towns in South Africa, smelled of Rajah curry powder. To her surprise she found herself face to face with the leopard that used to stand behind the sofa on Skinner's Drift, the frozen snarl revealing bubblegum pink gums and unnaturally white fangs, one paw raised as if the animal was about to swat anyone who came too close to the basket in front of it, which, according to a hand-lettered sign, held 'SEMI-PRECIOUS STONES FROM THE LIMPOPO RIVER'.

A figure appeared in the darkened doorway in the back of the shop.

'How much is the leopard?' Eva demanded.

'It's not for sale.'

'Jannie?'

'Eva!' He shook her hand, then moved into an awkward hug. 'The leopard's not for sale because it's yours! I have all the animals here. For safe keeping.' When he stepped out of their embrace, his cheeks were red and he softly said, 'I heard you were back . . . and I'm very glad.'

'I'm glad I'm back – sometimes!' Eva said with a laugh. She felt raw standing there in the curry-scented shop.

'We're just about to have lunch. Come, sit down with us.'

'That's sweet of you, but I should get going. I just need a Coke.'

'That's easy enough.' Katinka had entered the rear of the shop and she walked to the cool drink case and pulled out a Coke. 'But you also need lunch. You must stay.' She wore a nondescript olive-green, knee-length dress and flip flops. Her black hair, now streaked with grey, had been shorn to a sensible shoulder length and still she managed to look exotic. Perhaps it was her long neck, or the way she carried herself as if a crowded room of men were admiring her body and it was perfectly fine with her. She placed a hand on Jannie's arm. 'We insist. Don't we?'

''Fraid so,' said Jannie.

Eva acquiesced and followed the two of them out of the shop and across a small yard where several crudely shaped grey taxidermy forms were leaned against a tree. Their home was in a small outbuilding with pokey rooms, and there at a

mean, can I make it out to you and then you can give the money to him.'

'You won't be going to the farm?' Jannie asked in surprise.

She couldn't look at him when she said, 'No . . . no, I don't have the time.'

'That's a shame. Not even for a quick visit? I know he'd love to see you –'

'Maybe it's hard for Eva to go back there,' Katinka interrupted.

'Sorry, I'm not thinking. Of course, I'll give him the money.'

She signed her remaining four fifty dollar cheques and handed them to Jannie.

'Whew! I'll work it out exactly, but I can tell it's very generous. He'll be grateful. Can I tell him you say hello?'

Eva nodded. She closed her bag and folded her serviette and placed her knife just so on her plate. She wanted to leave. Immediately.

Jannie slipped the cheques into the breast pocket of his shirt. 'I do have some good news. There's abundant wildlife on the farm. No hunting so the bush is healing. Last time I was there I saw two cheetah, not even a mile from the farmhouse. Beautiful!' Jannie popped another nasturtium into his mouth.

Eva pushed her chair away from the table and stood up. 'It's been wonderful to sit with you.'

'You have to go?' he asked sadly. 'We want to hear about America.'

Katinka nudged him. 'Jannie, don't you –'

'Ah, that's right! Eva, wait just a bit. I must give you something.'

'If it's one of the animals –'

He laughed. 'No. But that's a thought. Do you want to see them?'

Eva didn't. But Dirk who had been sitting quietly all through lunch bobbed in his seat and made wild eyes at Jannie.

'I think someone would like to show them to you. Wouldn't you, son?' He plucked a set of keys from a shelf and handed them to Dirk.

Not wanting to disappoint the boy, Eva followed him to a store room attached to the shop. The aardwolf and several small springbuck heads were wedged in between boxes of Simba chips and bags of samp, the buffalo and the kudu leaning against the wall beside a tower of cartons of long-life milk. Eva couldn't decide if the scene was ludicrous or grotesque. 'Can you believe I grew up with all of these?'

The boy did not answer her, but pressed even closer to the door frame. He was staring at her with such grave curiosity that Eva could well imagine what he was thinking: This woman with the strange accent is the daughter of crazy, word-mangling, animal collecting *Oom* Martin?

The Louw family wasn't half as strange as the van Rensburgs.

'So, Dirk, are you going to the Laerskool Alldays?'

He nodded suspiciously.

'I went to the same school. Is old Mrs Booysens still teaching you arithmetic?'

Another nod, this one a little more forthcoming.

'She must be a hundred and two by now.'

A giggle.

Eva looked around as if to make sure no one was within earshot. 'I bet she still *poeps* when she bends down to pick up a piece of chalk.'

Dirk burst out laughing, a braying sound like a little donkey, and pranced back into the yard.

'What's going on?' Katinka called from the kitchen door-way.

'When you have a moment ask him about Mrs Booysens.'

'Ah, the farting teacher.'

The boy collapsed in a giggling heap of skinny limbs and

even Eva began to laugh. Until Jannie reappeared with a manila envelope.

'Something of your mom's,' he said, and he pulled a few gilt-edged pages part way out of the envelope to show her.

'Where did you find them?' she asked in a shaky voice, not sure if she even wanted them.

'Your dad asked me to sell some things to help him with the creditors.' He offered her a shoulder shrug of apology, 'And when I got the chest of drawers back here I found these taped on the bottom of one of the drawers. I recognized your mom's handwriting. I was going to give the papers to him, but then he went into the hospital. When I heard you were back, I thought, no, these are for Eva.' He slipped them into the envelope. 'I swear I haven't read them.'

'Of course you haven't. Eva knows that,' Katinka said.

Jannie pressed the envelope into Eva's hands. 'Are you all right?'

She nodded. Then, in a moment of honesty that surprised her, she admitted, 'It's hard being back.'

'You know what you need? A drive in the bush,' Jannie said as he and Dirk walked her across the yard to her car. '*Ja*. Promise me you'll come and see me before you leave. I'll drop everything and take you for a drive.'

'I promise.'

He hugged her goodbye. In the rear-view mirror she saw Dirk leaping into the air, waving furiously as she pulled away.

With one hand resting lightly on the envelope, Eva drove the few back streets in Alldays. She looped down Koorhaan, on to Arend and Dikkop, then back to Koorhaan. The houses were modest and depressing, surrounded by wire fences; a few *tannies* on their stoeps, wondering who was in the strange car circling their block; a few African gardeners on their knees, the good trustworthy *boys*, weeding around the dahlias, the roses. Summer had arrived early in Alldays. At two in the afternoon the heat was like a scorching gauze bandage wrapping the blister of a town. Eva felt panicky, she needed to sit some place cool, to at least gather her thoughts. She broke out of the fourth loop and drove back to the dirt road leading to Shangri-La, Johanna had mentioned that Kobus had sold it to an Austrian couple.

A quarter of a mile in and she was flanked by brilliant green lawns bordered with birds of paradise. Two tame duikers with matchstick legs trotted away as she parked her car near the entrance with its vaulted wooden overhang. An elegant black woman greeted her at the reception desk, then pointed her in the direction of the restaurant. Eva sat at a table overlooking the pool, sunbirds darted around the flowering vines climbing up the patio columns and a wall fountain trickled behind her. She'd stepped into the Africa of overseas currency, of duvets and bath tubs with jets and little bottles of English cologne, all the comforts offered to a wealthy hunter after a week in the bush.

She was the only person in the restaurant and, too embarrassed to just have a drink, she ordered a watercress and prawn salad along with her beer. She placed the manila envelope on the table. Her stomach felt as though it were caving in; people only hid things they were ashamed of, things they feared. The territory she shared with her father. Depending on her fluctuating guilt and longing and anger, she'd considered her mother either a fool or an innocent. Not yet ready to have her revealed, she finished the beer and ordered a frozen margarita. She drank half of it, then picked up the envelope and slipped the pages free. The intimacy of the first sentence stunned her.

17 DECEMBER
I barely know myself.

18 DECEMBER

Tonight this pen feels more dangerous than any of Martin's guns. Capable of unearthing things I'd rather not know about. But it is too late. I've been thinking it's Martin that I'm scared of. His vitality, his violence, his mad passion for his land, his exhilaration in fighting, in claiming what he believes is his birthright – a piece of South Africa. Yes, I thought I was afraid of him. But I am more afraid of Lorraine. She who shuffles the truth so fast, a magician with her feelings and here I am overwhelmed and confused. What is the truth? I do not love him any more. I love him beyond reason. Perhaps both. Does it even matter? They are equally terrifying.

19 DECEMBER

Another night. The pen is balking and I predict a demolition of sorts. To hell with it. In I go. Is he having an affair with Katinka? Some days I think, yes.

Eva's eyes scrabbled across the page as she tried to find purchase around the implications of that question. Her father and Katinka? She flushed with shame, recalling the lunch she'd just had. She'd been duped. Uncle Martin, Katinka called him and her bearing had been so confident.

Other days, no. The question is inside me, so desperate to come out. But why do I feel that it would be my asking it that would shatter us? That my suspicion is more damaging than his action. I tried it out in the garden today when no one was around. Martin, are you having an affair with Katinka? I barely recognized my own voice. This frail, thin sound.

20 DECEMBER

It's ten past one in the morning and these are my hours. The house is quiet. Martin on the sofa in the lounge. Eva down the hall in her room. Have I got used to it already, living on the edges? My life feels like a stone in my gullet. He took a loan from the Defence Department. Perhaps that galls me even more than the affair and tonight I am sure that he had one. He looks robust and I suppose there is something appealing in a man who can hardly speak, he can always be an enigma. But the loan. Why didn't he ask me? And would it have made a difference if I said I didn't want it? Would I have said that or would I have lied and agreed with him. If I had the courage I would tell Rolene I'm not interested in target practice. I would not skulk around, trying to hide my Englishness, I would not take

21 DECEMBER

on this Afrikaner mantle of toil, of suffering for one's land, of dripping one's blood into a patch of earth. Why is it that when an Afrikaner speaks English they take the most beautiful words and knock the edges off them, take the grace right out of my language. Roses, says Rolene, Lorraine grows such lovely rrrroses, and right there my beautiful flowers turn into lumps of clay. Funny, tonight I hate her more than the other one. If I had the courage I would not go to any more of their meetings. And I would not vote, I would tell Martin I do not want to support the NP. If I had the courage I would say, I beg to differ. Does he think he knows me? The way I foolishly believe I know him. Does he really think, of course Lorraine wants to stay and fight for our farm?

22 DECEMBER

This is what scares me, the memory of my mother. How I used to sit at our dinner table hating her. A little woman with dull brown hair while he sat there like a lord. I thought, I will never be like you. She seemed so subservient and meek. I will not be like that I said. But tonight at dinner I wondered if Eva thinks the same thing of me. Maybe her own variation. We were sitting there, Martin like a bird of prey at the head of the table, watching me, watching Eva. Something about him scared me. I think I was worried that he'd read the diary, that he knew that I suspected him of having the affair – God, isn't it madness that I am afraid, when he is the one who should feel that way. But I was frightened and I asked him an idiotic question, something about the river. I just blurted it out. Eva looked at me, an expression of such disdain on her face and for a moment I saw what I must have looked like to her. An inconsequential woman, a coward. For a moment I believed she knew about Katinka and that she had lost all respect for me. I then asked her something mindless, something about new clothes for the hockey season just so I could read her expression again. There it was. My mother is foolish and I will not be like her. After dinner I went upstairs and cried. I want her to know me, but it is impossible to talk to her these days. I feel I failed her as a child. Martin barely seemed to feel my love and when I saw how he flourished with hers I stepped aside. Somewhere, somehow I gave her to him. I want her back.

Her words stung Eva. She wanted to cradle that last sentence, she wanted to slip it into her mother's mouth. Why, why didn't she tell me? she wondered By the time she'd read through the pages again – slowly, without shock, this time acutely aware of her mother's struggle to define herself in the shadow of her father's beliefs – Eva's lament had subsided and she was thinking, yes, you tried to tell me, but I was too blind, too angry, finally too numb.

Her mother was right, as a young girl her heart had been knotted to her father's, and it was only when Eva was sixteen that she and Lorraine were flung together. At first Eva had denied her relationship with Neels, she felt incensed by her mother's intrusive questions. She was on the verge of hanging up the phone when something in her mother's tone of voice stopped her. Lorraine was genuinely worried. Neels had vanished.

That night Eva snuck out of the dorm after lights out and went to the stand of bluegum trees behind the pool, hoping to find him. Perhaps there was nothing to fear and he would be waiting for her. Her stomach tightened with an exquisite ache when she thought about making love to him. But the night was dark and lonely, Neels wasn't there and she began to worry.

When one of the prefects tracked her down during hockey practice two days later and told her that her mother was waiting for her in the headmistress's study, Eva knew what the news would be and she sprinted away in tears. They found her in the changing room at the pool, the prefect scolding her for alarming them so, her mother's arms folding around her.

Lorraine walked her back to the dorm, packed a suitcase and bundled Eva into the car. She slept in the back seat and when she woke hours later, the moonlit landscape of generous grassy plains that she saw through the window was not recognizable. Neels was dead and everything had changed. She sat up quietly, still holding her sorrow. Move too fast and she would shatter it, think too fast, too far forward or backward and she'd get into trouble. She held this sad thing, more fragile than a bird's egg and looked out the window at a lone windmill. Soon the headlights swept across a road sign. MKUZE 190K. SAINT LUCIA 255K. They were not going to Skinner's Drift, they were driving in the opposite direction. In the faint light from the dashboard Eva saw the determined set of her mother's face. After midnight they checked into a hotel on the muggy shores of Lake Saint Lucia where hippos grunted at daybreak and monkeys chattered in the trees. Lorraine decided it wasn't the place to be and they moved to a bungalow in a small resort on the coast. No animals' calls, just the pounding of the surf.

This mother creature, with her moon-shaped face and nervous habit of constantly tucking her hair behind her ears, looked after her. She made her eat two slices of toast with marmite in the mornings and expressed her concerns about swimming; they were near a river mouth, it had rained and it was common knowledge that sharks came in to feed in the murky water. This mother creature put her foot down, saying: 'You're not to go swimming. I forbid it. I can do that, until you're eighteen, forbid you to do things.'

At dusk the lonely fishermen who frequent shabby coastal resorts stopped at their bungalow and offered Lorraine spiny galjoen and opalescent grunters. They knelt on the lawn and chopped the heads off in front of her and Eva watched her mother blush. After dinner, Lorraine made a cup of tea and listened to the news on the radio; a bomb had exploded in a shopping centre in Kimberley and there were daily riots in the townships. She also telephoned the farm each night from the telephone box, returning after a few minutes to tell Eva that Martin missed her. Eva wondered if she said the same thing to him: your daughter misses you. And each night Eva lied. Instead of going to the rec room to play ping pong, she sat on the seaweed-strewn beach and drank cane and passion fruit with the son of the man who owned the resort. On the last night she let him yank off her jeans and have his way with her.

Eva assumed she would return to the farm for the next school holiday, but three months after Neels was killed a state of emergency was declared throughout most of the country. Patrols on the border farms were stepped up and soldiers drove the white children to school in *buffels*. Lorraine refused to bring Eva home. For the next year and a half she did not return to Skinner's Drift, and because farmers rarely leave their farms she did not see her father.

Money was tight and with the exception of a sweltering three-week long visit to a film set in the Karoo in the heat of summer where they watched Hendrik stagger out of flaming cars, they spent school holidays at rundown resorts. They took the bungalows without the view and just one bedroom. They showered at the public ablution block.

Lorraine was almost a stranger to Eva, so unlike her father. Talkative, emotional, maybe even worth knowing. Definitely worth laughing with, and they did that more and more, making wicked jokes about Lorraine's fishermen suitors who were there at every resort with their jerseys that reeked of bait tied around their waists and their offerings from the sea. Eva still woke up in the middle of the night, her heart galloping as she wondered what her father was doing alone, on the farm. Sometimes she'd look at her mother and feel her secrets rising like bile, about to spill out of her mouth. They played just behind her eyes, they turned her moods black, and the longing that coursed through her body for Lorraine would sour into loathing. She'd silently dare her to ask, Evie, what are you thinking about?

Then, like a tide, her anger would recede, and she'd be talking to her mother about her after-school plans. Lorraine wanted her to go to UCT. Eva agreed, tossing back and forth between the predictable BA and something more unusual like marine biology. One thing was certain, she wanted a break from text books and exams and with her mother's encouragement she decided to delay university for one year. It was Lorraine who picked her up on the last day of school and drove her into Johannesburg to a friend's flat; Lorraine who emptied her savings so that she could buy her first car and who said to her daughter, just before she drove back to Skinner's Drift, 'You're a beautiful girl, Evie. Live well, love, be good.'

Eva tilted her margarita glass and drizzled the last few drops into her mouth. She walked to her car, the envelope light between her fingers.

At the end of the driveway she let the engine idle for a moment. Someone had carved Viva Mandela! into one of the tusks at car-window level. And all around her the late afternoon light was softening the mopane scrub. Such a beautiful light, no matter how scabby or forsaken the place, that time of day had a way of smudging the land with mauve and gold. Skinner's Drift lay some forty miles away. The last time Eva had been there was for her father's fiftieth birthday, the weekend her mother was killed. She considered making the drive, at least to the edge of the plateau to see whether the Limpopo was flowing, but decided against it. She thought of what Jannie had told her. Two cheetah resting in the road, less than a mile from the farmhouse. Eva turned right and drove back to Louis Trichardt. Best to have the van Rensburgs off the land.

8

March 1987

Katinka sat cross-legged on the sofa in her lounge and placed a pair of castanets into a cardboard box. A cuckoo clock went in next, then a pair of thin silver spurs and a bottle of brandy with a pear floating in it. They were all gifts mailed to her from overseas by the hunters she'd met at Shangri-La. Irritable old Emily who cleaned her house three days a week and refused to do the bath because of her bad back would be the recipient, and who knows what she'd make of them. The sombrero was a good one, tightly woven and Katinka donned it one last time. She'd only worn it around the house and thought it looked rather fine. She was heading for the mirror in her bedroom when the telephone rang.

'Katinka?' a hesitant voice asked when she answered it.

'Yes?'

'It's Lorraine van Rensburg.'

Shit! she silently mouthed. Her affair with Martin had ended three years ago, but here it was, the accusatory phone call she'd been dreading.

'I'm sure you've heard about the party for Martin's fiftieth birthday?' Lorraine barely gave her time to reply before she barrelled on. 'It's tonight and somehow, in the chaos of planning it, I realized we forgot to invite you. Starts at seven. We'll see you then?' Lorraine didn't pause for her to respond. 'Wonderful! Bye!'

The phone went dead. Lorraine's words had raced into her life fast as noon-time lizards and Katinka's eyes flickered across the floor as if she were trying to locate them. Was it possible that Lorraine had no knowledge of the affair? Other people in the community certainly had their suspicions. Phone still in hand, she dialled Jannie's number and let it ring once before she changed her mind and disconnected the call. By year's end many of the locals would stand in withering judgement of her, so why not start now and face the looks of disapproval she'd surely garner when she arrived at the party.

Still feeling a little stunned, she cautiously opened her front door. No sign of her neighbour Mrs Botha who frequently glared at her over the amber beer-bottle shards cemented along the top of her brick wall. Just the sun sitting low in the sky, slanting the filigreed shadow of the pepper tree into the street. Lorraine had invited her to Skinner's Drift. She could scarcely believe it. She glanced at her watch; she had less than an hour to get ready.

She showered and walked naked into her bedroom, where she chose a black halter-neck dress with a swathe of golden bamboo stalks and Chinese characters rising up the left side.

Memories of her time with Martin washed through her – afternoons when she'd felt like a wild animal crouching at a still, remote pool, drinking his silence, trying to quench a thirst that could not be slaked. He'd been the one to end it after seven months, jawing and stammering out the sentence, *I'm sorry, I can't see you any more.* She knew it would have been easier for him to write a note and in the moment of his leaving she loved him more than any other time in their relationship.

Dirk's pension was not enough to live on and she took a job as a teller at Barclays Bank where she was horrified to overhear talk about Lorraine van Rensburg falling apart. 'She's on pills, you know,' Trixie Viljoen had said to the owner of the hardware shop as they waited in the queue. At the monthly Gossip and Guns Club – Katinka's name for the Civil Defence meetings, meetings that Lorraine no longer attended – she listened guiltily as the women lambasted Lorraine for wanting to leave the area. Then Lorraine did the unthinkable, she gave her rose garden to the stable boy. Her neighbours were appalled. 'It makes me sick to think of it,' Rolene said and she fired several rounds into the gorilla-like figure suspended between her palm trees.

After the State of Emergency was declared and Lorraine took Eva to the coast for her school holidays, the women indicted her for abandoning poor Martin. And when Lorraine returned from these jaunts it was with a tongue; she said that Rolene must be farming crocodiles to honour 'die groot krokodil' as slit-lipped P. W. Botha was known; while waiting in the queue at the post office she pounced on unsuspecting farmers' wives, asking how they liked their time in the SADF, and when they responded with a blank stare she cheerily informed them that they were South Africa's first line of defence. 'Why do you think we all received such big loans from the Defence Department? They wanted us here. And what a dreadful job we're doing what with the ANC blowing up OK Bazaars and all the trouble in the townships.'

The gossips gathered in a feeding frenzy. Does Martin even speak any more? Rolene wondered aloud over a potent ginger square. (Summer temperatures demanded that the G and G Club serve something a little stronger than a pot of Joko tea.) The man is hen-pecked. Ostrich-pecked! 'For god's sake, leave them alone!' Katinka snapped. 'Just because he stutters, just because she's English speaking it's okay to belittle them?'

She'd left that meeting, the last *she* would attend, early. Katinka had come to admire Lorraine van Rensburg, her outspokenness and the breezy manner in which she stood up to the packs of gossipers. She was an outsider, as Katinka had been before Dirk was killed and the community befriended her.

Katinka spun her damp hair into a braid that she coiled on

top of her head. She slipped into her dress and left the house barefoot, carrying her gold sandals until she'd crossed the gravel so she wouldn't nick the leather on the heels. Within minutes she was driving fast through an immense African night. She felt surprisingly calm, given that the wife of a former lover had invited her to his fiftieth birthday party, given that the day before she'd found out she was pregnant.

Katinka had not been to Skinner's Drift before, but she knew to take the dirt road as if she were going to Dolf's farm. On reaching the end of the plateau she saw the lights of a farm-house in the valley below and several cars ahead of her negotiating the switchbacks. Ten minutes later she reached the house and parked some distance away for a quick departure.

There were at least sixty people at the party; talk was that Martin didn't care about the festivities and they'd been arranged to please Lorraine, he was only interested in the lion hunt. For the first time in years lion tracks had been spotted on the banks of the Limpopo, then, late one night, one of his workers heard the unmistakable full throated *uuhuua! uuhuua!* of a lion. A hide had been erected on the western border of the farm and the morning after the party Martin, Dolf and Jannie were going to bait the animal.

The strands of party lights threaded through the security fence winked blue and yellow, and as Katinka walked towards the bougainvillea spilling off the fence a voice said, 'I heard you were coming.'

She peered into the darkness pooling to one side of the bush and saw Jannie leaning against the wire, a Castle dumpie in hand. He had been Dirk's closest friend, the shy sidekick of the handsome man who got all the girls. After his death Katinka had adopted Jannie. Or perhaps it was the other way around.

'I was invited,' Katinka said, 'just so you know.'

'*Ja*, Lorraine just told me.'

'She did?'

Katinka's self-assuredness faltered. She wanted to ask Jannie if he had an inkling as to why Lorraine had telephoned her at the last moment, but any reference to her relationship with Martin felt risky. The two of them had come close to a falling out when, several weeks into the affair, she had confided in him. 'And what about me?' Jannie demanded. Katinka was taken aback; it had never crossed her mind that Jannie might have those sort of feelings for her and she tried to console him by speaking of the value of his friendship. 'That's not what I meant,' he answered in a savage tone of voice that she'd never heard him use since. 'I am friends with the family. With Lorraine. You think I want to hear about this?' The only other mention of the affair was in passing, months after it had ended, when she said to him, 'That thing between me and Martin? It's been over for some time now.'

'You want a drink?' Jannie asked, and he tossed the dregs of his beer on the ground.

She nodded and followed him uneasily into the garden where flickering torches lit to keep the mosquitoes at bay elongated her shadow across the lawn. She immediately spotted Lorraine, dressed in a midnight-blue sleeveless dress, talking to a group of women, her hands flying erratically through the air. Jannie was heading right for her. He's doing it on purpose Katinka thought, and she tugged the waistband of his trousers just at the moment when he changed direction and veered towards the verandah.

'What?' he asked, a look of surprise on his face.

Liar, she thought, you know exactly why I did that. 'It's nothing. You're just drinking too much beer.' She flicked her finger against his small beer belly.

'Nonsense.' He gave his *boep* a little rub and walked on and she followed close behind.

Katinka had not overdressed for the occasion. Several women milling about wore dresses fancier than hers, while every man present, including Jannie, had donned a short trouser safari suit, a wider collar here, a darker shade of khaki there. Small black combs, rarely used because most men sported crew cuts, peeked out of dun-coloured knee socks hiked up their calves. The one standout in the crowd was a young woman with short blonde hair, dressed in torn jeans and a tight tiger-striped T-shirt. She sat to one side, wrestling something away from an Alsatian puppy, and when she raised her head Katinka realized with a shock that it was Eva. She'd given no thought to Martin's daughter during the affair, and yet now she couldn't help but feel that she were somehow responsible for Eva's inappropriate attire at her father's fiftieth birthday celebration.

Jannie elbowed his way through the crowd on the verandah until he reached the bar area where beers and bottles of rosé for the ladies jutted out of a zinc bathtub filled with ice, and the collection of drained dry jugs of red wine and bottles of rum and vodka was already impressive.

'Just half a glass and a little ice,' Katinka said as he reached for the rosé.

He handed her a plastic cup. 'I promised Martin I'd help him with the braai.'

'So, I'm on my own?'

He grinned, grabbed another cold Castle and a jug of wine and said, 'Tough as nails, Kat. You can handle this.'

Katinka stood close to one of the columns on the verandah and watched Jannie make his way across the lawn to an old drum cut in half. A grill had been laid across it and the meat was sizzling. He slapped Martin on the back and handed him the red wine. Martin took a sip then used the wine to douse the flames licking up the sides. When the smoke cleared and he turned around and raised the jug to his lips one more time, Katinka was shocked to see how worn he looked.

'Katinka!'

She started, crocodile-queen Rolene, her thin lips accentuated with a virulent shade of coral lipstick, was standing beside her with Detlef in tow. 'Smells good,' she said. 'And what a surprise to see you here.'

'Lorraine invited me.'

'Really?'

Katinka ignored the sarcasm. 'Hello, Detlef.'

He volunteered a brief smile. He had one of those Oom Paul beards that hug the jawline, and his face looked too open and oddly sexual.

'Best behaviour tonight,' Rolene said. Her eyes were fierce, they glittered and Katinka knew that Rolene had heard about her evening with the hunter from Kuwait. She steeled herself. 'Or maybe it should be our worst.' Rolene raised her glass. 'We're on display. Kobus brought two of his guests with him. Americans. You know what Americans are like, they always have to see a little local colour. You've met them?'

'No.'

'Kom, liefie,' Detlef soothed and he placed an arm around his wife's waist.

That's right, Katinka thought, calling off your dog before she bites.

But it was too late. 'Of course, you wouldn't have met them. They're white,' Rolene said, as her husband ushered her away.

Katinka was still smarting from Rolene's barb when Marikie Joubert, one of the three other single women at the party, waved hello. Marikie worked as a cashier at the hardware store in Messina and after ten years of ringing up packets of flea dip and boxes of nails for the bachelors in town, she had yet to land herself a husband.

'Where did you get that dress?' she asked and for once Katinka was grateful for her fawning admiration.

'A little place in Rosebank.' Then, because she saw how crestfallen Marikie looked, the poor woman would never make it to Johannesburg, she was destined to shop in crummy Truworths in Messina, Katinka said, 'Quite frankly, I think I overpaid. You can get dresses just as stylish at any of the chains. Even Truworths.'

'Oh!' said Marikie. 'Truworths!' While she bobbed her head and looked around as if searching for a witness to their exchange, Katinka slipped away. Keeping her eye on the where-abouts of the van Rensburgs, she moved to the outskirts of the party, drifting from a conversation about a church in the Free State that recently braaied a giraffe on a custom-built spit to raise money for an old-age home, to a heated discussion about the article in *Die Beeld* suggesting that F. W. de Klerk, the Minister of Education, wanted to open up a dialogue with the ANC.

By eight thirty large foil trays of impala sosaties, steaks, lamb chops with the fat blackened just so, and six puffadder-sized coils of boerewors bursting out of their skins were spread out on two trestle tables, along with parts of creatures that Katinka had no desire to eat: braised kudu livers, fried breast of crocodile, and pickled warthog legs bobbing in a barrel of brine.

The guests lined up to help themselves and the shrieks of laughter and rumble of deeper voices gradually gave way to grunting and satisfied slurping as morsels of marrow tucked into the crevices of chop bones were slowly sucked free. Katinka sat on a wicker chair on the verandah and poked at a salad of lychees, shredded cabbage, radishes and chopped dates. Lorraine's eccentricity extended to her salad recipes and she prayed that the creep of nausea she felt just below her ribcage would vanish. It didn't. A woman sitting opposite her shook her head vigorously, blonde curls swaying, as she wrestled a nugget of meat off a skewer. Dolf Claasen sat hunched on the verandah steps seemingly unaware of the bloodied juices running into his beard and there were the Americans, both wearing black cowboy hats, one gamely tackling a warthog leg, the other tearing into a steak to reveal a flesh pink interior.

Katinka shoved her plate on to a side table.

'Are you all right?' asked Marikie who'd nabbed the seat alongside her.

'Where's the toilet?'

'Down the passage, past the kitchen. Can I –'

Katinka hurried inside and jiggled the door to the downstairs toilet. It was locked. Her stomach lurched and she dashed upstairs to the bathroom where she splashed water on her face and lifted the lid of the toilet, just in case.

Perched on the edge of the bath to wait out her queasiness she noted the two toothbrushes and jar of Nivea face cream on the edge of the sink. She looked in the medicine chest. Bandaids, bottles of pills, an old tube of anti-wrinkle cream for eyes. Then she peeked downstairs and slipped into Martin and Lorraine's bedroom.

A bedside lamp was on, shadowing the horns of the mounted kudu up to the ceiling. On the bed she saw the evening's rejects, a black dress and a long pale green skirt. She touched the skirt, cotton, her heart thumping as she quickly put together a picture of the woman Martin had chosen and had returned to. On the chest of drawers she spied a gold lipstick case. She opened it. Coral. Every farmer's wife wore coral. The lipstick was ground down; she doubted Lorraine owned a lip brush, she must have dipped her little finger in it to apply the colour. She closed it and picked up the book on the bedside table. *The Minoan Civilization*. The pages fell open at a small photograph of a mosaic of a lean figure doing a handstand on the horns of a bull. She smiled at the grace of the curving figure, and when she glanced around, unconsciously wanting to share her joy, she sensed it, in the lamplit stillness, the entity that was Martin and Lorraine's marriage, nuzzling against the bed, panting softly against the walls, waiting for them to return. Katinka replaced the book and walked shamefully back to the party.

After the sosaties and boerewors were devoured and Lorraine had carried a cake with fifty flickering candles on to the verandah, dozens more bottles of beer were plunged into the zinc bath and the stereo was turned up. The accordion-driven *boere musiek* sent several couples to a makeshift dance floor fashioned out of large pieces of plywood placed on the lawn. Pumping their arms, spinning and stomping under a tent of stars they danced the sakie sakie, Lorraine's maid and two others pausing as they cleared the tables, giggling at their white employers.

The Americans had settled on the verandah steps. They glanced in Katinka's direction every so often. And there was Kobus shadowing his guests' every move. She hadn't been back to the lodge since her night with the Kuwaiti. She knew she must have offended Kobus. Usually he liked it when she stopped in for a drink, especially if he was just back from safari. A pretty woman for the men to flirt with after five days in the bush.

The older-looking American stood up. He was at least six feet tall and wore spurs on his cowboy boots. He took a few steps towards her, then stopped, snagged his fingers through his belt loops and frowned. Katinka heard it as well. Someone had a most peculiar laugh, a cackle. It grew louder, other guests began to notice it. The dance music faded and an ungodly sound, an orgy of giggling filled the air.

'Ek het julle lekker geskrik!' Dolf Claasen shouted. He

staggered to the edge of the verandah, a bottle of rum in his hand and spoke to the Americans. 'Feeding hyenas, man. We play that tape to get Martin's lion. *Ja*, forget about your fancy safari with Kobus. You must come with us tomorrow when the *boere* go hunting!'

The Americans raised their beers. 'Next time.' And with that Kobus slapped them each on the back and ushered them out of the garden and to his jeep.

The latest release from the Afrikaner crooner Ge Korsten with his tenor voice – all sunsets and crackling fires and flutes of champagne – lured everyone back to the dance floor. No one asked Katinka to dance, that didn't bother her, but poor Marikie looked devastated. Lips quivering, a large lace ruffle framing thin collar bones that looked as if they'd been scavenged from a kill.

Katinka stood up, there was only one thing to do, find Jannie who was no doubt hiding somewhere and insist that he dance with the poor creature. She headed across the lawn until she reached the dance floor where a drunken couple stumbled into her, the woman whacking the man on the shoulder while he exhaled a liquor-fuelled apology into Katinka's face. They staggered off and another twosome eased into their place. Martin with his arms wrapped around his wife. There was something child-like in the way he clung to Lorraine, his eyes creased shut, his head slumped on her shoulder as if he could rest there for hours. Swaying to the music they slowly circled until Lorraine was staring at Katinka.

Of course she knew about the affair. Katinka saw it in the peculiar little smile that almost crossed Lorraine's lips and instead ran into her wide-set eyes. And Katinka could do nothing but stand there and take the look, the hurt in Lorraine's eyes blossoming into a ragged pride. A step and another step and Martin, bloodshot blue eyes now open, was facing her. He blinked several times as if he couldn't quite believe it was her. Katinka wondered if he even knew she'd been invited. She felt both mortified and angry – how dare Lorraine toy with her like that – and she hurried away before Lorraine once again faced her.

In a darkened corner of the garden she gripped the security fence with one hand and threw up. The evening was a fiasco and she felt teary and wished she hadn't come. She made her way to a bench beneath one of the fig trees and sat down and unfastened her hair. Dirk had loved it so and she hadn't cut it since his death. With the dark spill of it laying in her lap, she fluttered her fingers through it, searching for tangles, all the while winnowing out memories of her husband, of the events that had brought her to this moment, hiding like a pariah in Lorraine van Rensburg's garden.

Dirk with his trim black moustache and neatly muscled arms, sitting at a tiny round table in the front row of the club. He looked aloof as if the evening's entertainment was beneath him, unlike his friends whose appetite was evident. She suddenly felt ashamed for dancing, but she fought back, what the hell, and put on such a show. She remembered the day he carried her across a browned square of lawn and into his spartan brick house in Messina; the afternoons that they'd driven to the Limpopo for naked swims, not caring if anyone saw them; and how miserable she'd felt when she met the wives of his friends, women with no style whatsoever, whose feet were calloused thick as hooves. Then, to suddenly realize that was all she had. After his death the few girls she'd stayed in touch with in Johannesburg suggested she return, but it seemed like such an effort. And now she was pregnant.

Again she considered having an abortion – surely it was the sensible thing to do – and again the faces of the two men came to mind. Dirk in black face, fuzzy wig on his head, cannibal smile, beer in blackened hands as he relaxed at

Oshakati base camp after a successful recce incursion. And the hunter from Kuwait, his long brown fingers cupping a brandy snifter.

Dirk had shown Katinka the photograph of himself, taken in the operational area, during a brief visit home the year before he was killed. They had made love and naked and slim-hipped he fished it out of his kit bag and tossed it on the bed.

'Who is that?' she demanded, unsettled by the brutality the photograph hinted at.

'It's me.' He stood in front of the mirror combing his hair.

'You?' She looked at her husband's reflection, the almost feminine arch of his brows, his small straight nose, and then turned back to the photograph, even more disturbed. 'But why – why must you disguise yourself like that?'

He flopped on the bed beside her and picked up a length of her hair as if it were a python and wrapped it around his forearm. 'Kat, we're fighting a war.'

Several times during his five-day leave, when he was in the shower, on the phone with Jannie, Katinka secretly slipped the photograph out of Dirk's kit bag. The crude disguise, the other she sensed in her husband, alternately transfixed and appalled her.

Six years later she'd sat in the bar at Shangri-La with Kobus and a few other locals who'd shown up to see the Arab with the British accent and skin so dark the receptionist had hissed, to anyone who would listen, 'since when are we letting kaffirs into the lodge'. Katinka did not want to be rude, but she could barely take her eyes off him. His dark face a palimpsest; the bowing of his head, his index finger running across his lips, and she felt as though she could reach through him to touch her husband. At times Kobus was almost dismissive of the man and Katinka guessed he felt uncomfortable with the dark-ness of his client's skin; now that his obligation as Professional Hunter was fulfilled, the buffalo already skinned, salted hide rolled up in Jannie's workshop, he wanted the man gone. The evening dragged on, she drank too much wine. When the hunter, so deft in the way he deflected all the subtle challenges that Kobus laid down, finally excused himself, she made her way to the small guest room that Kobus let her use when it was too late for her to drive home. The hunter caught up with her at the swimming pool. He told her that her hair was as black as the tents of the nomads who roamed the Arabian deserts. He asked her if she would be so gracious as to unfasten it and when she did and it poured over her shoulders and down her back he cried with delight, a hand reaching out to touch it and then politely withdrawing. It felt like utter insanity to follow him down the stone path to his luxury suite, past the birds of paradise, sinister looking in the shadows, and the damp-smelling ferns that tickled her legs. But when she reached for his shoulder to tell him that she couldn't, tears she didn't understand came to her eyes. She needn't have worried, he turned out to be a gentle man. In the night he appeared even darker and she relied on the brandied scent of his breath and the heat of him, the milky whites of his eyes, to know that he was there. '*Ahyuni*,' he murmured and he kissed her belly. It was an Arabic word, and when she asked what it meant he touched his heart and then gestured as if he were lifting it out of his chest. 'You are my eyes, through you I see.'

A rustling in the dry leaves beneath the fig trees broke Katinka's reverie. A voice said, 'Katinka, you're sitting alone?' and she turned to see Lorraine standing beneath the other tree.

'May I join you for a moment?' Lorraine asked.

Girding herself for the inevitable confrontation, Katinka said, 'Of course,' and she moved to the end of the bench.

Lorraine was forty-four, ten years older than she, and the

light glancing through the tree swept her high forehead. She looked noble, daunting, despite the fact that she'd pulled her blonde hair into a small pony tail. A breeze stirred the tree and she sat down, sniffing the air like a dog. 'The river is visiting us.'

The silence between them thickened. The muddy smell of the Limpopo intensified, fingers of earth pushing into Katinka's nostrils, and she blurted in an unnaturally high voice, 'Eva's turned into a lovely young woman. She has some of her mother's beauty.'

Lorraine snorted. 'Really? You who are the fairest of them all think I am beautiful?'

Katinka stared at her sandals. In all her life she had never uttered anything so trite, so cloyingly polite.

'Dammit! I've been nasty again. And I'm trying so hard not to be,' Lorraine muttered. She worried her wedding band with her thumb. 'I always thought *you* were quite beautiful, Katinka.'

Shut up, Katinka silently cautioned herself, you have no idea what to say so just keep your mouth shut.

'I want to be done with anger,' Lorraine went on. 'My lovely difficult daughter is growing up. Do you know that she's going to Johannesburg? Martin's step-brother got her some behind-the-scenes job on one of our TV soap operas. It's good. She needs a city. Martin is fifty and I suppose we'll limp along. And I want to plant something. I miss my garden.' She paused. 'Do you have any suggestions?'

Katinka shook her head.

'None? Nothing?' Lorraine sounded sad as if she had truly expected her to come up with an idea.

'I have a –' Katinka hesitated, thinking of the times that Martin had walked through her squeaking gate and scrunched across the gravel, 'it's quite silly – a gravel garden.'

'Gravel?'

'Drought resistant – Dirk's idea – but what I'd like is a pond with waterlilies.'

'Waterlilies?' A ferocious smile strayed across Lorraine's face. 'Waterlilies! My God, that would be quite something.'

'Yes, I always thought –'

'And lotus plants,' Lorraine interrupted. 'And a fountain! Yes, at night I'd lie in bed and listen to the play of water instead of the nightjars. I know I'm doomed to failure, but I keep trying to civilize this part of the world.' She rose unsteadily to her feet, dusted her hands across her dress, then looked Katinka in the eye. 'Would you like to see them?'

'I'm sorry – see what?'

'The roses.'

Katinka smiled wanly. She did not want to go tramping off to some African's quarters with Lorraine; she also sensed that declining was not an option. 'But the lion – isn't it –'

'Oh, miles away. Still on the Botswana side. Sleeping. But let's get some protection anyway.'

Katinka feared she might be in search of Martin, but she headed for the *braai* area where Jannie sat in a canvas chair, poking the embers with a long stick. He'd had enough of the party, Katinka could tell.

'You have a mission, dear Jannie. We –' She gestured to Katinka who stood a few paces behind her, and a startled expression flew across Jannie's broad face. Katinka wrinkled her brow and grimaced.

'We want to visit my – excuse me – Ezekiel's roses and we need an escort.'

'O-kay,' Jannie said warily.

'But first, a drink to take with us. I'll be right back.'

'What are you doing?' Jannie demanded when Lorraine was out of earshot.

'Oh, please! Why do you think it's my doing? This is her idea!'

'Shit!'

'Then, let's not go.'

'We can't.'

'And why is that?' Katinka asked. She was sick of Jannie's loyalty to the family.

'You know why,' he hissed.

'Oh, so this is my penance for the affair? I get to troop through –'

'Jesus, Katinka.'

'Are we ready?' Lorraine weaved towards them, a bottle of wine in one hand and a loopy smile on her face. 'Rosé, I can't stand the stuff but it seems fitting. Oops!' She wobbled, sloshing the wine, and Jannie held out a hand to steady her. 'A question.' She spoke *sotto voce*, a gleeful look on her face. 'Should we invite Rolene?'

'No,' said Katinka.

Lorraine giggled. 'I'm so tempted, but, no, you're right.' Once they were through the gate in the fence she prodded Jannie in the chest. 'You go in the middle.'

He obliged and Lorraine draped an arm across his shoulders. Katinka remained a few steps to the side of them. It was a four-minute walk along the dirt road, silvery grey beneath the gibbous moon. Lorraine sang the chorus to 'Me and Bobby McGee' and Jannie said things like '. . . but . . .' and 'are you . . .' and 'we shouldn't . . .' Katinka barely sipped at the warm air.

The musky smell of horses greeted them at the head of the footpath that led to the old stables. Jannie blocked Lorraine's way and finally managed a complete sentence. 'Are you sure about this?'

'Of course I'm sure,' Lorraine said crossly, and she walked around him.

Just beyond the darkened stables where the shadowy heads

of the horses nodded as they passed by, Lorraine stopped. Jannie almost bumped into her and Katinka just avoided him.

'Come on, Lorraine. Don't look at it.' He tried to lead her further down the path.

She shooed his hand away. 'If I want to look at it I will. In fact I'm going to stand here and stare at it.' She folded her arms, bottle of wine pressed to her chest. 'Do you see it, Katinka?'

A sway-backed donkey with broken-looking ears stood in the clearing beside the stables. Katinka guessed it belonged to one of the Africans.

'Do you know what it's for?'

'Lorraine!' Jannie pleaded.

'It's for the lion hunt tomorrow. You're looking at the bait.' She thrust the bottle into Katinka's arms and made her way to the bales of lucerne stacked against the stable wall.

'Bait?' Katinka whispered to Jannie.

'Don't. Don't you start as well.' He plucked the bottle from her and took a swig.

As Lorraine attempted to wrestle free a handful of lucerne she lost her balance and fell on to the bales. 'Oh shit, it's useless,' she spluttered.

Jannie handed the bottle back to Katinka. He helped Lorraine to her feet and while she made her way back to the path he gave the donkey a generous armful of lucerne.

'If I had the courage –' Lorraine laughed, a ha! sound. 'Oh, God, if I had the courage I'd set that animal free. I'd slap it on its rump –' She raised her arm in the air, mimicking the slap.

Jannie rejoined them. 'I fed it. Okay?'

Lorraine thought for a moment, then shook her head. 'No. Let it be on the record,' she said and her voice was surprisingly fierce, 'let it be on the record that I don't like this. Not one bit.'

They continued on their way. All three of them stumbled over a large root snaking across the ground. Lorraine swore again and a light flared in the old stables. She held a finger to her lips, then called out, 'Ezekiel, it's just me. The madam. Mrs van Rensburg. I've brought some guests to see the roses. I hope you don't mind!'

A light appeared in another small window. Low African voices were barely audible for a few seconds before the lights were abruptly extinguished.

They walked a few more paces around a small bend and for the first time Katinka saw the rose garden that had so disturbed the Limpopo valley farmers' wives. Moonlit roses in muted colours flanked the path and extended in neat rows into a small clearing in the bush. Lorraine moved amongst them like a swimmer, head dipping down to greet one ghostly blossom after another. And when she looked up and challenged Katinka – 'They're so beautiful! Come, come, see them!' – Katinka bowed her head and hoped Lorraine knew how much she regretted what she had done.

Jannie was biting his nails. 'She's tipsy, you know,' he whispered to Katinka. 'And they're so bloody thorny.'

'She's going to be all right. And I'm going to slip away. It's late.'

'Kat, no,' he said, and he gestured to Lorraine with one hand, as if to say, how the hell can I look after both of you?

'You worry so much about us women,' she chided. 'My car is just down the road and she says the lion's sleeping tonight. I'm going to believe her.'

The drive home took longer than Katinka had anticipated because she had to brake every few hundred yards for the nightjars sitting in the road like fans discarded at party's end. Dirk had taught her what to do. Switch off your head-lights and give the birds a chance to move on; if they don't, get out of the car and gently nudge them into flight. Twice she left her car and crouched beside them, fingertips briefly touching soft feathers before they flew silently into the night.

9

Jannie didn't mind the hours of waiting in the hide. It gave him time to observe the creatures in this natural clearing, close to the banks of the Limpopo, on the northwestern border of Skinner's Drift; lizards with electric blue tails sunning themselves on fallen tree limbs; the ants fanning from one column, into three, into seeming chaos when they encountered the dead donkey's innards splattered on the ground. Two blue butterflies, the size of postage stamps, pirouetted above the stomach contents, and a jackal with a pointed black-smudged muzzle waited in the shade to the left of the clearing, snapping at the metallic green flies.

Dolf Claasen sat slumped in the folding chair next to Jannie's, his head flopped forward. For the moment his snoring was an oddly pleasant counterpoint to the rustling and buzzing and occasional squawk, but if it grew too loud Jannie would nudge him quiet. Martin sat next to Dolf, lightly running his fingers up and down the stock of his rifle. He seemed to be revived and Jannie was glad. At the party Martin had looked out of sorts and lost, but who the hell would want such a fuss for a birthday.

As if reading his mind Martin turned to him and nodded and Jannie pushed the play button on the tape recorder at his feet. The hyenas cackled and shrieked, startling the birds, startling Dolf, and sending the jackal scurrying away in alarm. They'd been doing this on the hour since dawn and it was now noon.

Jannie had been annoyed with Martin. He should have hunted the lion first and then had his party. When the last guests left at one in the morning, Jannie had spread his sleeping bag on the verandah and slept till half past four. He and a badly hungover Dolf scrambled to get ready, while Martin headed for the stables to shoot the donkey. They heaved it into the flatbed of the bakkie and reached the hide just before six, an hour later than Jannie would have liked. They gulped their coffee, wrapped a chain around the donkey's hindquarters and hoisted it into a tree. Martin slit its stomach, the steamy contents sloshing to the ground. A rank smell, guaranteed to attract predators, billowed into the cool air whereupon Dolf promptly vomited.

This is what happens when I go hunting with farmers, Jannie thought. Although Martin had taken a leopard, an elephant, antelope, and, when he was a younger man, had stalked buffalo in Rhodesia, Jannie still considered him a farmer. A true hunter wouldn't drive around in his bakkie at night, headlights on high, to hunt impala, as he knew Martin sometimes did. An honest to god hunter wouldn't even bait a lion. But the smell of the bush at dawn – sun warming earth, the lingering musk of night animals, and the moist breath of the trees, something so subtle Jannie wondered if he imagined it – eased his irritation. Besides, Martin was his friend and Jannie was the forgiving sort.

With the midday sun above them, the reed hide grew stifling and sweat slopped off the men's faces. They sipped lukewarm water from their canteens and pissed into empty cool drink bottles that they capped to keep their scent at a minimum.

At around two in the afternoon, a lappet-faced vulture with a raw-looking neck landed in the tree, swivelled its head in an almost three hundred and sixty degree rotation and then hopped on to the donkey's rump and plucked at the sliced open stomach. The jackal leapt up and circled beneath the donkey, hoping for a fallen titbit. A bateleur eagle, then three smaller whitebacked vultures flew in. Once on the ground the vultures bounded towards the carcass with wings and necks outstretched. They hopped up, trying to find footing on the hindquarters, but the larger vulture chased them off and all four birds dropped to the ground hissing and screeching.

Martin suddenly raised his hand. He stared intently across the receding Limpopo, and as Jannie followed his gaze he saw what looked like a patch of shaded sand on the Botswana side of the river shake its head and rise to its feet. Dolf rolled his eyes, mouth half open as if swooning over a woman. Jannie grinned. The lion had probably been there all morning, biding its time. He checked his rifle, 358 calibre bullet snug in its chamber, safety off. He and Dolf would be ready, just in case.

The lion walked low-slung and slow across the sand to a place where the waters were just a few inches deep. It sloshed across, shook its paws and padded into South Africa. Martin thumped his fist to his heart and Jannie prayed: Dear God, let it be five to six years old, thick-maned, healthy, a good specimen for Martin.

It was. More magnificent than any of the lions Jannie had worked on in recent years. At the far edge of the small clearing, less than fifty feet from the hide, the lion stopped. Proud head large as the sun, lifting, swinging to face them, a slab of tongue hanging from its open mouth. It sniffed the air, growled, circled towards the donkey, front legs extending, extending again, to reveal the sweet spot where a bullet could enter the heart.

Now!

Jannie tensed his body and Martin fired.

The vultures took to the sky and the lion stumbled to the ground. The men remained in the hide, silent, intently watching one of the animal's front paws twitch and twitch. When the movement stopped, they approached with caution. Martin prodded at the eyes with his rifle while Jannie and Dolf stood a few feet back on each side, rifles at the ready. There was no need. Martin had fired the perfect shot, his lion was dead.

'Happy birthday! You lucky bastard!' Dolf hollered. He and Martin whooped and slapped each other on the back and danced a little jig. 'A *dop* to celebrate!' Dolf proclaimed and he reached into the bakkie to retrieve a half full bottle of brandy.

Martin looked sombrely at his lion, then exhaled a swooping whistle and turned to Jannie, huge lion-killer smile plastered across his face.

'Shit, man, shit!' he whispered and he and Jannie shook hands before moving into a rough embrace.

They toasted Martin's marksmanship and the elegance of the animal with swigs of Fish Eagle; the thick mane was almost as dark as a Kalahari lion. The only letdown was the tail. There was no tuft. Perhaps it got caught in a snare or was bitten off in a fight, Dolf suggested. Martin knelt next to his lion and examined the pelt for scars. Just three small scratches, each about three inches long on the hind quarters.

Jannie assured Martin that when it came time to do the mount he would doctor the tail. While Dolf and Martin finished the bottle, he slit the lion's belly; if the contents of the stomach weren't removed swiftly the animal would lose hair later on. He didn't want to take any chances, he knew trophy photos and more celebration awaited them back at the house.

The plan had been to leave the donkey for the scavengers, but when Jannie set about unchaining it Dolf protested. Even though the sawing cough of a leopard hadn't been heard in quite a while, he suggested they return later that evening. Perhaps Martin's luck would hold. They cleaned up the site and removed all their belongings, anything with the smell of man, from the hide, and with much effort – a rope slung around its belly and a 2x4 as a lever – they manoeuvred the lion into the back of the bakkie. Dolf and Martin sat with the animal and went to work on Dolf's hip flask while Jannie drove.

He was grateful for the time alone. Hunters never understood the nature of his job, for them it all ended when they pulled the trigger whereas for Jannie his relationship with the lion had just begun. Already he was thinking about the manner in which the lion had lifted its proud head, big as Africa, swollen with the blood of every animal it had ever killed. He had never seen anything so powerful and beautiful. He would try to capture it, the way that lion had swung its monstrous head towards them.

Often the skinning took place right where the animal had been shot and usually it was Gabriel, Jannie's African skinner, who did most of the work. But Jannie wanted every second of this lion for himself. He would skin it later on in Martin's cool room. It would take hours but he didn't care. Then he would salt the hide, roll it up, and leave it for a few weeks before starting on the mount. His friend Martin was going to have the finest example of his work, Jannie was certain of it.

Small groups of Africans had gathered on the side of the dirt road leading to the farmhouse and they waved as the bakkie rattled past. When a shot resounded Jannie braked sharply, thumping Dolf and Martin against the rear windscreen. Dolf leaned over the side and stuck his head through the passenger window. 'It's nothing, man. Just van Rensburg. He's proud as hell.' In the rear-view mirror Jannie watched Martin sight his rifle on something, then raise it and fire another round into the air.

He drove the last quarter mile at a crawl, letting his friend have his triumphant return. Not only had workers from Skinner's Drift turned out, but also those from the neighbouring farms. It was many years since a lion had been killed in the Limpopo valley.

Jannie parked in front of the house and the children swept into a tight group beneath the nyala tree. Dolf clambered out and Martin handed him the chairs. Jannie remained in the bakkie, his hands spread across the steering wheel, the memory of the lion still moving through him. The moment Lorraine looked at him he felt her gaze. He raised his eyes and saw her, dressed in shorts and a blue-checked blouse, walking through the gateway of the fence surrounding the house. Her hair was loose and messy, her arms folded tight across her chest.

He quickly opened the door and stepped out of the bakkie. He hoped she wouldn't make a barbed comment about the lion and he smiled at her. The night before after that crazy visit to the roses, Lorraine had made him sit in the garden with her amidst empty beer bottles and abandoned plates of food. She must have been quite drunk, even though she wasn't slurring her words too badly, because she spoke to him as if he were her confidant.

'You think I'm crazy, I know. Because I stayed. I knew about her and I stayed.'

Her reference to the affair made him uneasy. He'd never breathed a word of his knowledge to either Martin or her, and he said, 'Lorraine, you're the sanest person I know.'

She leaned in and cupped her palm on his cheek. The mascara she'd worn for the party had smudged into the delta of fine lines around her grey eyes and he suddenly wanted to tell her how beautiful she was and that he loved her. Not in any kind of sexual way, no something far more respectful than that. But he wasn't so drunk as to let such feelings escape and he kept quiet.

'It's a cruel country,' she went on, 'and I know' – her voice wavered – 'I know that my husband has a streak of cruelty in him. Yes, I do. My sometimes cruel husband loves this miserable, rotten and, yes, beautiful country. Far more than I ever will. And I . . . love . . . miserable, rotten, sometimes beautiful him.' Her eyes teared and she placed her forefinger on his lips as if she expected him to contradict her. 'Trust me, Jannie. There's an equation in there that makes sense.'

Standing in front of the bakkie, with a dead lion in the flatbed Jannie knew how vulgar the scene must look to Lorraine. He wanted to keep the peace, he wanted his friend Martin to have his celebration, and he wanted Lorraine to know that he knew that the killing of the lion distressed her. He was about to say something to her when Dolf, who was unloading the rifles, stumbled. The guns fell to the ground, a shot resounded and Lorraine was lifted off her feet and blown backwards. She hit the fence and fell to the ground, head twisted at a funny angle.

Jannie remained rooted, disbelieving beside the open door of the bakkie, staring at the red stain blooming furiously on her blouse. Then the African children screamed and he felt something burning cold plummeting into his heart, spreading vast wings, opening a razor sharp beak. He wanted to help her, but his legs wouldn't work and it was Martin who bellowed her name and reached her first. He fell down beside his wife and cradled her head.

Jannie ran to her. He crouched next to Martin who looked helplessly at him, his blue eyes seeming to crack with the horror of it. Jannie ripped off his shirt and covered her bloody chest, but the shirt was soaked through in seconds. Dolf ripped his off and laid it upon her and the blood darkened that one as well.

Martin stroked her cheek. 'L-l-lorraine,' he sobbed, and his hand fluttered over her chest, as if trying to staunch the flow of blood.

Jannie felt for a pulse in her wrist. Nothing. He pressed his fingers against her neck and blood trickled out of her mouth. 'Martin . . . Martin . . .' he said quietly, 'I think she's gone. But I'm going inside right now to call the doctor.' Left right, left right, he said to himself. His legs were working just fine and he broke into a run.

He telephoned Lourens at the Pontdrif police station and Dr Krieger in Alldays. Then he hurried upstairs to find something to cover her body. He yanked the bedspread off the bed she shared with Martin. Out of their bedroom window, he saw Eva pedalling furiously up the dirt road on a bicycle. The thing in his heart spread its wings even wider until the ache was almost unbearable.

Eva! He tried to will it be otherwise. But he couldn't. Lorraine was dead. Eva stopped in front of the gathering of Africans, she looked wildly from one to the other, then flung her bicycle to the ground and ran towards the house. Fifteen feet away she buckled over and Jannie knew she'd seen her mother's body. He raced down the stairs and through the garden. Grace was holding Eva, she wrestled and wept and finally sank into Grace's arms like a bundle of old clothes.

It was half past three in the afternoon. Birds sang and muffled sobs rose from the gathering of Africans. Lourens would be arriving in the next half hour. There would be statements and a funeral and days and weeks and months when what Jannie had seen and done, because he felt all three of them were responsible for her death, would revisit him and he wasn't ready. This long moment of waiting, with the unconcerned birds and the rhythmic lamenting of the Africans, was the safest place to be. But no, within twenty minutes he saw the dust billowing behind Lourens's patrol car. Krieger's old green station wagon was seconds behind.

By five o'clock statements had been taken and Krieger left with Lorraine's body. Lourens told Dolf to go home, get some rest, and Jannie offered to stay on the farm and be with the family. He moved grimly through what needed to be done; get the Africans to carry the lion into the cool room, hose the blood out of the bakkie and off the ground, find Martin some clean clothes.

He looked around. Martin and Eva were nowhere to be seen. He couldn't bring himself to call their names. The looming presence of the white house, the fruit trees in the darkening garden, Martin and Eva wherever they were – everything seemed so fragile, a raised voice could shatter it all.

He climbed the stairs to their bedroom again and stared at the chest of drawers. He didn't want to open one of hers. If Martin slept close to the door, because that is where the man usually slept to guard against any intruder entering the bedroom, then Lorraine would sleep on the window side and would probably use the closest drawers. Still he felt paralysed, a woman's personal items should remain private. This is ridiculous! he thought, and he roughly pulled on the handle of a bottom drawer. To his relief it was Martin's and he took out a pair of khaki shorts and a folded short-sleeved shirt and set about searching for his friend.

Jannie found him a short distance from the dirt road, no place special, just a man standing on his land, his dogs sitting erect beside him. He watched Martin for several minutes before approaching him, acutely aware of the cooling touch of the air, the calls of birds that preferred the darkness, the rising moon, the web of night in which his friend was being held. He searched for the appropriate thing to say and blurted out, 'I love you and your family.' Martin looked up at the evening's first stars. Jannie laid the clothes on the ground. He scratched Leeutjie's head. 'Do you know where Eva is?'

Martin turned to look at him, his face suddenly alive with distress. I'll find her, he said to Jannie without uttering a word.

Someone had switched on every light in the house and as Jannie walked slowly back along the dirt road he wondered if it was an African custom. To release the spirit. Maybe to call the family home.

He moved from kitchen to office to upstairs bedrooms, extinguishing all the lights, until only the verandah light and the lamps in the lounge remained lit. He poured himself a drink and sat on the sofa. He was surrounded by his handiwork, every one of the animals in the house, except for the buffalo that Martin had shot in Rhodesia, had passed through Jannie's workshop.

Jannie met Martin in 1975 when he was twenty-one and had just finished his mandatory two-year stint in the army. Some of his friends, like Dirk, had gone in for more but Jannie's spirit was low, he wasn't a fighter and he'd seen bodies defiled, acts of cruelty he didn't care for. He'd returned to the Limpopo area, taken a few part-time jobs, including driving Martin's truck. Even hunting had lost its thrill for him so he focused on his other interest, taxidermy. Word soon spread that he had a gift for it and Martin saved his kills for Jannie; in his house he wanted a display of all the animals that roamed Skinner's Drift.

Back then Martin sometimes telephoned him at five in the morning. 'You lucky bastard,' he'd stutter. 'There's something in my cool room and I want you to do it.' Jannie would gulp down a mug of instant coffee and stumble into his bakkie, eyes bloodshot from one too many at the bar of the Jacaranda Hotel. Ridiculous, he'd think, to be wakened by some crazy farmer who's driven around in his bakkie all night taking pot shots at whatever crosses his path. Then the sun would rise inflamed and furious, bringing the bush and the koppies and the rock figs and the sometimes glint of a river back to magnificent life and Jannie would hang his head out of the window and howl, because he couldn't imagine living anywhere more wild and beautiful, because he loved being the one summoned to capture the essence of the animal that had made the hunter want to shoot it in the first place. He'd park his bakkie in the shade, take a quick look in the cool room to see what beautiful creature awaited him and then breakfast with Martin, sleepy-eyed Lorraine who was often still wearing her dressing gown, and wild little Eva.

Weeks later he would return with the mounted trophy. A tiny impala, an aardwolf. It was the best of days when he arrived with the leopard. Eva would kiss the animals and he would join the family for tea. He would have preferred whiskey and Martin always offered one before pouring for himself, but even then Jannie had felt oddly protective of Lorraine. He didn't want her to feel left out so he sipped tea with her.

One afternoon, Eva, who couldn't have been more than seven at the time, trotted into the garden with a writhing snake in one hand. Lorraine screamed and dropped her teacup and Martin leapt up. Jannie's feet shot off the ground and he grazed his knees on the stone table. Terrible bush reflexes, best thing to do when you see a snake is to remain absolutely still.

'It's a mole snake!' Eva wailed. 'I made sure I knew what it was before I caught it. I promise!'

Halfway through an awkward scolding, Martin began to chuckle. Jannie watched the family knit itself back together. Martin scooped up his skinny daughter and sat her on his lap and Lorraine fetched Dettol and cotton wool from the house and insisted on doctoring Jannie's knees. For the next hour a teacup filled with whiskey was passed back and forth while Lorraine regaled Jannie with more of Eva's antics. Jannie was a lonely man and when he drove back to his lodgings behind the general store in Alldays that evening, he was longing for a family of his own.

It was past midnight when Jannie heard two sets of footsteps on the verandah. He raised his head off the sofa cushion, the briefest reprise from the emptiness in which he'd lain down. They didn't enter the house, instead he heard the scrape of a wicker chair being dragged across the stone floor.

Dawn came too soon. After some time he knew he had to get up and he went into the kitchen where he splashed water on his face. He made three cups of coffee, placed them on a tray, and carried it on to the verandah where sunlight was creeping up the stone steps and the moths that had made it through another night clung to the shaded walls. Eva lay curled on the wicker love seat, Martin sunken in a chair beside her. When she saw Jannie she sat up and made room for him.

'Did you sleep?' he asked, placing the tray on the low table in front of them.

She shook her head and he gently put his arm around her shoulders. She felt bony, fragile, she smelled of horses and sweet lucerne and he untangled a stalk caught in her hair. He looked at Martin, who had yet to acknowledge his presence, and was shocked at the change. His face was gaunt, his features some-how different as if in the night they'd been re-chiselled, eyes dulled and retreating, lines around the mouth gouged deeper.

'I've never arranged a funeral,' Eva said. 'Did you know she wanted to be cremated?'

Jannie shook his head. He knew Eva would be the one to make the phone calls. Martin hadn't said a word to him since the accident, even speaking in his presence felt like an act of betrayal.

There was nothing more that he could do. He told Martin and Eva that he would drive back to Alldays and telephone them that evening.

He'd reached the cattle grid and the weathered sign that read Skinner's Drift, when he remembered the lion. He switched off the bakkie and rested his forehead on the steering wheel until the engine stopped ticking and the sounds of guinea fowl fossicking in the bush filtered through the open window. Soon he would go for a walk, a long one, maybe for a whole day, it didn't matter where, as long as there was earth underfoot and he could trudge out some of the ache.

But not yet, he had to deal with the lion. He couldn't leave it in Martin's cool room and so he turned around and dipped back into the valley. He parked near the stables and once again followed the dirt path to Ezekiel's quarters until he reached the roses. In this cove amidst the bush with its snakes and scorpions, the huge peach and lilac flowers had a sense of mad courage about them, the way they reached for the sun, and Jannie began to weep.

Old Ezekiel, dressed in a worn black suit with too short sleeves and carrying a felt hat, approached him. 'Baas Jannie?'

He wiped his eyes. 'We have made such a bloody mess of everything.'

Ezekiel fingered the rim of his hat. And Jannie knew there was nothing the African man could say to appease his feelings of guilt.

'I've come back for the lion. Meet me at the cool room. I need to talk to Miss Eva. I don't want her to –' He turned away wearily in mid sentence and walked up the footpath. Already he could feel the weight of the animal.

He found Eva in the kitchen as he had often found Lorraine, sitting at the linoleum table with a mug of tea.

'I'm taking the lion. Just give me half an hour and we'll have it out of here.'

Eva nodded and Jannie noted how she was infused with her mother's essence, the finger tracing the rim of the mug, the refined nature of her sombre grey eyes.

It was a big awkward death that Jannie and Ezekiel and Mpho dragged on to a wheelbarrow and then hoisted into Jannie's bakkie. In Alldays he searched the deserted streets until he found three Africans who, after being convinced that the lion really was dead, helped carry it into the cool room that Jannie had built on to his workshop.

He could read the topography of the Limpopo valley in the lion's body; the bulk of the head with its thick mane rising like the sandstone rock formations on the edge of Skinner's Drift, the dip in the body between hind quarters and ribcage revealing a belly with fur pale as river sand.

He had no idea what to do with the corpse. Take it back to the bush for the scavengers? No, he feared someone might disturb the skull, make crude bracelets from the knuckle bones as he'd once seen in Swaziland. There were any number of locals who would take that lion – and desecrate it, give it to a shoddy taxidermist who would turn it into a rug for their lounge, head cocked forward with a frozen snarl.

The telephone in the hallway rang. He ignored it, then, thinking that it might be Eva, maybe Martin had done something foolish, he ran for it.

'Hello?'

'Jannie, it's not true, is it?' Katinka's voice was shaky. 'About Martin and Lorraine. Jannie . . . has she been shot?'

His silence was answered by a long shuddering exhalation.

'I'm coming over,' she said.

When Katinka arrived thirty-five minutes later, Jannie was sitting on a stool in front of the high wooden table where he did his finish work, waiting for his electric kettle to boil. A coffee can of assorted animal teeth, tubes of epoxy and several small cardboard boxes of amber-coloured glass eyes were scattered across the table.

Seeing her pale face and her tears lifted the numbness that had just settled over him and the very effort of speaking hurt. 'It was an accident.'

It seemed to take him at least half an hour to tell Katinka what had happened and there she was still staring at him with frantic eyes. 'An accident,' he reiterated. The kettle clicked off. 'I need coffee. You want some?'

She nodded, pulled up another stool and he made her a cup with half a spoon of sugar, the way she liked it.

'How is Martin?' she asked when he once again sat opposite her.

'Devastated. Eva is making the funeral arrangements.'

They sipped silently. Katinka reached across the work table and squeezed his arm. After a few seconds he pulled free.

'I have the lion. It's in the back.'

Katinka grimaced. 'Get rid of it!'

'I knew you would say that. But I can't. I have to skin it.' He stood up, opened a drawer beneath the table and removed a slim knife.

'Jannie . . . no.'

'It's funny, I've skinned so many animals, but this one is making me nervous.'

'Listen – you don't have to do it.'

'It's dead,' he continued.

'Of course it is.'

'No, that's not what I meant. All the animals are dead.' He fell silent. How could he explain to Katinka what happened when he was alone in his workshop, pinning a hide to a form, stepping back to dream a little, travelling down the path that the kudu followed each night to reach the waterhole, slipping into the crook of the tree where the leopard had dragged its kill. Then, believing he had some knowledge about the animal, its personality, moving back to the hide, adjusting it. 'This is going to sound crazy to you. Sometimes I feel their souls when I'm working on them. But I won't with this lion, its spirit left when she was killed.'

'Then why must you do this?' she pleaded. 'Let Gabriel do it. You always tell me he's got good hands.'

'I wish to God he would do it. And that is exactly why I must do it.'

'Then I'm going to wait here.'

'No, go home. I'll be in there for hours.' He reached for a thick khaki jacket hanging from a hook on the wall.

'I don't want to be alone,' she said simply.

Six hours later the skin of the lion lay on the table. Jannie salted it, rolled it up and placed it in a large pan. Gabriel would dispose of the carcass and Jannie decided that at some appropriate time in the future he would bury the skin.

The squat, whitewashed houses of Alldays stood Sunday quiet in the late afternoon light as he crossed the yard to where Katinka sat in one of his sagging deck chairs, his border collie at her feet. ·

'I'm done.' His back ached and he eased himself into the chair beside her. 'I need a drink, a lot of drink.'

'And food. When did you last eat?' Katinka asked.

He shrugged.

'Right, I'll get supper.'

Across the street, between the Jacaranda Hotel and the butcher shop, swallows were hawking insects. In the distance the Blaauberg had turned deep purple and a few rosy tinged clouds streaked the sky above the mountains. Regret after regret swooped into Jannie's heart. He wished he had been drunk enough to tell Lorraine that he loved her. He wished he'd brought her more croissants, and chocolate eclairs, rum babas, the strawberry tarts, any one of the little cakes he'd seen in Bertrand's Bakery as he waited to be served, his face growing warm because he smelled of sweat and potatoes and the fancy city women were giving him a wide berth.

Katinka returned with a tray and two beers and placed them on the ground in front of him, saying, 'I have now seen a bachelor's kitchen.'

He stared at the tray, the lone boiled egg, the slice of toast, the jar of pickled onions. 'It looks fine. You'll share it with me?'

'No.' She wrinkled her nose.

'A beer at least?'

'No. I'm pregnant.'

'What?'

'You heard me. Go on, eat.'

He peeled the egg and dipped it in salt. He fished an onion out of the jar and the sharpness of the vinegar cleared his head. He ate two more and glanced at Katinka who had slipped her feet out of her low-heeled sandals and was rubbing them across his dog's stomach. He remembered the day when Dirk had introduced his new wife. Jannie had expected to see a hardened vulgar-looking woman – he'd been disappointed in his friend when Dirk had told him about meeting Katinka at a strip club – but there she was in a pretty summer dress, a light floral perfume about her. And what a smile there'd been on Dirk's face, as if he were saying, 'Look! Look what has happened to me!' When Katinka confided in him, months after Dirk's death, that she was having an affair with Martin, he'd felt wild with jealousy. In the dregs of one drunken night he plotted his revenge, his seduction of Lorraine, a notion that had left him miserable and ashamed for days.

'Are you going to –' he hesitated.

'No. I can't. The father is that hunter . . . I know you've heard about it.'

'I don't know what to say.'

'I'm going to keep the baby.'

'So I should congratulate you?'

'Yes, because I've always wanted a child. No, because I've gone about it in the most cock-eyed way.'

'Eat the toast,' Jannie said.

He opened the second beer. There were two more in his fridge, they would have to do.

'Jannie?'

'What?'

'Do you have scissors?'

'Ja.'

'I need a pair.'

'Why?'

'So curious.' She took his hand and kissed it. 'Please.'

Jannie headed for the workroom. He gathered the large heavy pair that he used to cut skins and a tiny pair for trimming his nose hairs. On his return he found her standing, long black hair unfastened.

He held the scissors behind his back. 'No. I won't let you.'

She laughed and her hair rippled and gleamed in the last light of day. 'I have to.'

'But why?'

'It's too much for me. I need you to cut it.'

He shook his head.

'One, two, three,' she reassured him. 'Just like that.'

'How short?' he finally asked.

'I want you to see my neck.'

With twelve methodical snips Katinka's hair dropped to the ground.

10

March 1987

Mpho rubbed his nose. He coughed and cupped his hands over his mouth, and his mother, who had not been able to sit still since they returned from church, paused in her wanderings to ask, 'Are you sick?'

'No.'

'Good. Don't get sick,' she said and drifted back to her room.

Mpho pressed both hands to his face and breathed in deep. Something musky, something slightly rank. Mpho had the smell of lion on his hands.

Seconds later his mother was back. '*Tate?*' she called in a watery voice. The bed in the other room creaked and Lefu appeared in the doorway. 'Ai, I am going to miss her,' Nkele lamented. All afternoon they'd been seeking each other out and now they met in front of the kitchen table and shook their heads at each other. They looked at Mpho and he put on the solemn face appropriate for the day. They shook their heads once more and wandered away, leaving Mpho to stare at the slice of world visible through the open stable door, the footpath that jagged to the left for no reason, the grey flecked muzzle of old Lucky who was sleeping in his usual spot, pressed against the wall. Mpho's hands turned into paws, turned into fists that lightly pounded his thighs. Nothing fits any more, his home, his thoughts, his fierce heart beating in his too small chest.

★

While Martin, Dolf and Jannie had spent Saturday afternoon sitting in an airless hide, waiting for the lion to cross the Limpopo, Mpho had combed the ground behind the stables for the brass casing of the bullet that Martin had used to kill the donkey. Over the years he had gathered quite a collection of Martin's casings and he kept them in an abandoned hornbill's nest in a tamboti tree near their outside toilet.

Once he found the casing, Mpho ran home where he switched on his mother's transistor radio. He spat on the casing and polished it with his T-shirt until it gleamed. He squeezed it in his palm. The casing was warm from the day's sunshine, but Mpho imagined that it still held some of the heat of the gun. He listened. Above the gravelly moanings of the singer on the radio he heard two high-pitched voices. It was the twin sisters Nthato and Nthateng, dashing down the path to the first of the rose bushes. 'Tau! Tau! Makakaretsa has his lion,' they shouted.

Mpho sprinted after them. A swarm of children danced behind the slow moving blue bakkie, stamping their feet and chanting Li-on! Li-on! He saw Martin sitting in the back with Claasen. A rifle was slung over Martin's shoulder and Mpho guessed it was the one he used to shoot the lion. He leapt high, higher! and saw a flash of tawny fur. Martin fired the rifle into the air and the children squealed and scattered, except for Mpho who darted a few steps away, then stopped. He locked eyes with Martin who leaned forward and lowered his head as if sighting the gun. He pointed it at Mpho and Mpho could barely breathe from fear. Claasen was laughing and Martin smiled, an ugly hungry grin. He swung the gun high in the air and fired again.

The bakkie resumed its slow progress to the big house, the children once again trailing behind it like the ragged tail of a kite. But not Mpho. He was a different boy now, one who would not be humiliated like that, a boy who vowed to never again run behind a white man's car. He looked around as if he'd arrived on this road for the first time. New eyes staring at the horses that had been spooked by the gunshots. New tongue tasting the dust kicked up by the bakkie. A pocket of stillness inside him in which his anger sparked electric.

The sound of the third gunshot and the screaming set him running up the road. The African workers were clustered near the fence surrounding the house. Familiar arms wrapped around him, pulling him into the crowd. He could see the legs of the person who lay bleeding on the ground. It was Lorraine, he recognized her woven leather sandals. His mother clutched him and rocked from side to side and Mpho felt buoyed on a swaying sea. Then her hands slipped off his shoulders. She bustled past him, crying, 'Oh, Miss Eva!' Mpho stared at his bare feet. He felt alone and somehow stupid. But he was thirteen and he fought back his tears. He dug into the pockets of his shorts and squeezed the casing until it hurt.

Sitting at the rickety kitchen table, still dressed in his church clothes, he examined the cut on his palm, a small slice shaped like a crescent moon. His grandfather came into the room and dipped a mug into the bucket of water. And there was his mother, needing one as well.

Mpho slipped outside and ran through the high grass to the tamboti tree where he reached into the cavity and pulled out a handful of casings. He rubbed them on his trousers. What kind of bullet did a man use to kill a lion? How big would it be? How fast would it fly?

When he'd helped his grandfather and the other workers move the lion to the cool room, he'd only seen the animal in pieces, a jutting out hip, a dun-coloured tail. But this morning when he and Lefu helped Jannie move the lion yet again, Mpho had plenty of time to study the animal. He pulled on paws fat as small pumpkins, stared at the stiff purplish tongue, the huge yellowed teeth and worked his fingers deep into the lion's coarse dark mane.

He knew where Martin and Jannie had built the hide. The casing of the bullet used to kill the lion should be easy enough to find.

Early the following morning Jannie arrived at the old stables to tell Lefu that Martin would not be on the farm and his workers were to take the day off. 'Because of the tragedy.'

Mpho had just emptied the slops bucket and he stood to one side and listened.

'And when is the funeral for Mrs van Rensburg?' his grandfather asked.

'Tomorrow.'

'Baas Jannie, we would like to go. But we don't know where it will be.'

'Don't worry,' Jannie reassured him. 'I'll ask someone to give you a lift.'

Lefu pointed at the broom leaning against the leadwood tree. 'Sweep,' he said to Mpho.

It was going to be one of those days, as long as he lingered around the old stables Mpho knew his grandfather would find things for him to do. He whisked the dead moths, the chicken droppings and the leaves off the tamped-down earth, keeping an eye out for the moment when he could escape.

He heard his grandfather tell his mother about the day off. 'My heart cannot be open all the time,' she snapped. 'It keeps good kaffir store hours. Open for business two hours in the morning and one in the late afternoon!' Nkele laughed miserably at her own joke and then switched on her radio.

Mpho sneaked away, not up the footpath which could be seen from the kitchen table where his mother pointed the antenna this way and that in her search for reception, but through the bush in the direction of the river road. The hide was no more than a half hour away. He found a long stick to take, just in case, and whacked at the trees. *Wuk-wuk-wuk-wuk-wuk* cried the hornbills as they swooped above him.

He carried the stick like a spear, like a rifle. He marched close to the big house and trailed his stick across the diamond mesh of the security fence, a *tat-tat-tat* that brought the dogs charging. They hurled themselves against the wire in an explosion of tongues and teeth and claws. Mpho stood his ground. So many times in the past he'd flinched, terrified that the fence would not contain them. Now he dared himself to take his eyes off them. He opened wide to the music of their slobbering fury and looked across the rich green lawn to the white farmhouse. If Lorraine had been on the verandah she would have hurried to the fence, slipped off one of her shoes, thumped the dogs and apologized to him. But she was dead. For the first time Mpho sensed how different life on Skinner's Drift was going to be. He flung the stick at the dogs. '*Bona!*' he shouted in a wavering voice. '*Bona!*' He sprinted away, the dogs snapping and snarling. Half a kilometre beyond the farmhouse, he slowed to a trot, then to a walk. The river lay to his right, thin and blue and silent. If he followed it for another ten minutes he would reach the hide. He wondered if the dead donkey was still there. Lefu had told him that they hung it in a tree. Maybe hyenas and jackals were trying to eat it. He didn't have his stick. He looked around half-heartedly for another stick, then lost his nerve and followed the dirt road home.

Nkele washed the white shirt that Mpho had worn to church on Sunday. She ironed Lefu's suit and the one black dress that she owned, and early on Tuesday morning the family dressed for Lorraine's funeral. Lefu polished his star of Zion and pinned it to his chest, as did Nkele. Then they both took them off. They weren't going to their church, they were going to the white man's church. Maybe they wouldn't even be allowed in, maybe they would wait on the grass outside. It didn't matter, just as long as they were there.

Lefu didn't know what time their lift would arrive and Mpho carried a chair up to the dirt road and placed it in the shade where his grandfather would wait. He felt restless and itchy. Nkele slid her finger between the collar of his shirt and neck and grumbled, 'Always growing. Undo your top button.'

Later his grandfather walked down the path for another mug of coffee, then again for a finger pinch of Drum for his pipe. Still later for the thick slice of bread and mixed fruit jam that was his lunch. He took off his suit jacket and hung it carefully over his chair, and Mpho saw the damp patches of sweat on his back and the underarms of his shirt.

'Perhaps they are not coming,' Nkele gently said to her father and she filled his mug with tea.

He had one sip, then put it down. 'Listen! A car!'

Mpho listened, but all he heard were the chickens with their endless complaints. His grandfather hurried out of the old stable, shouting, 'Baas! Wait! We are ready!'

Mpho could not look at him for shame.

Nkele spoke bitterly. 'Mpho, this is the kind of day when I hate them especially. Yes, I wanted to go to Mrs van Rensburg's funeral. But there are other ways of paying respect. For your grandfather though, it is different. He is a man on this farm. It's three o'clock,' she said. 'Get out of those clothes. They are not coming.'

A week after Lorraine's death, Martin returned to Skinner's Drift. Mpho was walking along the road, a rusty bicycle wheel in his hand when Jannie's bakkie trundled past, and through the cloud of dust he saw the figure hunched in the passenger seat. At another time he would have dashed home to warn Lefu and Nkele, shouting, Makakaretsa is back! Not today. He walked down the footpath and made himself comfortable on the bench opposite the roses. From his pocket he took the half square of sandpaper that he'd pinched earlier that morning from Martin's workroom. Remove the rust, straighten the spokes and he felt certain he could sell the wheel to someone. He sanded with vigour until a voice behind him said, 'Boy!' There stood Jannie, hands shoved into the pockets of his shorts.

'Your father . . . Ezekiel . . . is he here?'

Mpho hated being called boy and how could Jannie be so stupid as to think that Lefu was his father. His father would not be humiliated like that, waiting all day for a lift that Jannie was supposed to have arranged.

He stood up and mumbled, 'My grandfather.'

'What?'

Correcting a white man was a frightening thing to do, but Mpho lifted his head and politely said, 'Ezekiel is my grandfather, baas Jannie.' Jannie looked puzzled and Mpho explained further, 'He looks after the horses —'

'I know . . . I know.' Jannie moved the bicycle wheel to the ground and sat on the bench. He slumped his head into his hands. 'Get him for me. And Grace as well.'

Mpho reached for his wheel and walked — he *walked*, he did not run — to the door of the old stables and summoned his family.

Jannie stood up and took off his old bush hat. 'It's terrible, coming back here and knowing she isn't —' He squashed the cloth hat in one hand and used it to wipe his eyes. 'Baas Martin is back. I want you to look after him.'

'We will, baas Jannie,' Lefu said.

'I'm worried about him. I've never seen a man so heartbroken. He looks like a ghost. I asked him to stay with me for a few weeks, but he wanted to come home. Eva's gone back to Jo'burg so he just has you. You must please look after him.'

Again Lefu said, 'We will, baas Jannie.'

Jannie patted him on the back. '*Ja . . . ja*, I know you will.' He turned to Nkele. 'I put groceries on the kitchen counter. Make him good things to eat. You know what he likes.'

'Yes, baas Jannie.'

'I don't know what plans he has for the farm, what he's going to plant next.'

'Tomatoes, baas Jannie. That's what he said last week.'

'Okay, good. You start that. I'll come back next week to make sure everything is okay.'

Mpho held the wheel behind his back, tapping it angrily against his calves as his mother and his grandfather bobbed their heads in unison. 'Thank you, baas Jannie,' they said.

That night Martin did not close the gate in the fence surrounding the big house. His dogs scratched at the kitchen door for hours, their yowling adding to the evening chorus of nightjars and jackals. Soon they discovered the open gate and a night-long rampage ensued, a baying Leeutjie hunted buck in the bush along the river and Shaka, the Alsatian puppy, nipped one of Thapelo's daughters as she returned from their outside toilet.

At dawn Lefu and Mpho accompanied Nkele up to the big house where she was to resume her duties. Mpho carried three large stones in the pocket of his shorts. If one of the dogs even came close to his mother he would pelt it. To his disappointment the two patches of fur on the kitchen steps whimpered as they approached.

'Baas Martin!' Lefu banged on the door. He called again and the dogs rolled on to their backs and whined. 'Give them clean water,' he instructed Mpho.

Mpho squatted next to the outside tap and spat on the ground. He filled the water bowl and placed it next to the dogs. Inside his mother was already sweeping the kitchen floor.

'Good,' said Lefu. 'Now, we work in the stables.'

★

Let the dogs starve! Let the crops wither! Lead the horses to the dried-up river, slit their throats, and watch five lions rise up out of the sand on Botswana side!

To Mpho's disgust, life on Skinner's Drift continued in exactly the same fashion as it had for years. Even though Martin was barely recognizable – roaming his farm without a gun, without even a sjambok – Nkele still cleaned and cooked and hung the washing from the line and Lefu and Thapelo and the other men still worked the fields. Everyone was as punctual as usual. They fell into bed exhausted at night, and walked miles to church on Sunday. It seemed to Mpho, who had reached the end of his time at Mrs Zietsman's farm school and now assumed much of the responsibility for the horses, that everyone worked even harder.

This suspicion filled him with a rage he could only express in futile punches to the unyielding haunches of the horses and in the hottest of tears. These secret crying episodes were often followed by a pocket of stillness during which he'd sit in a corner of the stables and ponder life on Skinner's Drift. What drove them so? He'd always thought it was Martin, the way he bullied and threatened them. But now there seemed to be so little to fear from him. Why did everyone still act frightened? He wasn't.

Am I frightened? Am I?

No. I used to be frightened, but now I am angry.

Pressed up against the cool stable walls whitewashed by his grandfather, he often thought about his father, not the man of the uncertain handwriting on the one letter his mother had received, but a father who carried his head high in the presence of the white man, a father who would never have waited all day, dressed in cast-off clothing, for a lift that never came. Mpho dreamed of going to Johannesburg to find him. They would walk the streets together in matching suits with wide stripes. They would wear brand-new shiny black shoes and eat hamburgers and buckets of chicken.

The twin sisters visited him at the stables to tell him about their new game – Hide and Seek with Martin as an unwitting participant. Nthato saw him, still in his pyjama bottoms, sitting under a tree next to the river. Nthateng spotted him standing in the middle of the dirt road for *hours*, looking around as if he had lost his way. And they were both certain that there was not one word left in him. Before, they said, words were piled up inside him like rocks and if he was very angry he would throw one at you. Mpho feigned disinterest, he was a man now, working on the farm. Childish games were not for him.

A few days after Martin's return Nkele stood in the kitchen, a quizzical look on her face. 'We have a visitor,' she announced. 'Or maybe it's a ghost. Van Rensburg is visiting the roses.'

'Leave him alone,' Lefu complained from his room. 'Ai, leave us all alone.' These days he returned from the fields exhausted, and often had to be wakened up for supper.

Nkele rolled her eyes at Mpho as if to say, Yes, I find your grandfather as tiresome as you do. She curled her finger and in seconds the two of them sidled up the path. Nkele ducked into the bushes at the edge of the clearing and when Mpho didn't immediately follow her she yanked him after her and hissed, 'Are you crazy?' He glared at her. His mother was hiding from Makakaretsa, even though this was their home, *their* plot of roses. He tried to pull free but she had a tight grip on his arm. There beyond the fragrant blooms stood glassy-eyed, dishevelled Martin. He wore a khaki shirt and his face looked as tired as one of Lefu's old shoes. 'Your grand-father is right,' she murmured when he finally shuffled away. 'We must leave him alone.'

And just like that Martin became a fixture, the late afternoon ghost in the ex-mealie field. Mpho charted his decline with furious sideways glances whenever he passed him. The same shirt with the coffee stain for six days in a row, the stubble growing into a rough beard, messier than the nests the buffalo weavers built. He felt cheated. How dare Martin shrivel up just when his anger had awakened.

And so Mpho fed his fury with the stoop of his grandfather's shoulders, with Lefu's hacking cough that woke him late at night. One evening, as he watched Lefu clench and unclench his fingers, growing so crooked and fat from arthritis, Mpho could no longer contain himself.

'Grandfather, why do you keep working so hard?' he demanded. 'Why, when Makakaretsa is going crazy. The potatoes could rot in the field and he wouldn't even care.'

'So perhaps you can work in the fields for me. Stable boy and field boy?'

'No,' Mpho answered sullenly. It was useless talking to his grandfather, a man with so little dignity he used the language of the boere. And here came the lecture.

'I don't see anyone else offering me work. And I see you waiting impatiently for the food that your mother and I bring –'

'I would eat less, if I had to,' Mpho interrupted.

Lefu found this hilarious and he shouted to Nkele who was kneeling next to the cooking fire just beyond the open door. 'Do you hear this? Your son is going to eat less!'

A peal of silky laughter floated back into the room. 'Is he starting tonight? Because I am very hungry and this is the best stew I have ever cooked!'

'I will earn my own money,' Mpho retorted.

'And where are you going to do this? With baas Claasen? Yes, that's a good idea. The pay packets on his farm are always short.'

Mpho shoved his chair away from the table. 'I do not need

to work for any of the *boere*! I will go to the city. I will ask my father to help me!'

'Mpho,' Nkele soothed.

'Yes!' He leapt to his feet. 'I will go and stay with a real man and he will help me. He will not make me stable *boy*. He will not make me sweep and clean just because – because he is old! And frightened!' Mpho stood on trembling legs, remorse and elation tugging at his heart. Never in his life had he been so disrespectful of his grandfather. He tried to summon up a picture of his lion.

'We should eat our dinner before it gets cold,' Nkele said in a small voice. She set two tin plates in front of Lefu and Mpho.

'Not yet,' Lefu said. 'Tell me Mpho, when did you become so angry?'

Mpho remained silent. He stared across the room at the chest of drawers where the two hardcover books that Lorraine had given him were stacked together with the diary for 1985 that his mother had yet to let him write in.

'Maybe a month ago? A year? No, I do not think that long. I would have recognized it. You feel it in your hands that jump at your sides. Yes? If those soldiers who searched our roads for land mines put their listening machine over your chest they would hear you ticking like a mad clock. And you think that I have not felt the same way?'

In the circle of yellowish light cast by their smoky paraffin lamp Lefu's face was alive with emotion, as if a wind were stirring a landscape that had been still for years. 'You think that when van Rensburg says that his stables are so dirty even a kaffir wouldn't sleep in them my throat does not burn, my arms do not become ropes that I could wrap around his throat? And you call me frightened. Frightened? Ai, Mpho!' With a sweep of his hand he sent the plates flying across the room and strode outside.

264

Nkele's eyes fluttered shut. She collected the plates, reset the table and served supper for two.

Mpho jutted his chin at her. 'I'm not hungry.'

She picked up the wooden spoon as if she were about to hit him with it and he joined her at the table. They ate in silence. Afterwards Nkele sewed buttons on a shirt and Mpho washed the dishes in the bucket outside. The night was warm and windy and his grandfather was nowhere to be seen. Just the dying cooking fire and Lucky and Lady nipping for fleas.

Hours later the stable door swung open. From where he lay on the floor Mpho watched his grandfather take off his trousers and put them in the cardboard box where he kept his clothes. He smelled of horses.

'*Koko*,' Mpho whispered. '. . . I'm sorry . . .'

Lefu squatted beside Mpho and placed a calloused palm on Mpho's shoulder. Despite the darkness of the night Mpho could make out the intensity of his gaze. And when Lefu moved his hand to his chest, Mpho felt as though his grandfather was reading all the confusion and sorrow and wild joy that he carried in his heart. Finally Lefu spoke. 'Finish your work early tomorrow. I have something to give to you.'

Mpho worked through his lunch and fed the horses an hour earlier than usual so he could meet his grandfather and mother at the old stables. Following Lefu the family walked to the last of the fields where Lefu had spent the day spraying the tomatoes for insects. There they left the road and Lefu led them to a thorn tree on the far side of the dam. He touched the trunk gently as if he were greeting a friend, then measured out twenty paces into the veld beyond. He knelt down and gestured for his family to join him.

Lefu smoothed the grass and took his grandson's hands and placed them firmly on the earth. 'A child is buried here.'

The back of Mpho's neck tingled and his hands lifted ever

so slightly off the ground. His grandfather spoke again, his words crackling like fire running through dry bush. 'I buried the body.'

'*Tate!*' Nkele yelped. 'You're scaring me! Whose child?'

'I do not know. I did not go to the police.'

Nkele did not ask why and Mpho knew that she was thinking that Lefu had done something terrible. He was, too.

'I did not go to the police because they might not believe me. You see, I had done things.'

Now Nkele squatted beside Mpho, a look of distress on her face.

'Such things! I stole Makakaretsa's horse!'

'No, no. He said you could ride. Remember?'

With a toss of his hand Lefu dismissed his daughter's words. 'You think I am stupid? A foolish old man who is confused?' He laughed and spoke directly to Mpho. 'This was before he asked me to ride with Miss Eva. In the night I was galloping on Donder. But when I was on his back his name was Makapelo! It was like flying, Mpho. I flew across this farm. But then when the rains came, a grave was washed away, a grave that I had not dug. I found the body and I knew it was one of our people.' Nkele tried to interject something and he raised a hand to silence her. 'White people are not thrown away like that. A white child goes missing and everyone is searching. I should have gone to the police, but I didn't.' Lefu sank back on to his heels. 'You are right Mpho. I was frightened. What if I go to Pontdrif and talk to Lourens and then they find out I have been riding? I think about going to Vivo. But the black policemen are worse than the white ones. I am telling this to you Mpho because –'

'But why didn't you tell Miss Eva?' Nkele interrupted. 'Then she could have gone to the police.'

'Ah, Dikiledi, I did tell her. And she was also very frightened.'

'Why?' Nkele persisted. 'The police will listen to a white person.'

'Because I think Makakaretsa shot the child.' Lefu leaned close to Mpho and Nkele. 'So many nights I think about this. Why does she have me bury the animals near the dam as if she is making a graveyard? Why will she not look at the body? Why does she say no, no it's a jackal. And when I tell her we must go to the police why does she get angry with me and tell me that there will be trouble if I do? She is protecting someone. And I think it is her father.'

Again he spoke directly to Mpho. 'This makes you angry?'

'Very angry!'

Mpho had so many questions. If his grandfather knew all of this why did he work so hard? Why was he so loyal and why did it not offend him that van Rensburg was visiting the roses? Lefu's eyes so penetrating, so commanding, made him hold his tongue.

'His wife is dead. Is that punishment? Some days I say yes. It is enough. Forget what you have buried here. But there are days when I say no, it will never be enough. Listen to me, Mpho. One day I will die and it is you who must remember the grave of this child. This boy or this girl.' He placed his hands on the ground and spread them wide. 'Too much blood on this farm.'

Mpho looked across the fields at the young potato plants pushing out of the earth, the sandstone cliffs catching fire with the low sun and the dream of going to Johannesburg, the walk down the streets of the big city with his father seemed just that.

'A cross,' Nkele said after some time. 'Please, we must put a cross on this grave.'

The grandfather who had spoken with such authority, shrank, grew old, the lines on his face obliterating the power that Mpho had sensed. And there was his mother, her shoulders rounded, her head bowed. Mpho knew why. He also felt it, as if the late afternoon air was infused with it, as if the river exhaled it, as if just by standing on the land they were subject to fear. Do not be near the roses when Makakaretsa is visiting them, and do not put a cross on the grave of the child. Yes, he is a shred of his former fierce self. But what if he comes back to life? What if we are told to leave Skinner's Drift?

'A stone,' Lefu said, and Mpho and his mother walked into the bushveld, returning with stones that they placed on the smoothed grass.

II

October 1997

The estate agent was encouraging. Foreigners were taking advantage of the weak rand and she'd sold two game farms in the past month. 'An American and a gentleman from Spain. That's what they want. Game farms. It's nice that the land can be cultivated, but that's of minor interest to most of our overseas buyers. River frontage is terrific. Have you heard about the proposed Peace Park?'

Eva hadn't.

Kathy Hamilton wheeled her swivel chair across the floor and pointed at a map. 'They're buying up farms to create a transfrontier park. Botswana, Zimbabwe, us. They envision lodges, a corridor so the animals can migrate. It's all terribly exciting.'

She plucked a pencil from a wooden holder adorned with a small sticker of the country's new flag. Behind her stood slim Nomzamo Siobo in her high heels and linen suit that must have come from Jo'burg, her brilliant smile flashing, Sell! Sell! And there was old Sterling Cilliers wearing a short trousers safari suit, a nose so bulbous, a face so gouged by life it looked as though a hyena had chewed him once then spat him out. Did they match up the agent with prospective clients? Nomzamo for the overseas buyers, Sterling if someone named Bezuidenhout and as sun ravaged as he came in wanting 'a little plot in the bush for a little peace and quiet', and Kathy Hamilton for agitated white women arriving unannounced late on a Friday afternoon and muttering something

269

about selling the family farm. Nelson Mandela smiled down at the trio from a large framed photograph on the wall.

'We need to look at this farm. Would next Tuesday suit you?'

'I leave for New York on Monday night.'

'Oh, no, we can do it sooner. I can clear some time tomorrow.'

'No, no, it's fine. My aunt lives in town. She can at least give you the keys and directions.'

Kathy wasn't sure about this and she spun around to convene with Nomzamo.

Through the window of Far North Realty, Eva watched Main Street jostling with late Friday afternoon energy. Pay day. The bottle stores would be busy, Checkers crowded with shoppers. Johanna had asked her to pick up a box of Maltabela and some dried apricots for her sosatie marinade. Martin was home.

Earlier that day Eva had wheeled him out of the hospital and helped Johanna settle him into the spare room. The old men with the camels had made it back on the wall, along with two SAA posters. One of a malachite kingfisher, the other of a herd of zebras. *SOUTH AFRICA! YOU WON'T BELIEVE YOUR EYES!* written in gold lettering beneath each of them. Her silent father had looked at the posters, at the burglar bars on the windows that lent the room a prison-like air. Eva waited for him to turn to her, to ask with his gaze, with a twist of his head, Why have you done this to me? I will go mad in here. But that was the father she'd left ten years ago, not this sunken man who obediently raised one foot, then the other, so his sister could remove his shoes and slip a pair of sheepskin slippers on his feet.

In the kitchen Eva told Johanna she needed to go into town for a few errands. She wasn't ready to talk to her aunt about selling the farm, about arranging power of attorney, but she knew she had no choice. A huge amount of debt and no sign of the good man Johanna suggested she marry.

As she drove down Main Street where young white men with six packs of Castle under their arms clambered into bakkies and laughing groups of black schoolgirls sashayed past, Eva had an overwhelming sense of not belonging. Even Johanna with her complaints and racial blunders had entered this new South Africa, she could talk about Mandela and Mbeki. And she'd voted. Late one afternoon when they'd emptied the teapot, Johanna poured two nips of Old Brown and confided in Eva. 'I voted for Mandela. The country was doomed and he's a good man. And they had him locked up for such a long time!'

Kathy Hamilton swivelled around in her chair to face her prospective client. 'Eva, it's no problem to change my schedule.' She pronounced it 'shedule'.

'No, it's all right. My aunt will happily give you the key and my last few days are going to be hectic.'

She took the necessary paperwork and promised to return it before she left. She gave them her number in New York and her address, then stepped outside into the pulsing energy of the street and headed for the Greek's. Only three more days of samosas and marshmallow mice.

Dinner was a sombre affair. After a few attempts at conversation both she and Johanna realized Martin was not going to speak. The silence about him was different, no longer brooding, no longer a cloud above his head, just silence as though he didn't have enough substance to create words. For the first time Eva sat in his presence without the electric charge of their wordless communication. There was nothing to read, no mood to pick up or anger to dodge. Martin was empty.

She ate her lamb curry and avoided looking at him, while Johanna chatted away. 'Eva's in New York now. I'm going to ask her to send us a little Statue of Liberty and one of that building the ape climbed up. The . . . the –'

'The Empire State Building,' Eva prompted.

'That's right.' Johanna poured a dollop of chutney on to Martin's plate. 'The state building.' She turned to Eva. 'He'd like that. And send us postcards. I want him to know where you are.'

'Eva works in films. Like Hendrik. Would you like to see one of his films tonight?'

'Let's do that *skat* – put one on for him.' She registered the fork clutched in Martin's hand, the untouched plate of food. 'Okay, *boetie*, you're not hungry right now. Then let's go to the cinema.'

They slowly trooped into the lounge, Johanna offering Martin an arm to hold on to. She showed him the photo on the sleeve that held the video: a grimy faced white man holding on to a rope dangling from a helicopter, machine gun at his hip. Eva switched off the overhead light. When the first helicopter blew up and a flaming figure staggered out of the wreckage, Johanna cried, 'There he is! Our Hendrik!' She rewound the tape and they watched the explosion three times. By half past eight, Martin was asleep in his chair and Eva was close to dozing off. She roused herself. Johanna declined her offer to help Martin to bed and Eva drove back to the hotel.

Turning into the driveway, she spotted Jock out for an evening stroll, dog tucked under his arm. He flicked the ash on his cigarillo. 'All quiet tonight. We survived the Truth. And you don't have to sneak around. The pilots are gambling in Venda. Friday night fun for the boys.'

Eva wondered if he had a lover somewhere in town and in a fit of affection she said, 'You should visit New York. I'll leave you my number.' She immediately regretted her offer.

He smiled as if he'd read her mind. 'I like the quiet life.

The mountains.' The glowing tip of his cigarillo arced through the night as he pointed at their dark shapes. 'What am I going to do in a city?'

In her room Eva dragged her suitcase out from under the bed. She packed the diaries, two rows of neat black bricks, and the black dress she'd brought in anticipation of a funeral. It was a start and she flopped on the bed. She fell asleep in her clothes, waking for a moment after midnight to switch off the light.

When Eva returned to Johanna's house the following morning, her aunt was at the stove, grimly stirring a pot of belching Maltabela. 'I had a sleepless night. He's not happy.'

'Give him time to settle in,' Eva urged.

Johanna shot her a look as if she recognized the attempt to mollify. She poured the yeasty-smelling brown porridge into a cereal bowl. 'Are you hungry? I have extra.' Eva nodded and helped herself while Johanna fussed over a breakfast tray, noisily switching the beaded lace doilies on the milk jug and the sugar bowl.

'No lumps,' Eva said in between mouthfuls. 'Maybe I should buy a box to take home.'

Johanna frowned at her.

'What?'

'I want you to get his dog.'

'Why . . . no . . .'

'Today. Drive to the farm.'

Her aunt was growing impatient with her, Eva could tell, and seeing that she was going to be taking care of Martin, Eva did not want to annoy her. But still, a drive to Skinner's Drift was out of the question. She moved to the sink and washed her bowl. 'I don't think I can. I have things to do. And we need to talk about power of attorney.'

Johanna seized the bowl from Eva's hand and rubbed it

vigorously with a dish cloth. 'Your father is in there. Dying! *Ja*, I'm not a fool, I can see he hasn't got long.'

And that's what you said when you telephoned me in New York! Eva almost snapped.

Her aunt wasn't done with her. 'Stop being so selfish and get that animal before I change my mind.'

A quick in and out, Eva told herself as she drove too fast through the Soutpansberg. Grab the dog, a young female bull terrier, and leave. She did not stop in Alldays. Sorry, Jannie, no time for that game drive. Two and a half hours after leaving Louis Trichardt, she turned left on to the dirt road leading to the border farms. The road was in bad condition, the car struggling for traction in the sand until she reached the corrugated stretch traversing the plateau. Dolf Claasen's old farm lay to her right. A few nights ago, Johanna had told her that he'd hanged himself months after Lorraine's death. 'I didn't want to tell you in a letter. I thought it might upset you.'

You're right, Eva thought as she rattled along the road. She was furious with him. It was one death too many, and she swore at poor dead Dolf. And just when she wanted to turn around, to say to hell with it, give eager Kathy an extra percentage point on her commission if she picks up the dog, Eva reached the edge of the plateau. In the distance, quiet as a painting, lay Skinner's Drift. The three circular fields, no longer perfect jade circles, were smudged with brown, the red-tile roof of the farmhouse barely visible through the trees. The dirt roads traversing the land looked narrow and slight and the last of the summer's rains glinted like silver bracelets on the Limpopo's sandy arm.

She followed the switchbacks, dropping slowly into the valley, her gaze slipping over odd-shaped rock outcroppings, familiar trees. She rolled them lazily through her mind, let them resonate with a hundred other memories, a hundred other afternoons when she'd returned to Skinner's Drift with her mother, with her father. Eva was home.

The road straightened out and she passed the horse camp, a lilac-breasted roller sitting like a jewel on the collapsed fencing. She was approaching the first of the fields when she caught sight of an African man standing in the bushveld beyond the dam. She slowed down. It wasn't Ezekiel, even from this distance she could tell this man was much younger. A worker from another farm, she surmised. Or, a more disturbing notion, a squatter. She considered walking through the bush to find out who he was. But that was what her father would have done, marched over, proclaimed his ownership, hounded the stranger off his land. She drove on, until she reached the path leading to the old stables where she slowed to a crawl. She leaned out the window and sniffed for wood smoke, she searched above the hum of the engine for the sound of a radio playing, chickens complaining. Anything to suggest that Ezekiel was home. After a few moments she drove on.

The fence near the carport was all but devoured by the bougainvillea, the gate was not locked. It groaned as she pushed it and the bull terrier leapt out of the old dog basket next to the kitchen steps and barked. The dog was slighter than Tosha with a brown saddle and two brown feet. Eva dropped to her knees and within seconds the dog was licking her face.

There was an air of abandonment about the house that seemed fitting, dirty white walls with long streaks of rust beneath the grille work on the windows. Accompanied by the dog she walked the garden, past sprawling fig trees and pawpaw trees tall and straight as ship masts and laden with green fruit. A pair of faded blue shorts was pegged to the washing line and the door to the cool room was wide open. Wild vines had crept up the security fence to embrace the

275

curls of barbed wire on the top and she could just make out the track on the other side along which the soldiers used to patrol.

She returned to the kitchen door. A quick look to check the condition of things and then she'd leave. The door was unlocked and she stepped into the warm musty smelling stillness. Her eyes adjusted to the dim interior and she saw the empty cans beside the sink, the thickly flowing stream of ants leading down the counter and into a crack in the floor. A camouflage shirt was draped over the back of one of the kitchen chairs, two Coke cans, a radio and a black leather diary on the table. Eva moved closer to read the date embossed on the front. 1985. She picked it up and fanned the pages, all of them blank until she reached the first one. 1 January had been crossed out and a new date pencilled in. 2 OCTOBER 1997. The previous day. Below that in handwriting that progressed from neat to increasingly scrawled, as if the person writing had become agitated, pressing the ballpoint pen hard into the page, she read:

Martin van Rensburg Shot an Afrikan Child on the Farm Called Skinner's Drift

This is the storie. My grandfather found the body in the donga near the dam after the rains. He knew it was one of our people because the body had been thrown away. My grandfather had been riding horses with MISS EVA. He beried animals for her near the dam and when he told her about the body she would not look at him. She said she would tell the police he was stealing the horses if he spoke to them. My grandfather carried this storie for many years. When I was thirteen and a man he gave it to me. He told me to remember the child. He said it is my responsibility. I am now in the army in Walmaanstal. I have not forgotten the child running, while Makakaretsa chases him in the bakkie, pretending he will drive over him, scaring him. Makakaretsa had a machine gun. He shot the animals, the jackals and the lion. The white people think we are animals and they shoot us. They throw our bodies away. They think they are safe. But I am not afraid. This is my land. I speak now. I will tell them what happened.

Amandla Awethu

JUSTIS IS MARTIN VAN RENSBURG PAYING FOR WHAT HE DID.

A knock startled her and Eva gasped and spun around, diary pressed to her chest. A tall black man stood in the doorway.

'You scared me! Can I help you?'

He wore a pair of camouflage trousers and his chest was bare. He shifted from side to side, his eyes wide as if he were straining to see into the kitchen. Then he straightened up.

'Miss Eva?'

She nodded.

He was silent for a moment and she registered the spade resting on one shoulder.

'You do not remember me?'

She shook her head and offered a smile of apology. 'I'm sorry – no –'

'Mpho.'

'Mpho!' He was barely recognizable as the little boy who played at the stables. 'Is your grandfather here?' she asked wildly.

'No. He's gone to the clinic in Messina.'

'Is he going to be all right?'

'I do not know. I wanted to go with him, but he told me to stay and look after the baas's dog.' Mpho gestured with his head towards the bull terrier stretched out on the kitchen floor. 'Our dogs, they can go hungry. But that white dog, she must eat every day.'

The way he'd said 'white dog', dragging the words with his lips and his tongue until they hung in front of her, unsettled Eva. She patted her thigh and the dog ambled to her side. She gripped the collar. 'Thank you. But I'm taking the dog back to Louis Trichardt in a few minutes so you don't have to worry about her.'

Mpho placed the spade on the ground and leaned an arm up against the door frame. He looked at the garden, then back at her, his eyes flickering down to the diary still in her hand. He was patient, he would wait all afternoon if he had to. Finally she asked him, knowing what the answer would be, but hoping, praying it were otherwise, 'Did you write this?'

He nodded. 'You drove past me. You saw me digging near the dam.'

This time she did not ask the question.

He answered it regardless. 'I'm looking for the body and when I find it I am going to the Commission. You see, Miss Eva, my grandfather was too afraid to go to the police. He thought he would lose his job. He's seventy years old now and he's still afraid. Otherwise he would let that dog go hungry. So I feed her and while I am here I switch on the radio. My grandfather's radio doesn't work any more because he has no money for batteries. I switch on the radio and they are talking about the hearings in Louis Trichardt. They are coming to Messina next. The Truth Hearings. And I will go and tell them what happened on Skinner's Drift. I am not afraid. I have no job to lose.' He held out his hand. 'The book.'

Eva didn't move.

He smiled for the first time and laughed. 'You think I stole this book? You think I walked through your house and stole things?'

'I haven't accused you –'

278

'Your mother gave it to my mother who then gave it to me. She told me I could write in it when I had something to say.'

Eva handed him the diary and he hoisted the spade back on to his shoulder. He was done with her.

She fought the urge to run after Mpho, to plead with him, offer him money, anything to stop him from digging. And as she watched him walk through the gate in the security fence, she remembered the afternoon so many years ago when she'd stood near the tomato fields watching Ezekiel dig the grave, something ugly, something like tar in her mouth. She'd chewed on it as she imagined Ezekiel walking into the police station at Pontdrif. *He's black and I am white and they will never believe him.* They would believe Mpho. The black man with the glasses, the Indian man and woman whom she'd seen at the Misty Mountain, they would listen to Mpho with his cold eyes, with his way of fattening his words with outrage. For a moment her outrage at his elaboration, his exaggeration of what had happened, hauled her out of her rising panic and she spun around and grabbed the camouflage shirt that she was certain belonged to him and flung it outside. The child wasn't hunted down. The child wasn't trapped in their headlights.

Then her knees seemed to loosen and she could barely close the kitchen door, visions of her father in jail, herself booked as an accomplice besetting her as she fumbled with the lock. She jiggled the light switch several times before the fluorescent, dulled by the layer of dead moths in the casing, flickered on. She circled the table, fist thumping against her lips. *It was an accident. An accident!*

Climbing into the bakkie that night with her dad she'd had a bad feeling. The atmosphere between the two of them had been charged since her return from boarding school. Martin alternately dismissive of her and almost begging for her company. She hadn't known how to deal with it, or how to handle her disappointment, her sorrow at knowing that she would leave her dad, that her dad was a simple man and there was more to life than Skinner's Drift, that the world beckoned and she wanted to go. The viciousness with which he emptied the clip of his revolver into the jackal banished all the guilt she'd felt after telling him that she would not shoot the impala. She sat there hating him. *Kill them all. I don't care, you cannot hurt me.* When the figure darted across the road later that night she knew immediately it was a child. She ran after him when he left the bakkie to look at what he'd shot and when he stood above the small body and fired two more shots, Eva wrapped her arms across her chest and rocked with warm sweet relief. Oh, thank God, it *is* a jackal! Then she stepped closer and saw the small dark arm flung across the ground.

Toenails clattering across the floor summoned her back to the present. Eva followed the bull terrier past the dining room, missing its stinkwood table and chairs, and into the lounge. End tables, lamps, the small desk where her mother used to write her diary entries – all must have been sold by Jannie. The room was bare except for a sofa, a TV on the floor and an old armchair into which the bull terrier promptly leapt. Eva stared at the makeshift bed on the sofa and knew this was where her father had spent his last nights. The blanket reeked of sweat, of spilled whiskey, but she didn't care. She curled up on it and began to cry.

Four o'clock arrived and she was still on the sofa, staring out the plate-glass window at the browning lawn. She should drive the dog back to Louis Trichardt and call South African Airways to change the reservation to tomorrow, put the surcharge on her credit card. Lock up the house and leave. Right now. But Eva could not. She hadn't known how worn thin her soul was and how desperate she was for the sounds of birds. African birds. And she felt quite hysterical when she thought about leaving without visiting the river.

At five o'clock she called Johanna.

'I'm still here.'

'I'm not surprised. It's home.'

'. . . I suppose so . . .'

'You sound a little *deurmekaar, skattie*. Are you all right?'

'I think I'm tired.'

'Then you mustn't be on the road. Spend the night. Go to bed early.'

'Okay.'

'I'll tell your pa you'll bring him the dog tomorrow morning.'

'Okay.'

'Eva – he's going to be happy knowing that you're on the farm.'

Eva hung up the phone. She had a sudden longing for the home of her early childhood; her mother breezing by, hands dancing as she talked about something from her day, and Eva's secret love, her dad, standing on the verandah, a drink in his hand, watching the arrival of the night.

She chided herself and stepped outside. The camouflage shirt was still lying on the ground and she glared at it and walked determinedly through the gate and circled the house to reach the dirt track running parallel to the river. Minutes later she was back for fear of running into Mpho.

Six o'clock, almost dark. A bushbuck barked near the river. The shadows in the garden vanished as the sun dropped away and Eva shut the gate. The padlock was in the closed position on the bolt. Best to lock the gate, she thought. She searched in the kitchen drawers for the key. In the room that they'd used as an office she rifled through a filing cabinet brimming with bills and letters from creditors. She looked around and registered the empty gun case. Her father had stopped hunting but, still, a farmer always had a gun. Had Mpho wandered down the hall and taken it? A shiver savaged the back of her neck. With night swaddling the farmhouse Eva closed the few windows that she'd opened and made sure all the doors were locked.

She switched on the TV, and sat on the sofa with a bowl of soup. Something was wrong with the antenna and she made it through five minutes of a snowy game show. What an idiotic idea it was to stay the night. Best to fall asleep as soon as possible, get up at dawn and leave. She investigated the collection of bottles beside the TV. All empty. Then she spied one next to the sofa that still held an inch or two of Fish Eagle. She drank straight from the bottle.

It was only seven o'clock. No one could go to bed this early. She contemplated calling a school friend, but she hadn't stayed in touch with any of them. Dial America? The robust purr of the ring, so much more assertive than the chirp of the South African phone system, comforted her.

'Hello?'

'Stefan? Hi, it's Eva.'

Eva could see him in his apartment in the East Village. He was jerking his head back slightly, tucking his chin in the way he did whenever he was surprised, pushing his glasses up the bridge of his nose. A bagel and a cup of coffee on his messy desk. Several seconds of silence passed.

'Eva? Hi.'

'I'm in South Africa.'

'Wow.' A long pause. 'That's far away. What's up?'

'The Truth Commission was meeting in the town that I was staying in. Louis Trichardt. And now they're' – she held her hand over the receiver and squeezed her eyes shut to fend off her tears – 'anyway, I thought of you.'

Another silence. 'That's great. You know, I haven't been following it much. I've been busy with –'

'Well, this is an expensive call. So I should hang up.'

'Wow. Well, thank you for thinking of me.'

No, 'Let's meet for a drink when you come back', no, 'Hey, I've been thinking of you.'

'Okay. Bye.'

'Okay. Eva, be careful.'

'Idiot!' she muttered after she'd hung up. She finished the brandy, then squatted next to the empties beside the TV. Not even a drop left in any of them. She stood up and caught sight of her reflection in the large window – a thin, unsmiling woman who'd just realized there were no curtains. Anyone could see in and she couldn't see out. She retreated to the doorway, all the while wondering what Mpho was doing. Perhaps writing in the diary about his visit with MISS EVA.

'Come, come,' she cooed to rouse the dog and she went upstairs. She opened the door to her room. It appeared untouched, her cowrie shell necklaces hanging from the mirror, the seed pod from the ana tree on the dressing table. A poster of a pair of hands nestling a white dove was still pinned to the wall above her narrow single bed, 'If You Love Something Set It Free' arcing above it in rainbow script.

The liquor hadn't helped and Eva felt frighteningly sober. There was nothing to do, nowhere to go but back to that night when she'd stood in this room, clawing her chest because she could not get enough air. If she'd only nudged her father into speaking then they could have dealt with it. But Eva could barely believe what had happened. Driving back to the farmhouse she'd had the sensation that her ears were blocked, she couldn't hear anything, not even the growl of the bakkie's engine. Usually they searched for something to nibble when they returned from a night drive and she went through the motions, standing in front of the stove, dipping a wooden spoon into the pot of sauce from their spaghetti dinner. The sauce was cold and she gagged. He stood behind her, shaking loose the ice from the tray in the freezer, and she said, I'm going to bed. A test to see whether she could still speak because she felt so strange. She vomited in the upstairs bathroom, catching the spill of it in her hands so it wouldn't splash in the toilet and make a noise and wake her mother. Eva knew she had to talk to her father, but she felt like her body was in pieces, like she couldn't put herself together to walk back downstairs. When she finally did, she found him sitting in his chair, locked somewhere far away with his thoughts. She knelt in front of him and asked what they should do. Ab-b-bout what? he stammered. Eva was too scared to say it. She left him in the lounge, and took a torch from one of the kitchen drawers and a spade from the workroom. She walked down the road praying that the child had turned into a buck because then everything would be fine and her father wouldn't get into trouble. But just beyond the fields of tomatoes, she came across the small body, one arm tossed to the side as if in sleep. The ground there was hard and stony and she dragged the child into the donga.

She was in the workroom, returning the spade when she heard footsteps behind her. She swallowed her scream. Martin hauled the impala that he'd shot out of the bakkie and dragged it by the horns, legs rocking back and forth, through the gate, across the lawn, past the rose garden and into his cool room. She followed. Help me, he said, and they hoisted the buck on to the metal table. He eviscerated it with precision. But that was a sloppy business, something a hunter usually does in the bush, and the impala's intestines and stomach contents spilled to the floor. Her father looked surprised. Don't worry, Eva said, and she shoved and scooped the mess into a bucket and carried it down the road to a tangle of bush where she dumped it. She found her father in the kitchen, cutting a slice of cheese and she tried again. Dad, I didn't know what to do and I buried –. She stopped. His eyes had the same dull sheen about them as those of the dead buck and he walked past her as if she wasn't here. The horror of the killing receded and Eva went back to her room with something that felt far more frightening, the sense that her father had cast her out of his world.

The farmhouse sighed, branches and people tapped against the windows and Eva's heart swelled with terror. Mpho and his friends climbed the stairs. They raped and tortured her. They cut her into pieces while she was still alive. In the pockets of time when she broke free of these lurid imaginings, she recognized how base and primitive her fears were, that they were the fears that had lurked in all of their bellies, had made her father fence the house, stockpile the guns.

Then her heart was once again straining and knocking at her ribcage. It could happen. Farmers were still being killed by disgruntled workers high on liquor and dagga, by those who believed that the land belonged to them. Why not a soldier seeking revenge for a dead child? Mpho was outraged. He was tall, his arms strong and he'd been inside the house. Maybe even in her room. She pulled her old duvet tight around her chest and listened.

Moonlight slid across the floor, casting the tip of the dog's tail in alabaster, then her rounded hind quarters. Eva extended her arm to the window and could just make out the face of her watch. Half past two and she had to pee. She considered wetting the bed. Finally she mustered the courage to open the bedroom door. The passage was dark and silent. Mpho was sitting downstairs on the sofa, listening to her footsteps. He was standing at the top of the stairs, watching her, his eyes so sharp that he could see the terror on her face even though she couldn't make him out. She forced herself to the bathroom, peed as quietly as possible, and raced back to the bedroom. She pushed the stool from the dressing table against the door, then stared at the wardrobe. Ridiculous, the dog would have woken up if anybody had slipped in.

Four o'clock and a glimmer of hope. If Mpho was going to kill her, he would have done it by now. This made sense to Eva.

The dark of four in the morning was different to the night of one a.m. Softer, easier to move through. This was the hour when she used to leave her bedroom to bury the animals. A glance at the door of her parents' room where her mother was sound asleep, down the stairs, past her father drunk in the lounge, out the kitchen door, the dogs snug in their baskets raising their heads, knowing it was her and sensing they were not invited, closing their eyes. The security fence had not yet been erected and the small gate opened silently.

She'd been in the stables, looking at the spade and going through what lay ahead – ride down the river road to where her father had shot the caracal – when blubbering tears came over her. She opened Casper's stall and muffled her cries in the horse's warm neck. She clambered on to his back and nudged him down the footpath. 'Ezekiel,' she whispered. 'Ezekiel!' And he appeared. He smelled of earth and fire and she wanted to reach down to touch his face, to believe he'd come to her. She wanted to tell him everything, wanted him to help her.

Dawn set the birds whooping and chucking and ratcheting and trilling. Eva waited until half past seven and then walked to the old stables. She hadn't seen her mother's roses since Lorraine had given them to Lefu, and the startling incongruity of a rose-lined path dipping down to the old stables with its rusting corrugated iron roof had her smiling. Two rangy dogs loped up the path to greet the bull terrier. And there was Mpho sitting outside in one of their cast-off chairs, his legs stretched out, enamel mug in his hand.

286

Eva walked up to the last rose bush. 'Good morning. I want to give Ezekiel a lift back to the farm. You said he went to the doctor in Messina. Is that right?'

Mpho tilted his chair against the stable wall. 'Do you know my grandfather's real name?'

Eva lightly touched one of the buds before answering him. Having survived her night of terror she felt stronger and he was starting to irritate her. 'Yes, I do. It's Lefu. Can you tell me where he is?'

'He had an appointment at the clinic.'

'Can you give me the address?'

Mpho tossed the dregs in his mug to one side and rocked his chair back on to level ground. 'You've never been to the township, have you? The street signs have all fallen down or have been stolen. You will have to ask directions when you get there.'

'Thank you,' she said and she walked away.

'Miss Eva!'

She stopped, but did not turn to face him.

'The appointment was yesterday. You will probably find my grandfather walking home, somewhere between here and Messina.'

Beyond Claasen's land Eva saw a thin man in a black suit being led by a child, a small dog trotting behind them. She slowed down, eyes searching. It wasn't him. She passed a man riding in a donkey cart, and a jaunty elderly fellow joking with two women dressed in bright white dresses for church. Where the dirt road joined the tar she saw two men sprawled in the long dry grass. Asleep or drunk, she couldn't tell. By the time the fifth old man hobbled towards her car she was feeling frantic. 'I'm looking for Ezekiel who works on Skinner's Drift. Lefu . . . do you know him?' He shook his head. He could not help her.

She found him twenty kilometres shy of Messina, standing on the opposite side of the road, waving his hat at an approaching bakkie. When it raced past he trudged back to a patch of shade under a thorn tree beside a stretch of tall game fencing. Eva stopped the car opposite him.

'Ezekiel?'

Even though his hair was ash-coloured, his face as wrinkled as the floodplain after the river had eaten it away, she recognized him immediately. He looked at her with eyes that were both curious and private, doffed his hat, and inquired in his deep voice, 'Madam?'

'Ezekiel! It's me, Eva!'

He leaned forward, using his walking stick as support. 'Naledi?'

'Yes! I want to give you a lift back to the farm.'

'Little Naledi!' he cried and an ember dropped into Eva's heart.

He reached for the rear-door handle and she said, 'No, no, sit with me. In front.' She pushed the bull terrier into the back. 'Oh, Ezekiel, I've been looking for you. I can't believe it's you!'

He settled into the seat beside her. 'Where have you been?'

'America.'

'You've come back?'

Eva couldn't bring herself to tell him she would be leaving soon. 'For a while. Yes,' she said and she put the car in gear.

He was shaking his head, looking out the window then turning to see her once again, his smile and laugh lines deep with joy. 'Naledi! You give me a surprise.'

'Were you waiting a long time for a lift?'

'Since last night. Tell me, how is the baas?'

'He's out of the hospital.' She remembered de Vet's comment about an African man visiting Martin. 'Did you go to see him?'

He nodded. 'He looked so sick. But he is well now? He is on the farm?'

Again Eva had to lie. 'Maybe in a few weeks he will come back. He's staying with Johanna.' When she'd spoken to Kathy Hamilton, she'd given no thought as to what would happen to Lefu when Skinner's Drift was sold. The farm had been his home for decades.

'Where is Grace?'

'She works for new people. Bristow. They have Claasen's farm now.'

He coughed, a terrible phlegmy sound, and she asked him what the doctor at the clinic had said.

'I must take some medicine for my chest. Also for my heart.'

'You have a prescription? Did you go to the chemist?'

He looked sheepish.

'Give it to me. I'll do it for you.'

He thanked her and they lapsed into silence, Eva figuring out just when she could get the prescription filled. And she wanted to give him more money. She'd borrow from Johanna. Lefu coughed again, his chest wheezing for at least a minute, and her plans stalled. Money had always been her answer. Ten rand pinched from her mother's handbag to bury a caracal and to appease her guilt. How much now so she could leave with a clean conscience? The silence that they were sitting in, driving along the thin grey road, past game farms and the occasional sandstone rock outcropping studded with a rock fig, felt increasingly uncomfortable.

'You must come back to the farm,' Lefu suddenly said. 'Skinner's Drift must grow things. You live in the big house. Grace will cook for you.' He sounded adamant, annoyed with her for leaving so many years ago.

Eva did not know how to respond. He could not mean it, not after all that had happened with her. Surely he was being polite, making the appropriate comments that a black man would make to the daughter of the baas. 'I don't know if I can,' she said at last. 'I've thought about it. But there have been so many sad times. Good times, yes, but also sad ones. Big sad ones. My mother. Neels. The drought, that was hard for everyone. I don't know if I could live there again.'

'A lot of sadness, Naledi.'

He stared straight ahead, holding his walking stick between his knees. She recognized his frayed brown trousers with the faint herringbone pattern as being the pair her father used to wear to Sunday lunch at Johanna's.

'Mpho is at the farm,' she said hesitantly.

'He's in the army.' Lefu did not lean back in the seat but sat upright, slightly forward.

'I know. I saw him in his camouflage uniform. Ezekiel – he's digging near the dam. He wants to go to the Truth Commission in a few days. In Messina.' The words Eva had been unable to utter for so many years sat simple on her tongue. 'He's looking for the child my father shot.'

Lefu retreated, his very essence sucking back into itself.

'I want to say that I'm sorry . . . and I know that's not enough . . . it's not nearly –'

'Ai, Miss Eva!' he cried. 'Why do you make me go back? Commissions? I know nothing. You must talk to Mpho. It is his business.'

His rejection of her apology flustered her and she soldiered on. 'I know I should never have asked you to go riding, to bury the animals. Sometimes I think that I wanted you to find out. And then you did and I . . . I threatened you. I'm sorry. We should have gone to the police. I was so scared. It will never be all right . . . and I'm still so scared!' Lefu had not looked at her and she pulled over to the side of the road, bumping to an abrupt stop. 'Please . . . please say something!' she implored.

He stared out the passenger window in silence, hands

wrapped tight around his walking stick. Eva knew then how much she'd hurt him.

'I don't blame you for not wanting to talk to me. No. I don't.' She turned the ignition key, forgetting that the car was running, and the starter motor complained. 'I'm going to drive you back to the farm. And I'll make sure you get some money. Jannie told me there were months when my dad couldn't pay you.'

Lefu's chest sounded worse, rattling with each breathe, and Eva felt hollowed out with shame. There were nights when she had said to herself, Yes, a child was killed on Skinner's Drift. But so many children were killed. In the townships, on the roads, perhaps even on other farms.

They turned on to the dirt road and jolted across the plateau. They were dropping into the valley when Lefu spoke.

'Naledi, you think I forget what happens on Skinner's Drift? The years it does not rain and everything is dying and the year when the Limpopo is big and the men from Zimbabwe come for the harvest and I watch them float across the river. They cannot swim and they are holding on to big branches. I remember it. I remember when I lived near the river, before the baas owned the farm, and I looked outside and saw a leopard walking past my home. And I remember the night I saw you on Casper. Yes, I was sure I was looking at a ghost. But then you asked me to ride with you. I could not say no. I knew it was wrong. But still I followed you. I remember the riding and each time I said to myself, Lefu you are mad, the baas will kill you if he finds out, and each time I followed you. I did not know why you wanted to bury the animals. I was frightened to know. I remember finding the bones. And I remember how frightened you looked when I told you. You kept saying it's a jackal. But I am not stupid, I know what I am looking at. And I think, did Naledi do this, is that why she is telling me it is a jackal? But I know her and she is good.

I think she is lying because she does not want someone else to get into trouble. And I know then it is the baas who has done something. This is what I tell myself when I am angry, when I do not understand how a child can be left like an animal. How can she do this, I ask, and the answer is always, because he is her father.'

Lefu paused before saying, 'And then you are gone and the madam is dead and Nkele works for someone else and Mpho is going to the army. It is just me on the farm with the baas and I am frightened to be alone with him. But I do not get angry. Is it because I know my grandson will remember the child? Or because I am old. I do not know. You want me to forgive you, Naledi. For what? For telling me I am black and I cannot speak, I cannot see. They all tell me that, people tell me that every day. You are not the first. And I forgave you a long time ago.'

They followed the last curve of the road into the valley and Eva searched for something to say. There was nothing. He forgave her and he wasn't angry, just worn out, exhausted. She glanced across the land when they passed the dam.

'I will sweep the verandah this afternoon,' Lefu said.

'No, you are sick. You must rest.' She parked at the footpath. 'Do you have the prescription? I'll get it for you tomorrow.'

He took a neatly folded piece of paper out of his jacket pocket and handed it to her. He opened his door and the bull terrier wriggled between the seats. 'Tosha,' he said and he patted the dog.

'You called her Tosha?'

'The baas did not give her a name and she reminds me of Tosha. She was a good dog.'

Lefu shut the car door and walked away, hat in his hand. And there was Mpho striding up the path to greet him.

'Ezekiel – wait!' Eva stepped out of the car.

Mpho had a hand out, ready to help his grandfather

home, but Lefu stopped. He handed his walking stick to his grandson.

'Ai, Naledi,' he murmured and he opened his arms to Eva.

'. . . he was a boy!' she sobbed. 'Oh, Ezekiel, he was a tiny little boy . . .'

Eva spent another night on Skinner's Drift sorting through her belongings, placing clothing and shoes and shell necklaces into old shopping bags that she left in the kitchen for Grace to distribute. She was on the road by eight, the dog sitting beside her in the passenger seat.

The women from Venda were unloading boxes of fruit and unwieldy bundles of carved wooden animals from a mini van when Eva reached the start of the mountain pass. She pulled over and bought two overripe pawpaws. Clouds still obscured the peaks of the Soutpansberg. She drove down the forested slopes and into Louis Trichardt.

She parked opposite her aunt's house and sat for a moment, looking at the old man sitting in the lawn chair beneath the jacaranda tree, the crocheted blanket from the room in which Eva had slept, and which was now his, draped over his lap. She'd been thinking about Lefu finding him after he'd had the stroke. Was he on the floor, incapacitated? Maybe he'd lain there for a day or two. She imagined Lefu's hands on her father's body, lifting him upright, raising a glass of water to his lips. In the quiet house he squatted beside Martin and told him that he'd called Jannie and the doctor was on his way.

With the bag of pawpaws in one hand and the other on the dog's collar, Eva ducked down and crossed the street and crouched next to the gate. She waited until the bull terrier saw her master and strained to join him. 'Who's that? Go get him!' she whispered. The dog raced across the lawn and leapt into Martin's lap and began licking his face.

Eva found her aunt in the kitchen. In her absence Johanna

had been baking and pickling, stewing and marinating and preserving. A Pyrex dish of sosaties, jars of green fig jam, two milk tarts freckled with cinnamon – the kitchen counter looked like the winner's table at *Boere Dag*.

'If he doesn't eat!' Johanna shook her fist, then sighed. 'That wasn't funny, I know. But last night he barely touched his food. And I ate and ate.'

Eva reached for a syrupy koeksister. 'I'm thinking of staying for another week.'

'Eva!'

'Only if you promise to make more pumpkin fritters.'

Johanna pulled a wrinkled hankie from between her breasts. 'I prayed, *skattie*, I asked –'

'Good,' Eva interrupted. 'But I need to talk to you about something. Later on today – maybe after dinner – with a bottle of sherry –' She placed one of the pawpaws on the kitchen table and sliced it open with the bread knife.

'Careful. That one looks *vrot*. You'll be running.'

'It's not for me. You need a pair of barbets in your garden.'

She carried the bruised-looking slices outside and placed them on the edge of Johanna's small lawn, close to some overgrown shrubs. The dog was standing on its hind legs, lapping water from the birdbath, and Eva rested her elbows on the back of the chair beside her father. 'Barbet bait,' she said and she mimicked their call, softly singing, '*Whoop-dudu whoop-dudu whoop-dudu.*'

Her father's hands sat like two frightened creatures in his lap. They were smaller than she remembered, the fingers tapered, and the nails had been cleaned up in the hospital. She'd never seen them like that. She reached for them and looked into his vague blue eyes. 'Dad – I went for a walk last night. I was on the farm and I went to see the river.'

Her voice, quiet at first, gathered in strength and she drew one last picture of Skinner's Drift for him, for herself. It was

late afternoon and she followed one of the footpaths mean-
dering across the floodplain. It took her over an hour to reach
the Limpopo. After every few steps, she stopped, to listen, to
feel the damp river air on her skin. Silence and space hung
like golden weights between the riverine trees, the ana trees
laden with pods and about to lose their leaves, and the nyalas
barely able to stop their branches from caressing the earth,
like women bowing down, skirts trailing across the ground.
When she reached the river, she splashed through the warm
shallow pools, all that remained of the previous summer's
rains.

Acknowledgements

Lisa Brower, Ruth Danon, Deborah Kampmeier, David Rosenstock, Elizabeth Tippens and Alice van Straalen offered invaluable feedback on early drafts.

A special thank you to Jennifer Egan, friend, mentor and brilliant critic.

Owen Sejake helped me find the right names for the African characters.

Thank you Marianne McDonald for pens to write with and houses to write in.

And thank you Bob Gottlieb for sending my manuscript across the ocean.

I am deeply grateful to Peter Straus for his faith in my work, and to Mary Mount for her eloquence in guiding my rewrites.

Thank you Nan Graham and Alexis Gargagliano for your deft and insightful feedback.

John, I am grateful for your patience and encouragement.

Mom and Dad, you continue to teach me the value of space and silence in a writer's life. Thank you for your unwavering faith and support.